PENGUIN BOOKS

The Pleasures of Winter

Evie Hunter is actually two authors who met at a creative writing workshop in 2010 and discovered a shared love of erotica. Since then, while they have both written fiction in other genres, they have also written a number of BDSM-themed novellas together. *The Pleasures of Winter* is their first collaboration on a novel. They plan for Evie to have a long and productive career.

The Pleasures of Winter

EVIE HUNTER

PENGUIN BOOKS

PENGUIN BOOKS

Published by the Penguin Group
Penguin Books Ltd, 80 Strand, London WC2R 0RL, England
Penguin Group (USA) Inc., 375 Hudson Street, New York, New York 10014, USA
Penguin Group (Canada), 90 Eglinton Avenue East, Suite 700, Toronto, Ontario, Canada M4P 2Y3
(a division of Pearson Penguin Canada Inc.)
Penguin Ireland, 25 St Stephen's Green, Dublin 2, Ireland (a division of Penguin Books Ltd)
Penguin Group (Australia), 707 Collins Street, Melbourne, Victoria 3008, Australia
(a division of Pearson Australia Group Pty Ltd)
Penguin Books India Pvt Ltd, 11 Community Centre, Panchsheel Park, New Delhi – 110 017, India
Penguin Group (NZ), 67 Apollo Drive, Rosedale, Auckland 0632, New Zealand
(a division of Pearson New Zealand Ltd)
Penguin Books (South Africa) (Pty) Ltd, Block D, Rosebank Office Park,
181 Jan Smuts Avenue, Parktown North, Gauteng 2193, South Africa

Penguin Books Ltd, Registered Offices: 80 Strand, London WC2R 0RL, England

www.penguin.com

First published 2012
003

Set in 12.5/14.75pt Garamond MT Std
Typeset by Jouve (UK), Milton Keynes
Printed in Great Britain by Clays Ltd, St Ives plc

A CIP catalogue record for this book is available from the British Library

ISBN: 978–1–844–88307–3

www.greenpenguin.co.uk

The Pleasures of Winter is dedicated to all of the Masters and submissives who so openly shared their personal experiences with us. Especially to D – rock, hard place and confidant.

Our grateful thanks to Ian O'Reilly of the BBC for the champagne and invaluable information about Honduras.

And to our neglected families who only complained slightly when we disappeared to write *The Pleasures of Winter* – normal service will be resumed shortly.

1

Abbie Marshall tucked the handset of the payphone under her chin as she scanned the display in Toncontín Airport. Despite the air conditioning, her T-shirt was already damp from the Honduran heat. 'You have to get me out of here.'

Every flight to the States was full and now she had a bigger problem. Two of them, to be precise. They had been on her tail since she left the hotel and the dark-eyed one with the scar on his cheek was horribly familiar.

She almost missed her editor's reply. 'I'm on it. Give me an hour and I'll –'

When Scarface rose to his feet, Abbie's heart dropped like a stone and she swallowed hard. This was an international airport. They couldn't just take her. Her gut told her something different. She had seen enough in the past two weeks to know that these men could do whatever they wanted, and no one would stop them. 'Josh, I don't think I have an hour.'

'How close are they?'

Abbie gripped the handset tighter. 'Would you be upset if I said thirty feet? I'm a sitting duck here. I can't get a signal on my cell. I'll find another payphone if I can't stay on this one.'

A string of expletives followed. 'I want you to stay on the line. Talk to me, Princess.'

Abbie ignored the princess jibe. 'I'm fine, I just . . . I'm fine. Tell Sara that I've got the story and I'll file it as soon as I get home.'

She eased the battered rucksack off her shoulder. It had seen her through some scary assignments – north Africa, Burma, Haiti. This might be the last trip for both of them. She had been in tight spots before, but nothing like this.

The flight to New York was announced and Abbie watched the passengers leave for the departure gate. Scarface returned from the bar and raised his glass in her direction. She wasn't any safer here than she had been at the hotel. In a couple of hours the last flight would be gone and the men would make their move.

'Abbie, you still there? *Abbie!*' Her editor's sharp tone jolted her back to reality. 'Listen. Go to the charter desk in the main hall. There's a private jet departing for Miami in thirty minutes. Jack Winter is on it. You can interview him on the way.'

'What are you talking about – interview Jack Winter?'

She heard an exasperated sigh on the other end.

'Do you want to get out of there or not? Standard Studios have been trying to put us together with Winter for months. He agreed to an interview, but we've never been able to get hold of him. It's your lucky day because of all the godforsaken places he could have turned up in, he's in Honduras. Or was. He's leaving on that plane tonight. The publicist is making sure you can get on the flight but she can't get through to Winter or his people. You'll just have to sweet-talk him when you get there. Now, *run!*'

Abbie closed her eyes. Apart from her work gear, her small rucksack contained nothing but a washbag and a change of underwear. There had been no time to grab anything else when fleeing the hotel. Her T-shirt was stuck to her body. And Josh expected her to interview a Hollywood heart-throb, a guy more famous for his hell-raising and womanizing than his acting?

When she opened her eyes again, Scarface was staring at her.

'I'm on it.' Abbie dropped the handset into the receiver and, picking up her rucksack, she ran.

The men were surprised by her sudden flight. She heard a chair scraping noisily against the tiles and a bottle crashing to the floor. Pushing her way through the waiting passengers, she fled across the lobby, ignoring the shouts of the men racing behind her. Abbie only slowed when she spotted the armed security personnel. Toncontín also served as a military airport and she didn't want to be arrested or shot by mistake.

A quick glance over her shoulder told her that Scarface hadn't been so lucky. The men had been stopped. Maybe she might get out of this after all. She hurried along the main hall. Most of the desks were closed and the man at the charter desk was pulling down the shutters.

'My name is Abbie Marshall. You should have had a call about this. I'm getting a ride on the Standard Studios jet.'

He glanced at his watch and gave her an apologetic smile. 'I'm sorry, Ms Marshall, but you're too late. The jet is ready for departure.'

Abbie looked over her shoulder. Scarface and his buddy had been released. 'Please, I have to get out of here tonight.'

As the man sized her up Abbie gave him a look that she

hoped conveyed the right mix of desperation and sympathy for his difficult job. Her life depended on changing his mind.

He made a snap decision. 'OK, but we'll have to run.' He ushered her behind the desk and through a small door at the back. She followed him along a maze of concrete corridors, through an emergency door and out into the night. The thick, humid air hit her face like a furnace.

'Hurry.' He grabbed her arm and dragged her along the tarmac until she thought her lungs would burst. Up ahead, she could see the sleek white outline of a waiting jet. Two figures in Hi-Vis waistcoats were pulling the portable steps away.

'No! Wait!' Abbie said. Waving her arms and yelling, she raced for the plane. The ground crew finally heard her and paused, leaving the steps in place for another few precious seconds.

She launched herself up the steps and through the door at the top, landing on her hands and knees. She stayed there, panting, trying to catch her breath before she had to deal with her fellow passengers.

'Are you OK?' asked a tall man, who helped her to her feet and gave her a reassuring smile.

Still trying to control her racing heartbeat and loud breathing, Abbie smiled back. 'I am now.' He was cute, with brown hair and blue eyes, and an Irish accent to die for.

An older man, already strapped into his seat, frowned at her. 'Were we expecting you?' he asked, glancing at his watch. His expensive suit didn't quite conceal the beginnings of a pot belly and his air of self-importance set her teeth on edge.

She stood up and dusted herself down. 'I believe you were. I'm Abbie Marshall, *New York Independent*. I'm here to interview Jack Winter.' She tried to make it sound as if that were the only reason she was on the plane.

'No so fast, Ms Marshall. I'm Mr Winter's agent. Everything should be cleared through me.' He pulled out his smartphone.

'This is Zeke Bryan,' the younger man said.

'Mr Bryan.' She nodded politely, but made no effort to shake his hand. '*New York Independent*. I believe an interview was agreed with us some time ago. Part of Mr Winter's contract with Standard Studios.'

The agent looked in two minds but before he could say anything else, the younger man flashed her a smile and said, 'Oh, give it a rest, Zeke, it's not as if we can't use some female company on the flight.'

The agent sat back in his seat scowling, and then looked away. It seemed she was free to proceed.

The young man held out his hand. 'I'm Kevin O'Malley.'

She shook his hand, enjoying his friendliness and easy manner. Abbie could understand all those stories about Irish charm.

He raised his voice slightly. 'Hey, Jack, come and meet our lovely guest.'

There was no response. Oh, great. Jack Winter was one of those prima donna actors who ignored everyone else. Reluctantly, she followed Kevin the few steps to the back of the plane, to be introduced to the infamous star.

When Kevin stepped to one side and she finally saw Jack Winter up close, she felt as though she had been hit by an invisible fist. Abbie had to make a conscious effort to keep breathing. Why had no one ever said? Or had she just not been paying attention? She dragged in a breath and tried to examine him objectively, like the professional journalist she was.

It was easy to see why women flocked to see his movies. Jack Winter was all masculine hard lines. He didn't carry an ounce of spare flesh but gave the impression of lethal power, barely under control. The actor's razor-sharp cheekbones and a strong jaw added to the tough-guy image. And yet, fighting that dazzling He-Man perfection, there was an irresistible sensual allure in the curve of his mouth. It wasn't right: no one should be that hot.

Somehow, it made it worse that Jack was staring out the window and ignoring everything in the cabin. Kevin touched his arm to get his attention.

Thick, dark brows framed the pair of startling blue eyes that turned in her direction. In the face of so much male beauty, Abbie was conscious of her own appearance. She was dirty, sweaty and in need of a shower.

He stood up, towering over her and making her feel dainty and petite. The photographs in the glossy magazines didn't do him justice: they couldn't show the overwhelming potency of the man. This close, she could feel the heat radiating off his body and caught the faint aroma of an expensive cologne. But even more distinctive was the subtle but still overwhelming aura of masculinity around him. No matter how familiar he was, nothing could have prepared her for that. Her breath caught in her throat . . .

'We're about to take off,' he said abruptly, and urged her into the seat opposite. He strapped her in before she could protest and redid his own seat belt. With that, the plane taxied down the rough runway. The engines whined as the jet left the ground and climbed into the sky, leaving the winking lights of Tegucigalpa airport far below them.

He offered her his hand. He had big hands, she noticed, with a strong, firm grip. 'I'm Jack Winter.' His voice was a low rumble and his accent was even more enticing than Kevin's.

Finally, he smiled. A smile as wicked as his reputation. Those sensuous lips curled, showing white teeth and a single dimple in his lean cheeks. His eyes blazed even bluer. She caught her breath. On the screen, he was handsome. In the flesh, Jack Winter was heart-stopping.

He continued to smile, waiting for a response. *Oh, settle down. You're not a star-struck intern on the lifestyle pages. He's just another job.* Abbie leaned forward and placed her hand in his. 'Abbie Marshall. Pleased to meet you, Mr Winter. Thanks for the ride.'

'Call me Jack.'

Abbie was in no frame of mind to do an interview. She had dealt with some frightening people in her day, but none had had this effect on her. Even in the face of gun-toting insurgents she had managed to keep a clear head. Not this time – both her pulse and her thoughts were racing. There was nothing for it but to get on with it. She reached down into her bag to pull out her recorder.

'I'll try to get the interview over quickly.'

His smile vanished. 'What interview?'

'The interview you agreed to give the *New York Independent*. That's why I'm here.'

Jack looked at her suspiciously. His aversion to journalists was well known. But she could see the flash of recognition in those steely blue eyes: the studio's publicity machine had set up an ambush and there was nothing he could do. It didn't mean he was happy about it. Abbie shivered as he gave her a long, steady look, assessing her coldly.

'Of course,' he said finally. 'I'm looking forward to a grilling.'

His dry tone and raised eyebrow told her that this wouldn't be an easy interview. What the hell had Josh dropped her into?

Kevin made his way to the front of the plane and returned with three bottles of iced tea. He offered Abbie one and she took it gratefully.

Abbie held up her digital recorder. 'Do you mind if I record this?'

Jack shrugged. He opened his bottle and took a long swig. 'Go ahead.'

Like a light being switched off, the charm was gone.

Abbey smiled encouragingly. 'I promise this won't take long, Mr Winter.'

Jack took another swig.

She switched on the recorder. 'So, why are you in Honduras?'

Jack gave her a blank stare before draining the last drops of iced tea. 'You haven't done your homework.' He sounded annoyed.

Abbie flushed. 'Sorry, I was kind of dropped into this, Mr Winter, but if you wouldn't mind filling me in on –'

'Lady, I've been up for thirty-six hours straight. I'm too tired for this.'

If Jack Winter wouldn't cooperate, this would be a short interview. Abbie could feel her temper rising and she took a deep breath before replying. 'I got this assignment thirty minutes ago. Just how much homework do you think I've been able to do?'

Jack pressed a button in the armrest of his seat and eased it back into a reclining position. 'Let's make it interesting. For each question you ask me, I get to ask you one. And you call me Jack. Agreed?'

'That is no way to conduct an interview, Mr . . . Jack.'

'Take it or leave it.' He closed his eyes.

She heard Zeke Bryan chuckle from further up the aisle.

Abbie sighed with frustration. Jack Winter might be Hollywood A-list but he was turning into a major pain in the ass. There was no way that she was going to let him get the better of her.

'Very well, Jack.'

He opened those amazing eyes and smiled at her. 'I'm all yours, Abbie. Ask your questions.'

'Why are you in Honduras?'

Before he had a chance to speak, Zeke Bryan interrupted. 'Jack was here to open a medical facility for the people of Tegucigalpa. We filmed *Jungle Heat* there last year and Jack promised to return when it was complete.'

His answer surprised her. A lot of the studios made promises to help the local people when they were on location, but they seldom delivered.

'My turn, Abbie. Why are you here?'

There was no harm in telling him. The story would hit the papers in a couple of days. 'I was covering a story about a link between drug cartels and political figures in the Honduran government.'

'A dangerous job for a woman.'

'Why?' She tried not to snap at him. 'Don't you think women should cover serious stories?'

She could feel herself shrinking under the intensity of his gaze. 'I didn't say that, but yes, I would consider covering a drugs story in Honduras to be a dangerous occupation.'

She couldn't even argue with that, considering Scarface and his associate. She decided not to mention that and forced her attention back to the interview. 'But you're famous for courting danger yourself, aren't you, Mr Winter? I mean, Jack.'

'I enjoy pushing my limits. Don't you find that you can learn a lot about yourself that way?'

'Is that a question?'

This time his smile was genuine. 'No, just an observation. Here's my question – since you obviously like going after big stories, what are you doing interviewing an actor?'

Was that a joke? She couldn't read him well enough to tell.

'Like you say, it's good to push your limits,' she said. 'I guess I was just in the right place at the right time. You know, taking on a role outside of my usual comfort zone. Haven't you ever done that?'

'Oh Abbie, you'd be surprised at my range,' he said.

Abbie had an uncomfortable feeling she was missing something.

'You're obviously committed to your career. Where does that leave the rest of your life? Tell me, are you married? Single? Still looking for the right guy?'

'Single,' she said. 'But I have a fiancé back in New York.' Abbie suppressed a pang of guilt when she remembered William. She hadn't spared him a thought in days. She would have to call him when she got to Miami.

'So, no serious relationships, then.'

Across the aisle, Kevin had been listening and guffawed. Abbie scowled at him. 'We've been engaged for four years.'

Jack whistled. 'Four years, and he hasn't managed to get you up the aisle. Doesn't sound like much of a fiancé to me.'

Abbie gritted her teeth. 'You've had your question, Jack. Let's talk about your relationships. Are you married or still looking for the right woman?'

She knew he wasn't married. Jack had a reputation for womanizing and now she could add being irritating and chauvinistic to his list of attributes.

Jack considered her question. 'I've never been married and never intend to be. As for the right woman, I don't believe there is such a thing. Only the one who is right for now.'

'And there have been a hell of a lot of those,' Kevin said as he got out of his seat and walked up the cabin again.

Abbie didn't know what possessed her to ask the question. 'How many?'

One dark brow crooked in surprise. 'It's my turn to ask a question, and as we're getting up close and personal –' He leaned in closer.

Abbie couldn't help swallowing as she looked at his mouth.

'When was the last time that you made love?'

She flushed scarlet. It was weeks, maybe months; she couldn't remember, but she wasn't going to tell him that.

'That's a very personal question.'

'That's not an answer.'

Kevin returned with more iced tea. Jack took the bottle from him without taking his eyes off her. She couldn't remember the last time she had felt so utterly exposed, but then she had never had a man like Jack Winter look at her so intently. He popped the cap while she played with her recorder and tried to ignore the question, but it seemed he wasn't going to let her get away with that.

'Well?' he said.

'It's none of your business,' she said through gritted teeth.

'In that case, the interview is over.' He stuck the bottle into the holder, pushed his seat all the way back, settled himself and closed his eyes.

Jack had watched Abbie blush like a virgin with a mixture of amusement and fascination and wondered how far he could push her. As he lay back, he ignored her outraged gulp and waited to see how long it would take before she cracked and told him what he wanted to know.

And he did want to know, he was surprised to find. Abbie Marshall wasn't his usual type, but there was something about her . . .

Even with his eyes closed, Jack had no problem picturing the shape of her face with its baby-soft skin and dusting of freckles. The women he normally dated wouldn't be seen dead with freckles, they'd have had them peeled and sandpapered away. Her mouth was wide and inviting with the perfectly even teeth of someone who had spent years in braces.

Her short hair framed her face, highlighting her eyes. He allowed himself a brief fantasy of running his fingers through that shiny dark hair, secure in the knowledge that he wouldn't be fighting half a pound of extensions and hair product. 'Don't touch the hair' was a mantra with his dates.

And those eyes: wide, green and sparkling with curiosity and intelligence. Oh yes, this was a woman who could stand up to him if necessary. He enjoyed the snap of animosity between them and if things had been different, would have enjoyed taking things further.

But she was a journalist. That was bad enough, even without the cut-glass accent which he recognized as Old Money. He was never getting involved with a woman like that again. He'd learned his lesson the hard way.

He heard her inhale.

'Mr –'

He opened one eye at her, shook his head and closed it again. Ms Marshall would learn that if she wanted to interview him, she had to play by his rules and answer his questions. His interest in her answer was beside the point.

She huffed and he couldn't resist a grin. She must have seen it because she huffed louder, but she refused to speak.

Gradually, the previous thirty-six hours caught up with him and despite the drone of the engine, he dozed.

The irregular splutter of the engines roused him. He opened his eyes and checked the cabin. Nothing looked out of place. Kev and Zeke had their heads together over an iPad and Abbie was curled up in her seat, her legs tucked under her in a way that his would never fit. When he glanced out the window, the engines looked as normal. But – he frowned – they were flying closer to the clouds than he would have expected.

The engine coughed again and the hairs prickled on the back of his neck. He got up and headed for the cockpit. On impulse, he snapped the safety belt around Abbie before he went.

She woke up and scowled at him. 'What are you doing?'

She sounded cranky and he wanted to smile, but his instincts were kicking in. 'Stay here, and keep that belt tight on you.'

'I don't take orders from you.'

'Take this one.' He didn't have time to explain his unease.

'Like I was going anywhere,' she said, but she settled back down, with the belt still around her.

Jack moved forward, noticing that there was a distinct slope in the floor of the cabin. Something was wrong.

The cockpit was tiny, not so much a room as a seat with a bunch of electronics behind a folding screen, and only enough room for one pilot. Jack forced the screen open and asked, 'Is anything wrong?'

The pilot, a silver-haired man with ruddy skin, was paler than Jack remembered. His face had a light sheen of sweat and there was a blue tinge to his lips. 'I don't feel so well,' he muttered. He gripped the steering column, but he seemed to be ignoring the urgent red lights blinking at him.

Under Jack's horrified eyes, the pilot's grip shifted and the nose of the plane dipped another few degrees.

'Got an aspirin? I've got a bit of a pain.' The pilot rubbed his chest, pressing hard on it, before grabbing the steering column again. The man kept his eyes glued on the sky, but ignored the instruments. He paled even further and sweat rolled down his face.

'Where are your meds?' Jack asked. Please let him have meds that would fix this.

The pilot's voice slurred. 'What meds?'

2

Fuck! To Jack's untrained eye, the pilot was having a heart attack. He shoved his way back into the cabin. 'Where's the first-aid kit?' he asked no one in particular. There should be aspirin in there.

Kev dragged his attention away from the iPad. 'The what?'

'The first-aid kit. I need aspirin.'

'I've got some paracetamol,' Abbie said. She moved to unbuckle her seat belt.

'Stay where you are,' Jack said and handed her the rucksack. He had no idea if it would do any good, but it was better than nothing. She fished though a pile of clothes, including some intriguingly lacy panties, and handed him a blister pack with two gone. 'Thanks.' He grabbed his bottle of iced tea to help the pilot wash it down. It would be warm, but who cared.

'What's going on?' Abbie asked as he moved back towards the cockpit.

'Nothing,' he replied gruffly. None of the others seemed to notice that anything out of the ordinary was happening and he wasn't about to cause a panic by telling them.

When he got back, the pilot's face was grey and he was struggling for breath. His grip on the steering column jerked and he slumped forward. His head hit something and the plane shuddered. Jack hauled him up to force the pills into him, but it was too late. The pilot had stopped breathing – and the plane was heading down through the clouds towards the ground.

Fuck. Fuck. Fuck. This wasn't good. Jack frantically tried to remember the flying lessons he had taken for *Fly Hard 3*. The first thing was to take control of the plane. He had to get it level and restore altitude. He pushed the pilot out of his seat. The man slumped forward, clearing the seat but blocking the foot pedals and far instruments. He tried to pull him out of the way, but he was wedged in place. This was going to get dirty.

Jack sat down in front of the controls, grabbed the steering column and pulled back on it, forcing the nose of the little plane up and away from the ground.

What was the emergency frequency number – 121.5? As soon as he had a safe altitude, he'd call for help.

He battled to keep the steering column pulled back, but the pilot must be pressing on something because the plane kept descending and pulling to the left. They dropped down into clouds and Jack found himself staring at a sea of white. The clouds muffled even the noise of the engines. If it weren't for the altimeter's rapidly changing numbers, everything would have seemed strangely peaceful.

Jack ran through every swear word he knew, and then stopped bothering while he battled the forces of gravity. His eyes watered from staring through the blanket of white, trying to pick out what was below them.

There was no doubt they were going to crash. The only question was, would it be a crash they could walk away from?

Without warning, the white gave way to green. Between

one blink and the next, they were out of the cloud and flying directly above the canopy of the rainforest. Jack wrestled the controls, trying to keep the plane level until he could spot somewhere to land.

The trees were directly underneath, so close that he swore a couple of them scraped the bottom of the plane. There was no way he could land. He checked his airspeed. Two hundred miles per hour. They were going to be mincemeat soon.

To the right, something caught his eye. A gap in the green. He banked the plane, hoping it might be a river. If that pilot could land a plane on the Hudson, he could do it too. God, this was even better than a river. It was a tiny airstrip, undoubtedly cleared by drug runners. He sucked in a breath; he might be able to land the plane.

He banked further, giving himself a bit of airspace before he began his descent. 'Buckle up and brace yourselves,' he yelled into the cabin. 'We're going down and it's going to be a rough landing.'

He ignored the others as they shouted back at him in alarm. The pilot was a deadweight pressing into his arm as he straightened their flight path for the landing. Jack pressed his shoulder against the man, trying to get at the controls. He eased back on the throttle to reduce the speed, and tried to line up with the airstrip. It was so small it was like threading a needle.

The ground rushed up at him, faster than he expected. He cursed, trying to keep the nose up. *Wheels are good, deploy the landing gear. Lower flaps, reduce speed, what else?* Too late, he saw that the landing strip had been sabotaged. There was a massive trench across it, guaranteed to crash any plane that tried to land. Frantically, he hauled on the steering column, forcing the plane away from the wheel-trapping trench and into the forest.

They were still carrying too much speed. Jack slammed on the brakes, but not before they smashed into the wall of green. All he could do was try to steer so that they didn't collide head-on with one of the giant trees that stretched up to cloud level.

The jerk of a wing hitting a small tree almost knocked him over, especially when it was followed soon after by another. *So, we're not flying out of here, then.* He was nearly blinded by the vegetation rushing at the cockpit window.

They were lucky they hadn't crashed into anything solid enough to pulverize them. Their speed was dropping and Jack began to hope they might get out of this alive.

The plane tipped forward, knocking him off his feet and crashing his head into the control panel. Only years of physical training kept him from tumbling straight into the window, which was now the lowest point of the cockpit. From the cabin he heard screams and a yell of pain.

When Jack got back to his feet, he saw that they had tipped into a gully of some sort. They were near the top of it, and only one broken wing caught on a tree had saved them from plummeting to the bottom.

Sweating, and ignoring the trickle of blood he could feel down his neck, he forced his way back into the cabin. The floor was tilted at a dangerous angle, but by grabbing the seat backs, he could make his way along.

Abbie and Kev were buckled into the seats, both white-faced and panting, but safe. Zeke Bryan was on the ground, clutching his arm and whimpering. His seat belt was unfastened. The dickhead hadn't done what he had told him.

'Zeke? How badly are you hurt?' he asked, as he tried to assess his injuries.

The older man glared at him. 'I broke my arm, you moron.' He held one arm tenderly with the other. 'What the hell were you playing at up there? Did you crash the plane?'

'The pilot had a heart attack,' Jack said shortly. He didn't have time for explanations. 'We need to get out of here now.'

'I'm not moving. Can't you see I'm injured?' Zeke sounded more like a petulant child than Hollywood's leading agent.

Jack's vision was fuzzy around the edges and his head hurt like hell. 'Fine, stay here and when the plane falls, you can fall with it.'

'Falls? What are you talking about?'

'We're at the top of a gully with a fair drop below us. If that wing goes, we'll fall to the bottom. I'm guessing it's a flood culvert and next time it rains, we'll be flotsam. It's time to get out of here.'

Jack made his way over to the door. By bracing himself with one foot on the floor and one on the wall, he was able to open it. He assessed their situation. They'd have to climb down from the plane, drop on to the ground and then scramble up the side of the gully to the relative safety of the forest floor. Oh yeah, this was going to be fun.

'How is everyone holding up?' he asked. The last thing he needed was a hysterical female on his hands, but it was

Zeke who was hyperventilating and changing colour. 'The hard part is over, now we just have to get out of here and we'll be safe,' he lied, knowing that the hard part would be staying alive.

Before he could say anything else, Zeke broke in. 'No, I'm not all right. I'm injured. I have a broken arm. I need to go to a hospital.'

'We'll get you to one as soon as possible. First we need to get out of here.' He gestured to Abbie. 'Ladies first.'

'Forget that,' Zeke told him. 'I'm injured. She's not. I need to get down out of here and find a doctor ASAP.'

Abbie shrugged. 'Fine by me.'

Abbie watched as Jack lowered himself carefully from the plane and dropped the last couple of feet. He skidded further down the muddy sides of the small ravine and had to climb back up. Anchoring himself on a couple of prominent roots sticking through the mud, he called up, 'OK, Zeke, come down and I'll catch you.'

Even with Kev lowering him and Jack guiding his feet, getting the agent out of the plane was a nightmare. He yelped and complained non-stop, occasionally screaming with pain. Jack caught him around the waist and lowered him to his feet before he helped him struggle up the few feet to the top of the gully. Zeke collapsed in a heap at the top, moaning piteously.

Jack then changed his mind about the order of exit. 'Kev, could you come down now and bring the first-aid kit with you?'

Whatever happened to women and children first? If

the plane moved again, she was going with it. *Tragedy as journalist survives plane crash, only to drown in river.*

'Sure thing.' Kev threw a small bag down to Jack, who tossed it up on to the bank. Then he guided Kev to a safe landing.

'Now you, Abbie.'

She took one last look around the cabin and patted her rucksack. Her laptop was safe, but where was her recorder?

'Just a moment, I have to get a few things.'

As she moved down the cabin, the plane shuddered.

'Now, Abbie,' Jack roared.

'In a minute,' she called. She dropped to her knees in front of the seat where she had been sitting. It had to be here. A shout from overhead startled her.

'What the hell are you doing? Get out of here now.' Jack had climbed back into the plane and was glaring down into her open rucksack.

'I'm trying to find my recorder,' she snapped. 'There's some stuff on it I really need.'

She watched as his jaw clenched and unclenched. 'We have crash-landed in the fucking jungle. It's a miracle we're not spaghetti sauce right now, and you are worrying about a bit of plastic? Forget the fucking recorder. Forget the laptop and leave your other stuff behind. We can't carry it.'

Abbie winced. Jack Winter in a temper was pretty terrifying, but she needed her notes. She opened her mouth to argue but he cut her off.

'You're leaving this plane now. Tell me what you need and I'll get it for you.'

'My recorder.' The plane lurched again, and she yelped.

'You have thirty seconds while I get some supplies. Then you are going out that door on your ass.'

Next thing, emergency parachutes and blankets were flying past as Jack tossed them through the open door. She saw him stuff his pockets with packets of nuts and miniature bottles of spirits and then filling a bag with bottles of water and pre-packaged meals.

She touched the digital recorder wedged under the seat, pulled it out and shoved it into her pocket. She could hear Jack moving in the cockpit. There must be something she could do to help him.

She was horrified when she saw the pilot's distorted body and the front of the plane so badly smashed up. For the first time since they landed, she wanted to be sick. She didn't know how Jack Winter had landed the plane safely. Her annoyance turned to admiration.

The pilot was twisted into an awkward position in the mangled cockpit. Jack braced himself with his feet on the control panel and tried to pull him out. The pilot was stuck. He winced as a piece of mangled plastic dug into his side.

Don't be such a girl, Marshall. Help him. She grasped the plastic and moved it out of his way, stifling a cry as she sliced her palm on the sharp edge.

'I don't think that we can move him,' Jack said.

Abbie stared at the man wedged under the instrument panel. It could be any one of them. 'We can't just leave him here. We have to bury him.'

'Abbie.' Jack's tone was sharp. 'I need you to hold him up while I try the radio.'

The pilot's body was still warm. Abbie tried not to look

at his face while Jack tried the radio, but it was as dead as the pilot. There was no help coming. They were stuck.

The plane shifted again.

'We're leaving here, right now,' he said.

Abbie couldn't move. Frozen to the spot, she could feel the plane shudder as it moved beneath her feet. Then Jack was grabbing her shoulders, urging her back into the main cabin. He paused long enough to rifle through the pilot's locker, removing a pack of cigarettes and a lighter, before pushing her to the door.

Jack yelled at Kev to be ready. He threw down the bag of supplies and then lowered her down. Even in this situation, she couldn't help noticing Jack's distinctive scent, musk and man, something that was uniquely him. Her breasts brushed his chest and she blushed at the intimate contact.

As he jumped down to the side of the gully behind her, the plane shifted again. With a creak of metal, the wing holding it in place twisted and the crippled aircraft toppled down. Jack gripped a root, desperately trying to prevent them being pulled down with it.

'It's OK. I've got you,' he said.

The crash as the plane hit was shockingly loud. The cacophony of sound grew louder still as every animal and bird in the area screamed in response. Anyone nearby would be bound to hear it. She clung to him for a long moment. Being held by Jack was like being in the eye of a storm. She had never felt so safe.

'Abbie.' Jack's voice took on a teasing tone. 'Much as I'm enjoying this, I think we'd better get out of here.'

Her eyes shot open. What was she thinking? She was

clinging to Jack Winter like a baby monkey. Abbie pushed away from him quickly, straightening her wrinkled clothes to cover her confusion. *I am not attracted to him. I am not attracted to him. I just banged my head.* Once she felt composed, she raised her eyes to his.

The sardonic expression was gone, replaced with a glint of amusement and something she couldn't fathom.

'What happens now? I guess we stay near the plane and wait to be rescued?'

Jack closed his eyes. 'Abbie.' His voice was strained, as if he were trying to keep it under control. 'What rescue? We are in the middle of the jungle. Miles from civilization. Our priority is survival.'

Survival? No. No way. This was not turning into one of those ridiculous programmes on TV where everyone ended up spending all day looking for something dry to burn and eating rats.

'They'll find us soon,' she said with more confidence than she felt. 'The pilot sent a Mayday and they'll –'

'There was no Mayday. There wasn't time.'

Her stomach flipped. 'Transponder?' she asked hopefully.

Jack ran his fingers through his hair. 'I don't know. You saw the front of the plane. It was pretty smashed up.'

Abbie took a deep breath. No one knew they were here. *Don't panic. Do not panic.*

'Come on, Kev has a medical kit. You can patch up that hand.'

3

Abbie battled shock as she sat at the top of the ravine while Kevin examined her hand. Keeping her head in a crisis went with the territory – an easily spooked journalist was useless – but she had just been in a plane crash. Now she was in the middle of the Honduran jungle with three men she didn't know, and all she could think about was what a great story it would be. *Forget the celebrity interview, look at the story I've got.*

She was savouring the brief moment of calm when Jack turned round and stared sharply at her and Kevin.

'I didn't realize this was a dating service,' he said.

'You think –'

She spluttered to a halt, lost for words. It was beyond ridiculous. On the plane she had been so overwhelmed by Jack Winter that she had allowed his attitude to slide. But now they were going to be stuck in the wilderness for who knew how long. She shuddered. She couldn't think about that – and she was just going to have to toughen up around him. Just because he was hotter than hell didn't mean he wasn't a jerk. And she knew how to put jerks in their place.

Kevin finished cleaning up her hand. He grinned at his friend and put his arm around her. 'Don't mind Jack. He likes to push people. Now me, I like to stroke them.' And he rubbed her back in a way that felt suspiciously like a caress. No – she was imagining things.

Jack scowled. 'Kev, we don't have time for you to chase pussy.'

Abbie felt like he had stung her and she jumped away from Kevin.

'How dare you? What century do you think you are living in? What sort of crude, distasteful, chauvinistic thing is that to say to anyone?'

She would have continued, but Jack cut in. 'And we don't have time for a lecture in feminism either. We've got to focus on survival here.'

'Exactly.' Zeke Bryan was sitting on the ground, holding one arm with the other. 'I need to get to a hospital at once. I have a broken arm. I need medical treatment, not to listen to this sort of juvenile squabbling.'

Abbie could see a flicker of annoyance on Jack's face, but then his expression reverted to neutral.

'Our priority is to survive,' he repeated. 'I have no idea if the plane is transmitting any sort of distress beacon. Anyone skilled in electronics?'

They all shook their heads.

'I've lost my cell phone. Any of you got a signal on yours?'

They checked and shook their heads again. Obviously they were too far away from a mast.

'We'll camp here tonight, and Kev and I will go down the ravine to bury the pilot in the morning. If anyone's looking for us they have a chance of finding us. If no one comes, we'll have to find our own way to civilization.'

Despite her earlier fury with him, Abbie couldn't help but admire how Jack took charge. He was a big Hollywood star, but obviously all those leading-men roles weren't just acting. He was tough and able to think in a crisis.

'No, I'm injured. I can't be moved,' Zeke said.

'I appreciate that, Zeke,' Jack said. 'But if help is not coming, we have no alternative. Now –'

'What do you mean, help isn't coming?' Zeke said. 'And what makes you such an expert?'

Abbie could see the effort Jack was making to restrain his temper with the whiny agent.

'I wouldn't say expert. But when we were filming *Jungle Heat,* I spent a lot of time with people who were and I tried to learn as much as possible. I know, for instance, that it's going to rain and get dark soon.'

The humidity was already pressing down on them like a blanket, making it difficult to breathe. The heat was making everyone sweat, but the heavy air was harder to deal with.

'So, the first thing we are going to do is make some hammocks and a cover for them.'

'Why hammocks? I can't sleep in a hammock,' Zeke said.

'Have you looked at the ground?' Jack asked. Everyone looked down to where their feet sank into the damp soil. The ground was just mud covered by leaves. 'And it will get worse when it rains. We need to be up above the ground then or we'll be trying to sleep in liquid mud.'

'What makes you so sure it's going to rain?' Zeke said.

'This is a rainforest. The clue is in the name. It rains here every day. Just because the canopy is hiding the clouds doesn't mean they aren't there. See that mist?' He pointed at the silver vapour softening the outlines of the trees. The others nodded. 'That's a good indication that rain is coming. We need to get to work.'

Jack grabbed the two parachutes that he had tossed from the plane and directed Kev and Abbie in how to use his Swiss army knife to cut them up to make hammocks and covers. The bright red material was thin but strong and should do the job. The strings could be trimmed to the right length to act as supports. It was fortunate he never went anywhere without the knife; they'd have struggled to make the hammocks without it. It was a top-of-the-range model he had bought when he made his first film. The tool for picking horse's hooves wasn't going to do them much good, but the magnifying glass, saw, scissors and file might come in handy.

He was glad of the chance to do something physical. He couldn't believe that in the middle of this crisis he was so affected by Abbie Marshall. The sight of her hand in Kev's had enraged him. That was the moment he knew she had gotten under his skin. It was insane; he had no business being interested in her. Not even for a quick fuck. Though if he was fucking Abbie Marshall, it wouldn't be quick – he would draw it out until she was begging for release. He caught himself again. He had to stop thinking like this. Quite apart from the fact that she was obviously a New York princess, the American version of Sarah O'Brien-Willis, the girl who had destroyed his life, she was a reporter. Privileged, entitled and inquisitive. A lethal combination. He could see that her sharp eyes missed very little, and he wouldn't be able to get away with his usual lies.

Not lies, self-preservation.

He was glad he had made her angry. If he couldn't have her, he could make sure she stayed away from him. He had worked on developing an iron-hard self-control, but something told him this woman might crack it. Kev was obviously interested in her. The best thing for everyone would be if Kev and Abbie paired up, but when he saw Kev flirting with her, he couldn't watch it.

He wasn't sure that any of the others realized how vulnerable their situation was. Zeke certainly didn't. But then that bastard only cared about himself. He had pushed his way to the front of the line, and left Abbie behind on the plane. Not that Jack regretted those moments when her surprisingly bountiful breasts had pressed up against him. Had the fool really expected that it would be just a matter of driving to a hospital? Only years of acting had kept Jack's thoughts off his face. He put his feelings aside for now: he would make the agent pay sooner or later.

He, Kev and Abbie worked quietly, anxious to get the camp prepared. He sorted through the rest of the stuff that he had grabbed from the plane. The ready meals and water would keep them going for tonight and maybe for breakfast tomorrow. He handed Zeke a couple of pain-killers and a swig of water. The agent might be a whiny bastard but he was white around the mouth.

The water bottles would do as canteens when they were empty. He tied string around the necks to make them easier to carry. He blessed his jungle instructor who had drilled him in the basics of survival, and who was directly responsible for his personal jungle pack which contained water purification tablets, gloves, matches, a compass, a map, knife, mosquito netting, insect repellent and gloves.

He searched his pockets a bit deeper and found a solitary condom.

He couldn't help it. He laughed, and the sound brought all eyes to him and what he held in his hand.

'You cannot be thinking –' said Zeke, appalled. 'This is not the time or place.'

Abbie flushed. 'Not if you were the last man alive,' she said.

Jack couldn't resist taunting her. 'Wait until you're asked. I could be keeping this for Kev.'

Kev laughed. 'Excellent idea. I'll take that,' he said and grabbed it from Jack's hand. 'After all, I'm more likely to get lucky than you are.'

Abbie sniffed. 'Did you forget that I have a fiancé? No one is getting lucky. Unless you two are a lot closer than I thought.' And she turned her back on both of them.

Jack and Kev exchanged glances and laughed.

'Pity that stewardess went off sick at the last minute. I know we said we'd be all right without cabin crew, but she looked like a girl who would have been game for a bit of jungle loving,' Kev said, winking at Jack.

Abbie's back stiffened, but she refused to turn round.

By the time the hammocks were finished, everyone was thirsty, hungry and tired, and the first shift in the light told him that night wasn't far off. Jack distributed the food, keeping the packets of nuts for the following day.

He sat on the trunk of a fallen tree. Its roots stuck up into the air, like an umbrella abandoned in a storm. The wood was soft and damp and he was fairly sure it moved occasionally with the thousands of insects that considered it home.

He put his jacket on the rough bark and invited Abbie to sit beside him.

Purely to prevent her having hysterics if she sat on a spider, he told himself. Nothing to do with his desire to have her close to him. To smell her all-too-enticing perfume, a perfume that owed nothing to bottles and was all woman. God, he loved her smell. Against his will, his body reacted.

To distract himself and to remove temptation, he handed her the small bottle of insect repellent. 'Here, use lots. You don't want to get bitten.' The eerie silence of the rainforest was broken by the hum and chitter of insects and the louder, more ominous drone of mosquitoes.

She gave him a dirty look but rubbed it on.

The smell was enough to douse his arousal but her mutinous obedience brought out something he needed to keep hidden. 'Good girl,' he told her.

Her back stiffened and her eyes flared. 'I don't know what century it is in Ireland, but here you do not call grown women "girl", not if you value your body parts.'

Kev and Zeke snickered but Jack just grinned. 'Oh, I value my body parts, and if you're especially good, you might get to sample them for yourself. Then you'll see what all the fuss is about.'

Abbie didn't know whether to scream abuse at Jack or pretend she hadn't heard. She could tell by his grin exactly what he was thinking. He was getting to her and he knew it.

She was glad of the distraction when he handed out the

meal packs from the plane. Each of them got a plastic tray with little compartments for breadsticks, olives, cream cheese, some unidentified deli meat and a tiny portion of mustard. They were snacks rather than full meals, but they were edible and would keep them going. She hated to think what they were going to do for food after this. She had had some survival training, but had never had to use it.

'I can't eat this, I have a gluten intolerance, my homeopath told me to avoid all wheat,' Zeke Bryan said.

'Then divide it out and we'll eat it,' Jack said.

She noticed that Jack ate quickly, keeping a wary eye on the sky. It was going to be dark in minutes.

'Find a bush, go do your business and we'll go to bed,' he said.

There was a horrified silence.

'Business?' Abbie said finally.

'Piss. Take a leak. Spend a penny. Whatever the hell you call it. Just do it, without getting bitten if possible, and get back here before night falls.'

Kevin laughed.

'That's impossible,' Zeke said. 'I can't use public facilities. I can't possibly, er, go in these conditions.'

Abbie almost felt sorry for the old creep. Of course, he knew he had to do what Jack called his 'business' out in the wild, but somehow he seemed to think if he protested loudly enough, everything would magically get better. That was showbiz. When she was a cub reporter she had spent three months as an intern on the paper's entertainment section and had raced out of it the first chance she got. Showbiz was full of big egos who lived in another world, one where they always had 'people' to fix things for them. It was why she couldn't help admiring Jack Winter even if he was a pain in the ass. He just got on with it. Zeke, on the other hand, had become a spoiled child, and it looked like Jack was rapidly losing patience with him.

'Fine, hold it all night. See if I care.'

Kevin grinned at her. 'Want me to come and mind your back while you're taking care of business?' he said.

She would have preferred to go off on her own, but she knew it was safer to have company.

'Yes, please. If you promise not to look. You can watch for spiders.'

'Cross my heart and hope to die,' Kevin said, making a cross on his chest in a childish gesture. He walked ahead of her until they were away from the other two and they found a clear spot.

When they were both done and ready to go back, Abbie took a deep breath.

Kevin smiled at her. 'Worried? Look, it's a hell of a situation but I've been in plenty of scrapes with Jack before and we always get out of them.'

Abbie smiled back at him weakly. The last twenty-four hours were catching up with her and she was at the end of her endurance.

'Of course, there's one guaranteed way to take your mind off things,' he said, stroking her arm, 'and it would be a pity to let that condom go to waste.'

Oh, for the love of . . . *Men!*

Abbie glared at him and stomped back to base. She could hear him chuckling behind her. Jack had set up two hammocks. Yet again Zeke was complaining.

'I'm not sharing a hammock,' he said. 'You should have made more. We have enough material for more.'

'But only enough mosquito netting to cover two. If you want to sleep in a hammock with no netting, be my guest.'

Jack looked up at her and Kevin, narrowing his eyes as he took in their expressions.

'Bags I'm sharing with the hot girl,' Kevin said.

Jack shook his head. 'You're not as heavy as I am. You and Zeke together probably weigh the same as Abbie and I do. So that's the way we'll have to pair up.'

And now my night is complete.

She wasn't sure she could face sharing a hammock with any of these guys. But the last person she wanted to share with was Jack Winter. In that instant, every cell in her body came alive. She had spent the last few hours trying to ignore how his edgy masculinity and overpowering presence made her feel. She had managed to distract herself by coming up with new ways to be infuriated by him. But all of that was for nothing, she realized now. There was no point. The first moment she had seen him, he had affected her. Now it was worse – his beauty was no longer just abstract, like a piece of art or a staggering vista that she could admire intellectually. Now it was personal. At the image of the two of them lying next to each other, her heart started to beat faster, and between her thighs she could feel an unwelcome pulsing. She was afraid she was going to hyperventilate.

'I'm fine,' she insisted. 'I don't think I could sleep anyway. I'll just sit here and –'

'Don't move, Abbie. Stay perfectly still.'

A quick glance at Kevin's shocked expression told her that Jack wasn't joking. Something rustled in her hair and she bit her lip hard, trying not to scream. Something was crawling on her.

'Abbie,' Jack picked up a stick and moved slowly towards her, 'whatever happens, don't move.'

Stick in hand, Jack lunged forwards. The stick skimmed the top of her head and something dark tumbled into the undergrowth at her feet and scurried away. Her heart thundered. 'Oh my god. Oh my god, what was that thing?'

Jack shook his head. 'You don't want to know.'

Abbie eyed the small clearing. Her vague notions about staying up all night rather than sharing with Jack vanished like mist. When the others went to bed, she would be alone. Alone with the creatures. *Plane crash survivor eaten alive by jungle creatures* wasn't the front-page story she had planned, but neither was *My night in a hammock with Jack Winter*. What would William say if he found out?

Jack was oblivious to her dilemma. 'I figure we have ten minutes before it's dark. Now, are you coming to bed or not, Ms Marshall?'

She had no choice. 'Lead the way, Mr Winter.'

4

Abbie watched as Jack lifted the mosquito netting and slid into the hammock, patting the minuscule space beside him. Oh god – she would be lying *that* close to him. They would practically be on top of each other. At least she was feeling a bit more in control. That spider had done her a favour. After her meltdown at the thought of spending the night beside Jack Winter, the fright had brought her back to earth. Still, her stomach flipped at the prospect of the night ahead.

She hugged her arms around herself. The evening had turned chilly. So she was going to spend the night with a bona fide Hollywood heart-throb. She could just imagine Kit screaming when she told her. If they got out of this. Her best friend and her cosy apartment in New York both seemed a long way away.

'Abbie, quit dithering and get into bed. I promise not to bite.'

She scrambled into the hammock and rolled against him. 'But I don't, Mr Winter, so keep your hands to yourself.'

His response was a snort of laughter. Jack leaned over her so that he could adjust the mosquito netting. 'There,' he announced. 'Snug as two bugs in a rug.'

'You don't have to sound so pleased about it, and watch where you put your hands,' she said. Abbie rolled over on her side and slid into the middle of the hammock.

Jack curved his body around hers and dropped his arm around her waist. 'Where do you suggest I put them?'

His hand slid to her hip in a slow sensuous glide. 'Here?'

Abbie swallowed. His hand was warm. In fact every inch of him was like a furnace, but the hand on her hip was dangerously close, making her very aware of her femininity. For a brief second she wondered what it would feel like if he touched her there. No. Absolutely not. Bad Abbie. She lifted his hand and moved it back to her waist.

'If you insist,' he said, but left it where it was.

They lay in silence, listening to the sounds of the jungle, and almost in the blink of an eye, night fell.

Jack shifted against her. 'Would you mind if I moved my other arm? I'm getting cramp.'

Abbie lifted her head and lay back down again. Oh my god, the man had biceps. William was . . . well, William was slight. There was no other word for it. He was an academic and more interested in working his mind than his body. William didn't need muscles.

'Much better.' Jack's warm breath fanned her neck, sending tiny shivers along her spine.

'Are you cold?'

'No. I'm fine, Mr Winter.'

She felt laughter rumble in his chest. 'Abbie, why are you calling me Mr Winter again? We're going to spend the night together. I think we're beyond the formalities.'

Put that way, it sounded ridiculous. They were stuck in the jungle. She was sharing a tiny hammock with him. Calling him Mr Winter had been a ploy to create a feeling of distance between them. But she realized it made her sound like a prudish spinster. 'Fine, Jack.'

His arm tightened around her waist. 'Good girl,' he mumbled against her neck.

She was about to tell him off when she heard a low snore. Jack Winter was asleep.

Abbie sighed, letting the tension slowly leave her body. She wasn't sure what she had expected. That he would paw her incessantly. That she would spend the night rejecting his advances. But here he was, sleeping like a baby.

The weird thing was that after all the turmoil she had gone through in the last few hours, she felt safe. He had been obnoxious earlier, but now he was gentle. The heavy arm around her waist was protective, his breath against her neck, comforting. Abbie relaxed against him. Her eyelids felt as if they had weights on them. Her eyelashes fluttered closed.

A low roar in the distance woke her and she jerked awake.

Jack lifted his head. 'It's miles away, go back to sleep. I won't let anything harm you.'

She settled back into his arms. She didn't know why, but somehow she believed him.

Abbie stirred. She didn't want to open her eyes yet, she was blissfully comfortable. William wasn't usually so amorous, but now, oh god, it was like that time on vacation when he had really chilled out and stopped worrying about his research and departmental politics. His hand cupped her breast, toying with her nipple through the thin fabric of her shirt, sending darts of pleasure around her body like tiny fireworks. His other hand cruised her hip, holding her in place while his hips rocked gently against hers, pressing a sizeable bulge against her butt.

'Mmm,' she moaned as she rocked against him, seeking more of the delicious pressure. His mouth moved against her neck, making soft circles with his tongue, and then he nipped her playfully with his teeth. Abbie sighed deeply and the hand on her breast squeezed tighter. It felt amazing. William usually ignored her breasts but, oh, he was excelling himself this morning . . .

Her eyes shot open and a series of confusing images filtered through the darkness. She wasn't in New York. This wasn't her apartment and those were definitely not William's hands making her feel so good. The first rays of daylight brought a cacophony of noise to the forest, but her shriek was louder. She slapped Jack's hand off her and rolled away from him, tumbling out of the hammock and on to the forest floor.

Jack's head appeared over the edge of the silk. His heavy-lidded expression left her in no doubt that he had been enjoying their early-morning encounter as much as she had.

'You, you . . . groped me.' Her voice echoed around the clearing.

'Relax, Abbie. I didn't mean it. I didn't know it was you.'

'Oh great. That makes me feel so much better.'

'I didn't hear you complaining.' Jack flashed an amused smile.

'Complaining, you arrogant –'

'What the hell is going on?' Zeke's head emerged from beneath the mosquito net. 'I've only just dozed off. Do you know how hard it is to sleep when you're injured? The meds have worn off and my chiropractor is going to kill me when he sees what I've done to my back.'

Oh great, just what she needed. Another day with the Hollywood hypochondriac. Darting a filthy glance at Jack, she headed for the bushes to take care of business.

Jack distributed the packets of nuts, and watched Zeke make faces and mutter things about nut intolerance, but he ate them. There was only one unopened bottle of water left, so they shared that, then he filled their empty bottles at a small stream and dropped in water purification tablets.

He carefully didn't touch Abbie when he handed her bottle back to her. That night of sharing a hammock with her, of having her lush behind pressed up against him, had been worse than he had expected. *A hard night any way you thought about it.* So much for his vaunted self-control. He had been reduced to pretending to be asleep to get Abbie to relax and had battled an erection for hours. Too bad his control slipped when he slept.

Waking up next to her, feeling her cuddled into his arms with her ass tight against him, that was too much to expect him to take without reacting. He knew his reputation, but he was only human, and Abbie Marshall's ass would tempt a saint. A dead saint. He had to stay away from her. Or make sure she stayed away from him.

Jack saw Kev's glance slide from Abbie to him and back. He obviously wanted to know what, if anything, had happened last night. They went back far enough that Kev would know when he was interested in a girl.

Not a girl, he reminded himself. A journalist, and a woman cut from the same cloth as Sarah O'Brien-Willis. Sarah had almost destroyed his life. He wasn't going to let Abbie Marshall do the same thing. And she would. He had no doubt about that.

He grinned. Oh, he knew just how to keep her pissed at him.

'Anyone still hungry?' he asked casually.

Zeke and Abbie both said they were. 'Not if it has wheat in it, though. Wheat gives me mucus,' Zeke said.

'Oh, I think I can guarantee there won't be any wheat in this,' he said. He noticed that Kev had guessed what was coming and was keeping his mouth firmly shut, but his eyes were alight with devilment.

Jack moved to the side of the small clearing and listened to the branches of fallen trees. The second one sounded promising. He broke off a piece of bark and pulled out a couple of large wriggling larvae. 'Breakfast is served. Wheat free.' He offered one to Zeke and one to Abbie.

Zeke backed away so fast he would have fallen off the log he was sitting on if Abbie hadn't put out a hand to balance him. Kev, who had known what was coming, had his phone out and captured the horrified expression on the agent's face, no doubt planning to upload it to YouTube as soon as they were home. Zeke was so occupied with the grub, he didn't even notice. *Nice one, Kev. A little retribution for allowing Abbie to stay behind on the plane.*

Abbie surprised him. She didn't scream or back away. But she did look closely as the larvae writhed in his grip and said, 'Ten dollars says you won't eat one of those.'

'You're on.' Jack popped one into his mouth and bit

down. The creature wriggled for another half-second before the juices squirted out into his mouth. It was vile. It took every ounce of his acting skill to keep his face straight and keep chewing. *Next time, I'm cooking it first.* But it was worth it for the revolted, disbelieving expression on all their faces. With a final effort, he swallowed.

'Ah, jungle food at its freshest. More protein per pound than grass-fed beef. Are you sure you don't want one?' He held out the other squirming larva to Abbie.

She shuddered. 'Not in a million years.'

He gave her a knowing grin. 'You'll eat them soon enough.'

'I'll pay you ten dollars a time to eat them for me,' she told him.

He held out his hand, waiting. She stared at him in disbelief before fishing a note out of her pocket and slapping it in his hand.

Well, that was one way to make her keep her distance.

He had been putting off the job he dreaded, but it had to be done. 'Kev, come on. Let's go down to the plane and bury the pilot.'

With Jack and Kevin gone, and Zeke Bryan lying back against a tree dozing, it was Abbie's first opportunity to take stock of the last twenty-four tumultuous hours. It was nothing new to her, having to operate on the fly and only getting to take in the full picture later. She was an experienced reporter, after all – she should have something to bring to the party instead of being told what to do all the time.

But when she tried to focus, her mind was a jumble of

images and emotions. Worse, she kept flashing back to her wake-up call that morning – Jack Winter's hands moving deliciously up her body, his fingers pinching her nipple, that bulge against her ass. She felt little flickers of pleasure again.

No! She couldn't let herself spend any more time in this state. She dug the Kindle out of her rucksack and opened the thriller she had begun reading a couple of days earlier. After a few minutes she was lost in the world of Norwegian cops and criminals. She was surprised when she heard the men's voices and realized an hour had passed.

They told her that when they got down to the bottom of the ravine, nature had done the job for them. They found the remains of the plane, torn apart and buried under a river of fresh mud. Abbie shivered at the reminder of the dangers of the rainforest.

It was going to rain soon, Jack said, so he got them to pack up their little camp as quickly as possible. He handed Zeke a small waterproof poncho. The agent was white about the mouth and moved with difficulty. Jack gave him another couple of painkillers and a slug of tequila. Not the ideal combination, Abbie thought, but she guessed whatever helped the injured man stay on his feet was worth it.

There was some silk left over from the parachute. Jack made a cap out of a piece and told them all to do the same. 'It will keep the insects out of your hair,' he said. He grinned when they all jumped to attention.

After her encounter with a spider the previous night, Abbie was determined not to repeat the experience. She went behind Jack to check how he had tied the knot. She was shocked by the dark stain on his shirt. How had she not noticed it before?

You've got blood down your back,' she said.

He twisted round to look and made a face.

'I forgot about that. I gashed my head in the cockpit when the plane was coming down. Didn't realize it had bled so much. You're not afraid of blood, are you?'

Abbie ignored the jibe. She wasn't as weak as he seemed to think.

'Sit down while I look at it,' she said in a voice that was gratifyingly cool and businesslike. 'You should have mentioned this last night. Did your survival training not mention the risk of infection out here?'

He grinned but sat, allowing her to fuss over him. She parted his hair, checking the cut. It was long, but was beginning to heal.

'It looks fairly clean. Lucky you've got thick hair.'

She rooted through their tiny first-aid kit and found an alcohol wipe. As she parted his hair again, she was suddenly aware of the intimacy of what she was doing. Her fingers seemed to have a will of their own as they lingered, taking longer than was necessary to locate the cut. She rubbed it with the wipe. The sting made him hiss.

'Big baby,' she scoffed and sprayed on disinfectant.

He looked up at her. 'Oh, I'm no baby.'

She flushed and busied herself packing away the kit.

Next time she checked, Jack was studying his compass. 'Time to move out,' he said. 'From what I saw from the cockpit, there's a lagoon and a settlement of some sort if we head north, so that's our best bet.'

She was glad someone had a plan. Before they could move, the heavens opened and dumped what felt like the contents of an ocean on their heads. They stood under a thickly leaved tree trying to shelter from the downpour, but it was like using a tissue to shelter from a waterfall.

'I always wanted to see Niagara Falls, but this is almost as good,' Abbie said.

They all huddled together. Yet again she found herself pressed against Jack Winter's chest. It had been a full day since any of them had been near a shower, so what she was smelling was pure essence of Winter and it had an intoxicating effect on her.

Almost as quickly as it started, it stopped. A few last heavy drops signalled the end of the rain. For now. Jack checked the compass again and led them out into the thick wall of vegetation.

Pictures didn't convey the reality of a jungle, she thought, as she watched him hacking away at the undergrowth. Each step involved several swings of his knife. It was a pity he didn't have a proper machete. Every foot of progress disturbed more insects and wildlife. Kevin chatted to her but she didn't pay much attention to what he was saying – she was too busy watching out for bugs. She was glad when Kevin brushed them off her head and back a few times.

Kevin and Jack swapped places and Jack fell in beside her. The four of them walked in silence, all focused on conserving their energies and simply making their way. Abbie suggested taking a turn leading, but Jack and Kevin just stared her down. She didn't push it – she wasn't confident she would be that good at hacking through the greenery.

By the time lunch came around, she needed to sit down. Jack lit a small fire, collected a number of larvae and grubs and put them on makeshift wooden skewers. She watched the bug kebabs cook, wondering how on earth she'd eat them but realizing that she had no choice.

'Not haute cuisine, but edible,' Jack said.

She wasn't sure. *Starving New York journalist forced to eat bugs – my jungle hell,* she thought as she took one off a skewer and reluctantly put it into her mouth. Imagining the headlines was the only way she was going to swallow anything. Oh god, oh god, she was going to be sick. She cast a sidelong glance at Jack. He was staring at her. Waiting to see if she would spit it out.

Not a chance. If Hollywood and his sidekick could swallow one of these babies, so could she. It was just like sushi.

Who was she kidding? It was a bug. A truly foul-tasting bug. She swallowed and flashed Jack her brightest smile.

'Would you like another, Abbie? Plenty more to go round.'

'No thanks, I'm good.'

The sound of retching made her stomach clench. Zeke was bent over a log, puking up his lunch. Abbie gritted her teeth, trying not to do the same. Kevin winked at her before going to fetch some water for Zeke.

Jack stretched his arms over his head and she caught a glimpse of a well-developed six-pack when his T-shirt lifted. Well, there was proof positive: he really had it. He didn't use a body double. Then she had another flash – those rock-hard abs pressed against her back, his hands roaming her . . . *Stop it, Abbie. Just behave.*

Jack winked when he caught her stare and she turned away quickly before he could see her blush.

'You OK, Zeke?' he called.

The agent stood up, his face pale and beads of sweat along his forehead. 'Of course I'm not OK. My gastro-enterologist will go crazy when he finds out what I've been eating. My digestive system is very delicate.'

Jack ignored that. 'Great. I'll take point. We'll walk for another couple of hours before we make camp for the night. Abbie, you can walk with Zeke, and Kevin will take the rear.'

'I bet he will,' she laughed, then realized she faced two hours of listening to Zeke now that he had her to himself.

'Can I take a turn with the knife?' she asked again.

'No,' both men chorused.

5

Jack struck the first blow at the green curtain and they set off into the unknown. Abbie chose not to think of how far they still had to go .

Zeke turned to her. 'So, what's a nice girl like you doing in a place like this?'

He was hitting on her, and with a line that corny? Abbie resisted the urge to break his other arm. He was old enough to be her father. She smiled sweetly at him. 'I was chasing down a connection between an international drugs cartel and Antonio Tabora.'

'Antonio who?'

'Tabora,' Jack's voice came from in front. 'He's running for the Honduran Congress. Charming, wealthy and dirty as hell.'

Abbie was surprised that Jack had heard of him. Tabora was being courted in the States as a new hope for Honduras.

'And did you find it?' said Zeke, only vaguely interested.

'I found enough,' she said. 'DEA agents have been working alongside the Honduran security forces to stop the trans-shipment of drugs. The State Department has put helicopters at their disposal to trace illegal landing strips funded by the Barrio18 and MS13 gangs. But I'm picking up hints of a leak in the State Department.'

The lawyers for the paper were probably going through her stuff with a fine-tooth comb at the moment. Suddenly she missed the newsroom. The other reporters, the lousy coffee and the occasional 'princess' jibe. What would they do when she failed to arrive in the office? Would they assume that Tabora's men had taken her?

And her family. Her dad would go crazy and her sister, Miffy, would let loose a big refrain of 'I told you so'. Abbie's style of gritty journalism wasn't feminine enough for Miffy. If she had to be a journalist, why couldn't she write about the art scene or fashion? Or better yet, stop parading the Marshall name through the papers and find some nice charity committees to sit on. Yada yada yada. That was what most of the women in their circle did – got a nice, undemanding job in a gallery or PR company before landing an investment banker or a lawyer and then embarking on a merry-go-round of charity fund-raising and competitive parenting. From the age of sixteen Abbie knew she would never be able to follow that path. Still, Miffy got on her case at every opportunity. She could just imagine the uproar when they got home after this escapade. If they got home.

Kevin came up behind her. 'You OK, Abbie? Jack's daily special staying down?'

'They were delicious.' She raised her voice enough for Jack to hear. 'Best I've tasted since I last ate in China-town.' She smiled at Kevin. He really was a charmer. 'What about you? I get the impression that you and Jack do a lot of double dating.'

'For sure. We've been friends since Trinity.'

'Trinity?'

'College.' He shrugged. 'Back in Dublin.'

'So, he really is from Ireland? I thought you just put on the accent to pick up women.'

Kevin kicked a tangle of vines out of their path. 'Nope, it's real, and Jack never needed to fake anything to pick up girls. Like flies around –'

'I am not deaf,' Jack shouted. 'And if you're interested, Abbie, you only had to ask.'

She cringed. She had let her curiosity get the better of her. Wouldn't make that mistake again.

Kevin grappled with an overhanging branch. 'He's not so bad, when you get to know him.'

'I have no intention of getting to know him,' she said primly.

Kevin gave her a sly grin. 'Well, you did sleep with him last night.'

'I did not sleep with him.' She could feel her face beginning to flush. Maybe she should have stayed with Zeke.

'So, you were awake, then. All night . . .' Kevin whistled.

Her right hand itched to punch something. 'I was not –' His snort of laughter brought her to her senses. 'You're a sly, underhanded . . .'

'Keep it up, I love compliments. And I'll tell you what else I'd love, Abbie –'

'You'd love a dig in the head from my fist.'

Abbie hadn't realized that Jack had returned. A large patch of sweat covered the front of his T-shirt and the damp fabric clung to his abs like a second skin. *Will you stop with the abs fixation. You're turning ab-normal.* She dragged her eyes to his face. His skin was flushed from exertion and his blue eyes could cut through her like a laser.

Jack handed the knife to Kevin. 'Your turn, bro.'

'That's what I was kind of hoping for.'

Kevin whistled as he took his place at the front. Abbie thought it was some Irish rebel song, but she couldn't be sure.

The journey was endless. Even with Jack beside her to help, several times Abbie stumbled over large roots hidden in the undergrowth. Her clothes were glued to her body and her hair to her head. What she wouldn't give for a shower. A nice, long, hot shower. Hell, even a cold one would do.

'Snake!' Zeke's shout dragged her out of her fantasy.

'Where?' Jack shouted.

Her gaze followed the direction of Zeke's pointing finger. Oh dear lord. She swallowed hard. She had seen them in the reptile enclosure in the zoo, but never a real one, and never one that big.

Jack and Kevin set off in pursuit. She hadn't thought that snakes could move that fast, but within seconds the men had disappeared into the foliage and all she could hear were their shouts.

'I can't do this any more.' Zeke took a seat on a log. 'The heat, the terrible food. No communications. How do people live like this?'

Beneath his perma-tan, his skin looked ashen. Maybe he really was ill? Abbie placed her hand on his forehead. He was hot, like everyone else, but he didn't feel feverish.

Zeke placed his hand on her wrist. 'You know, Abbie, maybe when this is over we can meet up and –'

It took a moment for the penny to drop. She hadn't imagined it earlier: Zeke was coming on to her and he meant it. When she slapped his hand away, he wasn't a bit perturbed. He smiled as if it were an everyday occurrence to paw someone thirty years his junior. Abbie stepped back. 'Oh, for heaven's sake. What is wrong with you?'

The green curtain of leaves parted and Jack and Kevin reappeared, both wearing matching expressions of triumph. 'How much do you love me?' asked Jack.

'Would you believe me if I said not a bit?'

He grinned at her. 'Suit yourself, but you better cosy up to me and Kev, because we have just caught dinner.'

Her stomach did a somersault. 'A snake. We're having a snake for dinner?'

'No, not a snake, Abbie,' Kevin said. 'A roasted snake. Trust me, it tastes just like chicken.'

The triumph of the returning hunters was marred by the sound of Zeke puking.

They pressed on for two more painful hours. Even with sensible boots that were well broken in, the soles of her feet felt as if they were on fire.

'OK, let's call it a night,' Jack said at last.

They were the sweetest words in the English language. Kevin organized the hammocks while Jack busied himself making a fire. 'Fetch me some leaves, Abbie. The long ones.'

She went off to get the leaves while he butchered the snake. Only when she was a few feet from the clearing did she realize that he had sent her away deliberately. Jack was protecting her? Hollywood had a soft streak?

The thought pleased her.

'Abbie, what the hell is keeping you?' he roared.

So much for his soft side. She hurried back to camp.

They had dug a small fire pit and the snake was now cut into rough chunks. Even Zeke had gotten over his upset stomach and was eying the meat with interest. 'Like chicken, you said?'

'Chicken,' Kevin repeated.

They watched as Jack parcelled the meat up in the damp leaves and placed it on a makeshift spit over the fire. It smelled wonderful and, despite her disgust, Abbie's mouth watered. They'd had nothing to eat all day but bugs and sour berries. This was a feast.

'I'll go bury the rest,' Kevin offered. 'We don't want to attract predators,' he said by way of explanation.

Predators. She hadn't thought of that. They were in a jungle and the only thing that stood between her and the dangerous environment was Jack and Kevin.

As if he could read her thoughts, Jack winked at her. 'Don't worry, babe, I'll take care of you.'

'That's what I'm afraid of,' she muttered.

She dreaded the night to come, not sure how she would react to all that rampant masculinity pressed up against her for a second night. But she had barely eaten half her portion of snake before fatigue crashed over her. She fought to keep her eyes open and was startled when Jack said, 'I've set up the hammock. Go to bed and I'll finish settling the camp for the night.'

She nodded gratefully, too tired to argue. The damp hammock was more welcome than the most luxurious bed she had ever slept in. For a few minutes, she held herself stiffly, waiting for Jack to join her. But exhaustion won. She was sleeping soundly by the time he came to bed.

There was something wrong, Jack realized, as they beat their way through the vegetation the next morning. When he checked behind him Abbie was looking up at Kev in a way that made his teeth clench. He had thought that if Kev and Abbie got together it would cure his inconvenient fixation. But now he knew that was the last thing he wanted. The previous night she had slept soundly beside him and he had gathered her in his arms. Despite himself, he wanted to protect her. They had woken together and for a brief moment had held each other's gaze before tumbling out either side of the hammock. He couldn't get away from it – he couldn't remember the last time he had wanted to fuck a woman the way he wanted to fuck Abbie Marshall. But even more than that, she had a quality that frightened as much as attracted him. She was sophisticated but still innocent. She had no idea how alluring she was and the more she did her superior-woman-of-the-world routine, the more he wanted to show her just how far down into the depths she could go with him. But that was impossible; he could never go there with Abbie. Yet still he was on the alert for any sign that she was falling for Kev's easy charm. It would kill him to see Kev with her.

Suddenly he realized what was different. For the first time in two days, Zeke had stopped complaining. He hadn't noticed it all morning, but now that they were settling into a routine the blessed silence had finally registered. He stopped to check on the older man. Zeke was white in the face. He had stopped complaining simply because he was beyond words. His breathing had become laboured and uneven.

'Kev,' he said sharply. 'I thought you were keeping an eye on Zeke.'

Kevin dragged his attention away from whatever Abbie was saying to look at the older man. 'Oh fuck,' he said.

That about summed it up. Jack made Zeke sit down and checked his arm. It was swollen and painful. Zeke flinched and whimpered with pain at any movement. Jack forced another couple of painkillers into him. He looked longingly at the paracetamol. His own head hurt like a bitch, but there were only six left, and Zeke needed them more than he did.

The muslin sling, now damp and thin, was just not up to the job of holding Zeke's injured arm securely. They needed to reinforce it, but with what? He ran a mental eye over all their gear. They had nothing that would give it the extra support it needed if Zeke was going to continue to walk.

Abbie gave Zeke a few mouthfuls of water and another slug of tequila. Her concern made her green eyes more brilliant than usual, and caused something to tighten in Jack's chest. He wanted her to look at him like that.

For a brief moment, he allowed himself the luxury of a fantasy where Abbie was naked in his bed, staring up at him with those luminous eyes and he . . . He cut off that train of thought. The things he wanted to do to her would have her running away screaming. And writing about it on the front page of her paper. Sometimes the pleasure was not worth the price.

But he still couldn't take his eyes off her, and when she brushed up against Zeke, he thought he could feel the caress of those nipples on his own skin.

That was it. 'Abbie, take off your bra.'

'What?'

The stunned expression on her face, the way shock caused her mouth to part, allowing him a glimpse of a tempting pink tongue, was an aphrodisiac in itself. Against his will, he felt himself harden. *Down, boy, this isn't the time or the place.*

'Jack, what are you –?' Kev was the one who protested. Then he caught sight of something in Jack's face which silenced him.

'Abbie's bra is mostly elastic, right? We can jerry-rig it so it will reinforce the sling and hold Zeke's arm more securely. He has to be able to walk. Let's face it, he mightn't be that heavy, but we can't carry him all the way.'

Zeke grumbled but he didn't protest. He was clearly close to his limit. If they had to, he and Kev could carry the older man, but that would leave Abbie trying to clear their path. Though she had offered, and she looked fit, she didn't have the muscle mass needed to cut a path through the greenery.

When he was wrestling the plane down, Jack had seen lights on the edge of a lagoon. He had been fighting to keep the plane airborne and not paying a lot of attention to the ground, so he'd only had time for a quick glimpse, but he believed those lights were their best hope. It was too much to hope it would be a proper town, but once they reached any kind of settlement there would be some form of communication so they could call for help. He had no idea how far away it was but calculated two or three days' trekking. They could do that, he hoped, even with the dangerous lack of provisions and equipment. Kev was the only one who knew how dangerous their position was and agreed to say nothing to the other two for fear of freaking them out. Trekking to the lagoon depended on all four of them being fully mobile. Zeke had to be able to walk if they were to make it out of there.

'Your bra, Abbie,' Jack said. 'We need it.' He spoke calmly, but his voice left her in no doubt he meant it. They didn't have time to deal with a lot of female fussing and arguing.

She looked from Jack to Zeke and back again. 'Oh, very well,' she said, surprising him, and awakening speculation that he would prefer to ignore. 'But you'll all have to turn your backs.'

He nodded. He would allow her that much. When he turned, the sound of rustling went on for far longer than he would have expected, and allowed his imagination to roam free. 'Kevin, eyes front,' she said sharply.

'Spoilsport,' Kev muttered. Jack decided that he was going to beat up his old friend soon. How dare he try to sneak a peek at Abbie? Then he imagined her nimble fingers unfastening button after button. The shirt sliding off her shoulders, exposing soft pale skin. The lacy bra underneath. Was it a front or a back fastener? Back, he decided, and visualized Abbie reaching behind to open it, the movement pushing her breasts forward as if they were begging for his touch. The bra opening, the straps falling down her arms, before Abbie removed the scrap of lingerie and finally revealed her breasts to his eager eyes. Each one would be a round handful, trembling slightly with each breath she took, and tipped with pale pink nipples. They'd be soft when she took off the bra, but they would tighten up once they were exposed to the air, and to his eyes. She would stretch, put her arms back, making them rise up level with his mouth. He would –

His erection pressed against the front of his jeans. *Relax. Think of something else. Insects. Think of eating larvae.* That did it. By the time Abbie said, 'Here it is,' and handed her bra to him, he was in command of himself again.

The sight of the lacy pink garment she held out almost shattered his calm, and the slight trace of Abbie's distinctive scent added to his problems.

'Good girl,' he said automatically. She gave him a look that would curdle milk, but he thought her breathing had deepened. God, he had to stop this.

'Stop glaring,' he told her. 'You've got a face like a slapped arse when you do that.'

'A WHAT?' If anything her glare darkened and her eyes glittered dangerously.

Kev guffawed. 'Don't mind Jack. He's got foot-in-mouth disease.'

Abbie moved to pull her bra back, but Jack snatched it out of her hand and turned to Zeke. He busied himself pulling the bra apart and using the elastic straps to reinforce the sling and immobilize Zeke's arm.

'Keep an eye on him,' Jack ordered her. He picked up the knife and prepared to set off again.

'You're not the boss of me,' Abbie said, but did what he told her.

That's what you think, lady. But he had sense enough not to say it out loud.

Abbie couldn't believe what she had just said. She sounded about as mature as a ten-year-old. Actually, she believed the last time she had told someone they weren't the boss of her was when she was in the fifth grade and Miffy was telling her she had to help her bake cupcakes for some fund-raising thing in her school.

Still, not for the first time, Abbie had to admit to herself that she was finding it oddly easy to let someone else take charge. Normally she was driven and focused. Apart from their engagement, which had been William's idea, she was the one who took the initiative and made plans in their relationship. And yet here she was with no clue what was happening and, in all honesty, no pressing desire to find out. She was dirty and uncomfortable and hungry, but not worried. She had a completely irrational belief that Jack Winter knew what he was doing. Her feelings seesawed wildly between disgust with herself for not being more assertive, and a perturbed acceptance of her own compliance. When – if – they got back to civilization, she and Kit would have hours of fun analysing what it all meant. She could see now why people paid good money to go on wilderness adventures: you really did find out stuff about yourself.

They were silent as they slogged through the forest, battling the thick humid air and the heat as well as the dense undergrowth. It was taking all their effort to keep going. Jack and Kevin took turns hacking out a track and bringing up the rear and she kept an eye on Zeke, helping him when he stumbled. No one had time or breath for more than random snatches of conversation.

With no conversation to distract them, the noise of the rainforest was astonishing: the constant whir and click of insects, the squawk and flutter of birds and the occasional roar of a jaguar. The first time they heard it, everyone tensed. 'Calm down,' Jack said. 'It's a jaguar. They almost never attack humans.' Just as they relaxed, he added, 'You are much more likely to get killed by a snake.'

It was impossible to judge distance in the jungle. Not only did they have to clear every foot of path before they could pass through it, they had to stop and try to shelter during the frequent downpours. Abbie's shirt dried quickly once the rain stopped, but her jeans and boots were a soggy torture.

She was also tormented by an awareness that the eyes of all three men were magnetically drawn to her chest. Now that she was braless, her breasts moved with every step she took. And of course when it rained her shirt stuck to her like a second skin and her nipples protruded. She decided to pretend it wasn't happening. It was the only way she could deal with it.

Finally Jack called a halt. Deep beneath the canopy of the forest, it was impossible to see the position of the sun in the sky, but she could detect a slight difference in the angle of the light. He said it was four thirty so they had about an hour before sunset.

Zeke was so spaced out she had to guide him down to a sitting position before checking him over. 'Mostly exhaustion, I think,' she told the other two.

'Where did you learn that?' Jack asked.

'Peace corps. And yes, OK, I was a candy-striper.' She felt herself flushing.

'What's that?' Kevin asked. Jack looked just as confused.

'If you don't know, you don't need to know,' she said and refused to elaborate. She just wasn't in the mood for the Florence Nightingale jokes if she told them she had done volunteer work in hospitals during high school and college.

She sat down under a tree, and realized that she must look nearly as bad as Zeke when neither Jack nor Kevin made any wisecracks.

'Sit there and have a rest,' Jack said. 'I think I saw some berries that I recognize. I'll pick some and we can have them for dessert.'

'Oh gee, which would I rather, live larvae or juicy berries? Decisions, decisions,' she said. But in spite of her jibe, she was relieved that he was being gentle with her. She closed her eyes and leaned back.

She allowed herself to drift. Kevin was starting to set up the camp for the night. He had unpacked the hammocks and was tying one end up to a tree. That was good – she couldn't wait for another long, deep sleep. She heard Jack's footsteps coming back and she stirred and yawned, stretching widely.

There was a movement beside her head. She opened her eyes, turned her head and found herself looking at the biggest set of snake fangs she had ever seen.

6

Jack's brain hadn't even processed the flash of brown when his body moved. The long snake was poised above Abbie in mid-strike when his stick hit it, knocking it sideways. It turned its attention from Abbie to him, whipping round so fast he didn't have time to blink. The fangs were barely three feet away from him.

'Jack!' Abbie's scream and movement distracted the snake for a vital fraction of a second. He hit it with the stick again. This time, he followed up by stepping forwards and standing on its head.

It thrashed and fought, nearly ten feet of muscle and viciousness. The skin was rough and the ridge along its back was sharp as a knife. One blow of its tail tore through his jeans and sliced his skin.

'Kev. Knife.' He barely got the words out while he fought. Then he had to take his attention off it for long enough to grab the knife Kev threw him. He fumbled the catch, but managed to get a grip before it fell. One solid downward plunge into the snake's spine and it could only manage one last strike before it died. Jack panted and tried to drag air into his labouring lungs before straightening up.

'Abbie, did it bite you?'

She shook her head, clearly too stunned to speak.

'Man, what the fuck was that?' Kev asked, coming over to examine the creature.

Jack took another look at it, hoping he was wrong, but he knew. Those reddish-brown triangular marks and the sharp ridge on its back were distinctive.

'It's a bushmaster. Largest venomous snake in the rainforest. Also known as a bull killer. One bite will kill in about ten minutes.'

Jack checked himself over for bites, but he knew he had escaped. If that monster had bitten him, he would be half-dead by now. No one walked away from a bushmaster bite. It was sheer chance that he had a stick when he came back to the camp. He had kept the stick he cut to reach the pokenoboy grapes so that Abbie could use it as a walking stick. If he hadn't had it she would probably be dead by now.

He looked longingly at the last mouthful of tequila. This called for a drink, but Zeke needed it more. Besides, he preferred Black Bush.

Ignoring Abbie's protests, he cooked the snake for their dinner. She was sufficiently recovered from the shock to ask if bushmasters weren't an endangered species.

He could hardly believe what he was hearing. 'So they are. I do apologize. Next time a poisonous snake is about to take a bite out of you, I'll let it.' He picked up its head and showed her the vicious fangs. 'This doesn't bother you at all, of course.'

'Reminds me of some of my relatives.' Abbie shuddered, but managed a small smile. She even ate a few pokenoboy grapes for dessert.

By the time darkness was falling, his sweat had cooled and his heart rate had slowed, but he was still riding the adrenalin high. That was the closest he had come to death in a long time. And it had been too damn close for Abbie. He shuddered again when he remembered the sight of the snake lunging for her arm. He doubted he would ever forget that.

He tucked her into the hammock beside him, determined to ignore her warmth and softness against his body, but the faint tremors that wracked her played havoc with his good intentions. He pulled her tightly to him. 'It's OK, baby. It's over.'

He held her, rubbing her back gently, allowing her to recover from the fright in her own time. He ruthlessly clamped down on those impulses that made him want to distract and comfort her in a completely different way.

For what seemed like an eternity, she shook in his arms, her curves pressed against him, her scent teasing his nostrils. He wrestled his demons, the part of him that wanted to drag her underneath him and unleash a different kind of adrenalin high on her unprepared body.

Then she tipped him over the edge. Abbie put her arm around his neck and pulled him down to kiss him. It was a light, fleeting kiss that even he recognized as thanks, but his inner beast didn't care.

At the first brush of her lips against his, he took over, pulled her harder against him, and plundered her mouth. This wasn't a gentle getting-to-know-you first kiss, it was possessive and raw. She had offered and, by god, he was going to take. He kissed her ravenously, unable to get enough of the taste of her.

She moaned, a tiny sound at the back of her throat, and it was like a flame to tinder. His control exploded. He plunged his tongue into her mouth, dominating her, giving her no room to retreat. She was his; he had won her by right of conquest. And when Abbie touched her tongue tentatively to his, he was lost.

He slid his hand from her back around to cup the fullness of her breast. She was so soft. Shoving his fingers under her shirt, he could feel the silkiness of her skin. He would never get enough of this.

He kneaded her breast gently and ran his thumb over her nipple. It tightened to a hard point that grazed his palm. She moaned again, twisting to press it more firmly into his hands. Oh god, she was as aroused as he was. He shifted, allowing her to feel his erection. Her hips bumped eagerly against his.

'Hey, Jack?' Kev's voice in the darkness was like being doused with cold water. 'Do those big snakes of yours climb trees?'

Abbie stiffened.

It was a moment before Jack could force his vocal cords to work, and collect his thoughts enough to answer. 'Not as far as I know.'

'As far as you know? Man, you don't know that they can't? Oh fuck!' Even Zeke managed a drowsy protest.

The moment was ruined. Abbie had moved as far away from him as she could get in a hammock. With a bit of coaxing, Jack thought that he could bring back that passionate woman who had kissed him so eagerly, but the interruption had given him a chance to remember why that would be a really bad idea. She might kiss like a dream and smell like distilled sex, but Abbie Marshall was still a reporter. He mustn't forget that.

She turned her back on him and clung to the edge of the hammock for the rest of the night. It was just as well.

I kissed Jack Winter. Oh sweet god, I can't believe I actually did that. Not only that, but I started it. That was one headline she definitely didn't want to see. She took a deep breath. It was a one-off. She was traumatized by the killer snake. She would have kissed anyone, and it wouldn't matter. The kiss could almost be considered medicinal.

She tried to ignore the small teasing voice that reminded her that she hadn't kissed Kevin or Zeke. Who was she trying to fool? Since the moment she had laid eyes on him, Abbie hadn't been able to ignore the sexual magnetism of Jack Winter. She had never felt anything like it.

She was a journalist – used to staying detached in extreme situations – so she had tried to treat him as an interesting phenomenon, worthy of study but not important to her. And she had tried to distract herself with the hour-by-hour struggle to get through the jungle. She had even tried to channel every feisty, independent heroine she could think of – from Buffy the Vampire Slayer to Veronica Mars. But in the end, there was always one man that got through the defences of the feisty heroine.

Abbie rolled over, trying not to wake him. The stubble shadowing his cheeks made him look dangerous and even more striking. It wasn't fair. She looked filthy and smelled rank. If she didn't find some way of washing soon, she would go crazy.

Abbie slithered out of the hammock and went to fetch her rucksack. The laptop was still safe in its waterproof cover. The battery hadn't died yet. Once they got to somewhere half civilized, she would get to work on the story.

'Morning, Abbie.' Kevin stretched and yawned. 'I don't suppose you have anything edible in that bag?'

'I wish.' She smiled ruefully. Abbie was struck by a sudden memory of the airport at Toncontín. She had broken a five-hundred lempira banknote to get change for the phone. She patted the front pouch of the bag. Please let it be there. She gave a small whoop of triumph when her hand fastened on the packet of gum.

She handed a stick of gum to Kevin.

He took it eagerly. 'Abbie Marshall, I love you and I want you to have my babies.'

Abbie batted her eyelashes. 'Why, Mr O'Malley, I didn't know you cared. Just how many little rug rats are we talking about?'

Kevin gave her an impish grin. 'About a dozen. I like big families. Of course we'd have to practise a lot, but I'd have no problem with that.'

'I would.' Jack's comment was almost a snarl.

Abbie glanced at him and then quickly back to Kevin. If anything, Jack looked even more dangerous than the night before and she didn't like the thunderous expression on his face. She offered him a stick of gum and said nothing.

Following a breakfast of berries and chewing gum, they set out on their way. Kevin took point, slashing his way through the undergrowth, whistling as he worked. Jack fell into step beside her. 'Cheerful bastard, isn't he?'

'And you're not?' She couldn't resist snapping back at him.

He slid an arm around her waist. 'Baby, if that's what does it for you, I can do cheerful.'

Abbie slapped his hand away. 'Please don't bother on my account. I wouldn't want you to get a pain in the face.'

Jack patted the rucksack. 'What the hell have you got in that thing?'

'Nothing. Just some water.'

Up ahead, Kevin stopped to catch his breath. 'Your turn, buddy.'

Abbie breathed a sigh of relief. Somehow she knew that Jack Winter wouldn't be a bit happy if he discovered that she had ignored his order to leave the laptop behind on the plane.

Within a couple of hours her shoulders were aching. She hadn't realized how much the straps of her bra had protected her shoulders. Sweat rolled down her back. Could it possibly get any hotter?

Jack's shirt was dark with sweat. 'OK, water break.'

Abbie kicked at the undergrowth to check for creatures before sitting on a fallen tree. She eased the rucksack from her shoulders, pulled out a water bottle and handed it to Jack.

'Good girl, thanks, I could do with that.'

Who the hell did he think he was? *Good girl, my ass.* She was sick of the jungle, sick of him and sick of being addressed like some kind of pet. 'Will you stop with the good girl thing, what do you think I am? A dog?'

Jack stopped drinking and wiped his mouth with the back of his hand. 'What's up with you? I only said thanks.'

'Keep your patronizing comments for your fans. I'm sure that they don't mind when you call them girl or pet.'

Jack moved closer, until he was towering over her. 'I seem to remember that you didn't complain last night.'

Kevin and Zeke were watching so Abbie resisted the urge to slap him. Bloody hell, if it got out that she had been up close and personal in a hammock with Jack Winter, she would never live it down. 'I don't know what you're talking about.'

'Really?' His blue eyes blazed with annoyance and a hint of something else. 'Would you like me to refresh your memory?'

Abbie stood up and smiled sweetly at him. 'No thanks, I'd rather have a date with the snake.'

They pressed on for another hour. Eventually Jack called a halt for lunch. Everyone was starving and even Zeke didn't complain about the prospect of another meal of cold snake. It was better than larvae. Abbie groaned as she pulled the rucksack off her shoulders. Jack caught her wincing and came over to her.

'OK, what's in the bag?'

'Nothing. I told you –'

Jack grabbed the rucksack and tipped the contents on to the ground. One bottle of water. One packet of water-purifying tablets. A small washbag. A plastic bag with used underwear. A Kindle, her cell phone and the heavy rubber case that protected her precious laptop. The digital recorder slid from the bag and landed at Jack's feet. He picked it up and shoved it into his pocket.

Abbie stared at the ground. She couldn't meet Jack's eyes, but she could feel the anger radiating from him as he loomed over her. 'What did I tell you?'

His tone was deadly calm and somehow that was worse than if he had yelled.

'Abbie.' His hand snaked out and he grasped her chin, tilting her head back. She had no choice but to stare at him.

'It is my laptop. I'm carrying it and it's none of your business.'

His grim expression told her that was the wrong answer.

'Hey, Jack, leave Abbie alone. If she wants to carry her –'

Jack silenced Kevin with a look and turned his attention back to her. The hand that caressed her neck was gentle. He brushed her hair away from her neck and, before she could protest, he had opened two buttons of her shirt and eased it off her shoulder. Her skin was raw where the strap of the bag had chaffed her.

'Look at me, Abbie.'

She raised her eyes to meet his piercing blue ones.

'Even a minor injury in this terrain can turn nasty very quickly. A laptop can be replaced, you can't. If you disobey me again there will be consequences. Do you understand?'

Abbie swallowed and nodded.

'You can have it back when we get out of here.' Jack released her, repacked the bag and walked away with it.

Abbie started after him. The nerve of him. Who did he think he was to take her bag and threaten her? Consequences indeed. She would show him consequences when they got back to civilization. 'Arrogant bastard . . .' she muttered under her breath.

Kevin smirked but she couldn't respond to his smile.

Mixed up with her anger was an annoying and confusing sense of hurt. Jack was disappointed with her. She had let him down. She hadn't felt so wretched since she'd accidentally broken a window in sixth grade.

Abbie ate a miserable lunch in silence. She could barely choke down the roasted larvae and even Kevin's handful of berries didn't cheer her up. Jack took point and they followed his path, moving steadily through the intermittent rain. After a couple of miles, the usual sounds of the jungle were replaced by something else. Falling water.

Kevin's face lit up. 'Do you hear that?'

Even the taciturn Zeke managed a smile. 'I vote that we investigate.'

'Seconded.' Abbie raised her arm, caught the scent of unwashed flesh and quickly lowered it.

'Hey, Jack,' Kevin called after him. 'We're going to take a detour.'

They diverted off the rough trail and followed a narrow meandering path through the forest. As the sound of the water grew louder, Abbie's spirits rose.

They broke through the cover of trees into the open area and a lagoon beyond. 'Oh wow.' Kevin began to unbutton his shirt.

Zeke sat down. 'I think I'm going to need a hand to get undressed.' He looked at Abbie.

'Not a chance,' she said, with a meaningful glance at his arm, still strapped up with her bra. 'You've exhausted my goodwill as far as clothing is concerned.'

She checked around her. Despite the enforced intimacy of their living arrangements over the last couple of days, she had no intention of stripping off in front of the men.

She struck out on her own, following the edge of the lagoon.

'Abbie, don't go too far,' Jack called after her. 'And be careful where you bathe.'

Abbie ignored him. She heard Kevin's whoop of joy followed by a loud splash. Seconds later Zeke roared his disapproval when he was splashed. Jack was silent.

The shallow pool was several feet away from the main lagoon. The water was crystal clear. Abbie looked behind her. She could still hear the guys horsing around in the water. There was plenty of time to have a quick dip.

She pulled off her trousers and boots quickly and dipped her foot in the water. It was warm, almost as warm as a bath. The temptation was too much. Abbie pulled her shirt over her head and pulled off her panties. If she was quick, she could rinse her clothing and leave it to dry on the rocks while she took a bath.

Within minutes she had washed everything and laid it out to dry. She stepped into the pool. The water was like silk against her skin. Abbie lay back and closed her eyes. God, it felt better than a flotation tank. She submerged and rinsed her hair. In the distance she could hear the shouts of the others.

'Just a few more minutes,' she murmured to herself.

The sun was warm against her skin and, supported by the buoyant water, Abbie drifted peacefully.

A shout from Jack roused her. 'Abbie, where are you?'

She floundered, desperately scrambling out of the pool. 'I'm fine. I'm fine. Don't come up here. I'm just getting dressed.'

Jack's low laugh was audible.

Abbie grabbed her panties. They were soaking wet; she couldn't put them back on yet. She brushed her skin and her fingers came into contact with a slimy protrusion. She slapped it away in panic, but it clung on.

'Ouch, ouch!' Abbie tried again but it felt like it was biting her. Her back and legs felt like they were on fire. Something moved in her hair and she screamed.

'Abbie?' She could hear the concern in Jack's roar.

'Don't come. Don't come up here.' But it was hard to keep the panic out of her voice. The things were biting her.

Jack slammed through the curtain of greenery. She yelped and tried to cover herself.

He approached slowly, palms upward. 'It's OK, Abbie. It's OK. I'm here now.'

Abbie couldn't stifle a whimper of pain.

'Turn round, baby, and let me see what the problem is.'

She felt a bewildering mix of fear and relief that he wasn't angry with her.

'Leeches,' he said and she cringed.

'Get them off me. Please, Jack, get them off me.'

Abbie heard a match striking and the acrid smell of cigarette smoke.

'Do you trust me, Abbie?'

She did trust him. Overbearing as he was, she did trust him. 'Yes.' The word came out in a pathetic wheeze.

'Good. Hold on to that thought. This is going to hurt them a lot more than it will hurt you.'

Abbie felt the heat of the cigarette tip as it neared her skin and heard the sizzle as it touched the leeches. The smell was sickening. One by one they fell to the ground.

How could she have been so stupid as to ignore Rules of the Jungle 101 – thou shalt not bathe in a pool with leeches. Now she was standing here, naked, while Jack burned them off her. She heard another hiss as Jack removed one from her thigh. God, he must be staring at her butt. 'Can't you go any faster?'

'I could, but it wouldn't be as much fun. Hold still.'

The heat of the cigarette made her flinch, even as another one dropped.

'You're enjoying this, aren't you?'

'Yep.' She could hear the laughter in his voice. 'It's the most fun I've had on a date in years. You, me, leeches and cigarettes. You can write this one up for the *New York Independent*.'

Abbie closed her eyes. She would be laughed out of the newsroom if the guys found out that she had to be rescued like this. 'I'm a news reporter. I don't write cheap gossip pieces.'

There was silence for a moment as her comment hit home. 'Yeah, you're right. Maybe the *National Enquirer* would run it. I'll give them a call when I get back to LA.'

'You wouldn't dare.' She held it together with an effort, but her endurance was running out.

Jack ran his hand along her thigh. 'Is that a challenge? You should know never to challenge me. You have no idea what I'm capable of.'

Jack's threat hung in the air as he continued to deal with the leeches. 'All done! You were very brave.'

His praise made her lose control entirely. Abbie turned and fell into his arms, sobbing like a baby. It didn't matter that she was completely naked while he was fully clothed.

All that mattered was the comfort of his arms around her and the strength of his broad chest as she sobbed into it.

'I know, I know,' he murmured.

Scary Jack was gone, replaced by strong Jack who would protect her. There was something about him. Despite his sardonic exterior, underneath there was a core of strength that she could lean on. She was filled with a certainty that he was a man who would never let her down.

'Baby,' he said, with his mouth pressed against her hair. 'The others will be here soon. Let's get you dressed.'

Abbie stood obediently while he dressed her, sliding her damp panties up her legs. She sat on a rock while he put on her socks, tutting when he saw the hole near her big toe.

Before he put her boots back on, he picked an orchid and tucked it into her hair. He stood back to examine the result. 'It's almost as beautiful as you.'

Abbie wanted to cry. The unexpected compliment was such a thoughtful gesture after the trauma of the leeches that she had to close her eyes against sudden tears.

He knelt down and put on her boots, lacing them up carefully. When she was dressed, he held her in front of him and looked at her sternly. Oh shit, scary Jack was back. She wanted to drop her eyes in the face of that uncompromising gaze, but knew that would make her a coward. His voice was as serious as a libel suit when he spoke. 'Abbie, I warned you that if you took stupid chances, there would be consequences. In future, you obey reasonable orders. Understand?'

Her urge to say something subservient and deferential appalled her. For an unnerving moment, she felt like a naughty schoolgirl in front of the principal. There was no way she was going to let Jack boss her around, so she smirked at him and said, 'Or what? You'll spank me? Come off it, Jack, I messed up. It's not as if anyone got hurt.'

His face hardened even more. 'You did, Abbie. You got hurt. This is not a joke. That's how people end up dead. If you hadn't already suffered from the leeches, there would be consequences. As it is, I think you've been punished enough, don't you?'

For a second, she wanted to drop her eyes. So she held his gaze. 'Trust me, there's nothing you could do which is worse than those leeches.'

He smiled, not a pleasant smile. 'Trust me, there is.'

Abbie snorted. 'Oh yeah? Bring it on, Hollywood.'

Before Jack could answer, Kevin arrived in the clearing. 'Do I smell cigarettes? I didn't know you smoked, Abbie. Got any spare?'

Jack gave him a narrow-eyed glare. Did the man specialize in those? Why had she never noticed that in his films? Although Jack Winter always played commanding lead roles, somehow she had never noticed this air of subtle menace on the screen. She was so busy wondering at the difference between the man in front of her and his screen persona that she almost missed him complaining about Kevin smoking.

'I haven't smoked for two years,' Kevin said. 'But this might be a good time to start again.'

Abbie tuned out the banter between the two men while she wondered how this side of Jack had never appeared in the papers or on the E! channel. For the first time, she wanted to do an in-depth profile, not of the movie star, but of the man behind the celebrity camouflage. And she wouldn't let him scare her off.

Back at the water's edge, Kevin and Zeke had lit a small fire and the tempting smell of grilling fish filled the air. Ignoring Jack, she flashed Kevin a bright smile. 'Fish. I think I love you. If I had to eat snake or larvae again, I'd probably turn into one.'

The prospect of a snake-free meal put everyone in a good mood. Even Zeke didn't complain about the lack of cutlery or the banana leaves they used for plates. When the meal was over, Abbie filled the water bottles and added water-purifying tablets. They were running low. If they didn't get out of here in a couple of days, they were going to have serious problems.

'Abbie.' Jack's voice caught her attention. 'Kevin and I are going to see if we can find some shelter for tonight. Make sure that you bury the fish guts. We don't want to attract any visitors.'

Abbie sighed. Jack was still in command mode. 'Fine, just as soon as I finish this.'

'Abbie.' This time it was Zeke. 'I need you to fix my sling again, it's slipping.'

What was it with the jungle? Was there some caveman pheromone in the air? Jack had gone all He-Man, now Zeke thought he could boss her around.

She packed the bottles into the rucksack and checked her phone. Still no signal and the battery was low. At least the Kindle was still working. She might get to sit down and read for a while.

'Abbie, my arm,' Zeke whinged again.

'OK, OK, the nurse is coming.'

She adjusted the makeshift sling. Kit would go crazy when she found out that the two-hundred-dollar bra she had forced her to buy had been turned into a bandage. So much for discovering her inner temptress. 'I'm sure that Carine Gilson will be thrilled that she's saving your arm.'

'I'll replace it,' Zeke said. 'Just as soon as we get back to civilization.'

'Gee, thanks. Just what I need. Something to remind me of this place.'

Abbie eyed the pile of fish heads and guts. A swarm of ants had decided to move in. She watched as they formed an orderly little army, pulling bits of fish away. With any luck she wouldn't have to bury any of it. The ants would take care of it for her.

A snuffling snore from Zeke revealed that he had dozed off. Perfect. Peace and quiet at last. She would read until the others returned.

She was lost in her novel when a deep-throated roar dragged her attention away from it. She dropped the Kindle. Zeke was still asleep, oblivious to the jaguar pawing at the remains of the fish.

Oh dear god. The scraps wouldn't be enough to feed a hungry cat and she couldn't remember if jaguars would attack humans or not. Why hadn't she buried the fish?

'Zeke,' she hissed. 'Please wake up.'

A snore was his only response. Abbie reached for a piece of stick from beside the fire and poked Zeke.

His eyes flew open. 'What the hell are you –?'

'Shhh, we have a visitor.' Abbie nodded in the direction of the jaguar, who was busy devouring the fish. It was almost gone. The cat raised his head, eying them thoughtfully.

Zeke dug his heels into the ground and began to inch away. 'Do something, Abbie.'

'Nice kitty, why don't you go away?' As the jaguar stepped forwards, Abbie grabbed her Kindle and rose to her feet. Maybe she could throw it at him.

Jack and Kevin burst through into the clearing, waving lengths of vine and screaming like hyenas. She had never been so glad to see anyone in her life. The cat turned and disappeared into the jungle as silently as it had arrived.

Kevin followed it to make sure that it was gone. Jack stepped over the pile of fish detritus and turned to look at her. Abbie winced. He had told her to bury it and she hadn't. She couldn't meet his eyes. He was mad at her this time. Really mad.

'Don't tell me, you love pussy but you hate cats?' She had no idea what got into her to come out with a crack like that. Hysteria, perhaps.

He met her feeble joke with a stony expression that chilled her.

'Jack, I –'

His hand locked around her wrist. 'Excuse me, gentlemen, I believe I need to have a word with Ms Marshall in private.'

7

Jack grabbed her wrist and hauled her off. She tried to resist being pulled along like a recalcitrant child, but he was impossible to oppose. It was like trying to resist a tsunami. He was a force of nature. A really pissed-off force of nature.

NYI reporter left bruised by Hollywood superstar. But she realized that, though his grip was manacling her wrist, it wasn't quite tight enough to leave bruises. She absolutely refused to admit that any tiny part of her liked his grasp on her. The look on his face and the set of his jaw warned her that whatever was coming would not be pleasant. Jack Winter was not thinking sexy thoughts. He obviously wanted to let fly at her without being inhibited by the other two. Well, so be it.

He dragged her into a cave she hadn't noticed. 'What is this?' she asked, hoping to distract him. 'Did you and Kevin find it?' She glanced around the cave, trying to distract herself from the six-foot tower of testosterone in front of her. The cave was dry and appeared to be spider-free. In the centre it was tall enough for Jack to stand upright. 'Nice, I like what you've done with the place.'

He ignored her flippancy and turned to face her. 'Do you have any idea just how badly you behaved?'

He seemed to be waiting for an answer, so she said, 'It wasn't that bad. Nobody got hurt.'

It was the wrong thing to say. Rage lit his eyes, but ominously, his tone become more measured. 'Nobody got hurt because I came back. If you had been on your own, you or Zeke would have been killed. All because you didn't do what I told you. What the hell were you thinking?'

Abbie was tempted to lie, to say she had forgotten or hadn't been able to do it. 'I had a million things to do. Zeke was moaning at me to fix his sling again and then when I saw the ants I –'

His dark expression didn't change a fraction, so she pressed on with the words, even though she knew they would make things worse. 'I didn't want to. I'm just sick of being ordered around. Really, it was your fault.'

For a second his eyes widened, then they became dangerous slits. 'I can't believe you just said that.'

She wished the cave were darker so that she wouldn't have to see the expression on his face. She was in a world of shit here. Then she braced herself. 'What are you going to do about it?'

'This.' She never saw him move. One moment he was standing there, looming over her like a bad-tempered teacher. The next he had picked her up and was striding to the side of the cave. By the time she had caught her breath, he had sat down on a rock and hauled her over his knees.

'I warned you there would be consequences, Abbie. Now you can deal with them.'

No! He couldn't possibly mean to spank her. She had joked about it before, but because the idea was a joke. It didn't happen in the twenty-first century to women like her. She fought like a wildcat, determined to get out of this undignified position and away from him. 'Let go of me, you bastard.'

He held her easily. 'You asked for this, Abbie, now you're going to get it.'

He was serious. He was actually going to do it. Abbie struggled furiously, not caring if she fell on to the ground, as long as she got out of this appalling situation. His thighs were rock hard, and dug into her chest and stomach. Blood flowed to her head, making her dizzy. She screamed with rage and tried to get leverage to push herself up again, but her hands and feet barely touched the ground and his grasp was implacable.

'Let go of me, you son of a bitch, you can't do this.' The rage was real, but she was disgusted to hear how breathless her voice sounded. She raked with her fingernails, trying to claw him, but only found the tough denim of his jeans.

She kicked as hard as she could and, in a sudden manoeuvre, found that he had changed position so that she was over one knee now with both her legs trapped between his. 'Let me go,' she screamed. 'I'll have you charged with assault, you bastard!'

'It's too late, Abbie, this is going to happen.' In contrast to her screeches, Jack's tone sounded maddeningly reasonable. He raised his hand and smacked her.

Ow! Her whole body jerked. 'That hurt!'

He laughed. The bastard laughed. 'What did you expect?'

His hand flashed down again, even harder this time. The sting blazed through her whole body, awakening nerve endings she didn't know she had. He did it again.

She gritted her teeth. She would get through this with dignity and silence.

The next spank was even harder. She grunted, unable to stay silent. The next one was harder and she grunted more loudly. To hell with silence, she couldn't bear this. She howled.

He did it again. She writhed, tried to get away. She tried to bite his leg, anything to stop this. Nothing made any difference.

She had sometimes wondered idly what people could possibly find sexy about spanking. She just couldn't imagine what could be arousing about being hit. Well, now she had her answer. Nothing. This wasn't sexy or sensual. This hurt. Jack's hand was like a slab of cement.

She tried to twist round to see if he had actually picked up something. Surely no human hand could hit that hard. 'Stop, stop, please stop.' She didn't know when her screams had turned to pleas, but it didn't stop him.

'You've earned this, Abbie.'

'Please, I've had enough.' The agony was building up, her backside was a stinging furnace. Who cared about dignity?

'We're only just warming up.' To her horror, he took the waistband of her trousers and pulled them down, dragging her panties with them. 'A good spanking should always be on the bare.'

No, he couldn't do that. It was humiliating. And it would hurt so much more. She hadn't been to Pilates classes recently and her ass wasn't in great shape. *What was she thinking?* He was hitting her and she didn't think her ass was good enough for him? Now she knew she had lost it.

He rubbed one hand gently over her bare backside. To her mortification, it felt good on her hot skin. She had to struggle not to lift herself against him, begging him to do it again.

'And now we're back to business.' He smacked her again. This one was sharper, more immediate, the sound of his hand on her bare skin louder in the echoing cave. She howled again.

When she managed to catch her breath, she asked, 'How many are you going to do?' She had no idea how many he had given her already, but if she had a number, she could grit her teeth and endure.

'As many as I think you need.' He spanked her again, the force of it driving her against his thigh, its solidity a strangely comforting contrast to the stinging heat of her buttocks.

Abbie gave herself up to the spanking. She couldn't stop it and would just have to endure it until he was finished. She didn't try to stay silent, but allowed herself to yelp and howl and let the sweat and the tears drip. She was aware she was a wet soggy mess, but no longer cared.

The only sound in her mind was the sound of flesh meeting flesh and her cries in response. There was no thought, only feeling. She was barely aware of her own voice saying, 'I'm sorry, I'm sorry. I won't do it again.'

Something about the spanking changed after that.

The spanks were different on different parts of her bottom. The ones that were higher up were worst and stung in a nasty way. She found herself moving, trying to direct his hand lower, to the point just above where her buttocks joined her thigh. Yes there, if he spanked there, it was almost bearable.

She moved again, raising herself on her toes slightly, trying to direct him without words. She would not beg him.

'Ah!' The angle of that spank was different, up rather than down, and it drove her against his thigh and caused a splinter of pleasure to dart through her. She scrabbled to get her toes under her so she could get that angle again.

He spanked upwards again, and this time the splinter was a spike. She cried out. He slowed the pace, spanked her more softly. Rubbed his hand over her burning skin.

She tilted her pelvis, begging without words. He spanked her again on the magic spot, but it wasn't quite enough. 'More. Harder.' She couldn't believe she had said those words, but he took it for the signal it was.

His hand flashed again, faster and faster, driving the breath from her body and pleasure through it. Abbie was vaguely aware that she was wet with her own arousal, but she didn't care. She had never felt anything like this before, had no way of coping with the overwhelming barrage of sensation flooding down over her. She gave herself up to it, allowing Jack to drive her higher and higher until, with a wail of pleasure, her climax broke over her, leaving her trembling and panting.

Oh god, oh god, oh god, what have I done? This had to be a bad dream, it couldn't be real. But she was still hanging almost upside down over Jack Winter's knee, his big hand rubbing soothing circles on her exposed backside. She allowed herself to lie there for another few moments, unwilling to face what had just happened.

'Well, who'd have guessed?' Jack's voice brought her back to earth, and the amused satisfaction in it made her stiffen.

She pushed herself up, and this time he made no move to stop her. He even helped her to stand upright. She winced as the movement tugged at the tender skin of her punished rear end. She couldn't meet his eyes and turned away, trying to pull up her trousers without revealing any more of her assets to him.

'Abbie –'

She never found out what Jack was about to say to her. A shout outside the cave interrupted him. 'Hey, are you two in there?'

Abbie fumbled, horrified at the thought of Kevin catching her with her trousers literally around her ankles, and drew them up. She sucked in her breath as the material rasped over the stinging skin. Her buttocks felt twice their normal size. She stared at Jack. 'Look what you you've done to me, I'm a wreck.' She kept her voice low, not wanting Kevin to hear.

Jack laughed. 'Relax, it wasn't that hard. You probably won't even have bruises tomorrow.'

Jack watched as Abbie spun away, turning her back and trying to fasten her trousers before Kevin arrived. She dragged her hand over her face, wiping away tears.

'You look fine, he'll never know,' he said.

She turned to give him a black look.

Daylight was fading outside, but he could still see the concern on Kev's face. 'We're in here. Everything's fine.' Abbie's dark expression made him want to laugh.

Zeke pushed into the cave and looked from one to the other. 'Are you sure?'

Jack held his breath. This was the moment when Abbie could destroy him. All she had to do was say, 'Jack Winter pulled down my panties and spanked my bare ass,' and his career was finished. He knew it, and undoubtedly, she did too.

He didn't regret spanking her. If ever a girl had needed it, she did. His blood still chilled when he remembered the sight of the jaguar only feet away from her, all because she had refused to do what he had told her. She deserved it, and if she had any sense of justice in her, Abbie would admit that. But she might still out him.

To his relief, she gave a curt, 'I'm fine,' and turned her back on Zeke as she managed the catch of her trousers under Jack's eyes.

Kev gave him a sharp glance, as if aware of what had happened. He probably was. Kev knew him too well.

'Abbie, are you all right?' His voice was gentler than usual. 'I'm going to set up the bedding here. Do you want to sleep beside me?'

'As long as you keep your hands to yourself.' She recovered fast, Jack had to give her that. 'I'm really not in the mood for another difficult male.'

In the bustle of sorting out bedding, arranging mosquito netting and getting Zeke settled, Abbie managed to ignore Jack. He could not ignore her.

He had loved spanking her. His hand still felt the impression of her gorgeous ass. God, that was an ass that begged for a spanking. He wished it had not had to be a punishment. He knew he had broken every rule in the book, because she hadn't consented to being spanked. But by god she had deserved it and he knew that, whatever she might say, her body had loved it. Whether she knew it or not, Abbie Marshall was a sub just waiting to happen. He would have loved to introduce her to the joys of going over the knee with an erotic, sensual spanking. Instead, it had had to be all business and no fun.

But she had come. He had heard the animal sounds she made as pleasure flooded her body and felt her shudder in orgasm. He knew it was possible to climax just from being spanked, but he had never made it happen. Abbie Marshall, uptight New Yorker, had come over his knee. He wanted to see her do that again.

She lay down on the far side of the cave, her back turned to him. It didn't matter; he couldn't stop watching her until the darkness of the cave blinded him.

Jack tried to sleep, but the erection which he had kept under control all through Abbie's spanking now tormented him. It rose against his belly, hard and unyielding, and kept him awake and wanting her. All through the night, he relived that extraordinary moment when she had climaxed under his hand.

He turned restlessly, trying to find a position where it would cease to torment him. In the silence of the cave, he couldn't even use his own hand to ease the ache. As soon as they got home, he would find an experienced sub and work out his frustration. He tried to focus on what he would do, but Abbie's face kept appearing instead.

He laughed silently. The idea of Abbie Marshall being part of his hidden life was so impossible that it was beyond fantasy. Even if she was a natural submissive who had no idea that she was.

Every time he fell asleep, he was tortured by dreams

of Abbie over his knee, of spanking her, of watching her come under his hand. He couldn't stand it.

As soon as the first light of dawn crept into the cave, he slid from under his netting and slipped out. The night-time drone of mosquitoes was still loud, but the new day was breaking. He headed down towards the lagoon, and stopped.

There was a boat on it. Some sort of canoe with two men fishing from it. 'Hola! Help!' he called. For a moment, he thought they hadn't heard, then they turned in his direction and paddled over.

They were saved.

8

Bleary eyed, Abbie made her way through the arrivals hall into Miami Airport. Zeke told her that she was lucky she was in the company of a celebrity, otherwise she would still be stuck in passport control. This whole star thing astounded her. There was no waiting. The airport authorities fawned over Jack and he accepted it as his due.

They hadn't spoken about what happened in the cave. She was still trying to make sense of it. That is, when she wasn't trying to shut the memory of it from her mind. How could he have done that to her, made her respond like that?

Jungle fever, she assured herself. Once she was back in New York she would deal with it.

'Abbie. My god, Abbie.' A slim blond man strode through the crowd.

William. She had never been so glad to see anyone in her entire life.

'Darling.' He swept her up in a hug. 'Everyone's been so worried about you. Miffy has been ringing the State Department every hour trying to get news of you.'

His arms loosened and he stepped back, wrinkling his nose. 'You look a bit . . . well, you look a bit –'

Sometimes he could be such a pain. 'Dirty? Smelly? I've been in the jungle for the last four days, William. What did you expect?'

'Now, don't be like that, chipmunk. I'm thrilled to have you back safely.' He gave her another, stiffer hug. 'I've reserved a suite at ONE Bal hotel so you can get cleaned up. And you might want to tell that newspaper of yours that you are safe, they keep pestering us.'

She nodded, already planning what she would say to her editor.

Abbie stole a last glance at Jack, who was surrounded by reporters and photographers. Even with several days' growth of beard and a sweat-stained shirt, he was breathtaking. But like the jaguar in the jungle – rare, exotic – he was far too dangerous to keep. It was time to put Honduras behind her and move on.

There was a sudden burst of laughter from the crowd surrounding Jack and she turned. Their eyes met and he gave her one of those stares. A Jack stare that made her insides quiver. She linked her arm through William's and turned her back on him.

Jack stared after Abbie's retreating back. It was ridiculous to be jealous of a wuss like that. Presumably he was the fiancé that Abbie had constantly waved in his face while they were in the jungle. Just one look was enough to tell Jack that the blond drink of water would never be enough for a passionate woman like Abbie. But it infuriated him that the other man was the one who could kiss her and take her home with him.

Jack wanted to kill him.

Then the blond bastard kissed Abbie, stepped back quickly and said something that made her mad. Jack was too far away to hear but by now he knew her body language. The other man had really pissed her off.

Jack grinned. Looked like he wasn't going to get lucky later. Just to make sure, he broke away from the gang of reporters who were popping camera flashes in his face and walked over to the pair. He tapped Abbie on the shoulder. 'Hey, haven't you forgotten something?'

'I'd love to forget everything.' Her expression was as stiff as her back.

'Even this?' He handed her the rucksack with her laptop inside it, and watched her face light up. For one moment, he hoped she would throw her arms around him and kiss him. Then dweeb wrinkled his nose and said, 'I don't believe we've met.'

Jack stuck out his hand. 'I'm Jack Winter. I've been sleeping with Abbie for the last four nights. Who are you?'

He watched the other man battle his reluctance to shake hands, but manners won out. He barely touched his fingers to Jack's. 'I'm William Dillard, Abbie's fiancé. And that joke was in very poor taste.'

'Will Dullard. Got it.' Jack stepped back before the other man could react. He didn't want to watch Abbie walking away again. Jack turned back to the press mob and flashes exploded in his face.

'Jack! Jack! How are you feeling?' Microphones were stuck in front of his face. God, he really hated this part of his job. The acting he loved, but he despised the whole publicity machine. But he knew how it worked, so he forced a smile on to his face and a twinkle into his eye and gave them the Bad Boy Jack Winter that they expected.

'I'm feeling just great now that I'm back in America, but

I've got to say, I can't wait to get home and have a cool glass of Guinness.' He winked at a female reporter and she blushed. 'Fancy keeping me company while I drink it?'

None of them had ever seen him drinking Guinness, but they were all convinced he got drunk on it every night.

There were a couple of questions about how they had survived in the jungle. Jack praised the survival training he had received when he was making *Jungle Heat*. Then a reporter asked, 'Is it true that you nailed Abbie Marshall when you were in the jungle?'

The question took him by surprise, and he responded with the stock Hollywood answer. 'No comment.'

The buzz increased and more camera bulbs went off in his face: as far as they were concerned, 'no comment' meant yes.

Abbie would never forgive him.

Abbie winced when she saw the pristine white cover on the bed. Everything in the luxurious suite was white, including the chairs. She couldn't even sit down to write her story.

'Everything OK?'

'Of course. Everything's fine, but I . . .' She glanced down at her mud-stained clothing.

'You'll be fine as soon as you wash and change,' William assured her.

'I don't have anything to change into.' And she wasn't going to go out looking like this. 'William, if I write down the sizes, could you go to the hotel shop and buy me something to wear?'

'Me?' William looked baffled, but he managed to smile at her. 'Of course. I'll get you something suitable.'

Abbie repressed a shudder at what he might buy, scribbled a quick list of sizes and closed the door behind him. She couldn't stay in these filthy things any longer. Maybe she could file the story naked before she climbed into the shower.

She pulled her laptop out of her bag and with it came the remains of the orchid Jack had given her. With shaking fingers, she tried to straighten the crushed petals. A burst of perfume gave her a jolt. For one instant, she was back in the jungle, Jack lacing up her boots and looking at her with those intense eyes.

She shook her head. She had a story to write. She opened the laptop and set to work.

Filing took longer than she expected. Her editor had follow-up questions, lots of them. 'Are you working on a colour piece as well about your time in the jungle with Jack Winter? It's a hot story.' Abbie could hear the amusement in his tone.

'Josh, come on, you know I don't do colour.' She shuddered at the thought of having to write about the days and nights spent with Jack. But somehow he talked her into writing a feature about her jungle adventures. 'OK, but not tonight. I'm beat. I'll be back in New York tomorrow. I'll do it then,' she told him. She hung up, wondering what she had let herself in for but knowing he was right: she had an exclusive, she should write about it.

She caught a glimpse of herself in the mirror. No wonder William had been shocked. She was sunburned, her hair was a mess and she looked like something from *National Geographic*.

The hot shower was one of the most blissful things she had ever experienced. Abbie washed away the filth of the jungle, soaping her body and her hair several times until she was certain that all traces were gone. Except for the marks on her ass. The redness had faded, but she could still see bruising from Jack's palm. She touched the skin there gently and felt a flicker of arousal. *Still!* She couldn't believe it. What on earth was wrong with her?

Abbie pulled on a hotel bathrobe to cover the marks. It would have to do until William came back with some clothes. From the bathroom she heard a tap on the outside door and a muffled voice. 'Abbie? It's me.'

She walked out and glanced at the two key cards on the coffee table. William must have left his behind. But when she opened the door it was Jack who was standing there. He had changed his clothes and his dark hair was still damp.

A wave of desire surged through her. He was wearing dark jeans and a crisp light-blue shirt that made his eyes look even bluer than she remembered. He smelled edible. Oh god – she needed to get a hold of herself. Jack Winter meant nothing but trouble.

'I thought you'd need this,' he said, holding something out to her. Her recorder. He had picked it up and put it in his pocket in the jungle.

She gathered her wits. Now that she thought about it, she should punch him for his behaviour at the airport.

How dare he speak about her like that in front of the cameras? Taking advantage of her moment of hesitation, Jack walked past her into the suite.

He looked around. 'No Dullard?'

'If you mean William, he's gone to buy me some clothes.'

Jack's eyes raked her up and down, taking time to rest on the bare skin at her throat. She had to remind herself to breathe.

'Pity. I prefer you naked.'

Abbie stifled a moan. He was trying to provoke her and she just had to control herself and not rise to the bait. She smiled sweetly at him. 'Your preferences are of no interest to me.'

Jack took a step closer. 'You want the same thing I do, Abbie, but I'm the only one who's honest enough to admit it.'

She backed away from him until her thighs hit the bed. This was not a good idea. Even though she was covered from neck to calf, Jack had a way of making her feel naked.

'Imagine it. Me running my hands over your bare skin before I put you over my knee. You wriggling that fabulous ass of yours, showing me what you need.'

Abbie swallowed. The pictures he painted in her head made her clench her thighs together. She couldn't speak and there was nowhere left for her to run.

Jack closed the distance between them and cupped the back of her neck in his strong hand, drawing her close until she could smell the soap on his skin. 'Don't fight it, Abbie. Let it happen. You know that you want this.'

She braced herself, expecting a ravenous, insistent kiss,

but this was different. Jack traced a path along the seam of her lips with his tongue and she opened to him with a soft moan. Jungle Jack was gone, replaced by a gentle seducer.

'This is not a good idea,' she said, even as her hands stroked the muscular planes of his back.

'Mmm,' he said, delving his tongue between her lips, teasing a response from her. His kiss was slow, lingering, as if he had all the time in the world.

She angled her head, seeking more contact. God, that man could kiss. She tried to tell herself that it was a mistake, that this shouldn't be happening, but a languid inertia swept over her. There was nothing else, nothing except Jack's kiss, tempting and passionate. A whimper escaped her mouth.

'That's better.' Jack tilted her head back until her throat was exposed to him, then he lowered his head and blew a breath against her heated skin. Her knees trembled. He had barely touched her but she wanted more and he knew it.

'Are you wet for me? Why don't I slip my hand inside your robe and find out?'

His hand traced a path along her shoulder, parting the robe and exposing her bare skin. He cupped her breasts with his hands before bending his head and taking one nipple in his mouth. The feel of his sucking mouth wasn't enough. She threaded her hands in his hair, dragging him closer. A low rumble of pleasure emanated from him. He suckled harder, switching from one breast to the other, grazing the tender flesh with his teeth.

'Oh god,' she cried out.

Jack released her nipple. His eyes were heavy-lidded with passion. 'Tell me what you need.'

'I want to . . .'

She couldn't say the word. How could she tell Jack Winter that she wanted him, that she needed him, to fuck her? That she would do anything he asked if he would only put his hands on her? Her voice came in a breathy sigh. 'Please.'

With deft fingers, he untied the belt and the robe dropped. Jack pushed her back gently until she was sprawled on the bed and he insinuated himself between her parted legs. He pushed one finger inside her and then another. Then he moved them in and out slowly, ignoring her attempts to make him speed up. 'Don't move, or I'll stop.'

Abbie froze. He couldn't stop now. One glance at his face told her that he would do exactly that. She tensed in the effort to hold herself still. When he removed his fingers and rubbed her clit with her juices, she almost leapt off the bed. Her whole body vibrated with need.

Jack dropped to his knees, using his shoulders to keep her thighs apart. At the first sweep of his tongue on her heated flesh, Abbie clawed at the coverlet, raking her nails against the cotton. His hot mouth laved her lips, making slow circles with his tongue, deliberately ignoring her clit. He circled the opening of her flesh before plunging his tongue inside her, licking and sucking until she gasped with pleasure.

Jack's attention returned to her clit, laving the little nub in slow torturous strokes that made her cry out. Then his fingers were inside her again, stroking the front wall of her pussy while his mouth sucked hard on her clit. She rocked her pelvis towards him, begging for more, and then she was lost. Pleasure crashed over her in waves, sending tremors throughout her whole body.

Abbie covered her mouth with her hand, trying to stifle her screams. His mouth and hand continued their wicked work, drawing out the last shaky pulses of her orgasm until she lay limp and sated on the bed.

He dropped a kiss on her stomach before rising to his feet. Abbie didn't have the energy to move.

'Poor baby. Wore you out, did I?'

She didn't protest when he helped her back into her robe and tied the belt in a neat bow.

The handle on the door jerked and William's voice outside in the corridor made her jump. Jack picked up the recorder and opened the door. 'Hi, Will, just dropped by to bring Abbie her recorder.' He put it on the side table beside the key cards and left without a backward glance.

William came into the bedroom, laden with shopping bags. 'Has he been here long?'

Not long enough. She struggled to engage that part of her brain that wasn't in a post-orgasmic fog. 'I was ages on the phone to Josh. I was just getting into the shower when he arrived.'

Luckily William had picked up the remote and didn't notice that her hair was already damp.

'You go ahead, chipmunk. I'll watch some TV.'

Abbie closed the bathroom door behind her and leaned

against it. What had she just done? She needed another shower. This time a very cold one.

After her shower she covered herself in moisturizer and pulled on the nightdress that William had bought her. It was white cotton with a high neckline. She grinned at her reflection. Even Miffy had sexier stuff than this, but at least it would cover the marks.

When she emerged from the bathroom, the TV was on in the background, William was stretched out on the bed channel-surfing and wearing a pair of silk pyjamas. A bottle of champagne lay in an ice bucket on the dresser.

There was something wrong with this picture. William was too small, too wiry, too blond. His silk pyjamas looked ridiculous, especially as she knew he wore them to cover a slightly concave chest. She had never minded before, but now she did. Reunion sex was the last thing she wanted.

It was months since she and William had slept together. Neither of them had a particularly high sex drive. They suited each other. Had suited each other. Something had happened to her libido in the jungle. Jack Winter had shaken something loose and she needed to get it back into the box where it belonged.

His smell was wrong. Not bad: William showered twice or three times a day, was religious about brushing and flossing and tongue-scraping, and invested in the most expensive colognes. Just wrong. When she got close to him, her nose wrinkled and she took an instinctive step back. He was perfect for her, but he wasn't Jack.

He patted the coverlet. 'I've missed you, chipmunk.'

Abbie cringed at the childish nickname, acquired before she had spent her teenage years in braces to cure her overbite. She didn't need to be reminded of that now. Jack would never call her that. *Stop thinking about Jack, he's gone.* But Abbie knew that she couldn't go straight from Jack's arms to William's. Something inside her shuddered at the thought.

She forced a smile. 'I missed you too, but would you mind if we didn't? I mean, I haven't slept properly in days and . . .'

He was immediately full of concern. 'Of course, how thoughtless of me. I only wanted to show you that I missed you. Let's get you tucked into bed.'

Abbie climbed between the sheets. The bed was blissfully comfortable, the pillows were just the way she liked them, but everything was too soft. As she drifted to sleep she imagined that she was swinging in a hammock above the jungle floor and a pair of strong arms were holding her close, protecting her. The faint scent of the orchid followed her into her dreams.

9

The early-morning flight to New York was uneventful. After the heat of the jungle Abbie felt cold. Winter was coming, and not the steely blue-eyed variety. *OK, stop thinking about him. When you get to New York you are not allowed to think about him any more.*

William snored softly in the seat beside her while she gazed out the window and tried to plan a feature story that did not involve rock-hard biceps, chiselled cheekbones and firm lips. The effort was lost on her libido.

Her heart lifted when she saw the small group waiting for her in the arrivals hall. There was her dad beside Miffy and the girls. Miffy's twins were holding cardboard signs painted with 'Welcome Home Abbie'. One of them was decorated with luridly coloured snakes.

The family reunion was interrupted when they were spotted by a pack of reporters who swarmed around them, all shouting questions.

'Ms Marshall. Abbie. Can you comment on the story in today's *Us Weekly*?'

A pudgy reporter shoved a camera into her face, ignoring William's attempt to protect her. 'Abbie, do you plan to see Jack again, or was it just some *Jungle Heat*?'

There was a chorus of sniggers at that one. Abbie's temper rose. 'Is there a point to these questions?'

A heavily made-up reporter stepped up, a pseudo-sympathetic expression on her face. 'Jack's fans simply want to know if it's true that you're an item?'

Taking Abbie's silence for assent, she pushed on. 'Four days and nights in the jungle. Tell me, what was it like to share a hammock with Jack Winter?'

Oh dear god, they knew. Everyone knew. Jack had told them. A lump formed in her throat. She could just imagine the amusement on Jack's face while he related the tale to some fawning interviewer. At the edge of the crowd, Abbie saw Miffy's mouth purse into an expression of distaste and realized this wasn't a welcome home party: it was a damage limitation exercise for the Marshall family.

William tucked her arm into his and Abbie flashed him a grateful glance and cleared her throat. 'My time in the jungle was an ordeal that I'd rather not repeat. I'm glad to be home with my family. I have nothing more to say.'

Ignoring the shouted questions and the flashing of a barrage of cameras, she pushed her way through the crowd, taking a small, perverse pleasure when she accidently stepped on a reporter's foot.

Her dad stepped forward, with his arms opened wide, and she ran to him. 'Oh, Daddy.'

'It's over, you're safe now.'

'Auntie Abbie, Auntie Abbie.' The twins jumped up and down, waving their drawings, vying for her attention. 'We made you pictures.'

Abbie knelt down, ignoring the tears pricking her eyelids. 'They're the best drawings I've ever seen. Is that a blue snake? Wow, I'm so impressed.'

Miffy gave her a stiff embrace and air-kissed her cheek.

'I really can't believe you've done this. Jack Winter of all people –'

'Now, girls.' Her father's calm tone silenced Miffy. 'We can talk about this later.'

The reporters pursued them through the arrivals hall until they escaped into the confines of their cars. Miffy and the girls went home, while William and Abbie were driven into the city by her father. For once, she was glad of the dark tinted windows of her dad's old-fashioned sedan. William hadn't said a word since the terminal. A scandal like this would upset his mother, and William would do anything to avoid that.

'Why don't you come home for a while?' her father said.

'No, Daddy, I'm fine. I have to work tomorrow. This will all blow over in a few days.'

They stopped outside Abbie's apartment and William got her rucksack from the trunk. 'Do you want to come in?' she asked.

William shook his head. 'I have a faculty meeting this afternoon, but I'll call you later.' He dropped a swift kiss on her cheek and then he was gone.

Abbie nodded to the concierge in the lobby. He handed her a sheaf of papers. 'Good to see you back, Ms Marshall. There are quite a number of messages for you.'

'Great,' Abbie said as she saw that the first one was from a researcher from the Letterman show. This was going to get nasty.

After making a pot of coffee, she opened a new document and stared at the blank screen. She had promised Josh a feature on her adventure in the jungle and the paper would be waiting for her to file her copy.

My Jungle Hell with Jack Winter she typed slowly. There, that wasn't so bad.

Six words down, only another one thousand nine hundred and ninety-four to go. Piece of cake. She got up from the desk and walked to the window to stare at the tree-lined street below. Maybe a run would settle her racing thoughts?

'No, Abbie, no running.' Echoing her thoughts, her cell phone rang. It was Josh.

'Abbie, do I look like an idiot? Every other paper is carrying a story about you and Jack Winter. We need that piece within the hour.'

'I'm on it.' She tried to sound cheerful.

She disconnected the call and sat down again. Damn Jack Winter. The sudden flare of anger motivated her. Abbie attacked the keyboard and began to write. It was cathartic – the jungle, the dangerous animals, sleeping outdoors, rescue. The words flowed from her. She detailed Zeke Bryan's injury, the near miss with the jaguar and all the other discomforts they had experienced. She skipped over the nights she had lain in Jack's arms and completely ignored the cave. Abbie did a last quick edit and pressed send.

Then she settled down to clear all the e-mails in her inbox. Junk, more requests for interviews; almost all of them were interested in her relationship with Jack Winter. *It's like living in a goldfish bowl*, she thought.

William had left a message when she got out of the shower. He had made reservations for dinner at Chez Martin and would meet her there. She wished he had picked somewhere less stuffy. Even the waitstaff looked like models and a tossed salad cost fifty dollars. Reluctantly, she pulled on a little black dress and heels.

The maître d' brought her to the table, right in the centre of the room. The Dillard name always guaranteed the best seat in the house. William was already waiting and rose when she approached. 'You look as beautiful as usual, my darling.'

Abbie knew she wasn't beautiful. When she went to the bother of dressing up and put on full make-up, she was presentable. It was the only time William ever complimented her. With a pang, she remembered how unkempt she had been after her swim in the jungle pool, and the sincerity in Jack's eyes when he presented her with the orchid and said it was almost as beautiful as she was.

That was over. Jack was part of her past. William was her present and her future. If only the thought wasn't so depressing. She sat down and the maître d' fussed over them, shaking her elaborately folded napkin and placing it across her lap, as if she were incapable of doing it for herself.

Their waiter arrived and presented them with leather-bound menus. As usual, her copy contained no prices. It didn't matter anyway. William insisted on ordering for both of them. She was too tired to argue.

'The porcini and truffle soufflé sounds divine.'

She smiled stiffly at him. 'You know I can't eat mushrooms.'

'Of course I do.'

But she knew that he hadn't been thinking of her at all. Food ordered, William then perused the wine list and, following an extended conversation with the sommelier, he turned his attention to her. Abbie cringed when she caught the amused glances from some of the other tables. A few people were whispering and she was sure she caught the word 'jungle'.

William reached for her hand. 'I think we need to have a little chat. I've spoken to Mother. She wasn't terribly happy about all of this gossip about you and Jack Winter.'

'And?' The idea of William's mother interfering with their relationship made Abbie's hackles rise.

'Well, Mother feels that you got yourself into this situation because of your job, and I tend to agree with her.' She opened her mouth but he kept going. 'It's about time you settled down and gave up all this dangerous trekking about the world. Why, look at Miffy, she has her charity work and the museum thing. You would see much more of her and the girls than you do now.' William patted her hand. 'What I'm trying to say, chipmunk, is that it's about time we got married.'

He gestured to the waiter, who brought a silver tray with two glasses and a bottle of champagne. Her heart sank. She was being mugged by Moët.

William rambled on. 'Mother wasn't pleased that I was prepared to forgive you. After all, the Dillard name has never been associated with scandal of any kind. But I believe that if you can show that you're sorry, she will come around.'

'Forgive me!' Abbie choked on the words. The thought of endless suppers for three, with Dolores Dillard looking down her snobbish nose at her, was too awful to contemplate.

William toyed with the stem of his champagne glass.

'But first, I need you to tell me that you weren't intimate with him.'

Here it was. The moment of truth. There could be no comforting lies. No pretending that Honduras never happened. William had been her friend since they were children. It had seemed so right at the time to get engaged. Everyone expected it. But even if she could lie to herself, she owed William the truth. He could be a bit uptight, but she was fond of him. She couldn't go through with the wedding, not while she felt so confused about her feelings for Jack.

'William, I'm so sorry. I can't lie to you. Jack and I . . .'

She couldn't say the words. She hadn't actually had sex with Jack, but what had happened felt somehow worse. Trying to ignore the hurt on his crestfallen face, Abbie touched her left hand. She wasn't wearing his ring. The Dillard family diamond had spent more time in the bank than it had on her finger.

'I'll have the bank return the ring tomorrow. I'm sorry, William.'

Abbie waited for the flood of guilt, but it didn't come. She should feel awful. Or broken-hearted. Instead, she felt free. Out of the corner of her eye she saw the waiter approach carrying two plates. She couldn't possibly sit opposite William and pretend that everything was fine. She grabbed her wrap and fled.

Outside, it was starting to rain. Abbie flagged down a cab. 'Take me to the nearest liquor store and after that you can drop me in the Village.'

10

Jack had had to fight to stay in one of Standard's serviced apartments. The studio had wanted to put him into a five-star hotel like the Waldorf where he would be constantly tripping over starlets and reporters. But right now he couldn't cope with that. He needed time to get his head straight. The jungle, the cave . . . walking out of that hotel room in Miami, Abbie all over his mouth and his fingers . . . her smell, her ripe ass, her glistening pussy, the sound she made when she was about to come. It was on a loop in his head and he couldn't stop it.

He didn't understand what had changed in Honduras. He'd had some hair-raising adventures before. After a few wild parties it was back to business as usual. This time, all he wanted was privacy to lick his wounds. Although it would help if he knew what his wounds were.

The basic apartment was normally used by travelling film crews. It had two bedrooms with minimal furnishing, a bathroom with a decent shower and a tiny kitchenette. Most important, it was empty and he had it all to himself.

He switched on the widescreen television and, out of habit, flicked to the E! channel. There he was, grungy and matted, smiling at the camera and, yeah – wait for it – suddenly looking shell-shocked and saying that damning 'No comment'. Hell, he almost believed himself that he had slept with her. Abbie would freak.

He made himself a big cup of coffee, one of the things he had really missed in the jungle: water that tasted of chemicals didn't cut it when he needed his caffeine fix. He almost missed the presenter's voice saying, 'Sources close to the couple in question reveal that, yes indeed, they did get hot and heavy. Ms Marshall, better known for her reporting skills than romancing the famous, seemed to have difficulty keeping her clothes on when Jack Winter was around.'

They flashed up a stock photograph of Abbie, buttoned-up and professional, interviewing President Obama. Then back to the airport in Miami, where she looked battered and exhausted. Jack liked that look better on her. Unbidden, his memory showed him a look he liked even better: Abbie naked after her swim.

The camera followed him when he broke away from Kev and Zeke to return her rucksack. He shouldn't have done that. Then he heard it. The sound was muffled, as if it had been amplified and there was a lot of background noise, but his words were clear. 'I'm Jack Winter. I've been sleeping with Abbie for the last four nights.'

Jack groaned. Oh yeah, that would do it.

He wanted to talk to Abbie, but realized he didn't have her cell phone number. He called Zeke instead. The agent was in a hospital, on drugs and very happy. 'Hey, did you see that news story about me and Abbie? I need you to call a press conference so we can put that right.'

Bryan chuckled. 'Buddy, there's nothing you can say that will change anyone's mind about that. The more you protest, the guiltier you'll look. Besides, it's great publicity. *Jungle Heat* will sell out, just on this. The hero of the film crashed in the jungle in real life, managed to get everyone out alive and nailed the leading lady. Pure box-office gold.'

'Zeke, you bastard! It was you! You tipped off the media. That's why you were so eager to get through to your office when we got to that town.'

His agent laughed.

Jack swore. 'Come on, Zeke. There has to be some way to take the heat off Abbie. She donated her bra to you. Don't give her a hard time.'

'Not as hard as you gave her, I bet.'

Jack growled in warning. 'Get her out of the headlines, Zeke, or so help me, I won't go to a single premiere for this movie.'

'So what? Everyone will just assume you're holed up with the nubile Ms Marshall, banging her brains out.'

'Zeke . . .'

Maybe the drugs were wearing off, or some shred of common sense still lived in Zeke Bryan's brain. He sobered slightly. 'OK, Jack, if you are serious about this, the best thing you can do is to avoid Abbie completely. Don't contact her, don't mention her and don't be seen with her. And start dating Kym Kardell.'

Oh fuck. Bryan was right. Kym Kardell, his co-star in *Jungle Heat*, would eat up the publicity and make sure that no one mentioned Abbie's name around him. Listening to her talk about manicures would rot his brain but it would be worth it. 'Sure, sign me up, Zeke. Whatever it takes.'

'I can't believe I managed to look that good with only two make-up artists and one hair stylist, can you?'

Kym Kardell never stopped talking. She clutched on to Jack's arm, smiled at the cameras, struck an instinctive pose, and still kept talking. He had to marvel at the amount of words she could manage without any content whatsoever.

And how come someone who could talk so much had never managed to remember the script? Jack had lost count of the number of ruined scenes because Kym had missed her cue or botched her lines.

They were standing on the red carpet at the New York premiere of *Jungle Heat*. Kym had mastered the art of posing while talking. 'Of course, those awful cargo pants would make a snake look fat, but I think I rocked the look, don't you? You could really see the result of my boot camp workout when I tied up my shirt to show my abs.' She was still talking, but now she paused as if she expected a reply.

Jack looked down at her. She was short and delicate as a china doll, with long black hair that took hours of styling every day, and which he had never been allowed to touch. The camera loved her huge eyes and pouting mouth, but in real life there was an unnerving lack of mobility to them. Too much Botox, he guessed, and tried not to think of a woman whose face moved naturally and who looked addictively good first thing in the morning, even without a trace of make-up.

He put his arm around her and leaned down as if he were about to kiss her. The crowd cheered and the cameras flashed hysterically. He held the pose for a couple of seconds, then straightened up, trying to look sheepish, as if he had been caught doing something naughty.

Kym smiled up at him, managing an adoring look that

she had never managed to produce in front of a film camera.

Jack had promised Zeke that he would go to the premiere with Kym, then take her out dancing afterwards and Zeke would make sure the publicity machine followed them. After a week of this, the public would be convinced Abbie was just a girl he met in the jungle. He hoped.

'Hey Jack, how's Abbie?' a reporter shouted at him.

He shrugged. 'I have no idea. I haven't talked to her since we landed in Miami.' But he wanted to. The strength of his desire to talk to Abbie scared him. She was the one woman he couldn't have. He had to forget her, even if it killed him.

'So, you're not seeing her?'

Jack managed to look incredulous and bored. 'Ms Marshall? Of course not.' He put his arm around Kym. 'I'm seeing this lovely lady. But keep it under your hat, please.'

It would be all over the media by tomorrow.

He wondered what Abbie would think.

Abbie lifted the empty bottle and stared at it. How could the wine have evaporated so quickly?

Kit hiccupped and tossed back her dark cornrow braids. 'OK, that's enough drowning our sorrows. You need to tell me what's really going on with you. And please don't tell me that you're broken-hearted about finishing with William.'

'I am broken-hearted –'

'Maybe, but not about William. Come on, this is me you're talking to, not some random woman you met in a coffee shop. That reminds me. I'd better contact the local branch of Husband Hunters and tell them that William is back on the market.'

Abbie threw a cushion at her. 'See if I care.'

'Well, that answers that question. Now, I can't wait for a minute longer. What happened between you and Jack Winter, and please don't say "no comment".'

'It's hard to say.'

She wasn't being evasive. Well, no more than usual. But if she could talk to anyone about this mess, it would be Kit. She was her oldest friend, and on those rare occasions when she got the urge to unburden herself Kit was the one she turned to. She had an uncanny instinct for knowing when to shut up and just listen. They had shared and analysed all the milestones – getting high, getting laid, getting launched into their careers – and everything in between. Kit never judged. And yet Abbie suddenly felt awkward, unsure how to explain Jack to her. She wasn't sure how to explain Jack to anyone.

A wave of heat moved up her neck and over her face.

'Oh my god, Abbie. Please tell me that you slept with him. No, wait. I need more alcohol first.'

Abbie heard her in the kitchen opening another bottle of wine and a bag of pretzels. They were going to have horrific hangovers in the morning. She didn't care. She had to talk to someone.

Kit poured two large glasses of Viognier. 'OK, shoot.'

Abbie swallowed. 'I didn't sleep with him, exactly. Well,

what I mean to say is that we did sleep together, in a hammock.'

'And was he – I mean, was there any activity in the horizontal salsa department? Oh come on, Abbie. I'm a visual person, I need details.'

'Is that a clinical term – "horizontal salsa"?' Abbie asked. 'Is that what you ask your clients? "How are things in the horizontal salsa department?" Impressive.'

Now it was Kit's turn to throw a cushion.

'Abbie, I didn't need to become a therapist to know when someone is avoiding the issue. Now, for the last time, what happened?'

'We kissed.'

Kit's scream could probably be heard two blocks away. 'Sorry, sorry. Go on. You kissed and . . .'

'We fooled around a bit.'

'What's a bit? Oh stop being such a puritan. Was he hot?'

She took another sip of wine.

'Jack Winter was hotter than hell.'

There, it was out. She had said it out loud. She was physically attracted to Jack Winter. Physical attraction was too feeble a term for what she felt – he had ignited something in her that was sheer torture: a glimpse of an unknown side of herself and a craving for more. It was an exquisite form of torment because she couldn't have more. He was Hollywood and she was New York. There was no point in dreaming. She had to get this out of her system.

'There's something else.'

Kit put down her glass and leaned forwards. 'Go on.'

'Well, he warned me about burying the fish debris after we ate one night – to avoid attracting predators – and, well, I didn't and a jaguar showed up. Lucky he frightened it away but he was absolutely furious –'

Abbie placed her glass on the table and paused before deciding to go through with it.

'He dragged me into a cave and he spanked me.'

Kit's expression was a mixture of shock and envy. 'Oh. My. God.'

'It's worse than that, Kit. I mean when he started to, you know, hit me I kicked and screamed and called him every name I could think of but . . . I don't know how to say this –'

'I'm a relationship counsellor – nothing that you could say would shock me.'

'I liked it,' she said miserably. 'I had an orgasm.'

'Oh.'

Kit's expression turned serious.

'Yes, "oh". The most intense O that I've ever had. And it's wrecking my head that someone like him could do that to me.'

'Oh, Abbie.' Kit abandoned her glass and enveloped Abbie in a hug. 'Had you any inclination before now? I mean, have you explored your submissive tendencies in other relationships?'

She pulled away from Kit.

'What are you talking about, my "submissive tendencies"? I'm not one of your weird clients.'

Kit looked at her with a mixture of affection and exasperation.

'Abbie, please don't take this the wrong way, but for a

woman of the world, you have some major gaps in your knowledge. What do you think I'm talking about?'

'I don't know. S and M, I suppose. The whole idea of it freaks me out completely. I mean, can you imagine me asking William to –'

They looked at each other before bursting into fits of laughter at the thought of William doing anything remotely kinky in the bedroom. Abbie mightn't have given Kit a blow-by-blow account of their sex life – or non-sex life – but she had told her enough. Sometimes, over a few glasses of wine, Kit had probed gently, asking her if she was sure a future with William was what she really wanted, but Abbie always fobbed her off.

Then Kit sobered up and became serious. 'Abbie, it's not about what people do, but who they *are* sexually.'

Abbie wasn't sure where Kit was going with this, but she stayed quiet and listened.

'There are some people who get off on dominance and submission – there's nothing wrong with it. It's normal for them. Some people have wild sex lives. And there's also a whole world of faithful couples out there who got together because one of them is a Dom and the other a sub.

'Abbie, having submissive tendencies doesn't mean you're "weird", and I've noticed that you have some.'

Abbie felt as if her head were about to explode.

'Look, you're not my client. I'm saying this as a friend. You may be able to jump on a plane and follow a story to hell, but when you're at home you're a wuss.'

'I am so not a wuss.' Abbie threw the cushion back at

Kit. It bounced harmlessly off the arm of the couch and landed on the rug.

'Oh yes, you are. Think about it. Who does everyone in your family dump on?'

'It's not like that.'

'Yes, it is. Who gave up her holidays to look after the twins?'

'But Miffy was sick –'

Kit stared at her. 'Abbie, the woman had flu. She has a husband and a staff of twelve. And what about those awful charity events you go to? Why can't you just say no?'

Ignoring the question, Abbie picked up a handful of pretzels. She could say no. She just didn't want to. It wasn't as if she had been railroaded into agreeing to marry William. She'd had a choice, hadn't she? And she loved Miffy and the girls.

Kit poured another glass of wine. 'I can see those little wheels turning inside your head. All I'm saying is that you've just broken up with William but you're not broken up about it. In fact, I'd go as far as to say you're relieved.'

She wasn't like that. She couldn't be so shallow as to break up with someone and not be broken-hearted.

'That is a terrible thing to say.'

'So throw another cushion at me. Look, Jack Winter has rocked your world and maybe that isn't a bad thing. Perhaps the Abbie who isn't running around trying to save the world should take a little time out for herself. If you like, I can put you in touch with someone. Just in case you want to find out more. I'll say no more. It's up to you.'

Abbie nodded. It might make Kit happy, but she had no intention of letting her submissive side out to play ever again.

Never again. I can't do this. I will strangle that woman if I ever have to spend another hour with her. Jack slammed the door of his apartment shut and contemplated locking himself in for the rest of his stay in New York. He could not spend any more time with Kym Kardell.

It was impossible that any woman could be that stupid. Abbie had more brains in her little finger than Kym had in her whole body.

Bad idea. *Stop thinking about Abbie.*

No matter whom he measured Kym against, she came up looking like a plastic doll. Even Sarah O'Brien-Willis had brains to burn. Now that he considered it, all the women he had ever been involved with had been intelligent. So that was his hard limit, an IQ in three digits. It shouldn't be that hard to find one in New York.

Jack tore off the tux and had a quick shower, just to get rid of the cloying smell of Kym's perfume lingering all over him. He didn't care how expensive it was, that stuff smelled nasty. Then, comfortable in sweats and a T-shirt, he settled in front of his laptop.

There were over forty e-mails waiting for him. He skimmed through them quickly. Some from fans. He cut-and-pasted a nice reply and tried to add something personal to each one. Two from children in the new school in Honduras, painstakingly written in basic English. He smiled and sent them a long reply. A short, stilted e-mail from his mother promising to write to him, and a long chatty one from his sister, bringing him up to date on everything that was happening in her life, and making him homesick for Dublin.

He sent her one back, telling her about the reality of life in the jungle. Not about what happened with Abbie in that cave, though. As he knew to his cost, there were some things his family couldn't face. Someday he would face the dark memories and go back. He had no intention of allowing his past to rule his life. But not yet. Give it another few years and maybe he would be ready.

A handful of business e-mails, some junk that had snuck past his spam filter, and finally he could open the messages he was really looking forward to. The FetLife e-mails. Jack was determined to reward himself for coping with plastic Barbie all night: he was going to hook up with someone who shared his kinks, have a great time and forget Abbie Marshall. This was New York, there had to be someone he could play with.

He opened his account and clicked into new messages. 'Dear Disciplinarian, I'm a naughty girl who needs a good spanking. Care to oblige me?' Jack checked her profile before replying. He had a firm rule about not getting involved with married women. But this one was completely blank. No friends, no fetishes, no groups, not even a single wall post.

He grimaced. He was willing to bet that was a reporter. No matter how hard he tried to keep his private life secret, sometimes rumours leaked out and journalists came sniffing. If they investigated a bit further, they'd know that he never got involved with someone who wasn't introduced through a friend. The risks were too high.

Just look at the debacle with Abbie.

No, he slammed the door on that thought. Enough obsessing about her. He clicked on a couple of other messages, chatted with friends, wrote birthday wishes on a friend's wall, noted that an old friend of his had a new Dom. Jack didn't know him, so he checked his profile to see what he was into and who he had been involved with in the past. Nothing suspicious there, he could relax knowing she had made a good choice.

His chat box popped open. It was Paloma, a former sub of his, the only one he'd had a long-term contract with. He had met her during his early days in New York, when they were both working off-Broadway. After what happened in Dublin, he had been frightened to have anything but vanilla sex. But Paloma had sensed something in him and she had freed him. He would always think of her warmly, though they were rarely in contact any more. He hadn't heard from her for over a year.

<Jack, is that you?>

He replied immediately.

<Who else would it be? How are things?>

<Not good.>

He waited for her to say more, but there was silence, so he prompted her.

<Tell me about it.>

<Yes, Sir.>

He grinned. He remembered the way just saying those words would settle Paloma.

<So tell me about it.>

This time the answer came quickly.

<I think T is going to break up with me.>

T was her current Dom. The last Jack heard they were very happy together.

<Why do you think that?>

There was a pause.

<He is acting strange with me. Yesterday we went out for a meal and he didn't let me call him Sir once.>

<Is that all?>

<And he didn't check what colour of panties I was wearing either.>

<That's bad.> Jack agreed. <What colour were they?>

<You're not my Dom any more.>

She was cheering up if she was getting sassy.

<But I'm still a red-blooded man and that's a spectacular ass you have. Anyone would be curious.>

<Just for old time's sake, I'll tell you they were black lace.>

<Good girl. Did T get to see them afterwards?>

<Yes, he liked them!!!>

<That sounds good. Maybe he was just having a bad day?>

<Perhaps. I'm still worried.>

Although she had moved on from him, he still felt responsible for her. And it would be great to catch up with her after so long.

<Can you meet me for a drink tomorrow night? You can tell me all about it.>

<Yes, that would be great. Would you like to eat Spanish? There's a new tapas bar near my place.>

After they settled the details, Jack looked again at the message from the 'naughty girl'. No reporters. Ever. He closed down the chat box.

11

Josh Martin pushed his coffee cup away from him. 'Abbie, just listen to me. I have no control over this. You're moving to Lifestyle and that's it.'

'Lifestyle? What birdbrain thought it made sense to put an experienced news journalist into a job that any first-year intern could do? For goodness sake, Josh, how hard can it be to dig up smut and gossip, and write features about fashion and design and the beautiful people?'

'I'm sorry about this, but it wasn't my decision. Jack Winter is hot news at the moment and since you're involved with –'

'I am not involved with Jack Winter.'

Josh raised his hands in mock surrender. 'OK, OK. I didn't believe that crap about you sleeping with him anyway. You're more intelligent than that.'

He got up and closed the door, shutting out the noise of the newsroom. 'Look, Abbie, I've been twenty years in the business and I can't understand it either. The board suddenly decided that you should be moved out of News and into Lifestyle. It's not something they normally do, but, hey, they're the board, they call the shots. Suck it up for a couple of months, and I'll apply to have you back in the newsroom again.'

Abbie huffed a breath. Why did she not feel reassured?

'And you know, just because you are in Lifestyle doesn't

mean you can't keep working on the Honduras story. Maybe if you move sideways into Lifestyle, it will take the heat off you and the weird shit will stop.'

She opened her mouth to argue, and then paused. Josh had a point. Someone had been working hard to stop her writing that story. She was used to harassment from people who didn't want her to write a particular report, but this time it had been worse than usual. Threats she could cope with, but the orchids were new. It wasn't hard to figure out why someone was sending her the national flower of Honduras; even though she'd left the country, they were still watching her. The flowers had become an almost daily occurrence at the newsroom. Sometimes they were perfect, sometimes torn and broken, each delivery more nerve-wracking than the last. She felt a pang that she had come to dread the sight of orchids. The moment when Jack put one in her hair was one of her happiest memories of the jungle.

'I'm not scared of them.'

His mouth tightened. 'Well, maybe you should be. You need to be more careful and if moving you to Lifestyle is the only way to get you to do that, then so be it.'

She nodded stiffly. If she had to go to Lifestyle, she would, even if it killed her. Just as she put her hand on the door, Josh added, 'And make sure you keep digging the dirt on Tom Breslin at the State Department. He's the key to nailing the story.'

She left the office and slammed the door behind her. Back at her desk, someone had left a copy of *Us Weekly* opened at page three. Circled in red was an exclusive interview with Jack Winter. *I am not involved with Abbie Marshall* shouted the headline. Abbie glanced around to see if any of the guys were laughing, but everyone was apparently buried in their work. Bastards. She picked up the paper and tossed it in the bin.

Fine. If they wanted her to move, then she'd move. Slowly. She refused to clean out her desk in the newsroom. Instead, she packed everything of value into her drawers and locked them. After a second cup of coffee and a muffin, she made her way upstairs.

'Ms Marshall, welcome.' Betsy Taylor had been editor of Lifestyle for more than a decade and her reputation was almost as tough as Josh Martin's.

'Hi, Ms Taylor, I'm not sure what I'm doing here.'

Oh hell. She knew exactly what she was doing here. Josh hadn't said it, no one had said it, but it was one of the unwritten rules. No serious journalist would get down and dirty with someone they were interviewing. They might say it was for her safety, but it was a punishment, plain and simple. The sooner she served her time and got back to real reporting, the better.

Betsy eyed Abbie's neat black trousers and button-down shirt. 'And how are we on fashion?'

'We're . . . not very comfortable,' Abbie said. *Put me in a jungle or a desert but please don't put me in heels and expect me to be happy.*

'Gossip?' Betsy asked.

'Political stuff?' Abbie said hopefully.

'No, darling.' Betsy pursed her lips. 'There is only one variety of gossip in Lifestyle. Who is sleeping with who, and what were they wearing while they were doing it.'

'Oh.' Abbie tried hard not to sound defeated. This was going to be worse than she thought.

'Of course, with your connections you have access to a lot of important people. Like Jack Winter. Now there is a story. Handsome Irish boy made good and a nice hint of danger to keep the pot simmering. I just love a tortured hero, don't you?'

Abbie's journalistic radar went live. 'What danger?'

'BDSM, of course. But he hasn't been caught. Yet. Our Jack runs with a wild crowd. Unfortunately they're all very discreet. See what you can find.'

A bespectacled assistant waved at the editor. 'Betsy, I've got Paris on the line for you.'

'Hilton?' Betsy said.

'No, France.'

With that, Betsy was gone, leaving a cloud of Jo Malone perfume in her wake.

What the hell? Jack was part of a BDSM scene? Even after what Kit had said, and despite all she had learned about domination and submission on the web, she had still managed to persuade herself that when Jack had spanked her it was because he was overcome with passion and fear for her life. The thought that this kinky stuff was his thing, that she was just one in a procession of women he spanked, made her feel ill.

She shouldn't have been surprised, she realized. He had been way too good at spanking. He knew exactly what he was doing. Years of practice, no doubt with lots of different women. That thought didn't make her feel any better.

And while Jack managed to keep all his little secrets, he had no problem with dropping her in it and making her a laughing stock. *Well, turnabout is fair play, Hollywood.* It was time his secrets came out. Within a week of meeting Jack Winter, she had lost her fiancé, her job and her reputation. It was time to start fighting back and she knew just how to do it.

Abbie found an empty desk, punched in Kit's number and got her answering machine. 'Kit, I need a favour. Remember you said you could put me in contact with someone about my, er, problem? Well, I need to talk to them and as soon as possible.'

The coffee bar was noisy. Abbie dropped her umbrella into the metal bin inside the door and scanned the place for Kit.

'Abbie.' She heard a voice calling her from across the room. In a small alcove, Kit sat with another woman. Abbie's heart thumped. She was really going to do this. Talk to another submissive. Not another submissive, she chided herself. You are not submissive.

'Paloma, this is my friend Abbie. Abbie, this is Paloma.'

Paloma was a surprise. Abbie now realized she had been expecting a scantily clad nymphet who looked like a porn star. Paloma was in her mid-thirties, subtly made-up with a rounded figure and a warm smile.

Kit excused herself, leaving them alone. For once, Abbie felt tongue-tied. What was she going to say to her?

Paloma's smile was understanding. 'I imagine this is all very strange for you?'

'Yes, I have no idea what I'm doing here. Kit thought we should meet.' The reality of what she was doing hit her. This was a real person, not a profile page on an internet site.

'Everyone has to start somewhere.' Paloma brushed her dark hair over one shoulder, revealing a silver chain with a small ornate padlock. Abbie had seen similar ones during her trawl of the internet sites, but this one looked old and expensive. Noticing her glance, Paloma fingered the necklace. 'Sir gave it to me to celebrate our third anniversary.'

'Oh, it's pretty.' Somehow she hadn't associated the whole whip-and-chain scene with anniversaries.

'Kit tells me that you want to make a connection with someone to explore your submissive tendencies?'

Put like that, it sounded very bald. 'Well, I don't know that I'm actually a – one of you or not, but yeah, I guess you could say that I'm exploring.'

Abbie knew that she sounded too vague. She needed an introduction into Paloma's world if she was ever going to nail Jack Winter. She had to convince Paloma to help her. 'Something happened to me while I was away on business. I met someone and we . . . well, he spanked me.' She held her breath, waiting to see how the other woman reacted.

She gave a slight smile. 'Spanking can be an intense experience. Was it your first?'

Abbie nodded. 'I can't stop thinking about it. I don't know if it was him, or what he did, and I have no idea how to deal with it. Look, I'll be honest, I'm a reporter. If this got out . . . well, my reputation would be –'

Paloma nodded. 'Yes, I saw you on the news.'

Abbie blanched and put her head into her hands for a shocked second. 'Oh god, you know who I am?' This was her nightmare, strangers knowing about her, laughing about it.

'It's OK. Discretion is the primary rule in the kinky community. I won't tell about you and you won't tell about me.'

Abbie finally made the connection. She didn't often go to the theatre, but she read the paper every day. 'You're Paloma Perez. You won a Tony a couple of years ago.'

Paloma nodded. 'Discretion, remember? And now I can guess who the man is.'

Abbie's mouth opened in shock, and her face heated up so much it felt like it was burning. 'I . . . I . . .'

She was lost for words. Paloma laughed gently, giving her time to recover. Finally, Abbie got control of herself again. 'Yes, but that's over. He has no interest in me.'

The other woman's knowing smile made Abbie grit her teeth. 'And I'm not interested in him. I just want to find out a bit more about this stuff. Maybe join a few websites, go to some parties or whatever.'

But Paloma shook her head. 'You'd be like a babe in the woods. You're not looking for a hook-up, no? You just want to find out more about yourself. You need a mentor.'

Paloma fingered the silver padlock again while she considered her response. 'Ordinarily, my Dom would be happy to talk to you. Help you explore your limits.'

Abbie rocked back in her chair. 'No, I'm not into that. No funny stuff.'

Paloma's laughter filled the tiny alcove. 'I meant online, Abbie. He's very good. But we're going through a difficult time at the moment. Things are a little fragile between us. But I can put you in touch with someone else. An old friend who is very experienced. I think you'd like him.'

'OK.' Relief washed over her. She would get to speak

to someone and maybe if she became convincing enough she would find Jack.

'Let me call him. You need to choose an online name.'

'Wild orchid,' she said quickly.

When she said the name, it sounded so silly, but she was reclaiming the flower from whoever was trying to scare her. It reminded her of Honduras and the jungle and the exotic flowers and, most of all, Jack. She shook the thought away.

'Fine,' Paloma nodded. 'I'll speak to my friend and e-mail you tonight.'

'Oh for fuck's sake, Jack, come out for a drink. You are no fun since you came back from Honduras.' Kevin slung his gym bag over his shoulder so he could punch Jack in the ribs.

Jack stepped back quickly. 'Are you a glutton for punishment? What the hell are you doing punching a man who's just done two hours of MMA training? That's how you get your teeth kicked in.'

Kevin ignored the not-very-subtle threat and headed down the steps to the street. 'You weren't the only one training in there. I can do my share of kicking.'

Jack followed him down, keeping a wary eye out for the paparazzi, but his luck was holding. 'You can't have been training hard enough if you still have energy for this.' He pulled the hood of his sweatshirt up over his damp hair, just in case.

'Some of us can stay in shape without doing a couple of hundred sit-ups, you know.'

'And some of us don't get a pay cheque if we don't keep in shape.'

It was all very well for Kev. He worked out just to stay fit, and didn't have to find a gym that wouldn't brag to the media that he was there or have reporters follow him into the sauna and shower. That had started a lot of Jack's reputation as a hellraiser. Well, he defied any reasonable man to stand there calmly while a little runt took photographs of his family jewels.

He grinned. At least the angle had been kind. He now had a reputation for being hung like a horse.

This gym specialized in mixed martial arts, had no sauna and the showers had the sort of crappy fixed heads that had gone out of style twenty years ago. But the dumbbells went up to 50kg, there were three power cages and the trainers were ruthless. Jack was limping and would be black and blue tomorrow.

He wondered if Abbie had bruised after that spanking. Maybe he should have told her to get some arnica. Fuck it, why did every thought, even about big sweaty personal trainers and ratty sneakers, come back to Abbie Marshall? He really needed to get laid, and so far, it wasn't happening. 'You're right, Kev,' he announced. 'It is time I went out for a drink.'

An hour later, he and Kev were holed up in an Irish bar on 3rd Avenue. They grabbed a table near the fireplace, and ordered food. Kev ordered Guinness for both of them. It wasn't Jack's drink but he couldn't be bothered arguing. He tried to remember the last time he'd had a drink, and couldn't. He was overdue.

'So, what's the story with you and Abbie?'

Jack choked on the house special, Traditional Irish Shepherd's Pie, and Kev slapped him, rather too enthusiastically, on the back.

'There is no story. We haven't seen or spoken to each other since we got back from the jungle.'

'Yeah, I've noticed you were busy. Doing Kym Kardell. Some guys have all the luck.'

'Jesus, if you had to spend ten minutes with that woman, you'd be poking pointed sticks into your ears rather than listen to her talk. There's a reason she's only in movies where she doesn't have to say much.'

'Oh come on, did you notice her boobs? Who cares what she says when she's got a rack like that?'

'And I know to the cent how much they cost her, how long her recovery took and how much they are insured for. Trust me, Kym Kardell is work, not play.'

'Unlike Abbie?'

So, they were back with Abbie, the one subject he didn't want to think about. 'Abbie is a reporter. You know how I feel about the press.' He picked up his drink and took a mouthful.

'In that case, you'll have no objection to me having a go at her?' Kev shoved a forkful of pie into his mouth and chewed. Jack wanted to shove the fork somewhere else.

'She's engaged. Remember? Abbie reminded us about her fiancé every time we spoke to her in the jungle.' Jack was aware that he sounded like every teacher he had ever hated, but he couldn't help it. The idea of Kev going after Abbie pissed him off.

'Nope, she's not engaged any more. Did you not hear? She broke it off with what's-his-name. So, now she's a free woman.'

Jack ignored the jump of his heart at that news. It was nothing to do with him.

'And I'm going to make a move on her.'

'Leave her alone.' The order came out before Jack could stop it, and Kev was watching him with eyes that saw too much.

'Or what? She's one hot chick. Her boobs are real and very nice too. Great job getting her bra off, by the way.'

'Leave her alone,' Jack repeated.

'Sorry, bro. She's available, she's hot, and you screwed up with her.'

Jack had no conscious awareness of what happened next. Later, he blamed it on a combination of MMA training, too much alcohol on an empty stomach, and Kev being really annoying. He punched him. Hard. Kev flew backwards, leaving a path in the sawdust floor, before picking himself up and launching himself at Jack.

By the time the bar staff managed to separate them, the police had been called and they were both arrested. Zeke came to bail him out of jail. He wasn't surprised by the gauntlet of paparazzi and television cameras he was going to have to run to get out of the precinct. It was always news when a celeb was arrested, even bigger news when he was arrested for slugging his best friend and breaking up a bar. The only good thing was that so far no one had asked either of them what started the fight – two Irish guys fighting in a bar; there didn't need to be a reason.

It was after dark when Zeke bailed him out, and Jack was almost blinded by the camera flashes going off in his face. He scowled and put his arm up to hide his eyes. God, sometimes he really hated his life. Acting was his passion, not this film-star crap.

A camera swung into his face, and he cursed and knocked it out of the cameraman's hands. The owner protested, outraged. 'Hey, that's a brand-new Hasselblad. Have you any idea how much that cost?'

'So, sue me.' Jack had had enough of this. He turned to Zeke. 'Get me out of here.'

Ten minutes later, they were on their way, not to Jack's tiny apartment, but to Zeke's upstate mansion, his New York home. Electronic gates, state-of-the-art security system, ten-acre grounds and colonnaded grandeur made it a dramatic contrast to the bustling streets of the city.

'Cosy little place you've got here,' Jack said. 'It'll be lovely when you've done it up.'

Zeke stared at him blankly.

Jack sighed. He sometimes forgot how people here just didn't get the Irish sense of humour.

A butler opened the door. He bowed. 'Mr Bryan, nice to see you again.' But he barely gave Jack a nod of the head. A bar fight followed by a few hours in the cells hadn't left him looking his best.

'Coffee, lots of it,' Zeke ordered. Did he think that Jack was still drunk? Then he led him into a beautifully designed replica of a nineteenth-century library. Jack was willing to bet that Zeke hadn't read a single book in it.

Zeke said nothing until they were sitting down with coffee, then he rounded on Jack. 'Are you out of your mind?

Don't you care about your career? Do you want to earn a living bussing tables? Well, just keeping carrying on like this and you'll get there.'

Jack put down his cup. 'It was just a minor fight. Nothing serious. I'll pay the damages.'

Zeke waved that away. 'I've already done that. Who cares about a broken chair? No, what I'm complaining about is the way you constantly go out of your way to ruin your reputation.'

'It was a scuffle, Zeke. No one would have cared if I weren't Jack Winter.'

'Well, you are. And I'm hearing rumours that you're involved in other stuff.' He paused. It wasn't like Zeke to be embarrassed about anything. 'Weird stuff.'

Jack took a mouthful of coffee. 'What weird stuff?'

'You know. Kinky stuff. Spanking.'

Jack wanted to laugh. Some of the films Zeke had been involved in casting were seriously twisted, with people being killed in disgustingly inventive ways. And he was stuttering over a spanking. God forbid he found out some of the other stuff. 'It's not a big deal.'

'Yes it is, Jack. They're remaking *The African Queen*. You're up for the lead, but not if this gets out. It's going to be a PG film. You have to behave yourself.'

Jack was glad he was sitting down. *The African Queen*. That was one of the biggest roles in film history and would break him out of the pretty-boy movies he had been doing. If he got that, they would have to take him seriously. It was the role he had been waiting for since he came to Hollywood.

'OK, Zeke, what do I have to do to get it?'

'Stay clean. Don't go anywhere, don't talk to anyone, and stay out of trouble. Live like a nun.'

For the chance to play Charlie in *The African Queen*, Jack would agree to anything. He nodded. He would live like a nun.

12

Jack stared at the display on his smartphone. Three missed calls from Paloma. That was odd. He hoped she was all right. He called and she picked up on the first ring. 'Are you all right?'

She sounded surprised at his urgency. 'Yes, of course.'

'I had three missed calls from you. I was worried.'

'Sorry, Sir.' He could hear the contrition in her voice.

'I'm not your Dom any more.'

'Old habits, you know? Besides, you were so much stricter than Tomas is.'

He wanted to grin but kept his voice stern. 'I'll get strict again if you don't tell me why you rang. You can still do corner time.'

'Ugh. I hate that. I hope you're not mad. A friend of a friend has just discovered she is a sub, and she's upset. I told her to talk to you.'

'Paloma –' How could he tell her why it was a bad time for this?

'After all, you are responsible.'

'What?' Jack's brain stopped working. It couldn't possibly be Abbie. She had freaked when he had spanked her. 'Are you sure?' he said.

He could hear the smile in her voice. 'Come on, Jack, how many girls did you spank in the jungle? She hasn't been able to stop thinking about it. She needs to explore, find out who she is.'

'This is a mistake. Abbie Marshall is pure vanilla.' Yes, the same Abbie Marshall who had a screaming orgasm when he spanked her.

There was a pause while Paloma considered that. 'I don't think so. But if you don't want to do it, I'll find someone else to mentor her.'

'No!' That came out before Jack had time to think. Of all the subs in New York, how the hell had Abbie ended up talking to Paloma? 'I don't want anyone else near her. She's like Alice in Wonderland, wandering around getting into all kinds of mischief. God knows who she'd end up with. At least I can keep an eye on her and make sure she's all right.'

Paloma laughed. 'I knew it. You wouldn't shut up about the jungle the other night. Abbie's profile name is Wild Orchid. I didn't tell her who you were. She's expecting a message from a Dom tonight at ten. If you don't want to be there, I'll find someone else.'

'No, you won't. I'll be there, and put the fear of God into her for this. And Paloma, I swear, if you were here, I'd have you over the table for a punishment spanking.'

She laughed. 'Promises, promises,' she said, and hung up.

Abbie closed the cover of her Kindle with a snap and glanced at her watch. It wasn't time yet. Another hour before she had to go online and talk to a complete stranger about sex. What had she let herself in for? She hadn't expected Paloma to get back to her so fast. She thought it would be weeks before someone would contact her.

She padded to the kitchen and opened a bottle of wine. She would need alcohol if she was going to do this, but not too much: Abbie mixed with alcohol equalled way too much frankness. Look at what happened the night she had talked to Kit.

She logged on to her Yahoo messenger account. Three tabs opened quickly, all sending her messages. Abbie almost closed the computer.

'Idiot, they're probably spammers.'

She took another peek. No 'Disciplinarian'. Just offers of computer games. Abbie didn't know whether to be relieved or not. Forty-five minutes to go. She would have a bath. That would relax her and when she came back she would chat with him.

She wished she had more time to talk to Paloma. What would she say to him? Would he expect her to call him Sir? No way, she was not addressing a complete stranger as Sir.

After her bath, she pulled on a pair of pyjamas and a dressing gown. Her watch said 10.15pm. Perfect, she didn't want to appear too eager. Abbie logged on. No messages from him yet. She took a breath. 'Here goes.'

<Wild orchid: Hi there.>

<Disciplinarian: You're late.>

Oh god, he was there. And he was annoyed. What was she going to do? *Stop being so stupid and talk to him, Abbie. It's not as if he can see you.* She rested her fingers on the keyboard and began to type.

<Wild orchid: I'm sorry.>

<Disciplinarian: Why are you here?>

<Wild orchid: You tell me.>

Abbie reached for her wine glass. That sounded cheeky and childish. She typed again.

<Wild orchid: Sorry, didn't mean that. I spoke to Paloma and she said you might be able to help me.>

<Disciplinarian: Paloma is a good judge. What do you expect from me?>

Abbie took a sip of wine. She should have been more prepared. What did she expect from him? Not this. Not some strict, voiceless stranger on the other side of cyberspace.

<Wild orchid: I'm not really sure. I haven't done this kind of thing before.>

<Disciplinarian: This kind of thing?>

<Wild orchid: You know.>

<Disciplinarian: No, you have to tell me.>

She could almost feel his contempt. He must think that she was an idiot. Abbie took a deep breath.

<Wild orchid: BDSM. OK, I met this guy. Let's call him Kevin, and we kind of sparked off each other. Lots of sparkage.>

Jack spat out his coffee all over his computer screen. Kev? She didn't just say that she and Kev . . .? No, no, no, that was all wrong. He wiped the coffee off the screen, trying to calm himself before he replied to her.

<Disciplinarian: Kevin? That's an unusual name.>

By god, if it was Kev O'Malley that she was talking about he was going to kill him.

<Wild orchid: Yes, he's Irish.>

It was Kev. He would tan her ass for that. How dare she get involved with Kev? He paused a moment, remembering the jungle. He didn't think Abbie and Kev had spent enough time together for anything serious, but he didn't want her even thinking about Kev like that. He typed.

<Disciplinarian: Tell me about him.>

Jack was mad to know what she had to say. As if to torment him, there was a long pause that made him wonder if she was going to answer. He typed again.

<Disciplinarian: One of the principles of D/s relationships is honesty. You don't lie to me, even by omission.>

<Wild orchid: Shit, do I have to?>

<Disciplinarian: I have certain expectations. When you are talking to me, you will not use unbecoming language. Please remove the word 'Shit' from your vocabulary.>

It was true, he did hate that word. But even more important, it was a tiny thing that would demonstrate to both of them whether she could comply.

<Disciplinarian: Then we'll talk about what you are doing here.>

<Wild orchid: Sh –, I mean, sorry.>

He wanted to punch the air. *Oh yes, sweet Abbie, you're going to be mine.*

<Disciplinarian: Good girl.>

<Wild orchid: I want to know if what happened to me was because of the man or what he did.>

<Disciplinarian: What happened?>

<Wild orchid: He spanked me.>

Wild orchid is typing appeared on the screen.

<Wild orchid: And I liked it.>

Jackpot! He had known she had come, had dreamed of seeing her orgasm under his hand, but he had wondered if she would admit it to herself. Was it possible that Abbie was serious about this, that she wasn't just trying to get a story?

She had to know that he could save this dialogue. In fact, he would save it, just as a precaution if she couldn't resist printing something about him. He could make sure she suffered just as much as he did. What should he ask now? He couldn't tell her he had been there for it.

<Disciplinarian: Was it a proper spanking?>

<Wild orchid: I don't know what that means.>

<Disciplinarian: OTK?>

<Wild orchid: What is OTK?>

So she really was a BDSM virgin.

<Disciplinarian: Over the knee.>

His favourite way. Some women didn't like it, but to him, nothing beat the intimacy of an old-fashioned over-the-knee spanking.

<Wild orchid: Yes, it was. OTK, lol.>

<Disciplinarian: If you are a sub, you'll hear that one a lot.>

<Wild orchid: I'm not sure if I'm a sub or not. That's what I'm trying to find out.>

<Disciplinarian: What makes you think you might be a sub? Or might not be?>

He waited to hear what she would say. He had spotted some subtle signs that made him fairly sure, but wondered how self-aware she was. And if she would tell him.

<Wild orchid: Oh, several reasons. I have a demanding job. I'm bossy, opinionated and too independent – according to my sister Miffy. That doesn't sound like a sub, does it?>

<Disciplinarian: Yes. The best subs are intelligent, capable and assertive.>

<Wild orchid: Oh. I thought that they wore collars and did what they were told. But doesn't submissive mean weak? Letting someone else boss you around. I don't think I could do that.>

Jack smiled at the idea of anyone bossing Abbie around, and not expecting to get an earful. But he wanted her to submit to him. His dick hardened at the thought.

<Disciplinarian: No Dom wants a doormat. It's a relationship. A strong Dom needs a strong sub. Submitting to a Dom is a choice, it's a matter of trust, not a sign of weakness.>

<Wild orchid: Oh.>

<Disciplinarian: Surprised?>

<Wild orchid: Yes, very. I'm still not comfortable with the idea. But I think that I need to explore it.>

Jack hardened even more at the thought of Abbie exploring her submissive side. He shifted on his uncomfortable wooden chair. Thank god there was no one else in the apartment to see him sprouting a hard-on while he typed.

<Disciplinarian: Did you get turned on when you were spanked?>

<Wild orchid: That's none of your . . .>

Wild orchid is typing.

<Wild orchid: Yes.>

<Disciplinarian: Good girl.>

He was genuinely proud of her. That was a difficult thing to admit.

<Disciplinarian: Honesty is hard, isn't it?>

<Wild orchid: Yes.>

<Disciplinarian: You can't live a lie and be happy. You have to face who you are.>

<Wild orchid: And how do I do that? Lots of people depend on me. I can't just change overnight.>

<Disciplinarian: Who depends on you?>

Abbie had never mentioned anyone except the perfect William Dullard while she was in the jungle, and only the dweeb had turned up to meet her in Miami.

<Wild orchid: My family – my dad, Miffy and her girls. I'm a strong person, they depend on me.>

<Disciplinarian: What age are you?>

<Wild orchid: 27.>

She looked a little younger, but the assurance in her manner made it easy to believe.

<Wild orchid: And work. I've just come back from South America. Did Paloma tell you I'm a reporter? I do hard news and foreign stories. I've even interviewed the President on foreign policy.>

For some reason, Jack hadn't expected her to admit that she was a reporter. She should have more sense than to give a stranger so much personal information. Even if he hadn't known her name, she had just given him enough to track her down. He would spank her for that later. But first . . .

<Disciplinarian: You're a reporter? Is this for a story?>

<Wild orchid: Nononono. Nothing like that, honestly.

But I can't talk to anyone else and I don't know what to do. I don't want to feel this way.>

<Disciplinarian: Why?>

The question hung on the screen, blinking back at her. The big question. Was it because of Jack? Had he made her feel this way or was Kit right? Maybe she had submissive tendencies. How could she have reached the age of twenty-seven and not know about it?

A vision came into her head of some of the scarier sites she had surfed on the net. Collars, whips, ropes, people dressed in leather. She was definitely not like that. Abbie took a gulp of wine. *Mental note to self, do not buy any more of this stuff.* The question flashed on the screen. He was still waiting for her response.

<Wild orchid: Because I don't know if I can feel this way with anyone else.>

Nothing happened. Her answer sat there, laughing at her. Maybe she was wasting his time. Maybe he had gone away. A message popped up on the bottom of the screen: *Disciplinarian is typing.*

<Disciplinarian: Tell me how you feel about him.>

Abbie had never felt so relieved to receive a response. She leaned her elbows on the table and cupped her chin in her hands. What was she going to say to him? *The truth, Abbie. Just tell him the truth.*

<Wild orchid: Don't laugh at me, but I think about him all the time. I know that it's stupid and I wouldn't talk like this to anyone else. It's just not me. I've even broken up with William, my fiancé.>

<Disciplinarian: Why?>

<Wild orchid: Because I slept with Kevin.>

Oops. Typed on the screen like that it looked terrible. Like she was some kind of cyber-slut who ran around sleeping with random guys. OK, she'd better clarify that. She was about to expand on her response when he came back.

<Disciplinarian: While you were engaged to William?>

Abbie typed furiously.

<Wild orchid: Yes. Well, when I say slept with him. I meant as in sleeping – not, you know.>

<Disciplinarian: Are you saying you didn't have sex with him?>

<Wild orchid: No I didn't, but I wanted to.>

<Disciplinarian: Tell me about Kevin.>

<Wild orchid: I can't tell you a lot because he's famous and I wouldn't like to betray a confidence. Anyway, he's not my usual type. He's basically a pain in the ass. But I liked him, he made me feel safe and I'm not used to having someone to lean on. Does that sound weird?>

<Disciplinarian: No. It sounds like a D/s relationship. Did you enjoy it?>

<Wild orchid: Sort of. Well, maybe not at first – he was too domineering. Wanted everything his own way.>

<Disciplinarian: Like any good Dom.>

<Wild orchid: It wasn't a D/s relationship.>

<Disciplinarian: He took care of you, kept you safe and spanked you when you needed it. Sounds like a relationship to me.>

Relationship. Abbie stared at the word on the screen. They weren't in a relationship. Jack was off, god-knows-where, probably with some beautiful starlet, and she was here talking to a stranger, trying to pick up the pieces.

<Wild orchid: I didn't mean that. I meant that he is not in my life now.>

<Disciplinarian: Why not?>

<Wild orchid: He's Hollywood. I'm New York. He wasn't offering any kind of a relationship. It was just a one-time thing. He's probably forgotten all about me.>

Disciplinarian is typing.

<Disciplinarian: Tell me about William.>

<Wild orchid: William and I met when we were four years old. Our mothers played bridge together. Anyway, I was the quiet sister but that didn't seem to matter. William and I always ended up together. Graduation, college, all the social stuff. It just seemed right when we got engaged. Our families expected it.>

<Disciplinarian: Did you enjoy having sex with him?>

What? How could he ask that? Even Kit didn't ask her questions like that. She sat back on the couch. A minute ticked by. He did not have the right to ask her that stuff. She would give him a piece of her mind.

<Wild orchid: That is a terrible question to ask.>

<Disciplinarian: It's relevant.>

<Wild orchid: Sex isn't everything, you know. People can have a very good relationship without sex.>

<Disciplinarian: Absolutely. But not if you are planning to marry him, have his children and sleep with him every night. So, tell me about sex with William.>

<Wild orchid: You are so . . . I can't think of a word for it.>

<Disciplinarian: Lol.>

<Wild orchid: Are you aware that I've only known you for 56 minutes?>

<Disciplinarian: So what?>

So what? Abbie's temper rose. He was almost as annoying as Jack. She would refuse to answer the question.

Disciplinarian is typing.

<Disciplinarian: Will it be different in 60 minutes? Tell me about sex with William.>

<Wild orchid: There's not a lot to tell. It's not that we haven't, you know, done it, but it's not the most important part of our relationship. William is nice, he's gentle. He says that we shouldn't get hung up about sex.>

<Disciplinarian: You said that you were bossy, opinionated and independent. How is that a good match for nice, gentle William?>

Abbie bit her lip. Put like that, it sounded awful. She knew that she could be all of those things, but it wasn't as if she bossed William around. Well, not all the time. Her fingers raced over the keyboard.

<Wild orchid: That is so not nice.>

<Disciplinarian: This is not about being nice. It's about finding the truth. Who is Wild orchid?>

<Wild orchid: Wild orchid is me. A part of me. The part of me that I left in Honduras. I think I need to go now.>

<Disciplinarian: Good night. Log on tomorrow at 10pm. Don't be late.>

<Wild orchid: K.>

<Disciplinarian: Good girl.>

She was tempted to write a snappy response to his 'good girl' remark. He was almost as bad as Jack. But it was too late, he had already gone offline. She read over the last few lines of their conversation. How had a stranger done this to her? Made her open up to him in a way that she couldn't with anyone else. Was it the online thing? Perhaps there was safety in geography. She didn't know where he was and they would probably never meet.

13

Abbie's cell phone buzzed as she stepped into the coffee shop. She reached into her purse and pulled it out. Wrong one. She fished out the other one and glanced at the display. It was Betsy again. She was tempted to take the battery out and crush it under the spike heel of her shoes. Josh Martin on his worst day wasn't half as demanding as the queen of the Lifestyle section. Abbie let the call go to voicemail. No wonder the woman was a size zero. She never took a lunch break.

Kit waved at her from their usual table and Abbie flopped down into the chair opposite. 'You know, life was easier in the jungle. Have you ordered yet?'

'Yep, two vegetarian specials.'

Abbie pulled a face. Kit was a health-food freak.

'So?' Kit poured two glasses of water from a carafe. 'How is cyberspace? Have you made contact with Paloma's friend yet?'

Abbie was relieved when the waiter arrived with two colourful salads. She wasn't sure if she wanted to talk about this yet.

'You've gone back into your shell again.'

'No, I haven't. I'm just – what would you say? – I'm processing.'

'And?'

Abbie put her knife and fork on her plate. 'I'm not going to get away with this, am I?'

Kit titled her head and smiled. 'Not a chance. Tell me what's going on with you.'

She speared a piece of tofu. 'I've made contact with him.'

'Him who?'

Abbie leaned forwards. 'His name is Disciplinarian.'

Kit gave a very unladylike snort of laughter. 'Sorry. I didn't mean that but with you and the spanking, well I –'

Abbie could feel the blush rising from her neck. 'Why don't you stand on a chair and announce it to the restaurant? I don't think the girl at the till heard you.'

'Don't be so sensitive, Abbie. It was a joke. Now, tell me about D.'

Abbie pushed her salad around her plate. 'He doesn't let me get away with anything. I have to tell the truth. I can't use bad language and he wants to talk about my sex life with William.'

'Anything else?'

'What do you mean, anything else? I haven't even spoken to you about that stuff.'

'Maybe it's easier to talk to someone in cyberspace. The good thing is that you're talking to someone.'

A meeting with Betsy and the team distracted her, but by late afternoon she was pensive again. Abbie pulled her coat around her as she left the office. Despite the threatening rain clouds, she decided to walk home. It would do her good to chase away her unsettling thoughts. Kit was pleased that she was talking to someone. She wasn't so sure. D was like a battering ram, breaching her defences, and she wasn't sure if she wanted someone poking around inside her head. She stopped by the local deli and picked up calzone for dinner. She ate in front of the television, trying to kill time until she could log on.

<Wild orchid: Hi>

He responded almost immediately.

<Disciplinarian: How are you this evening?>

<Wild orchid: I'm good. Work was busy. I'm learning a new job.>

<Disciplinarian: And what are your thoughts after yesterday?>

Nope, the old *let me distract you by telling you about my new job* ploy hadn't worked with him. They were back to talking about her feelings again.

<Wild orchid: Confused, I guess. I can't believe I told you all that stuff. I had a few OMG moments by the water cooler today.>

<Disciplinarian: But you came back for more tonight. So, what caused the OMG moments?>

Where could she start? Talking to him like this had opened up a ton of stuff. William, the wedding, her family. She wasn't sure whether she was ready for another session of Let's Torture Abbie.

<Wild orchid: I don't talk about my feelings with anyone. Even people I know – except my best friend, Kit. And that usually involves alcohol – lol.>

<Disciplinarian: Are you drinking now?>

Trust him to pick up on that. It wasn't as if she was out every night drinking cocktails until 2am.

<Wild orchid: Yes. White wine. But just one glass. Dutch courage.>

She took a defiant sip before typing again.

<Wild orchid: You're a bit scary.>

<Disciplinarian: You're scared of me?>
<Wild orchid: Yes. Terrified.>
<Disciplinarian: Why?>

Abbie stared at the computer screen for a long minute. Why was she so scared? What was so hard about talking to someone? He wouldn't be here if he wasn't interested.

Disciplinarian is typing.

<Disciplinarian: Tell me your thoughts.>

<Wild orchid: Well, I was thinking about William. None of this was his fault. We sort of drifted into an engagement and now I've ruined his life.>

<Disciplinarian: How have you done that?>

<Wild orchid: His mother had a wonderful wedding planned – twice.>

In stark black and white that looked bad. It wasn't as if she had asked her to organize anything. Dolores Dillard simply took over and William was happy to let her. The first time she had gone to North Africa and got stuck there. Not turning up for a fitting with Vera Wang which had been booked months before had been the first nail in the coffin of their mother-in-law/daughter-in-law relationship. Dolores had been furious that she hadn't just resigned from her job when they got engaged.

<Wild orchid: It's all my fault.>

<Disciplinarian: Because you broke up with him? Even though he wasn't satisfying you in bed?>

God, the man was obsessed. Sex, sex, sex. Didn't he ever think of anything else? He was worse than Kit. She got it that they weren't online to chat about her interest in Honduran drug gangs. But did it have to keep coming back to her sex life? She tried to distract him.

<Wild orchid: We're back to bed again. Lol. Did anyone ever tell you that you're obsessed?>

<Disciplinarian: Frequently. It's one of the things that makes me a good Dom. Tell me about going to bed with William.>

<Wild orchid: I'm not sure if I really want to talk about this.>

Correction, I so *do not want to go there.* What was the endless fascination with William? It wasn't as if he had been her first boyfriend. There had been that guy she had spent the night with in Mexico during spring break. She didn't remember much of it except that he was from Sweden, doing a world tour after college. They hadn't actually had sex. Too many mojitos. Maybe D would like to hear about that instead?

<Wild orchid: He wasn't my first, you know.>

<Disciplinarian: You're avoiding the question. If you're not interested in doing this, we can stop now. You can find someone else to talk to.>

He wouldn't. He couldn't cut her off like this. Abbie typed furiously.

<Wild orchid: No, no. It's OK. William and I got engaged when we finished college. We were going away together to work on an elephant project in Namibia. Anyway, my dad is a bit old-fashioned. You should have seen William's face when he said, "Bring her back the way you found her." So we got engaged.>

<Disciplinarian: And did he?>

<Wild orchid: Did he what? Oh sorry, you mean did he . . . We did it when we stopped over in Paris. Have you ever been there? In a little hotel that William found. We

had a great view of the Eiffel Tower. It was romantic, I guess.>

<Disciplinarian: What happened?>

<Wild orchid: We went for dinner – Le Jules Verne at the top of the Eiffel Tower. Afterwards we went for a walk and then we went back to the hotel and . . . Well, it was nice.>

<Disciplinarian: Nice?>

What more did he want? An anatomy lesson? She had just told him about her first time. What could she tell a Dom about sex that he didn't know already?

<Wild orchid: Nice.>

<Disciplinarian: Did you come?>

<Wild orchid: I can't believe you just asked me that.>

Abbie was tempted to throw a cushion at the screen. If she didn't reply he would go all Dom again. She had asked him to help her, not burrow into every little part of her brain. The man was worse than a therapist.

<Wild orchid: No. I did not come, but not everyone is as obsessed about sex as you are. It didn't matter to me. What did matter was that we were together, that William and I were starting out on a big adventure. It can't always end in fireworks.>

Disciplinarian is typing.

<Disciplinarian: Really? Tell me more.>

She could feel a lump in her throat. So what if she didn't come? So what if life inside the Marshall/Dillard boudoir wasn't like the Kama Sutra? Lots of people didn't have an orgasm every time they had sex. Lots of her friends didn't have sex at all. D was just winding her up. Trying to see how far he could push her. He was just like Jack.

<Wild orchid: I don't want to do this any more.>

She slammed the laptop shut. Abbie sniffed loudly. This had been a mistake. A huge mistake. She reached for her cell phone, but it was already late. She couldn't call Kit now. Abbie eyed the power cable. What she wouldn't give to be within two feet of Mr Disciplinarian. Memories of Jack flashed into her brain. His arms around her at night protecting her. His hand on her –

'Shit.' She dragged her hand through her hair. She couldn't go on like this. There had to be some way of getting Jack out of her head. She would have to talk to D.

Fuck, fuck, fuck. Had he pushed her too hard? She had just gone offline, with no indication that she would be back.

He pushed himself back from the laptop, unable to sit still, and paced around the apartment. He wished there were something lying around on the floor that he could kick. He reviewed the conversation. Had he allowed his jealousy of that dweeby jerk to make him push her too hard?

He shook his head. No, there was something there. She would chat away and answer his questions, but when it came to nice, perfect William, she got tense. There was something about going to bed with William that was freaking her out.

Jack wanted to ask her more about the cave, and the spanking he had given her. He wanted to hear her impression of it, and he would get her to tell him, sooner or later. But first he had to deal with the dweeb and whatever it was about their relationship that was niggling at Abbie.

He poured himself a glass of whiskey, added some ice and went back to the computer. She was still offline, so he forced himself to answer a couple of e-mails. He even checked his Twitter account. Wow, two million followers and climbing. He added a quick tweet. 'Just back from an evening out with the beautiful Kym Kardell. Think we managed to escape the paparazzi this time.' That should keep Zeke happy.

His Yahoo icon flashed. Bingo. It was Abbie.

<Wild orchid: Are you still there?>

He paused before he answered. She could suffer a bit too.

<Disciplinarian: Yes.>

<Wild orchid: Sorry about that, I just freaked out.>

<Disciplinarian: Are you over it now?>

<Wild orchid: Yes. I'm just not used to talking about my feelings and other stuff.>

<Disciplinarian: Who do you talk to?>

<Wild orchid: Kit, sometimes, but I'm on the road a lot. Or I was until they transferred me.>

<Disciplinarian: Where did they transfer you to?>

<Wild orchid: New York Lifestyle – ugh. And all because they think I'm sleeping with Kevin.>

<Disciplinarian: You don't approve?>

<Wild orchid: Noooooo. Have you any idea what it's like to work with a bunch of bitchy women who spend the day thinking about nothing but clothes and hair?>

He laughed so hard he almost choked on his drink. He was willing to bet that no one in her newspaper could come within an ass's roar of Kym Kardell when it came to thinking about clothes and hair.

<Disciplinarian: I can imagine.>

He smiled.

<Wild orchid: No, you can't. They expect me to wear heels in the office – those tall ones that make you feel like you're standing on a skyscraper. And a SKIRT. I am not a skirt girl – feel my pain.>

The image of Abbie in high heels and a skirt did predictable things to his cock. He took a drink and allowed himself a brief vision before he put his hands back on the keyboard.

<Disciplinarian: I like skirts. I prefer my subs to wear skirts. And it's always dangerous to ask a Dom to feel your pain.>

<Wild orchid: Oh.>

<Disciplinarian: When you present yourself for a spanking, I expect you to wear a skirt.>

<Wild orchid: Present myself to who? To you? But I don't even know you.>

<Disciplinarian: But we are getting there. Aren't we?>

<Wild orchid: I suppose, a little. What happens next?>

<Disciplinarian: You have to decide. Do you want to be my sub? Online only for now. Until you are ready to take it further.>

He held his breath while he waited for her reply.

Wild orchid is typing.

<Wild orchid: Yes and yes.>

Jack almost came on the spot. It took a huge effort of will to make himself type again.

<Disciplinarian: Good girl.>

He allowed that to sink in for a moment.

<Disciplinarian: There are things I expect from you:

I expect you to be honest with me at all times. No lying, either actively or by omission.>

She couldn't really object to that. Although with Abbie, he wouldn't put money on it.

<Disciplinarian: I expect you to be online every evening at 10pm, unless we have arranged otherwise first. Answer direct questions directly. No swearing. Is there anything there that you have a problem with?>

<Wild orchid: No.>

<Disciplinarian: No, Sir.>

<Wild orchid: No.>

Wild orchid is typing.

<Wild orchid: Sir.>

Jack laughed. He was so looking forward to this.

14

The call came just as she finished filing a story on the rise of Danish fashion designers. Abbie reached for her personal phone. Maybe it was Jack? A mad thought, but right now everything came back to him. When she saw Miffy's name on her screen she was tempted to ignore it but there was no point postponing the inevitable.

'Hi, Sis, is Dad OK?'

'He's fine. He's taken JJ and Robyn for the weekend, so I thought that we might meet for lunch.'

Abbie glanced at her watch. It was almost noon and lunch was Miffy's preferred setting for an ambush. She braced herself. 'OK, where do you want to meet?'

'Bergdorf Goodman, of course. It feels like ages since I saw you. I've got us a nice table where we can have a chat.'

She could just imagine it. Miffy's favourite table was at the window with a view of Central Park. This wouldn't be a casual lunch date, more like an interrogation. They hadn't yet analysed her break-up with William. And she knew Miffy would have plenty to say about that.

Millicent was four years older than her but acted more like it was forty. She always thought that she knew what was best for her. Miffy had always been a bit bossy, but after their mother died, she went into overdrive. It was her way of coping. Most of the time Abbie didn't let it get to her – at least, she thought she didn't – but the prospect of having to come up with an acceptable version of what had happened with William filled her with dread. Still, it had to be done.

'OK, but remember I'm at work, I can't stay too long.' Miffy never quite got the concept of working hours.

'Wonderful.' Miffy rambled on, not listening. 'I'll see you there at 1:15.'

It was 1:20 before Abbie raced through the homewares department on the seventh floor and into the crowded restaurant. The place was full of out-of-towners. At least it was loud. The sound would drown out Miffy's constant complaints.

'Abbie.' Miffy stood up and air-kissed her on both cheeks. 'Lovely to see you. I've ordered a glass of Veuve for both of us. Sit, sit, you can tell me everything that's happened since poor William.'

Poor William? Abbie was about to turn round and go home again when a waiter materialized behind her, slid back her chair and Abbie took a seat, wincing as she was pinned against the table. There was no escape now.

Miffy smiled at the waiter as if he were an old friend. 'We'll both have Lobster Mac and the Harvest Salad.'

Great, why doesn't she ask me if I want to go to the bathroom before I sit down? Another waiter appeared with their champagne. Abbie took a moment to try to settle herself. She was just going to have to get through this.

Miffy took a sip of her drink and replaced the glass on the table. She laced her fingers together and rested her chin on her hands. 'Darling, tell me everything. I still can't believe it. You must be devastated about losing William.'

Abbie took a sip of her water. 'I'm good, actually.'

'Good?' Miffy sounded horrified. 'How can you say that? You've practically been engaged since second grade.'

'Maybe that was the problem.'

'But William adores you and Dolores Dillard is simply distraught. I saw her at bridge on Thursday and she could barely hold her cards.'

Abbie almost choked on her champagne at the thought of scandalizing bridge night. She could just imagine the undercurrent of spite as the ladies who lunched pretended to be sympathetic.

'It's for the best, Miffy. Honestly.'

Miffy sat back in her chair. 'It's that man, isn't it? Jack Winter? He's done this to you. He's attractive, I'll give you that, but he's not our sort of people, is he?'

Our sort of people. Now there was a thought. Abbie gave a little inward shudder. Just who were 'our sort of people'? Was Kit right? Was she simply a wuss who was under the thumb of her family? After all, Miffy wasn't really concerned about her, but about some set of unwritten rules about what was appropriate for their family.

Even though Jack was arrogant and overbearing, in the short time they had spent together she always felt that he was utterly focused on her. He listened to her like no one else ever had, not even Kit. Abbie stifled a smile at the thought of a Jack/Miffy encounter. Alien versus Predator came to mind.

'I'm not seeing Jack,' she said.

Miffy looked almost disappointed. 'But he's here, isn't he, in New York? I saw his face on the front of the *Post*.'

The waiter arrived with their food and refilled their

champagne glasses. Abbie dug a fork into her meal and wished she were somewhere else. 'I have no idea.'

'So you're not . . . I mean . . .' Miffy stared at her, but not a muscle moved in her face.

Abbie sighed. More Botox. Her sister couldn't frown any more with the amount of stuff she had in her face.

'No, I am not sleeping with Jack Winter.'

At the table beside her, a fork clattered to the floor.

'There's no need to be vulgar, darling.'

Miffy toyed with her food, moving it around the plate until Abbie wanted to slap her. How could she be on another diet? She was barely a size two. The waiter whisked away Miffy's barely touched plate and brought their salads.

'Now, darling. I know that you don't want to listen to advice. I mean, if you did, you wouldn't still be working at that newspaper and running around the world getting yourself into all kinds of ridiculous scrapes.'

Miffy examined the greenery on her plate. 'Go back to William. I'm sure if you ask him to forgive you, he will. You can have a winter wedding. Somewhere quiet. But do it soon, darling, before he meets someone else.'

Abbie almost choked on her salad. It was the ultimate humiliation – love advice from her sister.

'You're not getting any younger, you know,' Miffy said as she stuck a fork into her tiny dish of salad dressing first before attacking the carefully arranged circle of leaves.

'If you just want to casually run into him, William will be at the Van Gogh exhibition opening next weekend. I've booked some tickets for you. It's a very good cause. You've no idea how much it costs to stage an exhibition like that.'

More tickets. Abbie didn't want to think about how much they would cost. If it wasn't tickets for the museum, it was the opera or some other charity that she was involved with. Why did Miffy always think that she could do this to her?

Because you always let her. Idiot.

'I'm not sure about the weekend . . .'

'Darling, you know that I only want the best for you. Don't let your involvement with that man destroy your only chance of happiness.'

Message delivered, Miffy sat back in her chair. 'Now, after we have coffee, we can do a little shopping. Miu Miu have some darling shoes and you simply must try them.'

15

The party at the Honduras Friendship Society was not the sort of thing that Jack Winter normally attended, so Abbie was astonished when she got there and saw him stepping out of a car on to a red carpet.

Betsy had sent her to cover the event on the basis that she had a better chance than anyone else of getting an interview with Jack Winter. Abbie hadn't believed he would actually show up.

When she saw him, she couldn't help but drink in the sight of him. He looked stunning in a tuxedo. She was torn between gazing at the way his sharp cheekbones gave an air of danger to a face that was almost too beautiful to be real, and imagining the body underneath the handmade suit. In the end, she settled for his eyes. Jack's eyes were so blue, so intense, that she would be tempted to claim they were coloured contacts if she hadn't seen the exact same blue in the jungle.

His thick hair had been cut and styled, but nothing could make this man look tame. She shivered. Every time she saw him, he reminded her of the big cat that had prowled so dangerously close in the jungle. They were both beautiful and lethal.

And you are going to bring him down. When she was finished with Jack Winter, he wouldn't have hordes of adoring fans chasing him around with notebooks begging for his autograph. People would know he was the sort of man who dragged women into caves and spanked them.

But looking at him as he bent down to talk to an elderly woman, she couldn't get herself riled up as she had been before. Right now, she wasn't sure what she wanted from him. A tiny part of her wanted him to drag her away and do it all over again. She blamed D and his questions for keeping her libido awake and sending it in directions she didn't want it to go.

Jack moved towards the building and then spotted her standing on the steps. He paused and his eyes widened for a second, then he started to move towards her, all that heart-stopping intensity focused on her.

She forced herself not to flinch and to hold her position. Jack would not intimidate her. At least this time, for the first time since she met him, she was properly dressed. She wasn't a fan of heels and pencil skirts, but they looked good, and her red silk blouse was both dramatic and comfortable. She had styled her hair and gone for a smoky look with her eye make-up.

The expression on Jack's face said that she had succeeded, but when he approached her, he was a model of decorum. 'Ms Marshall. How nice to see you again. What are you doing here? I thought you'd still be working on that Tabora story.'

She scowled, though she was pleased he had remembered what she was working on. 'This wasn't my idea. My editor wanted me to get an interview with you.' She clutched her digital recorder, the one he had returned to her.

He bowed. 'I'm always ready to service you –'

She gasped. Just when she thought she was safe, he came out with something like that.

'But I'm not doing any interviews tonight. Still, you might make some good contacts for the Tabora piece.'

She turned away from him and marched up the steps, conscious of his eyes on her back, then took her place in the press row.

The speeches went on for longer than she had expected. It seemed that every political figure connected to Honduras was making the most of the press turn-out prompted by Jack's presence to talk about nothing at great length. She recorded and took notes. It might be boring but there were a few snippets worth following up.

As the night dragged on, she got restless. It didn't look as if she was going to get out by ten. She fidgeted, torn between the need to get back to her laptop on time, and reluctance to leave the party while Jack was there. Even at his most aggravating, he drew her towards him so that she hated having to leave.

Get a grip, Abbie. This obsession is not healthy. She knew it, but it didn't help when she was in the same room as him. Despite herself, she watched him all night. She noticed that Jack checked his watch as often as she did. No doubt he had another date set up for when he was finished here. The thought hurt her on a level she hadn't expected.

Finally it was time for Jack to say a few words. He stood up, looked at the audience and spoke. Abbie jerked upright so hard she thought she had twisted something in her back. Jack in the jungle was imposing. Jack at the pool was gentle. Jack in the cave was scary. Jack in her hotel room was sexy. Nothing had prepared her for this.

Jack in front of an audience was mesmerizing. His speech was short, reminding them of the people he had met in Honduras and why they needed help, but the way he delivered it made the hairs stand up on the back of her neck.

She was getting aroused. In front of a hundred people and not even touching him, she was getting turned on. God knew what she would have done if Kevin O'Malley hadn't slipped in and sat down beside her. 'Sorry I'm late, but I'm glad you kept the best seat for me.' She laughed, as much in relief from the sexual tension as anything else.

From the podium, Jack's flinty gaze caught hers and she could tell that he wasn't pleased. He wrapped up his remarks quickly. She checked her watch – 10.05pm. D was going to be unhappy. Tough, she had a charming Irishman beside her handing her his card, and an irate one who was scowling at her from a podium. She had too many men in her life.

Jack posed for photographs afterwards, and Abbie enjoyed just watching him while Kevin made ribald comments about the other guests. Then a photographer asked Kevin and her to pose with Jack. Reluctantly she agreed. She hated being photographed, especially after the stories about their supposed jungle dalliance. Still, that was more or less yesterday's news. *In more ways than one*, she thought with a pang.

As she stood there she was pretty sure that Jack was sniffing her hair. He was unbelievable. She checked her watch again.

'Got another date?' he murmured to her. 'Just tell him I've got dibs on that ass.'

She glowered at him. 'You are a pain in the ass.'

'And you love it.'

Kev put a protective arm around her and smirked at Jack. 'You're losing it, bro.' He turned to her and said, 'Come on, I'll give you a ride home.'

She nodded and picked up her bag. She was not going to hang around like a pathetic loser, waiting to talk to Jack, even if leaving him hurt like a knife wound. The strength of her desire to stay wherever he was frightened her.

She was glad she had D to take her mind off Jack Winter. She wondered what he would say when she logged on late.

'So, I was wondering if we could have lunch together soon, catch up on what's been happening since Honduras?'

Abbie dragged her attention away from the traffic and back to Kevin. It was 10:45. D was going to be angry, if he had bothered to wait for her.

'That would be nice,' she said, distracted by the cab that had just cut in front of them.

'Great. How about lunch on Saturday?'

'Saturday?' She had envisaged a quick coffee midweek while she tried to keep up with Betsy's ever-increasing demands. Oh, why not? Kevin was nice and it wasn't as if she had been inundated with requests for dates since she broke up with William. It would be the perfect opportunity to talk to him about Jack.

'Saturday would be lovely.'

'Great, I'll pick you up at noon.'

The car pulled up in front of her apartment building and she reached for the door handle.

'Abbie.' Something in Kevin's tone made her turn round.

He dropped a light kiss on her cheek before pulling away quickly. A smile quirked the corner of his mouth. 'I'll see you on Saturday.'

The kiss hadn't been anything other than friendly, but there was an undercurrent of something else behind his smile. Abbie shook her head. She would think about Kevin later, right now she had to deal with an angry Dom.

Back in her apartment, she switched on the laptop and waited for it to boot up. Kicking off her shoes, she hurried to the bedroom, dragging off the blouse and unzipping her skirt and the hated pantyhose as she went. She didn't have time to change. Oh, what the hell, it wasn't as if he could see her.

She grabbed a glass of water and hurried back to the couch to log on. The chat-room icon winked at her. Abbie took a deep breath and began to type.

<Wild orchid: Hi, sorry I'm late. I had to work.>

<Disciplinarian: You didn't let me know. If this is to go anywhere, we need to establish some rules.>

<Disciplinarian: Be on time. If you can't get here at the time we arranged, send me an IM to let me know.>

<Disciplinarian: Change your font when you are chatting to me. I prefer Arial.>

<Disciplinarian: Once we are chatting, do not leave without permission. Ask before you leave.>

<Disciplinarian: No bad language.>

<Disciplinarian: Answer direct questions directly.>

<Disciplinarian: I think that's enough to be going on with, don't you?>

<Wild orchid: Change my font? Why?>

<Disciplinarian: Because I like Arial, and I'm the Dom. What's wrong, don't you know how to change it?>

<Wild orchid: Of course I can but . . .>

<Disciplinarian: Why were you late?>

<Wild orchid: Betsy told me to cover a party at the Honduran Embassy. I didn't think it would go on for so long.>

<Disciplinarian: You could have IM'ed me. I'll deal with that later. Tell me about the party.>

<Wild orchid: I didn't think of IM. I thought I'd be home on time. The party was the usual – long speeches and political factions trying to score points because of the media presence. Same old, same old. I've been at a million of them.>

<Disciplinarian: Is that all?>

<Wild orchid: No. You remember I told you about Kevin? Well, he was there.>

<Disciplinarian: How did you react? Did your panties get wet?>

<Wild orchid: I refuse to respond to that question. Kevin pushed my buttons as usual.>

<Disciplinarian: Got you wet?>

She was torn between indignation and laughter. How did he do this to her?

<Wild orchid: I am so not answering.>

<Disciplinarian: I thought you agreed that you would be honest. Tell the truth, no lying by omission.>

<Wild orchid: He makes me feel hot and aroused. Just like he's always done, but I hate feeling like this.>

<Disciplinarian: Why?>

<Wild orchid: Because . . . because it leads nowhere.>

<Disciplinarian: Do you want it to lead somewhere?

<Wild orchid: That's impossible. I've seen the papers. He has a ton of other women in his life. I'm just someone he liked to torture.>

She paused. That was true. It was just a game to him.

<Wild orchid: Anyway, I've decided to try to move on. I have a date on Saturday.>

<Disciplinarian: With who?>

<Wild orchid: It's with Kevin's friend, Jack. He's nice.>

She got a perverse pleasure from switching the names around.

<Disciplinarian: Jack is nice?>

<Wild orchid: Yes, he's sweet and he's a great listener. I like him.>

<Disciplinarian: Sweeter than William?>

<Wild orchid: He's not a bit like William. Jack is lots of fun. We're going to lunch.>

<Disciplinarian: You've been a busy girl, haven't you?>

Was it her imagination that there was an edge in that line? Abbie wished she could hear his words, not just see them written down. What sort of voice did D have? She'd bet it was a deep rumble, strong and authoritative.

<Disciplinarian: Have you been exploring your submissive nature?>

<Wild orchid: I haven't had a lot of time to think about it. I had lunch with Kit today. We spoke about old boyfriends. She says that I've always dated the same guy – they just had different names.>

<Disciplinarian: And none of them were Doms. None of them gave you what you needed.>

<Wild orchid: How do you know that?>

<Disciplinarian: If they did, you wouldn't be here now.>

She hated to admit it, but it was true. Kit had said it, and now D was saying the same thing. It was time to admit that there was a side to her personality she had never acknowledged. She took a breath.

<Wild orchid: OK, say if I wanted to explore this. What would happen next if I was in a D/s relationship with you?>

<Disciplinarian: I'd set the rules. And you would obey them. And you'd like it.>

Rules. Her breath left her body. She didn't know if she was scared or aroused. She had to keep it light, not let him know how his words affected her.

<Wild orchid: OK, I like this game. What's the first rule?>

<Disciplinarian: You tell me what colour panties you are wearing. Every day.>

<Wild orchid: You want to know about my underwear?>

<Disciplinarian: Yes.>

<Wild orchid: I suppose I could do that, but it won't be very exciting. I can tell you now. They're either black or flesh-coloured.>

<Disciplinarian: Well, that ends now. Throw them away and buy pretty ones.>

<Wild orchid: All of them?>

<Disciplinarian: Yes, and send me a report every morning when you get dressed, so I know what you're wearing. First rule, no drab underwear. Pretty colours. And you have to tell me about them. Is that too difficult?>

Abbie stared at the screen. Is that too difficult? He had

no idea what he was asking. The mysterious D wanted control of her lingerie drawer and expected her to hand it over, just like that? Maybe this was a test to see if she was submissive. Her hands hovered over the keyboard.

She was torn between anger and an intense desire to giggle. In a way, it was flattering. No one ever had the slightest interest in what she wore. William often told her she looked beautiful, but he never really looked at her. OK, Marshall, are you really going to do this?

<Wild orchid: OK, I'll go shopping tomorrow.>

<Disciplinarian: Good girl. What colour panties are you wearing now?>

<Wild orchid: Black, oh, and I'm wearing a scarlet silk chemise – to match the outfit I was wearing earlier. Miffy bought it for me last Christmas.>

<Disciplinarian: I like the chemise. But the black panties have to go. Take them off.>

<Wild orchid: What?>

<Disciplinarian: Take them off. I'll wait.>

He had to be kidding. Would Jack be like this too? Wanting to take control of her. She slid her hands along the bare skin of her thighs and toyed with the edge of her underwear. *Come on, if Jack was here, you wouldn't hesitate.* She pulled them off in one swift movement and tucked them behind a cushion.

<Wild orchid: OK, they're off.>

<Disciplinarian: Tell me how it feels.>

<Wild orchid: I will not.>

<Disciplinarian: Are you excited?>

<Wild orchid: I'm not answering that question.>

<Disciplinarian: Then we're finished.>

How could she have thought he was a little bit like Jack? He was a whole lot like him. Stern, uncompromising, wanting his own way all the time. If she said no, he would probably stop talking to her and where the hell would she find someone else? Some of the people on the BDSM sites she had looked at were just plain scary. God knows what they would ask her to do.

<Wild orchid: It feels strange, a bit naughty.>

<Disciplinarian: Are you aroused?>

<Wild orchid: From talking to you like this or from meeting Kevin?>

Hah. See how you like that.

<Disciplinarian: About sitting there bare-assed, waiting for my next command.>

He was really pushing this. He wasn't going to let her get away with anything.

<Wild orchid: Yes.>

<Wild orchid: Yes, Sir.>

<Disciplinarian: Good girl. Does your ass tingle? Are you hoping for another spanking?>

He had to be joking. Had he listened to a single thing she had told him all evening?

<Wild orchid: As I told you, Kevin and I were a one-time thing. It's not going to happen again.>

<Disciplinarian: Have you been able to stop thinking about it?>

The cursor blinked steadily at her for almost a minute before she could type again. He was right. She hadn't been able to get Jack out of her head, and meeting him tonight had only made matters worse.

<Wild orchid: No.>

<Disciplinarian: Someday it's going to happen again. With me.>

<Wild orchid: Oh!>

With him? D wanted to spank her? Her blood raced as if she had just downed a dozen espressos. They were actually going to meet up. She would have to speak to Paloma. She couldn't just meet some stranger and let him spank her.

<Wild orchid: I thought that we were only going to be like this. Online, I mean.>

<Disciplinarian: We are, for now. How was your ass after the last one?>

<Wild orchid: Fine, it was a little bruised but that's gone. I can't believe I'm telling you this.>

<Disciplinarian: And that you're thinking about the next time.>

<Wild orchid: That too.>

<Disciplinarian: The next time you'll be prepared. A skirt, white panties, and you'll be completely smooth.>

<Wild orchid: Oh!>

<Wild orchid: You expect me to . . .>

She sometimes went with Kit to a salon, but she wasn't a Brazilian kind of girl. She didn't wear the type of clothes that necessitated it and that type of girly maintenance while on the road, or in a war zone, simply wasn't possible.

<Wild orchid: Why?>

<Disciplinarian: Because I like it.>

<Wild orchid: And white?>

<Disciplinarian: White is the colour of submission.>

<Wild orchid: My submission, to you?>

Abbie watched the words dance across the screen.

Disciplinarian is typing.

He wanted her to submit to him. Physically as well as mentally. She could feel her heart thudding in her chest as she waited for his response.

<Disciplinarian: Yes. How are your thoughts?>

<Wild orchid: Confused. It's like you're inside my head, but at the same time, I'm physically attracted to Kevin. It's really weird. Oh, hell, I don't know how I feel. I think I'd better go now.>

Disciplinarian is typing.

<Disciplinarian: Remember to send me a message tomorrow.>

Abbie shut down the laptop. It was late, and she didn't know how she was going to sleep after this. Too much was happening all at once. Meeting Jack, talking to D. It was as if someone had taken the calm, logical Abbie Marshall and locked her up. The person left behind was a simmering crock-pot of confusion.

When she was alone, she wanted Jack. When she was with him, he acted like an ass and she wanted to kiss him and slap him all at the same time. If she was completely honest, she wanted to try the spanking thing again. *Oh Abbie, you are in so much trouble.*

16

As soon as Abbie had signed off, Jack rang Kev. He wanted to rip his throat out for poaching his woman. The fact that Kev often moved in on his old girlfriends, offering tissues and sympathy, was beside the point. Abbie wasn't an ex. Kev had no right to lay a finger on her.

Kev wasn't answering his phone so Jack was left stewing overnight. At 6am he headed for the gym. He badly needed to kick the shit out of someone. It was busy and he warmed up by jumping rope until he was sweating, then thrashed the hell out of a defenceless punch bag. Sweat dripped down his back, his knuckles were raw and his feet hurt, but he was nowhere near ready to stop. The energy generated by his jealous fury refused to abate.

He grabbed a set of heavy chains, draped them around his neck and alternated giant sets of press-ups and pull-ups. He was vaguely aware that some of the other gym rats has stopped training to watch him and were placing bets on how many he could do before he collapsed. He didn't care. The thought of Abbie eating with Kev, maybe kissing Kev, drove him on. When he finally hit muscle failure and had to release the bar, he collapsed, shaking and sweating and fighting the urge to puke. There was a general round of congratulations from the spectators and half a dozen of them helped him lift the chains off his shoulders.

'Way to go, bro. That was spectacular.' Kev slapped him on the shoulder.

Jack forced himself to his feet. 'Keep your damn hands off Abbie.' It wasn't what he had intended to say, but it was too late to be polite.

Kev smirked at him, unrepentant. 'Too late. You had your chance.'

Jack charged at Kev. His initial charge seemed to take Kev by surprise, knocking him to the ground. But Kev recovered fast, leaping up in time to defend himself against another attack.

'What the hell's got into you?' he asked.

Jack swung again. 'I said: keep your damn hands off Abbie.'

This time Kev was prepared and danced out of the way. 'Are you mad?' He snapped out a side kick which caught Jack hard enough to knock him back.

Jack recovered enough to step in with a hammer fist and front push kick. Both were hard enough to hurt. Kev retaliated with a superman punch and the fight was on. For five exhilarating minutes Jack got to beat Kev up. It felt good.

Kev was no slouch, and he wasn't knackered from doing a stupid number of chain pull-ups, so it was an even match. But Jack was not prepared to back down and kept coming. Finally, Kev got in a lucky throw and Jack found himself falling backwards into the ice bath.

He hit the surface with a shout and went under. For a couple of seconds, the heat of his own sweat and rage kept him warm, then the icy water shocked him senseless.

He came up, cursing and splashing cold water and chunks of ice over all the spectators nearby. He tossed a handful of icy water at Kev and started to laugh.

No doubt about it, he could make a fool of himself in grand style.

He struggled out of the ice bath before the security staff got there. Bathing with your sparring shoes on was not permitted.

Kev gave him a hand and supported him to the changing room. 'Feeling better now?' he asked.

Jack considered. 'Yes. But I meant it. Keep your hands off Abbie.'

Kit was waiting outside Journelle when Abbie climbed out of the cab. 'Am I late?' she asked anxiously.

'No, I've just got here. So, what got your panties in a bunch that you had to meet me today?'

Despite the chill in the air, Abbie could feel her face flushing. 'It's him, D. He's sent me lingerie shopping and you know I hate places like this. The last time you brought me on one of your splurges I spent two hundred dollars on a bra that ended up as a sling.'

Kit clamped her lips together, trying not to laugh. Her eyes flashed with mirth. 'Oh, Abbie.'

She pushed the door open and the doorbell rang, announcing their arrival. Abbie stared at the white oak floors and purple silk curtains. One part of the store had been set up to look like a library. *As if anyone is going to try on lingerie in a bookstore.*

'Ladies.' An effusive assistant came to greet them. 'What can we do for you today? Have you something special in mind? A wedding perhaps?'

Abbie shook her head. 'No. No wedding. I need to replace all of my stuff. It got lost. On a flight,' she added lamely.

The assistant smiled. 'That's no problem. We have dressing rooms down the back with robes for you to change into. But first, perhaps you could give me an idea of styles that you like.'

Abbie stepped on to one of the sheepskin rugs that dotted the floor and selected a pair of plain black seamless panties.

Kit shook her head. 'He said lingerie, remember?'

She put the hanger back on the stand. Kit was right. Anything flesh-coloured or black was out.

'If you'd like some items for casual wear, we have some lovely Fleur't LuLu boyshorts and of course we have matching T-shirt bras to go with them.'

Abbie looked at the price tag. $35 for a pair of panties? She ignored Kit's smirk. It was better to get this over with in one trip. She knew that D would probably hate the comfy stuff. 'Fine, I'll try a set in size 36C, but I need something more feminine.'

She looked around the display. Egyptian cotton pyjamas vied with Swarovski-crystal-adorned chemises with a four-figure price tag. Definitely not her. She would feel like a Christmas tree. It was time to put herself in the hands of a professional. 'I need some silky, lacy stuff. The kind that guys like. Nothing scratchy, nothing that has beads on it and absolutely no thongs.'

The assistant gave her a speculative look that made Abbie feel like she was auditioning for the lead role in *Pretty Woman*. 'You say that you've lost all of your lingerie?'

Abbie nodded. 'Everything. Consider me completely panty-less.'

'Lovely. Fitting room three, then. You'll find a robe inside to change into. I'll bring you everything you need.'

The private dressing room was spacious. The lighting didn't make her feel too uncomfortable and they had placed a dish of Italian white chocolates next to the fluffy white robe. The assistant appeared frequently and whisked away any item she agreed to. It was almost enjoyable.

Two hours later Abbie's purchases were elegantly boxed and wrapped with a bow. They were the last customers to leave the store. 'I can't believe I just spent twelve hundred dollars on lingerie.'

Kit laughed. 'Think of it as an investment. What do you want to do now? Go for a drink?'

Abbie glanced at her watch. She had finally persuaded someone from the State Department to talk to her about the Tabora story and they had promised to call her at eight. 'I'd love to, Kit, but I have to work tonight. How about a rain check?'

'No problem, but I want a full report on how you get on with the lingerie.'

'You wish.' Abbie giggled.

She was still smiling when she reached the next junction and stood at the street corner waiting to cross the street. Food was probably a good idea. Maybe she could grab something at the deli on her way home. A couple of hours' work and then she would get to speak to D.

Just as the lights changed Abbie felt a sharp blow between her shoulder blades and she careened forward on to the street. Everything seemed to happen in slow motion. Her hands hitting the asphalt, the sound of a woman screaming, the boxes from Journelle scattering on the street, the front wheels of a cab approaching with frightening speed. Frozen to the spot, she shut her eyes, waiting for the impact.

Brakes screeched. When she opened her eyes again, the chrome bumper of the cab was inches from her face. The blue-turbaned driver was shouting at her, words that she couldn't understand. She was still alive. It took a few moments for the knowledge to sink in, and then she started to shake.

A pair of tourists wearing *I Love NY* sweatshirts collected her fallen shopping and helped her to her feet. They sounded like Jack and Kevin and the lilt of their voices brought her to the verge of tears.

'I'm fine, honestly,' she said, as they insisted on checking her scraped hands and knees for damage. Her teeth chattered but she got the words out.

The middle-aged woman handed her a tissue from her pocket. 'That was an awful fall. You just take it easy for a minute. Do you need to go to a hospital?'

Abbie shook her head. 'No, I'll take a cab. I just want to go home.' She needed to be alone. No, she needed Jack. The Jack who had tended to her so gently at the pool. But since she couldn't have him, she wanted to be alone.

The grey-haired man hailed a cab and they helped her into it with her shopping. Only when the car pulled away did Abbie realize that she hadn't even asked their names.

The shock was beginning to wear off and cold reality set in, bringing with it something she didn't want to face. She hadn't fallen. Someone had pushed her into the street, straight into the path of the cab.

If it hadn't been for the driver's skill, she would have been under the wheels, another pedestrian jaywalker who didn't quite make it. She felt the tears coming and she reached into her pocket for a tissue. Her fingers came in contact with something waxy and she drew it out carefully.

The orchid was bruised and damaged. A strange thing to find in the pocket of a road-traffic victim, but otherwise unremarkable. Nothing that a coroner would pay heed to. It would just be noted as an odd coincidence, that someone who had recently returned from Honduras carried its national flower.

Abbie paid the cab driver and hurried across the lobby, desperate for the silence and safety of her apartment. She locked the door and put on the deadbolt. Only then did she allow herself to cry.

After a while, she stripped off and climbed into the shower. As the warm water washed over her, stinging her bruised knees and hands, she thought about her story. Was this connected? When she got out, she wrapped herself in a robe and went looking for some sticking plasters.

The red flashing light on the answering machine caught her attention and she pressed the play button.

'Ms Marshall, this is Tom Breslin from the State Department. Sorry I missed you. I won't be able to give you that interview after all, I'm being transferred.'

She couldn't stop her hands from shaking. Was that her story gone?

One thing that journalism had taught her was that there was no such thing as coincidence. She would have to go through all her files again and that would mean spending the next day at her desk in the newsroom. She wouldn't be able to meet Kevin for lunch. It would have to be dinner instead.

17

He couldn't leave it alone. Jack had managed to control himself all through another boring work lunch, knowing that Abbie was with Kev, wearing a pair of pink silk panties trimmed with black lace. Like a good sub, she had sent him a report on her underwear that morning. He had nearly choked on his espresso when he read it.

Now all Jack could think about was that scrap of pink silk moulded to that spankable ass. He wondered if she was wearing a matching bra. This evening, he was going to add an order that she describe the bra she was wearing as well as the panties.

Just as long as nobody else got to see either of them.

Jack excused himself from the mayor, ducked round the corner and rang Kev. 'Well, how was lunch with Abbie?' He tried to sound casual.

'Oh, we didn't go.'

Jack stood up straight. 'Why not? Did she change her mind?' He fought to keep the elation out of his voice.

Kev laughed. 'No, nothing like that. Something came up and she had to work today, so we're meeting for dinner instead. She told me about this amazing little Italian restaurant near her apartment, Mamma D'Inzeo. I'll tell you all about it if I get lucky.' He hung up before Jack could react.

Jack clenched his fists, so furious he could barely

contain it. Kev, the traitorous bastard, was going out to dinner with Abbie. Lunch could be a casual thing, just a couple of friends meeting up. Dinner in an 'amazing little Italian restaurant' on a Saturday night was a date. And Abbie was wearing pink silk panties with black lace.

'And now, please welcome our guest of honour, Mr Jack Winter.'

An assistant of the mayor came round the corner, hustled Jack back to the podium and thrust a microphone into his hand. Hell, he had to do this first. He grabbed the microphone. 'Thank you for inviting me. It is with great pleasure that I declare this –' he took a quick glance around. Where the hell was he? '– arts project open.' He whipped the flowers out of the hand of the astonished child in the white dress, kissed her on the cheek, posed just long enough to have a few photos taken and headed for the exit.

There was no way Kev was going to get near Abbie's silk panties.

By the time Jack found Mamma D'Inzeo that evening, it was dark and the restaurant was already full. He peered in through the window at the diners and saw Kev leaning over to say something in Abbie's ear and her laughing in response.

It was a scene he had seen countless times over the years. When he broke up with the latest model or starlet Zeke pushed in his direction, Kev was there to console her and assure her that she was desirable and attractive. They made a great double act. But not this time. He and Abbie were not finished. Kev was not having her.

He pushed the door open and headed for their table. A short, round Italian woman with steel-grey hair stood in his path, blocking him. 'Do you have a reservation, sir?'

It was so long since Jack had needed a reservation that it took him a moment to understand the question. He tried to brush past her, but she moved in front of him. 'Your reservation, sir?'

'I'm not eating. I just need to go over there.' He pointed at Abbie's table.

'Miss Marshall's table? I'll see if she is expecting guests. Wait here.'

Jack followed her to the table, to be met with twin scowls. 'What are you doing here?' Kev asked.

Jack drank in Abbie for a moment before he answered. She had done something to her hair. It was caught up on one side and glittered with health. Her mouth was wide, red and alluring. Oh, the things he yearned to do to that mouth. Her eyes snapped up at him, and every annoyed breath caused her breasts to swell. The thin silk of her blouse was modest enough, he supposed, but on Abbie, it was an invitation to sin.

Kev was sitting too close to her in a quiet booth of the aromatic little restaurant – sitting at such an angle that he could look right down Abbie's blouse.

'I've come to join you,' he told Abbie. 'After all, I figured you were talking about me, so I might as well give you the inside information.'

He was delighted to see a deep flush on Abbie's cheeks. She had been talking about him. She shot him a look that would melt iron. 'Well, I see that the ego has landed.'

Kev glared at him. 'Yes, go away, Jack. I'll see you tomorrow.'

Jack wanted to sit beside Abbie, but the determined Italian blocked his path, so he slid in beside Kev. 'No, I'm good. I haven't eaten anyway, I'll join you.'

Abbie was speechless. The Italian maître d' looked to her for confirmation that she should bring another menu. She was too shocked to do anything but nod.

She and Kevin had just ordered. They had water and a glass of wine each, but no food yet. Jack had timed his arrival well to make sure they didn't get past the small talk.

He turned to her. 'So, have you recovered from your time in the jungle?'

She nodded. She wondered when she was going to recover the power of speech.

'Did Zeke replace that bra of yours? Gotta say, I loved watching you without it.'

Her fingers were trembling as she picked up her water glass. She sipped slowly, hoping to buy enough time to calm her nerves.

'I'll ignore that, and try to pretend that we're all polite adults,' she said finally.

She hated scenes and this had all the makings of a very big scene. Jack had a nasty smile on his face and Kevin looked furious.

'So, Kev, didn't you say you had somewhere to be?'

'Yes, I did. Right here, having dinner with Abbie. Go away, Jack, you're being a prick.'

'I thought we discussed this in the gym?'

Kevin fished a sliver of ice out of his water and held it up. It obviously meant something to them.

'So we did,' Kevin said. 'If you want more ice, just tell me. Until then, go away.'

'Let's ask the lady what she wants. I bet she wants me to stay, don't you, Abbie?'

She wanted Jack all right – she was wet just looking at him – but she was also mad as hell. Who did he think he was?

'Right now, I'm tempted to tell both of you to go away. Kevin at least had the manners to invite me out for a meal, instead of just barging in and interrupting a perfectly nice dinner.'

He picked up her hand where it grasped the water glass, felt her pulse and looked into her eyes. 'You don't want a man with manners. You want someone who will let you walk on the wild side, who knows what you're really like.'

She pulled her hand back. 'You have no idea what I am really like,' she said, sounding prim even to her own ears.

'I know you like wearing pink silk panties,' he said.

It felt like her entire body blushed. How did he know that? *Oh god – no!* Oh god – it couldn't be.

'You're D?' she said incredulously. 'You've been stringing me along all this time.'

Jack shrugged.

She felt as if the air had been sucked out of the room. Time seemed to stand still. Jack just looked back at her, expressionless. Kevin was looking from her to Jack and back again.

She picked up the jug of water, poured it over Jack and

then grabbed her bag and dashed out of the restaurant. He caught up with her before she got to the end of the block.

'Abbie, wait,' he said, reaching out to touch her arm.

She whirled and she barely recognized her own voice as she shouted at him.

'Don't touch me. You're a lying bastard and I want nothing to do with you.'

'And you're the one who's just soaked me.'

He did look a mess, as far as Jack Winter could ever look a mess. She felt a brief moment of satisfaction.

'I did, didn't I? And I'll do it again if you annoy me.'

'First we talk.' He refused to let her get away from him and held her wrist as they turned into the entrance of her building.

'You're not coming up with me,' she said.

'You owe me a towel at least.'

The concierge was busy helping an elderly woman in a wheelchair, so she couldn't get him involved. And there was no other option. She'd just have to let him up to dry off.

As soon as the elevator door shut behind them, he grabbed her, hauled her against him and slammed his mouth down on hers. No, no, no – it wasn't going to be that way. For a second, she defied him, pressing her mouth shut.

He traced the seam of her lips with his tongue, demanding entry. She held out for as long as she could and then it was over. She had to have him. She kissed him back, just as ravenously. He tightened his arms around her. His tongue and his lips feasted on her. She arched against his long, beautiful body, her fingertips digging into his shoulders.

They were lost in each other when the elevator jerked to a halt and the doors opened. Jack seemed oblivious. Then he raised his head a bare half-inch from her mouth. 'What number?'

She was dazed from his kiss, her mouth soft and slightly bruised. She had to think for a moment. What was her number? 'Four-two-three.'

Her hands shook when they got to the door so he took the key from her hands and put it into the lock. As soon as they were inside and the door closed, he grabbed her again.

This time the kiss was open-mouthed and voracious. Jack fisted his hand into her hair, holding her still so that he could devour her. Abbie fought to put her arm up around his neck so she could pull him closer. Her lips sought his and matched him move for move. One of her hands was trapped between their bodies and she shoved it in between the buttons of his shirt so she could touch his skin.

He dropped one hand to her ass, caressing and kneading it, forcing her to feel his erection. She rose on tiptoe and rocked.

'Oh god, Abbie,' he said, before burying his face in her neck. He sucked it, then pressed open-mouthed kisses against it, as if to soothe the small hurt. He was marking her, but she didn't care. She wanted him to mark her.

Abbie felt like she was on fire. She shoved her hands up through his hair, tugging him back to her mouth. When she had him where she wanted him, she yanked his shirt out of his trousers and pushed her hands up under it. Her hands slid up his back and then round to the front, tangling in the springy hair on his chest.

He nipped at the spot under her ear and she moaned, tipping her head to offer him that vulnerable point again. He obliged, harder this time, and she moaned again.

She could feel his erection jerking. She had to touch it. She slid her hand down to his zip but before she could do anything he shoved his hands up under her silk blouse and caressed her skin. Then he dropped his hands and pulled at her skirt.

'You didn't tell me about these,' he said suddenly.

Abbie had no idea what he was talking about. She was just hypnotized by his mouth.

'No pantyhose,' he said. 'Horrible stuff.'

He tugged and she heard them tear. He continued to rip them from her. The sound of the tearing was electrifying. She wanted him to tear everything off her body. She wanted to feel him all over her.

Suddenly he stopped and looked around. They were in her sitting room, which was large and sparsely furnished. He pulled her over to the end of the couch.

'Bend over. Hold on to that cushion, don't move your hands.' He eased her into position as he spoke.

'What are you doing?' she said.

'Eyes front.' He was back in control now. She could barely imagine the picture she made. Her pantyhose were in ribbons but she was still in a pair of heels that forced her ass up in the air. Moving slowly, he took his time, easing the skirt up until it was around her waist, leaving her bare except for the pink panties.

Jack moved in closer, so that he was standing almost

between her feet, and tapped them. 'Wider.' Obediently she shuffled her feet apart. He did it again. 'More.' She struggled to move them another few inches and still stay in position.

'Good girl.' He caressed her ass, and then with a ruthless jerk, tore the panties off her. 'I'll buy you more.'

She heard the tear of a condom wrapper and then felt him fall on her. The first lunge was mind-blowing. He possessed her so completely, it was like nothing she had ever known before. Her nerve endings felt as if they would melt under so much pleasure. She let out a shuddering cry that seemed to make Jack hesitate. She pushed back, silently begging for more. He thrust into her again, holding her hips, controlling the tempo. He wouldn't let her rush ahead as she wanted.

All she could think was that this was what she longed for, what she needed. She begged him to keep going.

He raked his nails along her back and she groaned. When he pinched her nipple through her silky lace bra, she gasped and reared up.

'Stay in position,' he growled. 'Hold the cushion.'

Obediently, she dropped back but her grip on the cushion was so tight it threatened to tear it apart.

'Yes, Sir,' she said.

That was what it took to get what she craved so desperately. Jack couldn't resist speeding up, lunging into her faster and harder. He drove into her again and again and she rose to meet him.

'More, please,' she cried.

That was the end. Jack hammered into her, without finesse or skill, but she was too far gone to care. With a wail that could be heard in the street, she came.

18

Oh dear god, what just happened? Abbie's fingers clutched at a handful of feathers from the burst cushion. Jack's warm body lay on top of hers. He was still inside her, still breathing heavily. He dropped a light kiss on her shoulder.

'You OK, Abbie?'

'Yes . . . I . . .' She had actually done it. Made love with Jack.

She felt a sense of loss as he withdrew from her and stood up. 'Let's get you into bed,' he said.

'No.' Ouch, she hadn't meant to sound whiny. He would think that she was one of those needy women who would beg him to stay for the night.

Jack picked her up and set her on her feet. He pulled her against his chest, using one hand to tilt her head back. 'Did I hurt you?'

'No, you didn't hurt me.'

'Would you like me to?' A wicked grin dispelled his serious expression. Abbie remembered the cave in the jungle, the slap of his hand against her tender flesh. The sudden heat of impact.

'Do you know that your pupils have just dilated?' Jack gave a low laugh. 'I'll take that as a yes.'

He bent and hooked his arm under her knees, lifting her against a wall of solid muscle. 'Bedroom?'

'Through there.' She pointed.

He deposited her on the bed, and before she could ask, he closed the curtains and turned on the bedside lamp. His hot stare made her tremble and Abbie moved her hand to cover herself.

'Don't.' The word was a command rather than a request. She felt like a rabbit in the headlights as his eyes raked her from head to foot.

She had no idea where her torn panties were, two buttons were missing from her silk blouse and her smart skirt was a mass of creases. And somehow she was still wearing her new heels, the ones Miffy had made her buy.

'I like these,' Jack said, his voice gravelly. 'There's something about a woman in heels. I think we'll leave these on.'

His fingers moved slowly along her instep, until they encountered a snag where he had ripped her pantyhose. 'These, however, have to go.'

Her skirt and blouse followed the shredded pantyhose on to the floor.

'Now, this is pretty.' Jack paused when he reached her lacy brassiere, brushing his index finger across her lace-covered nipples. Just that light touch sent a shot of pleasure through her. She moaned and arched up into his touch.

'Does it make you feel sexy to wear something like this, Abbie?'

'I –' Oh god, her brain had turned to mush and if he didn't stop touching her she was going to melt.

'Answer me.' His tone took on a sharp edge that sent a shiver down her spine.

'Yes, it does.'

'Good girl.' His lips slowly circled one nipple and then he sucked hard on it.

The sensation was delicious – hovering on the edge between ecstasy and pain. Jack released her, unclipped the bra and tossed it with her other clothes.

'You're beautiful.'

She didn't feel the least bit beautiful. She was naked, vulnerable, wearing nothing but a pair of dark-red Miu Miu shoes. Jack was still fully clothed. Her hand crept across her breast to cover herself.

Her action earned her a sharp tap on the hip from Jack. 'Hands above your head, Abbie, and keep them there.'

The edge of danger in his tone made her comply. 'What happened to your palms?'

'I fell,' she admitted. 'I hurt my knees too.'

Jack kissed each palm. 'I'll kiss your other injuries later.' Then his hand tilted her head back, his thumb stroked the edge of her jaw. 'Look at me, Abbie.'

She blinked and swallowed hard under his intent gaze.

'For tonight, you're mine.'

Releasing her jaw, he trailed his hand over her chest, cupping her breast, taking a slow path over her abdomen before pausing to cup her mound. One broad finger pushed inside her and Abbie took a sharp breath.

A second finger joined the first and his thumb brushed against her clit.

Abbie arched against him, seeking more pressure. She was so sensitized to his touch from their earlier encounter, it wouldn't take much to push her over the edge again.

'Bad girl.' Jack withdrew his fingers and pressed them

to his mouth. 'Hot, sweet little Abbie, I can see that you're going to need a lesson about who's in charge here.'

Jack left Abbie and went to find her kitchen. He had almost laughed at her expression when he asked her where it was. Finally, he had Abbie where he wanted her and where he knew she wanted to be. They had the whole night and he was going to make her see fireworks. Before that, she had to eat.

As he moved around her kitchen, he thought that Abbie had surpassed his expectations in every way. If that's what it was like the first time they made love, he could barely imagine what could happen between them. He had been astonished and even more aroused than he thought possible by the fragility of her skin – so pale and soft. It was an invitation for him to do his worst to her. And that luscious backside that had haunted his dreams for two weeks, he wanted to touch it more than he wanted his next breath. Those green eyes that flashed with desire. He wanted to see what else he could make those eyes do.

He had fought the dark impulses that wanted to strip her naked, tie her up and mark her as his. But her cry of 'More, please' was an aphrodisiac that would have aroused a statue of a saint, and god knew he was no saint. She had been so hot and wet, her softness contrasting with her strength as she pushed back to meet him, and when he felt her delicate inner muscles holding him like a fist, driving him over the edge, he had been lost in ecstasy. If that was vanilla sex with Abbie, he didn't dare dream what would happen when they went darker.

After about fifteen minutes, he was ready. Two glasses of wine from a bottle in her empty fridge. And a plate of French toast for her.

When he got back to the bedroom she was sitting up, curious.

'I seem to remember that I made you miss dinner,' he said.

Abbie giggled. 'I haven't forgiven you for that yet. Do you know how hard it is to get a reservation for Mamma D'Inzeo on a Saturday night?'

'I'll make it up to you,' he said. 'But first, we need to have a discussion about your refrigerator.'

'What's wrong with my refrigerator?'

'There isn't enough food in it to keep a sparrow alive and I hate skinny women.'

'You want to feed me?'

The thought seemed to make her giddy. 'So, what delights have you conjured up?'

'I thought that madame might like some French toast with maple syrup to keep her strength up.'

Abbie reached for the fork.

'Ah ah, no touching the food. No hands. I want to feed you.' He cut a piece and pressed it to her lips.

'What's that flavour?' she mumbled, as she chewed.

That's what he liked to see – a woman too busy eating to worry about manners.

'Vanilla, for my vanilla girl,' he said, grinning, and pressed another mouthful to her lips.

Abbie swallowed it quickly. 'I am not vanilla.'

'Aren't you?' he said.

They held each other's gaze, both realizing the deal that was being negotiated.

Abbie spoke hesitantly. She seemed to be choosing her words carefully. 'What if I wanted to try other flavours? What if I was willing to taste something else?'

Jack cut another mouthful of toast and fed it to her.

'You don't know what you're asking. You don't know what I'm like.'

Abbie refused the last mouthful of food and he popped it into his own mouth instead. She was blinking away tears.

'What if I wanted to find out?' she said. 'What if I wanted to get to know the real Jack Winter, the one you're so scared to show me?'

It was so tempting, to bring her into his world. It was what he had wanted since that day in the cave. And yet, now that she was offering herself, he hesitated. Did she really understand what she was letting herself in for?

Abbie reached for his hand and placed it on her naked breast. Her nipple hardened instantly beneath his touch. 'What if I said that I wanted to play by your rules?'

Maybe she did understand, but he had to be sure. 'I'm a lot darker than you can possibly imagine. This is not a game, it's part of who I am.'

She sat up and reached for him, winding her arms around his neck, threading her fingers though his dark hair. She nipped at his bottom lip and he groaned. He wasn't immune to her. Pulling his head down to her, she kissed his mouth roughly until they were both breathless. 'I want you. Show me how you want me.'

'Lie down, Abbie,' he said, and then went to her closet

and riffled through it until he found what he was looking for. He returned to the bed with a handful of silk scarves.

'Are you sure that you want this, Abbie? Because once we start, it will only finish when I say so.'

'Yes, I'm sure.'

'Good girl. I suggest you visit the bathroom now. You may be tied up for a while.'

Abbie fled.

The bathroom mirror confirmed her worst suspicions. Her hair was wild. Her mascara had melted and her lipstick had vanished. She had cuts on her knees and a bruise on her neck where he had nipped her. But she looked like a woman who had just had the most incredible lovemaking of her life.

She stared in disbelief at her reflection. That couldn't be Abbie Marshall. She was naked in her bathroom, except for a pair of heels, and Jack Winter was in her bedroom, waiting to tie her up and do god-knew-what to her. A feeling of sick excitement invaded her stomach. She was going to do this. She would prove to Jack that she wasn't vanilla. She swished some mouthwash around her mouth and spat it out.

She didn't want to take too long. Jack was waiting for her.

The look in his eyes almost made her retreat back into the bathroom. It was so hungry, so filled with anticipation that she shivered. What had she let herself in for? But there was no going back. If she stopped now, she would never forgive herself.

He tied the first scarf around her eyes. It wasn't pitch

black, but it was disorientating enough to make her sway. She shivered, conscious of her nakedness and his closeness. She could hear his breathing, feel the brush of his shirt against her sensitized skin.

'Easy there.' Jack pulled her against his chest. He was still fully clothed and the feel of his denim-clad legs against her bare thigh raised goosebumps along her back. 'Lie down, Abbie.'

She moved a little awkwardly, finding her balance was off now that her eyes were covered. She lay obediently on the linen comforter. Jack took each wrist in turn and looped the silk around it before fixing it to the wooden headboard. He inserted his fingers under the loop, checking her circulation. Abbie heard the rattle of crockery as he carried the tray back to the kitchen. Then there was silence.

It was hard to tell how long he was gone, but time dragged, increasing her nervousness. Finally the bedroom door opened.

'Oh, Ms Marshall, you are a sight for sore eyes.' Jack's Irish accent made her nipples peak. 'I'm going to taste every inch of you.'

She felt his warm breath on her ankle. He wasn't joking. With infinite slowness Jack kissed his way along the inside of her calf, pausing to pay homage to the tender spot at the inside of her knee before kissing the inside of her thigh.

'Oh god,' she groaned.

'Did I give you permission to speak?'

'No, I . . .' Abbie felt a sharp tap against her thigh. 'No, Sir.'

'Good girl. But now that you've disturbed my concentration, I'm going to have to start all over again.'

The mattress shifted as he moved to the end of the bed and began the same torture on her other ankle. Soft kisses, gently sucking and licking her skin, followed by the occasional sharp nip that made her whimper.

She felt his mouth on her inner thigh again and Abbie fought the urge to squirm. Her breathing became ragged. Every inch of her body tingled. She desperately wanted to come. 'Please.'

'Poor Abbie.' The vibration of his voice against her skin almost sent her over the edge. 'Are you wet for me?'

Rising frustration almost made her suggest that he go find out himself. But she knew instinctively that he would take that as a challenge. 'Yes.' The word came out of her parched throat. 'Yes, Sir.'

'Good.'

She felt the mattress move again and then Jack was kneeling beside her, pressing chips of ice against her lips. Abbie felt his hand caress her forehead tenderly. She heard the crunch of ice again and opened her mouth.

Instead of a chip against her lips, his ice-filled mouth fastened on her nipple. The cold grip hit her like a vice and she arched her back and screamed. His warm hand cupped her other breast, tweaking her nipple between his fingers. Abbie struggled against the sensory overload and received a sharp nip for her efforts. She felt the melting ice and water run between her breasts and Jack's tongue lapping at every drop.

'You have such sensitive breasts. I think I'll have to buy you some nipple clamps. Would you like that, mmm?

Imagine the sensation of blood rushing back to your nipples when I remove them.'

Abbie couldn't help it. She groaned again. His mouth continued its torturous path along her abdomen, pausing to blow a puff of ice-cold air on her shaven mound. She arched her hips, wanting his mouth there.

'Responsive little thing, aren't you? Let's see what else you like.'

Abbie tensed when she felt him getting off the bed. What was he going to do this time? More ice?

The feel of his warm hand between her legs almost lifted her off the bed. She arched against his touch, groaning with relief when she felt his finger slide into her. 'Oh god, please. Please, Jack. Please, Sir'

She was almost incoherent now. He rewarded her with a slow pump of his finger. Just enough to madden her, but not enough to take her over the edge. 'Bastard.' The word escaped from between her lips and she heard a low laugh and the sting of a sharp slap against her thigh.

'You have no idea, Abbie. I haven't even begun.'

At the first brush of the feather against her skin, Abbie squirmed against her bonds. 'No, don't do that. Please, I'm really ticklish.'

Jack straddled her hips and his weight pressed her against the bed. 'You really shouldn't have told me that.'

Pleasure and pain. The gentle brush of the feather and the sharp pain of its quill as he used it to draw slow circles around her nipples, and lines on her breast and along her abdomen. Her nerve endings didn't know how to respond, sending her brain confused messages so that she had no idea if she hated or loved it. Her cries of pain alternated with moans of pleasure. Her world closed down to Jack and his hands. She had no sense of time.

'My sweet Abbie. I think you deserve a reward.'

She couldn't reply. He had become her world, the light at the end of the tunnel. Every brush of pleasure or pain was within his control, she could do nothing but tremble and wait to see which he would give her. It was like floating.

A jolt of pleasure shot through her when she heard the rasp of a zipper and she squirmed, rubbing her damp thighs together. The bed creaked as it took his weight, and then they were skin to skin. The glorious muscular length of him stretched against her.

'Jack.' Her voice was hoarse from crying out.

'I'm here, baby.'

His mouth crushed hers without warning. There was no tenderness, only dark, inexorable need. She felt his hand in her hair, angling her head so that he could take her mouth as roughly as he pleased. Hot kisses rained down her neck and breasts, making her arch against him in need, but this time there was no teasing.

At the first pass of his tongue between her legs she cried out. He lapped at her as if he wanted to devour her, with hot, slow swirls of his tongue that never quite touched her aching clit.

'Please, Jack. Please let me come.' She didn't care that she was begging. She only knew that she would die if he didn't give her some release soon.

'What do you want?'

'Fuck me. Please, fuck me.' She never thought she would say those words out loud, but she had no dignity left.

As if her words were a starting pistol, Jack moved. He moved up her body, kissing her with abandon and taking her mouth greedily.

Jack knelt between her thighs. Abbie couldn't stop trembling. He slid into her in one slow thrust and she cried out. She dug her nails into the scarf. He eased out slowly and thrust hard again.

Her body rocked against his. God, that was good. His thrusts increased in momentum as control slipped away from him. There was nothing but the sound of flesh slapping against flesh and his harsh grunts. This was no tender lovemaking, but a fierce, rough taking.

Jack was marking her as his, and her body responded. Her skin tingled at his every touch and her blood raced. The intensity of the moment converged in one shattering surge of pleasure. Her inner muscles gripped his cock, her clit pulsed as if it were on fire, stars exploded behind her eyelids.

When she came round, she was lying in his arms, untied and with her eyes uncovered. Abbie felt his heart thudding against her cheek and his mouth against her hair.

'You OK, Abbie?' There was a hint of nervousness in his voice that she hadn't been expecting. She had gotten close enough to catch a glimpse of the hidden Jack and she knew that he wasn't referring to the sex.

She snuggled into his arms and pressed a kiss against his chest. 'I'm fine. It was amazing.'

After a while she heard a soft snuffle. Jack Winter was asleep in her bed.

19

Something jerked her out of her sleep. She turned to find Jack was sitting up in the bed, shaking. She sat up and switched on the bedside lamp.

'Didn't mean to wake you. Go back to sleep.'

She touched his chest. His skin was cold and clammy. 'Are you sick?'

He shook his head. 'Nothing like that. It's just a bad dream.'

She stroked his arm. Even in the dim light he was pale. Whatever he had been dreaming about had really scared him. 'Are you sure? I can make you some –'

Jack brushed her concerns away. 'I'm fine. I'll just grab a glass of water.'

He kissed her on the forehead, turned off the lamp and left the bedroom. Abbie lay awake, listening to him move around the sitting room. She heard the sound of the refrigerator door opening and closing and then there was silence. She rolled over, but she couldn't sleep without him.

To hell with sleeping. She grabbed her robe and padded out. The sound of Jack's voice stopped her in her tracks and she paused just inside the bedroom door to listen to the one-sided conversation.

'No, I'm fine. I just wanted to hear your voice . . . How can you say that? I do miss you, you know that.'

His words, the affectionate tone of his voice, made her stomach drop as if she were on a roller coaster, plummeting down the ramp. Jack had left her bed so that he could call another woman.

'No, I'm in New York this time. Pre-pub for the movie. You know how it is. Same old, same old.'

Abbie heard his easy laugh. This Jack was tender, comfortable with whoever he was speaking to at 4am. Another nightbird? Or maybe someone in another country.

'OK, put her on.'

There was a short pause and Jack paced the floor of the sitting room as he listened to the voice on the phone.

'A snow globe? You want a snow globe?'

She heard the teasing lilt in Jack's voice. The American accent was gone and he sounded much as he had done in the jungle when he was talking to Kevin. His guard was down. Jack sounded as if he were speaking to a child.

She didn't know that Jack had a family. His bio was sketchy about his earlier years in Ireland. Maybe there was a family. Perhaps Jack had left someone behind when he had come to seek his fortune in Hollywood.

The publicity machine played up his wild, party-boy image. The unattainable bachelor who would never settle down. Maybe Jack already had settled, and that was why he couldn't commit. Abbie wanted to drag herself away from the door but a sick sense of fascination made her wait, hungry for more torture.

'I'll buy you the prettiest snow globe in all of New York, I promise. The prettiest snow globe for the prettiest girl. Now, put your mum back on.'

His voice changed, no longer adult to child. 'Ciara, I

gotta go. It's some godforsaken hour here and I have to fly to LA tomorrow, I mean today . . . Maybe, I don't know.' Jack's tone became impatient. 'I said I don't know. Don't push me on this.'

Jack flopped on to the couch, picked up a handful of feathers and let them drift between his fingers on to the floor. Abbie touched the swell of her breast. The marks he had made with the quill were still there, a series of faint red lines, one of which looked like the letter M.

Abbie tensed. Jack was speaking again. 'I'll think about it. OK? Look, I really have to go . . . I love you too, Ciara.'

Jack returned to the kitchen and Abbie heard the sound of the refrigerator door opening again. Turning on her heel, she fled back to bed.

Even before he woke up, Jack was aware of the unfamiliar warmth cuddled in at his side. He didn't have to open his eyes to know it was Abbie. Her shape and smell were imprinted on his brain. What rattled him more than the instinctive recognition was the fact that he had slept with her in his arms, and it felt right.

Jack Winter didn't do nights. He Dommed, he fucked, he had a good time and then he went home. He did not climb into bed, cuddle his sub all night long and fall asleep with her in his arms. But this was Abbie. No matter how hard he tried to keep aloof, she caught him at gut level.

He couldn't believe he had slept again. Usually after that dream, he stayed awake all night. If he was in LA he'd go down to the beach and run outside for hours until he was too exhausted to stay awake – anything to exorcize the memories of that cell, with the reek of the primitive toilet and the added torture of his claustrophobia. The prospect of spending years of being locked up like that still haunted him and dragged him, shaking and sweating, from the deepest sleep.

He had planned to fuck Abbie again, just to relieve the frustration generated by his old terrors, and then go out running. He couldn't believe he had fallen asleep.

Maybe I should keep her. He had no idea where the thought came from, but he dismissed it immediately. He didn't do long term. He was very good at being a sessional Dom. He had subs in three cities he could call when he was in town. But as soon as the session was over, he was gone.

Abbie was unfinished business, that was all. Last night he had given her a tiny taste of life on the dark side, and she had loved it. He knew that she would want more, just as he knew that she would baulk if he ever allowed her to know the real him. At heart, she was a vanilla and feathers girl, and he was leather and steel.

She stirred in her sleep and rolled over, slipping one arm around his waist in an embrace that wasn't as confining as he had expected. He could relax for a few minutes before he got up and showered.

His cell phone went off in the other room. He had left it there after talking to Ciara. Jack scrambled out of bed, hurrying to get to it before it woke Abbie. He had tired her out; she needed her rest. He was smiling when he answered it.

'Jack, my boy, I'm back in LA. Where are you?' Zeke Bryan's voice was almost as loud as his neckties.

'I'm still in New York.'

'Well, get that ass of yours home as soon as you can. I've got you an audition for *The African Queen*.'

Jack exhaled sharply. This was the role he'd been waiting for. 'I'm on an LA flight in three hours' time. When is the audition?'

'First thing tomorrow morning. I've set it up with the casting company that they'll see you first, so you'll be in ahead of the horde. Did I do good, or what?'

'What do you mean, "horde"?' Jack asked. 'How many are going for this role?'

Zeke scoffed. 'Charlie Allnut? Every major actor and every wannabe is lining up to get this role. It's a sure-fire Oscar nomination.'

'I know. That's why I want it. I can only do dumb-ass action-man roles for so long before they dry up. I need something that doesn't depend on having eight-pack abs and a silicon-enhanced leading lady.'

'Don't knock it. Those roles pay the bills, both yours and mine. Just remember, your call is at eight tomorrow morning. Make sure you're on time.' His voice dropped. 'And keep your nose clean.'

'Don't worry, I'm as pure as the driven snow,' he said and ended the call.

A husky laugh sounded from the doorway. Abbie stood there, wearing a sheet and nothing else. 'Pure? After what you did to me?' She was heavy-eyed, with faint bruises on her skin and a bite mark on her neck, and she looked sweet and good enough to eat. He wanted to take her back to bed and mark her up some more.

'Compared to what I usually do, oh yeah.'

Her eyes widened, with a combination of speculation, fear and interest.

But he didn't have time. 'I'm sorry, Abbie, I have to go.'

Her face shut down. She was trying hard not to look upset. 'I don't want to, but I have an audition in LA in the morning. I have to be there.'

'That's OK. I know you're busy.' She was busy looking down at where her fingers were pleating and unpleating a fold of cotton sheet.

'But not so busy I won't expect you online at ten tonight.'

She looked up then. 'But –'

He kept his voice stern. 'You thought I'd let you off?'

'Well . . .'

'Not going to happen. But I have another account on Yahoo. Any time you need to chat to me, call Michael Delaney and I will answer.'

He had no idea why he gave her that account name. It was his private one.

'Who is Michael Delaney?'

He didn't want to think about that. 'No one. Just a name I use.'

He changed the subject. 'Are we clear? I'll expect you at ten sharp. And Abbie?' She met his eyes. 'We are going to take this seriously.'

She nodded. He dressed quickly and kissed her before he headed to LA.

Abbie couldn't wait for the weekly service clean. She dug out the vacuum cleaner and swept up the feathers. She would probably be finding them for weeks. They had already made their way into the bedroom and bathroom. Little souvenirs of Jack, all waiting to ambush her.

She washed the dishes he had used the night before and poured the iced water into the sink. She looked around her. The apartment was restored to its pre-Jack state and she had never felt so miserable. She needed caffeine and Kit.

The coffee shop was crowded with Sunday morning customers, all enjoying brunch. She flopped down into a chair opposite Kit and a waiter arrived to take her order. 'No fruit, no healthy smoothies, I need blueberry pancakes and coffee, lots of coffee.'

Kit sat back in her chair. 'Aha, the post-coital special. How was your date with Kevin? Or do I need to ask?'

Abbie flushed. She had completely forgotten about Kevin. He had taken her out to dinner and she had abandoned him. She flipped open her phone. She had to call him and apologize.

'Abbie, put the phone away and talk to me.'

The waiter returned with coffee and Abbie took a grateful sip, savouring her first caffeine hit of the day. 'The date with Kevin didn't go so well.'

'Let me guess. Jack?'

'How did you . . .?'

Kit stirred her berry smoothie with a straw. 'You have that Jack expression on your face. The one you wear when he's on your mind. So, tell me exactly what happened and please don't spare the details. I'm a professional, I can take it.'

'Bitch.' Abbie grinned at her. 'I'm so glad I'm not paying you $200 an hour. I'd be flat broke in no time.'

'Honey, I will pay you $200 an hour to hear what Jack Winter is like between the sheets. Now, spill.'

'Well, I went to Mamma D'Inzeo with Kev –'

'Skip dinner, hon. I've already eaten. Fast forward to the Jack part.'

Abbie cringed when she remembered the restaurant. She would never get a reservation there again.

'Jack turned up at the restaurant and caused a scene.'

Kit's eyes widened. 'Bad Boy Winter hits New York. I wish I'd been there to see that. OK, what happened next?'

'We had an argument in Mamma d'Inzeo's and . . .'

'Back up there a minute. Please pinch me and tell me that Ms Prissy did not have a screaming match in a public place.' Kit's delighted laugh could be heard three tables away.

Abbie flushed. People were beginning to stare at them. 'Will you please be quiet?'

'Sorry, sorry. Oh god, I wish I'd been there.'

'There was a moment when I wished you were there too, so I could give you a piece of my mind.'

'Huh?'

'He let slip that he's the Dom your friend set me up with. He's the one I've been telling my secrets to every night, the one who's supposed to be helping me explore my submissive side.'

'Oh, Abbie,' Kit said. 'I don't know what to say. Paloma is very discreet about her Doms. I didn't know she knew him, though I suppose they would have been on the same scene here before he went to LA. I'm really sorry.'

'It's OK. You're forgiven.' If it hadn't been for Kit, she wouldn't have connected with Jack online.

'So, what happened when you found out?'

'I threw a jug of iced water over him.'

Kit covered her mouth. Her cornrow braids bobbed up and down as her shoulders shook. After a few seconds she regained her composure and took a long sip from her smoothie.

Abbie was tempted to giggle. Looking back on it, she supposed it had been kind of funny. She never would have thought that she would do something so melodramatic. She caught an interested glance from the couple at the next table. There was no way that she could share the details of her encounter with Jack here. They needed to find somewhere private. They chatted about other things and then Abbie paid the bill and they stepped out into the November sunshine. The air was crisp and cold. She pulled her scarf around her neck, fighting the chill of the breeze.

Kit waved down a cab. 'We can go to my apartment, it's closer than yours.'

The tiny apartment had been Kit's home since college. The loft held her eclectic collection of finds gathered on her travels in Mexico and India. A colourful silk batik throw covered one wall and a curtain of beads screened the galley kitchen. Kit busied herself in the kitchen brewing a pot of tea while Abbie settled on a cushion-laden couch: another of Kit's charity-shop finds.

Abbie pushed a pile of *Psychiatry Now* journals aside to make room for the tray. The samovar had lost its gilt a long time before Kit had found it. She poured the steaming tea into mismatched cups and lit a candle.

The tea smelled of winter spice and reminded Abbie

of Christmas. She wondered about the child – she was certain that Jack had been speaking to a child – who had demanded a snow globe. What if Jack already had someone? What if he was married?

She didn't want to think about that. It was almost a relief when Kit commanded her to talk. She sat back in her chair and sipped her tea, waiting for Abbie to speak.

'We spent the night together, or rather, we fucked.' She smiled wryly at her choice of words. 'Actually, we did quite a lot of other things too. By the time –' Abbie swallowed hard. 'By the time he was through, I was begging him to, you know. I never knew it was possible to feel like that, Kit – to give up so much control to another person – and it scared the life out of me.'

'So it was good, then.'

'Good doesn't begin to describe it. I screamed for him. I never wanted it to stop.'

The slow tick of a grandfather clock marked time in the room while she tried to gather her thoughts together. Lying in Jack's arms. Finding him shaking in the middle of the night. The phone call to the woman and child. She knew almost nothing about the real Jack. Except that she loved him.

What she had experienced with William was a shallow reflecting pool. Jack was a deep ocean that she longed to dive into. She wanted to explore every dark abyss and find the core of the man: the Jack who enjoyed pain. The Jack who spoke so tenderly to a child. The arrogant, insufferable, movie-star Jack. She didn't know where to start.

'Do you plan on seeing him again?'

Kit's question cut through her reverie and Abbie

shrugged. 'He flew back to LA this morning, but we'll chat tonight.'

'That's good, Abbie. The fact that you're keeping in contact is positive. Just try to take things slow.'

'I think it's too late for that. I'm in love with him.'

Home had never looked so big, or so empty. Jack had landed, met Zeke at the airport to get the details of his audition the next day, and had finally got back to his Hollywood mansion. His dogs, two German Shepherd bitches named Blackie and Brownie – it was always a mistake to let your three-year-old niece pick names for dogs – had welcomed him with limitless enthusiasm and drool.

They had barked madly when they realized he was home, and raced up to greet him, jumping all over him and almost knocking him over in their excitement. He laughed, rubbed their ears and allowed them to rough-house. He wondered if they would be too vigorous for Abbie. She was a lot smaller than he was. They might knock her over.

Where had that thought come from? He scowled. He had an audition to prepare for, he had to stop thinking about her. Abbie was a career New Yorker. She didn't belong here, and wouldn't be meeting his dogs.

Of course, a nagging little voice that sounded a lot like Kevin reminded him that he didn't belong here either. He had bought this house five years earlier and had barely touched it. His name might be on the power bill, but it wasn't really his home. The only things he had changed were the gym in the basement and his playroom.

His invitation-only, strictly adults-only playroom. He tried to imagine Abbie there and failed. His vanilla girl would run away screaming at the sight of his A-frame and spanking bench. He took a quick look in as he passed it on the way to the kitchen. All his crops, canes, flails and ropes were neatly hung, waiting for him to use them. Blackie tried to wriggle her way into the room but Jack pulled her out.

'Come out of there, you brat.'

She whined like a puppy. Jack laughed and rubbed her head, but wouldn't allow her in. Neither of the dogs was allowed in, but that didn't stop them being insanely curious.

Tyrell, his personal trainer and personal assistant, strolled out of the kitchen. 'Good, you're back. I've got a two-hour training session planned for you: weights, cardio and Pilates.'

Jack groaned. Tyrell was ruthless in the gym.

Tyrell grinned nastily. 'And after that, the real torture starts. You've got a full body wax, then a facial scrub, eyebrow shaping, hair styling and a spray tan.'

Jack cursed. The glamorous life of a Hollywood A-lister. His sister thought it was hilarious that he had to spend more time on his beauty routine than she did.

20

By the time he finished his workout and endured hours of manscaping, the only thing keeping him sane was the prospect of getting online to Abbie. He counted down the minutes until it was ten in New York, and then logged on. She was already online, waiting.

<Michael Delaney: Good evening, Abbie.>

<Wild orchid: Hi, Sir.>

That was all it took and his cock swelled. Even after hours of workouts and torture, Abbie only had to write the word 'Sir' and he was erect.

<Michael Delaney: How are you feeling this evening? Sore?>

He didn't think he had hurt her, but there had been marks on her skin this morning.

<Wild orchid: You have to ask me that?>

<Michael Delaney: Tell me your thoughts.>

<Wild orchid: Confused, I guess. I would have liked to spend more time with you before you had to go back to LA. It feels weird to have become so close and then for you to disappear.>

<Michael Delaney: I'm sorry I had to leave you like that. Did you enjoy the night?>

<Wild orchid: Honestly? Yes. I've never done anything like that before.>

<Michael Delaney: Nothing that generated so much cleaning up afterwards?>

Jack allowed himself to smile when he remembered the state of her apartment after they were finished. Her sitting room was awash with feathers and her bedroom was a mess.

<Wild orchid: Ha ha. My cleaner doesn't come until Wednesday. Lots of domestic stuff today, lol.>

<Michael Delaney: Did you get any work done? How's the Tabora story?>

<Wild orchid: They're running it as a special on Saturday. The State Department won't confirm who made the decision to fund Tabora. Even calling my contacts at home for an off-the-record conversation, I can't get anyone to tell me what's going on. Since the DEA is saying that 80% of cocaine entering the country is being shipped through Honduras, it's looking very suspect. Josh is fed up waiting to run the story. Now he's threatened to say that they refused to comment. They won't like that.>

<Michael Delaney: Poor you. Working on a Sunday. Especially after being so busy on Saturday night.>

<Wild orchid: I'm used to it. But your concern for my well-being is touching. Luckily I'm off tomorrow so I'm looking forward to a big sleep-in.>

<Michael Delaney: You've earned it, baby. Will you get the byline when the story runs?>

<Wild orchid: Yes, for sure. Maybe it will get me out of fashion hell and back to the newsroom.>

<Michael Delaney: But it might get more drug runners following you around with guns.>

He was impressed by her commitment to her work and how good she was at it. He would never forget the first sight of her jumping into his plane. In the jungle she had admitted that the interview with him was just a ploy to get on the plane, and that time she had only gotten away from the bad guys by the skin of her teeth. It worried him.

<Wild orchid: I can take care of myself.>

<Michael Delaney: I want you to be careful.>

He was surprised by how much he wanted her to be careful. He never interfered with his subs outside their sessions, but this was different.

<Wild orchid: Look, don't worry. It couldn't be as bad as the time I did the story on people trafficking. That was scary. I had to stay with Kit for weeks.>

<Michael Delaney: Now I'm getting worried. I don't want you to stop what you're doing. You're obviously good at it. But just don't be stupid. Who looks after you?>

That was the question that mattered. It seemed to him that no one looked after Abbie. He was surprised by how much he wanted to.

<Wild orchid: I'm a big girl, Jack. I'm pretty good at taking care of myself.>

<Michael Delaney: I want the right to take care of you too.>

<Wild orchid: I like the sound of that.>

<Michael Delaney: I want you to think about signing an agreement with me.>

<Wild orchid: What sort of agreement?>

<Michael Delaney: A D/s agreement.>

<Wild orchid: Oh. I read about those. Do we need one? Is it not too soon?>

<Michael Delaney: I don't think so. I know what I want. I think you do too. Putting it down in writing gives us the freedom to test our limits safely.>

<Wild orchid: It just seems a bit strange putting down rules for a relationship. Relationships should be spontaneous.>

<Michael Delaney: And how well did that work for you up to now?>

Wild orchid is typing.

<Wild orchid: Touché. OK. You win. Do I have any input or are these the Rules According to Jack?>

<Michael Delaney: I'll send you the agreement. It's short, and sets out what I expect and what you can expect. And you can tell me your thoughts.>

<Wild orchid: F**k my thoughts. Why do you keep asking me that?>

<Michael Delaney: Someone should. I want to know what you are thinking, and feeling. And how you feel about doing it all again, but pushing your limits next time.>

<Wild orchid: Not sure if I like the sound of that, lol. My soft furnishings may not survive.>

<Michael Delaney: We'll take it in easy stages. For instance, what colour of panties are you wearing today?>

<Wild orchid: Sorry, forgot to tell you. They're green, with a little white bow.>

<Michael Delaney: As punishment for forgetting, you have to show me. Switch on your webcam, pull up your shirt and show me.>

<Wild orchid: What!>

He could feel her shock and outrage vibrate through the internet. God, he loved pushing her.

<Michael Delaney: It's not difficult. And it's what I want you to do. It would please me to see your panties.>

<Wild orchid: You are such a>

He wondered what names she had been about to call him. Something very refined, he was sure.

<Wild orchid: OK, give me a minute.>

Yes! She was going to do it. He held his breath while she fiddled with her laptop. A box opened up, showing a quick glimpse of Abbie's face. Her mouth was slightly open and she looked flushed. She was turned on by this. The angle changed and panned down Abbie's T-shirt, something loose with a bold design, to her yoga pants. What would she do now?

She untied the drawstring, shimmied and allowed the black pants to fall out of sight, leaving her in a skimpy pair of green panties. Sure enough, there was even a little white bow, which trembled with each breath. His erection surged to hard, throbbing life.

She stood there for a minute, displaying herself to him, before she switched off the webcam and typed

<Wild orchid: Happy?>

She had no idea how much.

<Michael Delaney: Good girl. I'm so pleased with you.>

<Michael Delaney: Read the agreement and contact me tomorrow night.>

<Wild orchid: Yes.>

Wild orchid is typing.

<Wild orchid: Sir.>

He groaned. He was facing a cold shower before bed.

The buzz of her cell phone woke her and Abbie patted the bedside table trying to find it. With one eye open, she stared at the display. It was Kevin, and it was almost noon. She had tried his number several times the previous day but he hadn't picked up and she still owed him an apology for the horrible evening in Mamma d'Inzeo's.

She rolled over. 'Hi, Kevin.'

'Awake at last. You must have had a late night.'

'Um . . .' She didn't want to admit how late or why.

'How is Jack?'

So much for keeping their relationship discreet, but he was probably in contact with Kevin almost every day. 'He's fine, gone back to LA to audition for some big part.'

'Poor bastard. It's still the most nerve-wracking part of the business. So, what do you say we meet up and have coffee? I can't ask you to dinner again. Jack would kill me.'

'Lunch would be good.' Abbie rattled off the address of her favourite coffee bar and tumbled out of bed.

Ninety minutes later she was sitting opposite him at the same table she and Kit had shared the day before.

'I'm sorry,' they both chorused in unison and then laughed.

'Sorry, Abbie. I wouldn't have hit on you if I had known that you were still involved with Jack. He won't tolerate anyone else near his women.'

His women. Was that what she was? One of Jack's women.

'I didn't realize I was,' she said.

He gave her a speculative look. 'Oh, I think you're a lot more than that. He nearly fired Zeke Bryan when he found out he had leaked stories about what happened with you in the jungle. I've never seen him so mad.'

Jack had already told her, but it was good to hear Kevin confirming that he hadn't betrayed her.

'And as for women, he hasn't got up to anything since he got back from Honduras, and believe me, that says a lot for Jack.'

'What about Kym Kardell?' She hated asking, it made her sound so needy, but the thought of the beautiful film star tormented her. This was the sort of woman Jack was used to. Not someone ordinary like her.

Kevin laughed. 'It's a show. The studio tells him to date her, so he does. He can't stand her, and anyway, she's dating her make-up artist.'

Abbie buried her face in the menu, trying to hide her confusion. 'You've known Jack for a long time?'

'Since we were at college. I came out here the year before Jack. He did some off-off-Broadway stuff for a year or two until he was spotted and Hollywood came knocking.'

'And his family?' She knew she shouldn't have asked the question when Kevin's expression became guarded.

'Still in Ireland,' he admitted. 'But you should really talk to Jack about that. He values his privacy more than a lot of things.'

'Can I ask one question?'

His pained expression told her that he would rather that she didn't.

'Please, Kevin, just one and I promise I won't pry any more after that.'

'Abbie, there is no guarantee that I will answer it, but shoot.'

She took a deep breath. 'Who is Ciara?'

'Ciara?' Kevin laughed. 'She's Jack's sister. I had the hots for her when we were in college, but he wouldn't let me date her. He was a protective bastard, even then.'

Kit arrived and settled herself into the seat beside Abbie. 'Who's a protective bastard?'

'Oh hi, Kit, this is Kevin O'Malley. We met in Honduras.'

Kevin stood up and offered his hand. 'Pleased to meet you. Can I grab you a coffee or anything?' He gave her braids and print dress a once-over. 'No, let me guess, herbal tea?'

Kit raised an eyebrow. 'Nettle, if they have it. If not, I'll have some green tea.'

Their table was beside the counter, so Kevin stood up to order the tea and Abbie and Kit talked weather.

'So, what do you do, Kit? Something arty, I bet,' he said as Kit poured from the teapot he had put down in front of her.

'I'm a relationship counsellor.'

'I bet you're busy. New York is full of people with nothing better to do with their time but talk about their relationships. I can't understand why they don't talk to their friends.'

Kit's sweet smile belied her sharp tongue and Abbie could see that Kevin was going to be on the receiving end of it.

She took a sip of tea before regarding Kevin thoughtfully. 'Maybe people need counsellors because their friends are assholes who don't listen to them.'

Ouch. Kit didn't pull her punches. Abbie sat back and let them at it.

Kevin was unabashed. 'And the money doesn't come into it. Tell me, how much do you usually charge a Billy No-Mates for a session?'

'Is that a patient inquiry? Would you like to speak to someone in a supportive and caring environment?'

'And have you poke around inside my head? No, thanks,' Kevin snorted.

'You're right. Maybe there's not a lot to poke, but I do like a challenge.'

Kit sat back in her chair and Abbie caught a glint of amusement in her eyes. Wonders would never cease. Kit actually liked him. Kit drained the last of her tea and stood up. 'In case you change your mind, here's my card.' She winked at Abbie. 'Catch you later.'

As the waiter cleared the teapot and cup away, Abbie noticed that Kevin was still turning the card over and over in his hand. 'Sassy bitch,' he muttered.

Abbie grinned at him. 'Does that mean you'll call her?'

Kevin pocketed the card. 'Absolutely, but not for a professional consultation.'

21

Abbie stared at her screen in disbelief. Despite everything she had done in the last few weeks – and how ready she thought she was to be Jack's submissive – now that she saw her future set out in writing, she felt sick. She knew that agreements like this were standard. During one of her internet trawls she had come across them. But it was one thing reading about them in theory and another to read something that she was supposed to sign up to.

She read over the document in front of her again. It didn't change.

Memorandum of Agreement

This agreement is entered into by Jack Winter (hereafter referred to as the Dominant) and Abbie Marshall (hereafter referred to as the submissive).

It is understood that both parties enter this agreement freely and are fully conversant with all of the implications that such an agreement entails.

Purpose

The purpose of this agreement is to put into place a written accord between the two parties to promote harmony in the relationship and to enhance the lifestyle of both. The relationship will be conducted in a loving, attentive and discreet manner. Both parties agree to take whatever actions are necessary to ensure its continued success.

Confidentiality Clause

By entering into this agreement, the submissive agrees and acknowledges that she will never publicize, comment on or otherwise divulge any details of this agreement or the relationship, save with the express permission of her Dominant. In return, he undertakes to do the same. To underpin this clause, the submissive agrees to enter into a bond in the sum of ten million dollars.

The Rules

The submissive consents to her submission to the Dominant, and in return he accepts the role of her Dominant. By agreeing the Dominant undertakes to accept the submissive's submission, and assume the responsibilities of protecting her from herself and from outside harm. These rules are designed to enhance the quality of the submissive's life and will vary from time to time as her conduct and circumstances demand. The submissive agrees that she will:

Never lie, directly, indirectly or by omission to her Dominant

Be courteous and considerate to him at all times

Not use unbecoming language

Dress modestly unless otherwise directed to do so by her Dominant

Strive to get eight hours' sleep each night

Ensure that her refrigerator contains food at all times

Obey her Dominant's orders without question

Accept that her failure to adhere to the Rules will result in punishment.

Offences punishable by scolding & spanking

Causing embarrassment to her Dominant

Overuse of foul or expletive language

Not adhering to agreed dress code

Failing to recognize the benefits of compromise by being argumentative and disagreeable – the final decision is his, whether she agrees or not.

Offences punishable by cane or crop

Placing herself in danger by failing to take sensible precautions in her work life

Any other rule set by the Dominant after discussion with the submissive

Persistent and continuous breaches or misdemeanors will result in other forms of punishment.

Holy Shit! Abbie pushed away from the computer desk. What the hell had she gotten herself into? Dress modestly, have food in the refrigerator, no unbecoming language? Well, he could go fuck himself. She cursed defiantly. There was no way that she could agree to this – she had to talk to Kit.

Kit waved to the waiter and ordered another nettle tea. 'You know, we really should buy shares in this place. What was so important that you couldn't e-mail me? I feel like I'm living here.'

Abbie shoved the pages across the table to her. 'Read that and tell me that I'm not crazy.'

She watched Kit's face as she read through the agreement slowly. Kit didn't look shocked. In fact, Abbie was sure that she was trying not to laugh.

Eventually, Kit raised her head. 'Well? What's the problem?'

'What's the problem?' Abbie snatched back the paper. 'Have you seen what he wants me to do? The dress code, the food thing, my language. What is wrong with my language? Jack uses swear words like commas.'

'Seriously, Abbie. It's pretty much a standard D/s contract. Apart from the ten million.' She whistled. 'He obviously values his privacy.'

Kit leaned forwards. 'Look, the guy is a Dom and he wants to take care of you. I've counselled D/s couples and, considering the lifestyle, his demands aren't excessive. I've seen a lot more extreme. The tenets of a BDSM relationship are safe, sane and consensual. This is all about an exchange of power.'

'But how is drawing up a contract a healthy part of a relationship, Kit. You're the expert. You tell me.'

'You know, every single relationship has its rules, but usually they're not spelled out. A lot of the people I see wouldn't be in difficulty if they were more upfront. It's one of the things I admire about the BDSM scene: people think seriously about what they want and need.

'This is an agreement, Abbie, not a sentence. Nothing happens unless you consent to it. If there is something in it that bugs you, then negotiate with him. This is not about

Jack taking over your world, it's about you giving control of certain aspects of your life to him.'

Kit pushed the page across the table. 'What parts do you have problems with?'

One demand in particular set her nerves on edge. 'The work one,' Abbie said. 'It's bad enough that my family want me to give up reporting and live off my trust fund. I can't do that, Kit.'

'It says he wants you to take sensible precautions. I'm not sure I see the issue.'

'But I do that already. The Honduran thing was a plane crash. I had no control over that.'

'OK, what about that people-trafficking story last year? You had to move out of your apartment.'

'Only for two weeks.'

Kit frowned. 'Abbie, the guy sent you a body part in the mail.'

She couldn't deny it. Kit was right. That had been a really bad case, but those men were in prison now. Well, most of them.

'Look, this is between you and Jack. If you don't want to sign it, then don't sign it.'

Kit was right. All she had to do was not sign it, but if she refused then Jack Winter would probably disappear from her life completely and she didn't want that. There was nothing for it. She would have to talk to him.

Jack was waiting when Abbie logged on that evening. He had been thinking about this moment all afternoon. The morning had gone well – better than well. Although he knew that he wasn't the only A-lister going for the *African Queen* part, the three casting directors had been visibly excited after he read with Maria Richards. He shouldn't have been surprised to see that a two-time Oscar winner would be playing the leading lady. But what surprised everyone – even him – was how well they sparked off each other. The senior casting director, Hank Lawson, told him he could expect to hear from them before the end of the week. Lawson was known as a straight-up guy so he was sure the part was in the bag. Between that and meeting Abbie, his life seemed to have taken quite a turn in the last few weeks. Of course, that depended on what Abbie made of the contract. He could imagine it freaking her out.

<Wild orchid: I got the agreement. I think we need to talk.>

<Michael Delaney: Of course we'll talk. What do you have a problem with?>

<Wild orchid: I haven't done this before and, well, some of the stuff is . . .>

<Michael Delaney: I don't want to frighten you, but nothing sounded terrible to me.>

<Wild orchid: I know, Jack, but it was a bit scary seeing a contract. Have you done this before? With other subs?>

<Michael Delaney: It's usually not necessary. I'm making an exception for you. But yes, if I have a sub, both of us have to know what we are agreeing to.>

<Wild orchid: So, ten million dollars? You must trust people a lot. Lol.>

<Michael Delaney: Would you, in my place? You are a

reporter. Your instinct is to write. I've seen how you can't rest until you've finished the story.>

<Wild orchid: I guess not. I wouldn't betray you, Jack, but if you think like that, then . . .>

<Michael Delaney: Then it won't matter, will it?>

<Wild orchid: It's not just that, well, there is other stuff there. You want to decide how I dress?>

<Michael Delaney: I won't do anything to embarrass you. But I won't let you dress as if you're ashamed of being a woman. You're smart, intelligent and passionate. Your clothes should reflect that.>

<Wild orchid: Oh, please, no. Not skirts.>

<Michael Delaney: You look great in a skirt. And so tempting. You know you have a world-class ass? It's a crime to hide it.>

<Wild orchid: Lol. You are so bad.>

<Michael Delaney: You have no idea . . .>

<Wild orchid: OK then, skirts, sometimes.>

<Michael Delaney: When I say. Lol. I won't make you wear them riding or ice-skating.>

<Wild orchid: Gee, thanks. Now, about food . . .>

<Michael Delaney: I don't want you starving yourself, or living on coffee because you don't take time to eat properly. I'm not dictating what you eat. I'll leave that up to you.>

<Wild orchid: It's a news thing. I have to be able to jump on a plane any time. Do you know what a three-week-old lettuce looks like? That's why I have a cleaner once a week.>

<Michael Delaney: You live in New York, the city that

never sleeps. I'm sure you can buy food occasionally. Or you could move out to LA. Your paper has an office here.>

Jack stared at the screen. What had he just typed? He never asked women to move to be near him. But with Abbie, it seemed like the right thing to do.

<Wild orchid: LA? Would you like that?>

<Michael Delaney: The idea is growing on me. I'd be able to keep a much closer eye on you. What are your thoughts on the idea?>

<Wild orchid: Oh, I would like to spend more time with you. The weekend was too short.>

<Michael Delaney: And I could introduce you to some of my favourite toys.>

<Wild orchid: That sounds a bit scary. I presume you're not talking about action figures.>

<Michael Delaney: Well, they do see some action!>

<Wild orchid: Now you are teasing me.>

<Michael Delaney: We can test your limits. See if you really are pure vanilla.>

<Wild orchid: I am not vanilla. Well, maybe a bit. A lot. But I haven't done anything like this before.>

<Michael Delaney: I know that.>

<Wild orchid: Will there be other people there? Other women? I'm not sure how I would feel if I saw you with someone else.>

<Michael Delaney: That's what's bothering you? Not what I might do to you in my playroom?>

<Wild orchid: You tied me to a bed and tortured me with feathers and ice, and you spanked me. What else did you have in mind?>

Every instinct screamed at him to stop, but Jack typed.

<Michael Delaney: You know, it might be better if you didn't agree to that contract. I'm not sure if I could be gentle enough if I had you to myself.>

It was true. Something about Abbie brought out all his demons. No matter how much that stupid therapist he had visited told him that his sexual drives were healthy and normal, he worried that they were too strong for Abbie to cope with.

<Wild orchid: You said punishment with a cane.>

<Michael Delaney: Yes.>

Maybe that would give her pause. She had to think about what she was letting herself in for.

<Wild orchid: Anything else? Only I've seen pictures on sites and, well, it looks like it hurts.>

<Michael Delaney: Well, maybe a crop, or a belt, or a flail. You'll like the flail.>

He hardened at the thought of Abbie naked while he played the flail gently up and down her defenceless back. Or even over her front. How would she react then? He couldn't wait to find out.

<Michael Delaney: And I reserve the right to improvise other punishments if appropriate.>

<Wild orchid: Like what?>

<Michael Delaney: Let's say I find you have an empty refrigerator. I would find a food-based punishment.>

<Wild orchid: That's not too scary. What will you make me do? Eat cauliflower? Lol! (Seriously though, I hate cauliflower.)>

<Michael Delaney: Ever heard of figging?>

There was a long pause while Abbie went off and

looked it up. He grinned, picturing her reaction when she found out what he meant. He wasn't disappointed.

<Wild orchid: Oh, no. Nonononono. You wouldn't. Having a finger of ginger up my ass. That's just too disgusting for words.>

<Michael Delaney: Not from my point of view. You'll wiggle that ass so much I'll have a permanent erection.>

<Wild orchid: OK, I will keep some food in the fridge.>

<Michael Delaney: Pity. But I'm glad you're going to eat.>

<Wild orchid: You are evil! So, how do we do this? The Jack and Abbie show. You're there, I'm here. That's an awful lot of distance between us.>

<Michael Delaney: Oh, we'll manage. Sign and return that contract, and we can begin. I'll push your limits, and you'll enjoy it. Mostly.>

<Wild orchid: There's just one thing.>

<Michael Delaney: Yes?>

<Wild orchid: How long is the contract for? I mean, is it a month, six months?>

<Michael Delaney: Do you want a time limit?>

<Wild orchid: I'm not looking for a commitment but you are asking me to trust you.>

<Michael Delaney: A D/s contract is a commitment.>

<Wild orchid: To hand control of parts of my life to you. I guess what I'm saying is . . .>

<Michael Delaney: And I undertake to take care of you.>

<Wild orchid: Then maybe we should have a date first.>

<Michael Delaney: A date?>

<Wild orchid: Yes, a date. It's what couples do.>

<Michael Delaney: When they're living in the same state. Or even the same time zone.>

<Wild orchid: A date. You know, something that doesn't involve being thrown out of a restaurant, or watching a movie that you're in.>

<Michael Delaney: I'm in so many . . .>

<Wild orchid: Lol. If I sign the contract, I want us to go on a date. I want that written in. Maybe two dates.>

<Michael Delaney: OK, we can definitely add that to the contract. But I get to say what happens to your panties on that date.>

<Wild orchid: I want this to be about more than sex, Jack. Call me old-fashioned.>

<Michael Delaney: Trust me, you'll enjoy the date a lot more if you know your panties are in my pocket. Think of feeling the breeze caressing your pussy when I can't.>

<Wild orchid: Stop that! Do you always know if you're going to get lucky at the end of the night?>

<Michael Delaney: If I have you, I know I'm lucky.>

<Wild orchid: What a lovely thing to say.>

<Michael Delaney: It's all for show. Deep down, I'm evil. Remember that.>

<Wild orchid: I'll take that under advisement. Now, I have to go to bed or I won't get eight hours' sleep.>

Abbie signed off and Jack laughed. This was going to be fun.

22

The package was delivered to her desk at 3pm. Not an orchid this time, but a large black box tied up with a ribbon.

'Someone loves you,' said the delivery man as he handed her a docket to sign.

Abbie scrawled her name and lifted the lid, snapping it down quickly when she caught a hint of lace. It had to be from Jack. Ignoring the interested glance from the reporter at the next desk, she hurried to the ladies' room.

Luckily, there was no one else there. The dress was black lace, lined with flesh-coloured silk, the stockings were hold ups and the impossibly high black heels were her size. The accompanying card instructed her to be ready at 5pm, and that she should wear nothing else, except the lipstick provided. It was signed with a J.

Abbie turned the card over. The back said, 'You asked for a date.'

What was he up to? Jack was three thousand miles away. Why would he do all this?

She struggled through the next ninety minutes, barely able to focus on anything she was doing. At four thirty, her cell phone buzzed.

'Are you still at your desk?'

'Yes, some of us have work to do.' She giggled. 'So, what is this? Another cyber date?'

'You'll have to wait and see. Go to the ladies' room and change. Be on the roof of the building at five.'

'The roof?' He had already hung up.

Box under her arm, Abbie hurried back to the ladies'. A few other women were in there touching up their make-up before heading out for the evening. She locked herself in a cubicle, pulled down the seat and perched on the edge of the toilet. The whole thing was ridiculous. Men were useless at knowing what size a woman was. There was no way that the dress would fit. And what was she going to do on the roof? Get picked up by hot air balloon?

She shoved her sensible work clothes into her tote bag, then pulled the dress over her head and closed the zipper. First round to Jack. It stretched and it did fit. The stockings were sheer and although the shoes were high, she could just about walk in them.

Abbie teetered outside and stared at her reflection in the mirror. It was sexy without being vampish. She grudgingly admitted that Jack had good taste. She opened the lipstick. 'Pure Scarlett': the name was enough. *I take back what I just said.*

She tightened the belt of her coat and took the elevator to the top floor. A light wind drifted across the rooftop as Abbie scanned the skyline. A dark speck in the distance came closer and Abbie heard the sound of a helicopter. Only the board of the newspaper used the flight pad. Jack wouldn't dare.

It seemed that he would dare. The pilot waved to her and she raced across the rooftop and climbed inside. Thank goodness for low maintenance haircuts: the wind from the blades was as strong as being out in a gale. She settled herself in the seat beside the pilot and tucked her safety belt around her waist.

Jack wasn't on board. The pilot took off, while she battled a wave of disappointment and watched the New York skyline vanish from view.

The pilot didn't say a word to her, but occasionally his eyes strayed to her stocking-clad legs and high-heeled shoes. 'Can I ask where we're going?' she said.

'No, ma'am. I've been told to tell you that it's a surprise.'

She inched back in her chair. 'OK, surprise me.'

Darkness had fallen when she caught her first glimpse of the illuminated falls at Niagara. She felt a rush of pleasure. He had remembered their brief conversation from the jungle.

A dark limousine was waiting at the heliport, but there was still no sign of Jack. Her heart fell. As the car pulled up outside the hotel, she checked her cell, but there was still no message from him. Abbie was escorted to a two-storey suite on the twenty-second floor. The rooms were luxurious and a log fire was burning in the fireplace of the living room. Outside on the balcony, she had a spectacular view of the falls.

Everything was perfect, except that she was alone. What was this? Why had he brought her all the way here? She could have been miserable and alone in New York.

Her new shoes were beginning to pinch and she kicked them off. She was tempted to take off the dress and toss it over the balcony when she heard a discreet knock. She hurried to open the door.

'I'm sorry, madame, but Mr Winter has been delayed.

He has requested that dinner be served here, rather than the restaurant. Would you care to order?'

Jack was coming. Abbie smiled. 'Can you repeat that please? You lost me at delayed.'

'It's the first time Mr Winter has stayed with us. Is there something special that you would like? A tasting menu, perhaps?'

Abbie was tempted to request a side order of bugs or roast snake for Jack, but she relented. He was on his way. She would see him tonight. 'A tasting menu would be good, but no mushrooms. And have the sommelier pick some wine to go with it.'

'Of course.' He nodded.

She was halfway through a glass of wine when the door opened. Jack's hair was damp from the rain and his shirt was wrinkled, but it was the expression on his face that made her heart jump. He had a faint shadow of stubble which gave him an edge of danger and his eyes were darker than usual.

Abbie launched herself at him. 'God, I missed you.' His scent, woodsy and masculine, made something in her belly clench with anticipation.

His mouth took hers in a hungry kiss that left her breathless. 'Sorry, I wanted to meet you off the helicopter, not have you hanging out here alone.'

'It's OK. I'm so glad you're here.' She kissed him again, running her palms along the hard planes of his back, scratching him lightly with her nails.

He gave a low growl of pleasure, before gently pushing her a foot away. 'Behave. This is supposed to be a date.'

'A date?'

The corner of his mouth quirked up in a smile. 'You said we had to have at least one date. So, I figured dinner, maybe watch a movie. You know, like vanilla people.'

Abbie stepped away from him. 'Have you seen the heels on my new shoes? Perhaps I should introduce you?'

He raised a brow in mock horror. 'There will be no kink tonight. Now, how about dinner. I'm starving.'

As if they had heard him, the door opened and two uniformed waiters brought in their dinner. They laid the table, poured wine, lit candles and left. Jack dimmed the main lights, leaving one table lamp to cast a glow over the room. Outside, the torrent of rushing water was illuminated with the colours of the rainbow.

'You remembered what I said in the jungle. About the falls, I mean.' Abbie still couldn't get over it. William couldn't remember that she was allergic to mushrooms, but Jack remembered one chance remark about Niagara Falls.

'How could I not? *Niagara* is one of my all-time favourite movies. The destructiveness of sex and all that.'

'And is sex destructive?' she asked.

A wry expression crossed Jack's face. 'It can be. That's why I want you to be sure before you enter an agreement with me. We're both adults, but starting a D/s relationship can be an emotional roller coaster.'

He was nervous too. She hadn't thought of it that way before. Jack always seemed so confident, so sure about everything. 'How many subs have you had before me?'

Jack's laughter echoed around the dimly lit room. 'I'm no angel. There have been a lot of women, but most of them were just D/s hook-ups. I've only had two serious relationships before you. Paloma and someone back home.'

Abbie almost dropped her fork. The idea of Jack and Paloma in a relationship had never entered her head. With her rounded figure and nondescript features, Paloma seemed an unlikely mate for a superstar. 'She didn't strike me as your type.'

The words were out of her mouth before she could stop them and Jack frowned. 'D/s isn't about types. It's not about supermodels running around with duct tape over their nipples or dressed head to toe in latex.'

'I'm sorry. I didn't mean it that way. It was just a surprise.' It was too late, the brooding expression was back. She had upset him and it was the last thing she had intended to do.

She tried to restore the mood as they bantered over dinner and he seemed to come back to her. But not fully. After finishing his meal, Jack pushed his plate away. 'Would you like to go for a walk? Maybe see the falls up close?'

'I'd like that.' She went hunting for her abandoned high heels, but Jack advised her to wear whatever was comfortable. She got into her work shoes.

Outside the hotel, they walked in an awkward silence. Jack had made a big effort to organize the night. The dress, the transport, the venue. Everything had been designed to create the perfect date and somehow she had ruined it. Abbie tucked her arm through his, trying to reconnect with him, and she was comforted when he covered her hand with his. 'I didn't mean to . . .'

Jack squeezed her hand. 'I know. I guess we both have

things in our past that will surprise the other. I'm just asking you to trust me when I say that I only want what's best for you.'

'I do trust you.'

He rewarded her statement with a hungry kiss. 'Oh, Ms Marshall, I hope you don't regret it.'

The misty rain turned to a steady downpour and Abbie was glad that she had left the high heels behind. They hurried back to the hotel and crossed the lobby, ignoring the glances of recognition that Jack received. The elevator had a mirror, where she could see her damp hair was sticking to her face. Her lipstick was gone and standing beside Jack's dark beauty, she looked ordinary.

'I told you to stop judging yourself.'

Abbie stuck out her tongue at her reflection. 'So, spank me.'

Usually that would have been enough to provoke him. She found herself hungering for his dark gaze, the one that told her that he planned to do some very naughty things to her. Instead, he dropped a light kiss on her cheek. 'Not tonight, Abbie.'

The ground floor of the suite had been cleared in their absence. The candles had been extinguished and a metal guard placed in front of the fire. Abbie glanced nervously at Jack. On the basis of previous encounters, he should have had her pinned to the wall by now. Her dress should have been a crumpled heap on the floor. Instead, he was controlled, almost detached. It bugged the hell out of her. 'Is something wrong?'

He sat on the couch and patted the cushion beside him. 'Of course not. Come here.'

Abbie snuggled beside him, trying to quell the butterflies fluttering inside her. Jack dropped an arm around her shoulders and reached for the remote control of the TV. He had to be kidding. He had travelled three thousand miles to watch a movie? Jack flicked idly through the selection available.

She glanced at her wristwatch. It was almost 10pm. She would have an early start to get back to the city on time and god knew when Jack had to leave. She had no intention of sitting through a movie.

In a wriggling manoeuvre, she slid across his lap until she straddled him. She couldn't resist running her hands across his shoulders. So broad and solid. All that power beneath her hands was intoxicating, but his stillness was unnerving. Jack laid his head on the back of the couch and closed his eyes. At least he hadn't rebuffed her attentions. She nipped along his jaw where the skin was thin and sensitive.

He didn't react. What was going on?

Abbie opened one button on his shirt, and then another, tracing a path with her tongue on his bare skin until her mouth closed over his nipple and his eyes jerked open. Ah, a reaction.

Jack picked up the remote control and switched off the TV. 'It looks like you have an evil plan to seduce me.' The words were encouraging, but he sounded strangely distant.

She tried to infuse a hint of devilment into her voice. 'You have no idea.' What was up with him tonight? His passive behaviour was so at odds with the way he was usually.

He ruffled her hair. 'Let's go to bed, then.'

They climbed the stairs together but without touching. Jack switched on the bedside lamp and unbuttoned his shirt. Abbie stared at him. His stomach rippled and flexed with every breath, and the muscles on his chest and arms were sharply defined. His body never failed to amaze her, nor the amount of time it took to keep it that way.

She waited for him to take command, to order her to undress, but nothing happened. She cleaned off her make-up, stripped off her dress and climbed into bed beside him.

Jack rolled over and kissed her with breathtaking intensity. Ah, this she knew. She relaxed against him, trusting him with her body. He stroked and caressed her until she was helplessly squirming against him, wordlessly begging for more. He kissed his way down her body, tasting and nibbling until she moaned and begged. He watched her every reaction, varying his attentions from tender to rough, utterly focused on bringing her pleasure. But there was something missing.

His first hard thrust inside her almost brought her to orgasm. She clung on to his shoulders as he rode her with merciless intent. Abbie clawed at his back, thrashing wildly beneath him until her entire being turned into one rushing torrent of sensation and she came.

When she opened her eyes again, Jack was staring at her.

Her stomach flipped. Something was terribly wrong. Maybe this was break-up sex, if there was such a thing. 'Please tell me that you're not breaking up with me.'

He pressed a damp kiss on her forehead and smiled. 'Never.'

She lay against him in silence until the helicopter came

to collect her. She expected, in spite of the noise, to sleep all the way home. It had been a long day, she'd had amazing sex and had to work in a few hours. Instead, she spent the journey staring out into the night, battling an inexplicable sense of unease.

Abbie spent the day in turmoil, unable to make sense of what had happened the night before. She knew that their relationship had changed, but she wasn't sure whether she liked it. She tried Kit's cell, but then remembered that Kit was on one of her New Age retreats and out of contact except for emergencies. There was no one else she could talk to. Except Jack. She would just have to wait till ten.

By the time she logged on, she felt wrung out and almost past caring.

<Wild orchid: Are you there?>

<Michael Delaney: Yes, Abbie. How was your day?>

<Wild orchid: You said you wanted honesty?>

<Michael Delaney: Always.>

<Wild orchid: Well, my day was miserable. I know I did something wrong last night but I don't know how to fix it. You have to tell me.>

<Michael Delaney: You did nothing wrong.>

<Wild orchid: Don't say that. I know I'm not imagining things. Just tell me what's wrong.>

<Michael Delaney: You wanted a vanilla date, remember? That was vanilla, Abbie. I just wanted you to know the difference.>

<Wild orchid: What are you saying?>

<Michael Delaney: Remember, you said you wanted our relationship to be about more than sex.>

<Wild orchid: Yes.>

<Michael Delaney: And then you were surprised that Paloma had been my sub – because you didn't think she looked 'the part'. Am I right? Be honest.>

<Wild orchid: Yes.>

<Michael Delaney: Well, that made me wonder if you get me at all. If you get yourself.>

<Wild orchid: Sorry? I don't understand.>

<Michael Delaney: The way I am with you is not just about sex. The sex is an expression of what I am. I had to accept that a long time ago and I paid a high price for it. If you think everything that's happened between us is just about some kind of role-playing then you don't understand D/s.>

Wild orchid is typing.

<Wild orchid: Jack, I'm so sorry. I don't know what to say.>

<Michael Delaney: That's OK. You're new to this. It's not that I always have to be in charge when we make love. But for me, spending a night being the perfect vanilla boyfriend is a bit like acting. I can give a very convincing performance, but it's not real. That's what you felt last night.>

<Wild orchid: Oh.>

He had finally opened up to her. She felt closer to him now than she had the previous night when he was making love to her. Jack wasn't trying to break up with her, he had been trying to show her the difference between D/s and vanilla, and now she knew it was no longer her favourite flavour.

<Wild orchid: OK. You've given me a lot to think about. So, I guess we'll have no more dates, then!>

<Michael Delaney: Lol. We just have to redefine dating.>

She felt absurdly happy that he was laughing. She felt like she'd been run over by a truck but it was OK now. Everything was going to be all right.

Michael Delaney is typing.

<Michael Delaney: One more thing. You missed being ordered around last night, didn't you?>

<Wild orchid: Yes.>

<Michael Delaney: Yes?>

<Wild orchid: Yes, Sir!>

<Michael Delaney: That's my girl. Sleep tight.>

23

Abbie wasn't sure what woke her. She'd been working flat out for the last week since her vanilla date with Jack, and the clock on the side table said 3.15am. She should be asleep. She lay awake, listening. The noise came again. It sounded like drawers being pulled out.

For a moment, terror froze her muscles, then she forced herself into action. How had she not heard them get in? She must have forgotten to bolt the front door. Jack would kill her, if they didn't get to her first. She slid out of bed and made her way quietly to the bedroom door. The noise came from the kitchen this time. She could hear the sound of the refrigerator being opened and closed. *OK, calm down, they're outside and you have a lock on the door.* Her father had insisted on it after the last time she'd had a break-in. She turned the key and slid the deadbolt into place.

She had to call the police. Abbie patted the floor beside the bed, searching. She'd been rereading the texts from Jack on her personal phone before she fell asleep; it must be here somewhere. She didn't dare to turn on a light. Her phone beeped as it came to life and she smothered the sound against her chest and tried not to breathe. She heard the sound of glass breaking and a male voice cursing.

With shaking fingers, she dialled 911.

'Emergency Services, how can we help you?'

'There's someone in my apartment,' she whispered down the phone.

'Ma'am, can you speak up?'

Abbie crawled along the floor until she had reached the furthest spot from the bedroom door. 'There is someone in my apartment. Please come.'

She could barely keep the fear out of her voice.

'Ma'am, you need to give me your name and address and I'll send a car. Where are you now?'

'In my bedroom. I've locked myself in,' Abbie whispered. She rattled off her name and address.

Another crash came from outside. Louder this time. They would hardly expect her to sleep through that. 'Please hurry.'

The operator stayed on the line, trying to soothe her. 'Ma'am, just hang on there, there's a car in the area, someone will be with you shortly.'

Abbie waited for what seemed like for ever, keeping her eyes firmly on the locked door, watching the doorknob turn first in one direction and then the other. Outside, she heard the blare of a police siren. The doorknob twisted again. Then, she heard a loud thump and the sound of raised voices.

'Cops coming,' a gruff voice muttered and Abbie heard a door slamming. Her first instinct was to open the door, but what if they were still there? What if they were just pretending? She sat on the floor, hugging herself, trying to stop shaking.

'Ma'am, are you still there, ma'am?'

Abbie pulled the phone to her ear. 'Yes, I –'

'The officers are in your building, ma'am. Just hold on.'

'Thanks. Thank you for staying on the line.'

'You're welcome, ma'am.' The call disconnected.

Abbie jumped when a loud rap came on the bedroom door. 'Ms Marshall? This is the New York Police Department.'

Afterwards was a nightmare. Her apartment had been torn apart. She couldn't tell what had been taken. Her computer disks were spread around the floor, her cushions had been ripped apart and all her books had been tossed around, pages torn and their spines broken.

One of the cops picked up an antique silver frame. 'Well, they weren't looking for valuables. Can you tell if anything is missing, ma'am?'

She scanned the shelves again. Two portable disk drives were gone, but her precious laptop was still in the bedroom. Some photographs from Honduras were trampled into the rug, alongside a torn orchid. The broken glass from the frame glittered on the petals of the flower.

Bile rose in her throat. It was the same people, it had to be, and now they knew where she lived. She couldn't ignore it any longer. She had to tell the police.

She watched the officer's face as she talked and what he thought was a routine burglary turned into something far more sinister.

'Ma'am, have you someone you can call? A friend, maybe?'

'Yes, I'll grab a few things. I don't want to stay here.'

She called Kit, glad to hear a friendly voice on the other end of the line. Kit told her to come over immediately. She packed an overnight bag and wondered if she could put off calling Jack until the morning. She could just imagine the dire punishment that awaited her if she did. No, it had to be done. She took a breath and pressed his number on the phone, praying that he was still awake.

'I've had a break-in,' she said quickly when he answered. 'The police are here.'

'What? Are you OK?'

She looked around at the mess. 'The cleaner won't like it but I'm fine. I can't talk for long.'

'Are you hurt?'

'No. I locked myself in the bedroom.'

'Get out of there. I warned you about taking chances.' God, he was turning into a Neanderthal again. Curiously, it made her feel better.

'I wasn't planning to stay here tonight. Jack, I think it was connected with the story about Honduras.'

'Honduras?'

'Well, it's the only news story I'm still working on. They're hardly concerned about my crimes against fashion.'

She heard a snort on the other end of the line. He was definitely going to put her over his knee for that remark.

'Abbie, I'm not joking. You are to take all necessary precautions. Or I'll do it for you.'

She hugged her coat around her. 'I'm going. I'll stay with Kit for a few days. I'll let you know when I arrive.'

'If you do anything stupid, you are going to make the acquaintance of every single implement in my playroom. You will be typing standing up for a month.'

He sounded as if he really meant it. 'I'll be fine. I just wanted to hear your voice. I'll call you when I get to Kit's.'

'Text me when you leave your apartment, and when you get to Kit's. And don't go anywhere on your own.'

She ran downstairs to get her cab, feeling strangely reassured.

Jack was playing pool when the phone rang. Worrying about Abbie had been driving him crazy all day, even through his call-back audition for *The African Queen*. He had to let off some steam. He was in his favourite bar which, despite Californian anti-smoking laws, always seemed to be dim and smoky, even in the late afternoon. He was dressed in a baggy lumberjack shirt and wire-rimmed glasses, with his hair brushed over his face. If a tourist managed to find his way here, he'd be hard-pressed to recognize Hollywood heart-throb Jack Winter.

Most of the patrons here were bikers, truckers or farm workers. It was a hang-out for locals. When Jack asked people to call him Michael, no one blinked. The beer was good, the women were friendly and the nachos were spicy.

There was twenty dollars on the table, and Jack had lined up a tricky cross shot. He cursed the phone, but didn't think of ignoring it. Only a handful of people had this number. He checked the display, hoping it was Abbie, but Kev's ID glowed on the screen. Reluctantly, he answered it.

'About time, you bastard,' Kev snarled. 'Where the hell do you get off, busting up my date and then ignoring my calls?'

'Sorry, Kev, I wasn't ignoring you. I just had my phone

switched off.' In this bar, he couldn't mention the *African Queen* audition.

'And did you have your brain switched off when you crashed my date with Abbie?'

Jack shoved his hand through his hair, not caring that it might make him easier to recognize. 'Yeah, about that –'

'Don't try to weasel out of it.' Kevin's annoyance came clearly through the phone. 'You might have had a thing with her in Honduras, but you told me it was all over. So, what the hell were you doing coming on like a caveman?'

'Change of plan, Kev. It's not over. I know, I should have told you.' He lowered his voice. 'Have you seen her? How is she with all this shit?'

'Abbie's fine. She's living with her friend the Crazy Cornrow Girl in an apartment in the Village that looks like something off the Psychic channel. I mean, she has dreamcatchers in the kitchen. How long is she planning to stay there?'

A large trucker yelled at Jack. 'Hey, Mick, are you going to play pool or chat up your girlfriend?' He made kissy noises towards the phone, and his jowls, almost hidden by a ginger beard, quivered.

Jack pulled the phone away from his ear for a moment. 'Hold your horses, this is important.'

The trucker made an obscene gesture while Jack put the phone back to his ear. 'Go on.'

'She is going to drive me demented. She's on kissing terms with everyone in New York. It's not just the men, it's the women too. Do you think she could be a lesbian? I mean, that would be cool, I've always wanted to watch some lesbian action, but it would be nice to have some warning, you know?'

Jack felt as if he'd fallen down the rabbit hole. 'What are you talking about? Lesbian? Of course she's not. What other men?'

'Four men came up and kissed her in an hour. And three women. Not polite air-kissing either, real kisses. There could have been tongue. And one of them felt her ass.'

What the hell? 'Are you sure?' How could he be so mistaken about anyone?

'Of course I'm sure.' Kev sounded indignant. 'I was there. Hell, the only reason I didn't shoot clips for YouTube was because she'd have called me "Mr O'Malley" in that annoying way of hers, and then set the cops on me.'

'Mick!' roared the trucker. 'Put down that goddamned phone and pick up your pool cue, or forfeit the game.'

'Go fuck yourself,' Jack told him. 'I need to hear this.'

He turned his back on the trucker. Abbie was kissing strange men?

The next moment he was whipped round and pinned against the pool table. A pair of bloodshot eyes stared down at him. 'Did you just tell me to go fuck myself? Do you know who you are talking to?'

'A drunken asshole with beer breath?' said Jack, too pissed off to watch his words.

A growl from two guys standing at the bar was his only warning. He blinked, and was doubled over when a meaty fist slammed into his belly, knocking all the breath out of his lungs.

A second blow to the chin cracked his head back, and

the row of rings on the chunky fingers acted like a knuckle-duster. When Jack shook his head, drops of blood scattered.

He braced himself against the edge of the table and kicked out. His boot connected with the trucker's thigh, knocking him backwards and producing a cry of pain.

'Why you little bastard.' With a roar, the trucker threw himself at Jack. With the pool table at his back, there was no escape and Jack braced himself for three hundred pounds of drunken fury. He landed a punch, which made the other man wheeze, then got pitched over on to the table beneath his opponent.

The pool table, old and battered, couldn't take the strain and collapsed under them. Jack hit the floor first, with the trucker on top of him and splinters of table leg scraping his skin. He twisted out from underneath and scrambled to his feet, but the trucker grabbed his ankle and pulled him off balance.

By the time Jack had sorted out the misunderstanding with the trucker, he was a mass of bruises and under arrest. He used his phone call to ring Kev. 'What the hell do you mean Abbie was kissing other men?'

'What?' Kev sounded baffled. 'Not Abbie. That fruit-cake friend of hers. All Abbie does is hang around indoors and play with her computer.'

Jack sat impatiently waiting for Abbie to log on. He needed to see her, to reassure himself that she was safe and happy. Well, as happy as anyone could be when a powerful bad guy was gunning for her. He was still astonished at her sangfroid when it came to threats to her safety.

She took it all in her stride and complained that he was worrying over nothing.

He cursed when he remembered the faint tremor in her voice when she had told him her apartment had been broken into. If he hadn't been due at a press conference for *Jungle Heat* the next morning, he would have dropped everything to be at her side. He still wanted to blister her backside for not taking better care of herself.

But her disregard for her personal safety was going to end. Abbie had signed and returned the agreement. *She's mine to care for now. And I will, whether she likes it or not.* He was already plotting how he would make sure that his sweet sub stayed safe.

At precisely ten New York time, Abbie logged on.

<Wild orchid: Good evening, Sir.>

Despite his irritation with her disregard for her safety, he couldn't help smiling.

<Michael Delaney: Good evening, Abbie. How are you feeling?>

<Wild orchid: Fine. I'm at Kit's but there's been nothing happening since the break-in. It's all a storm in a teacup. I'll go back home soon.>

<Michael Delaney: No, you won't. Not until I'm convinced it is safe. Where is Kit? I want to talk to her, make sure she is taking precautions.>

<Wild orchid: She's out on a date.>

<Michael Delaney: What? She's supposed to be there looking after you.>

<Wild orchid: Jack, I'm a big girl. I don't need anyone to look after me. Anyway, it's with Kevin, she'll be home in no time.>

Wild orchid is typing.

<Wild orchid: Besides, it means I'm all alone in the apartment.>

<Michael Delaney: Don't think I don't know what you're doing. But as a distraction, that works. Prove it. Switch on the webcam.>

24

Abbie debated disobeying him. It wasn't as if he could do anything about it, since she was in New York and he was in LA. But it might be more fun to tease him. Just to annoy him she took her time about switching on the web-cam. She grinned at him.

His voice, slightly distorted by the poor speakers on her laptop, was still enough to give her chills. That Irish accent was pure sex. Then she listened to his words.

'You failed to provide a lingerie report this morning. You know what that means.'

Sh –. She stopped that word from even crossing her mind. She had enough problems as it was. She wondered what he would do tonight. 'Aw, come on. I had a lot on my mind.'

Yeah, that was going to work. Jack's face was set in that stern 'I am the Dom' expression that always gave her a nervous thrill in the pit of her stomach.

'So did I. Waiting for your report. Wondering if there wasn't one because you weren't wearing any. The thought was giving me a hard-on in the call-back audition. I was doing a scene with Maria Richards and she appreciated it far too much.'

Abbie couldn't help it. She giggled at the idea of the queen of Hollywood getting excited by Jack, while she, Abbie Marshall was the one who had him on her webcam, planning to do something depraved. He didn't disappoint her.

'Come on, you know what you have to do. Take them off and show them to me.'

'Take them off?' she protested. 'Last time I just had to show you while I was wearing them.'

'You didn't learn your lesson, so the penalty increases. Take them off and put them on the desk.'

She couldn't deny the thrill that ran through her at the idea. Her thighs flexed against a tickle of arousal, but she wasn't going to tell him that. 'You're a baaaad man.'

What could she do to stop him getting too cocky? She moved away from the computer and considered. He wanted her panties. Fair enough, she hadn't sent him the report. But she could play him at his own game. She took them off and slipped back in front of the computer. She held them up. Blue lace, he ought to approve of that. 'Happy?'

Of course it wouldn't be that easy. Jack said, 'No, I think you should take off the skirt as well.'

'Are you out of your mind?' She was going to kill him.

'You don't have to show me. The desk will hide everything.' He almost sounded reasonable. 'I just want to know that you are sitting there, naked and available. My imagination will do the rest.'

Unfortunately, her imagination was pretty active too. The thought of sitting there, in front of Jack, bare from the waist down, made her pulse pound. She was surprised by how tempting the idea was.

'If you insist,' she said, trying to sound reluctant. She got up, unzipped the skirt and wriggled out of it, but managed to angle herself when she came back to the desk so that he couldn't see anything. Before he could speak and demand proof, she dropped her black skirt on the desk. 'Satisfied now?'

His laugh was evil. And tempting. 'No, but I'm sure I soon will be. How do you feel sitting there like that?'

She wished he hadn't asked her that. She had been trying to ignore the sensations that were unsettling her, but he had asked a direct question. She had to answer him. 'A little bit cold. And a little bit scared. What if someone comes in and catches me like this? A lot excited. The air is moving around me; it almost feels like someone is blowing on me.'

'On what?'

Oh, he was evil. 'On my pussy.' It was a struggle to get the words out.

Jack smiled at her, an untrustworthy smile that alerted her. 'Hook your feet around the legs of your chair.' She did, and moaned. The position, which sounded so innocent when he said it, spread her legs and left her feeling completely exposed. 'That's it. You can't cross your legs or press your thighs together.'

She tried to close her thighs, and found she couldn't. The position focused all her awareness on how exposed she was. To her embarrassment, she felt a trickle of moisture. Kit would kill her. This was an antique chair.

'Good girl. I'm very pleased with you. Did submitting to my order make you all creamy?'

She swore that his words made everything worse. She had never been so conscious of how wet she was. Reluctantly, she nodded.

He went on, relentless as an avalanche. 'How are your nipples? Are they hard? Open your blouse and see.'

Oh, he was so bad. It didn't help that her breasts were heavy and aching, just dying for some contact. Abbie put her hand up inside her blouse and caressed them, teasing the sensitive nipples into further hardness. But again she angled herself so that Jack wouldn't be able to see what she was doing under her silky blouse.

She grinned at him. 'Nope. This is not doing a thing for me. I'm as calm as a nun. Bored with all this. Getting a bit chilly, even.' Let's see how he reacted to that.

'We'll have to fix that. Go to the freezer and bring back a cup of ice.'

'Ice? Why?'

'Why do you think? Don't sit there hesitating. It's not as if I'm telling you to go and pick some nettles.'

Nettles? For a moment her brain fogged up. What could he possibly want with nettles? Then she remembered skimming over something when she was looking up figging, about a Dom who made a sub put nettles down her panties. No, oh no, that was so not happening. Ice she could handle.

Carefully, she got up, manoeuvring herself so that her bare butt would be out of the shot. Never mind that he had already seen it, spanked it, kissed it, drew pictures on it; she wasn't showing it to him tonight. She used the break away from the computer and Jack's commanding gaze to calm her breathing and slow her pounding pulse.

She hunted around in Kit's freezer until she found the icemaker and scooped a cupful of ice from it. She hurried back to the sitting room and Jack. Why was it that every time she saw him, he took her breath away? Even on the small screen of her laptop, he dominated the room, dominated her. There was no point in trying to hide it.

'Good girl. Now rub one ice cube over your nipples. Just enough to get them hard and tight.'

As if they weren't already. Abbie smiled. 'Yes, Sir.'

She slowly opened the front catch on her bra, cupping her breasts and smoothing her hands over them. She kept up the tease, doing it all out of view. Somehow, she kept her face straight when he leaned forwards, anxious to see more.

She picked up an ice cube and touched herself with it. It was so cold it almost burned the tender skin of her breast. She hissed and took a couple of deep breaths to absorb the sensation. And still she kept the blouse in position so that Jack couldn't see. She was on a roll tonight. She knew she would pay, but the idea of tantalizing him like this was delicious.

'They're very hard now, Sir.'

He would make her pay for this, and she didn't care. A reckless surge of audacity made her want to bait him even more. Maybe it would be enough to bring him back to New York.

It took Jack a moment before he replied and then his voice was rough. 'Very good girl. Now put the ice back, and imagine it's my hands on your breasts.' She was, she was. 'I'm cupping them, feeling the weight of them. So pretty. Pull back that blouse so I can admire them.'

She had intended to torment him for longer, but the vivid blue of his eyes and the roughness of his voice were too much. Her fingers shook when she undid the last buttons.

'Now put your hands back on the keyboard. Don't touch yourself any more. That's my job. Tell me what it feels like to have my hands on your breasts.'

What was he doing? Obediently she put her hands on the keyboard, as if she were about to type. The position immediately made her aware of her exposed breasts. Her arms brushed the side of them, the nipples ached for attention. She shivered, wanting something. Something more.

'Oh, that feels strange,' she murmured.

Jack was continuing. 'Now my hands are sliding down your stomach. So soft. So ticklish. And you can't stop me because your hands are on the keyboard.'

Abbie shifted in her seat and fought the need to cross her legs. Instead she shifted restlessly, swinging her chair from side to side, too aroused and needy to stay still. 'Jack, stop doing that.' She giggled, a nervous sound that had nothing do to with laughter. 'It feels weird.'

'Now I'm thinking about your pretty pussy. So soft and bare and defenceless. And so open and wet. No, don't close your legs. How does it feel?'

She didn't want to tell him. She was glad she didn't have to type, or she would be reduced to gibberish. 'You really are very bad,' she said, and was astonished at how breathless her voice was.

'You're swinging around in your chair a lot, Abbie.' Did he miss anything? He was relentless. 'Have you a problem? Still feel like a nun?'

She fought the urge to laugh hysterically. If any nun

were caught like this, she'd be expelled from the convent. Jack was there waiting for her answer.

'No, I do not have a problem.' She was proud she managed to talk coherently.

'You have to hold still now. I'm sliding a finger down your pretty pussy, and feeling how wet you are. Naughty girl. You like this, don't you? You're panting.'

Abbie wanted to kill him. He was right. She was so wet she was horrified to think of the state of Kit's chair. She'd have to buy her a new one. But right now, all she cared about were the curls of heat in her belly that were destroying her ability to think.

'Good girl. You're doing so well. Stay still like that while I slide my finger inside you.'

She panted, trying to catch her breath, feeling a phantom finger easing her open, moving inside. Her thighs flexed as she fought to contain the feelings pulling her in different directions. And no matter how much she wanted to move, she kept her hands poised over the keyboard.

'So hot and wet.' Jack's praise pushed her arousal up another notch.

'Oh, yes,' she moaned.

'Pick up one of the ice chips, run it down your neck.' At last, a chance to move, to grab control of herself again. The ice chip was shockingly cold, and her breath strangled in her throat. Drops of melted water dripped from her neck and down her shoulder. Jack's voice continued, 'Now hold it flat against your breast, circle your nipple.'

Oh god, it was so cold, she didn't know whether she loved it or hated it.

'Yes, just like that.'

Abbie gasped; her submission heated her up even more.

'Good girl. So good. Now rub over your nipple, while I suck the other one. Feel the contrast of heat and cold.'

Her hands were over her breasts, one hot and shaking, the other holding the melting ice. She shuddered. The contrast was frying her ability to think.

'Get another ice cube, slowly draw it down over your belly. See how pretty the drops of water are on your skin? Now lower, let it just glance off your clit.'

Blindly, she obeyed his instructions. His voice alone pushed her to places she had never been. The cold was shocking, making her jump and squeal. She closed her eyes. She couldn't cope with the sensory overload of Jack's face and voice and the cold of the ice against her overheated skin. She fought for breath, but no matter how aroused she was, she didn't attempt to close her legs.

'Oh yes, sweet Abbie. Just like that. Do that again.'

Abbie cried out, an incoherent cry, not sure if she was begging for him to keep going or stop.

'Now, push the ice cube inside you. All the way. And imagine my hot mouth on your clit, kissing and sucking it. Oh yes, just like that . . .'

The combination of heat and cold overloaded her nerve endings. She had no idea if she was in pain or ecstasy, she just knew that her body was out of her control.

'Yes, oh yes. Jack. I want you.' Wetness, from the melting ice as well as her own arousal, soaked the chair.

Just as she was about to come, Jack said, 'Stop. Take your hands away.'

No, no, no, he couldn't mean that. No, it must be a mistake.

She forced her eyes open and stared at the screen. 'What?'

'Take your hands away. I didn't say you could come.'

'I can't come? But you . . .'

His face was stern. Jack was in full Dom mode. He had issued an order.

For the space of ten breaths, Abbie fought with herself. Finally, she sat upright in her chair, feet together on the floor. She glared at him. 'Do you think this is funny?' She prayed he couldn't see the shaking that still rocked her body. Dom or no Dom, she was going to rip him apart.

A key sounded in the front door. She heard the deadbolt being thrown. Oh god, it was Kit. She couldn't let them find her like this.

She would deal with Jack Winter in the morning. Right now, she needed a cold shower. She grabbed her stuff and ran into her bedroom. As she dumped it on the bed, she realized she didn't have her panties. She had left them on the desk. Sweet god, if Kevin or Kit found them she would never be able to look at either of them again. She crept back towards Kit's living room.

'I just don't know why you have to be so touchy-feely all the time.' She could hear Kevin berating her friend in the hallway. 'You're supposed to be a head doctor, you know, not a masseuse.'

Kit laughed. 'What can I say? That's the type of girl I am. Why? Are you jealous?'

Kevin barked a short laugh. They were still in the hallway and neither of them had noticed her. Abbie inched towards the desk. The blue panties were lying there for anyone to see.

'What if I am? Jealous, I mean.'

Abbie stopped mid-stride. Kevin and Kit? They had to be kidding. Kit had a sassy mouth and she wasn't afraid to use it. Sure, since they met a couple of weeks earlier they sparked off each other, but she had never seen Kit get serious about anyone and she was willing to bet that Kevin was the same. She inched closer to the desk and reached out, clasping the scrap of silk between her fingers. Now, to get out of here before she was spotted.

'Maybe I like it that you're jealous.' Kit's tone was husky.

No. Abbie stood stock-still. This was *so* not her friend. Not her and Kevin. Mesmerized, she stopped to listen. *You will go to hell for this, Marshall.*

'Maybe you should show me just how jealous you are.'

'Maybe I should.'

The sounds of kissing were unmistakable. Abbie heard the rustle of clothing and Kit's low laugh. She crouched down low and fled to her room.

The following morning, Kevin was still there. She didn't have to ask how their date went. Kit smirked at her over the breakfast bar like the cat that got the cream. Although Kevin chatted amiably, his eyes followed every move that Kit made.

They were waiting for her to leave for work before they started round three, or was that four? Abbie gulped down a coffee, made her excuses and left. Everyone was having far too much sex and none of it was going her way. Unless she counted the cyber sessions.

She couldn't believe that Jack had stopped her from coming. Was he trying to torture her libido to death? She had barely thought about sex before Honduras, now she was like a cat on heat.

When she got her hands on him again, there were several things she planned on doing to him. Most of which involved handcuffs, ice and massage oil. Jack was going to pay for turning her into a rabid sex kitten.

She took several deep breaths as the elevator ascended to the twenty-third floor. It was 8.45am, and not a single message from Betsy yet. Had Earth been invaded? Maybe a race of fashion zombies had taken over the world while she was sleeping.

The elevator doors opened. Betsy's assistant was standing there, waiting for her. 'She wants to see you.'

Abbie barely had time to drop her coat over her chair before she hurried to Betsy's office. Did that woman ever sleep? She had been at her desk when Abbie left at seven the previous night.

The door was open. Betsy issued commands while two nondescript men listened attentively. A sheaf of black and white images were spread across the conference table. Betsy perused them like a connoisseur savouring a fine wine. 'I like this one. Go with the shot of them leaving the hotel together. You can't see her face in the car. Good work.'

With a curt nod she dismissed the men. The guys were known in the office as the night shift. Betsy's personal paparazzi. She let them loose each evening on her latest target.

'You wanted to see me?' Abbie asked.

'Don't sit down. I want you to go home and pack.'

'Pack? For what?'

'LA.' Betsy didn't lift her head from the photographs.

Abbie pinched herself.

'Any particular reason?' She tried to sound casual.

'The *African Queen* story is hot. And there are a few other big things coming up that we need you to cover.'

'But don't we have someone there already?' This was beginning to sound a little bit suspect.

Betsy replaced the photograph on her desk and looked at Abbie sternly. 'Josh Martin took me to lunch. He told me about the break-in at your apartment and the other stuff.'

'He had no right to –'

Betsy frowned. 'He had every right to. Why didn't you tell me? Those flowers have started to turn up here too.'

'Oh.' She knew that the deliveries had stopped for a few days. They were obviously back.

'Look, this may just be a crackpot with a flower fetish but I can't take that risk with one of my reporters. You're being transferred to LA. Don't worry, you'll be back by Christmas. Now, go pack.'

She had almost reached the door when Betsy called her. 'And Abbie, I haven't forgotten Jack Winter. Just in case you happen to run into him on the *African Queen* story.'

25

Jack's phone buzzed when he was in the shower after a gruelling workout at the gym. By the time he picked up, it had gone to voicemail. The caller ID said Abbie. Ever since hearing about the break-in and the threats, Jack had been on edge. He needed to be there to protect her.

Still dripping wet and naked, Jack called Abbie back. 'What is it?' he barked, without identifying himself.

'Oh!' She sounded surprised. There was a lot of background noise where she was. 'I thought I would let you know that I'm being sent to Los Angeles to cover the story about *The African Queen*.'

'You're coming here?' Against his will, his dick swelled.

'Well, to LA.' She sounded tentative. 'If that's OK with you?'

Oh yes, that was so OK that the other guys in the changing room were pointing at where his erection tented his towel. He turned his back on them and lowered his voice.

'Does the thought of coming here to me please you?'

'Yes, Sir.'

He had thought he couldn't get any harder. He was wrong.

'Then prove it. Are you still hot from last night?'

There was a pause. She must be in the newsroom with colleagues around her. 'Yes, Sir.' Her voice was a husky thread of sound.

'Good girl. Now go into the ladies', take off your panties and make yourself come. I want to hear it.'

There was a stunned silence for a second. God, he loved producing that reaction in her. 'You mean –'

'Oh yes, I do. Off to the ladies' with you. Now.'

'But there might be other people there.' She wasn't refusing, Jack noticed, just negotiating. And her voice had changed. This was turning her on. His wild orchid might be vanilla, but she had a wild side, wilder than she realized.

'Then you'll just have to be very careful, won't you? Loud enough so that I can hear you, quiet enough so that no one else can.'

'Yes, Sir.' That almost finished Jack. He was stuck in the changing room, still naked, though now a lot hotter. He couldn't find anywhere private to enjoy this phone call. While the sounds coming through the phone changed as Abbie left the newsroom, walked down a corridor and moved into the bathroom, he found himself a small changing cubicle. It wasn't much, but it had a door with a lock. He settled in and flipped the occupied sign.

'I'm here,' she whispered. Her voice had gone thin, breathless.

'Now, take off those panties.' He could hear her put the phone down and the rustle of clothes as she obeyed. He loved that sound. He heard a muffled curse and then she picked the phone up again.

'They're off.'

'Good. Now pull your skirt up.' More rustles. 'Up all the way. To your waist.'

'It'll get wrinkled,' she said.

'So what? It's only an hour until you go home, right? No one expects you to be pristine.'

More rustling.

'It's up around my waist.'

He closed his eyes to savour that image. Abbie standing there with her skirt up around her waist, those long legs made even longer by a pair of fuck-me heels. 'Are your legs bare or are you wearing stockings?' he asked. His voice sounded hoarse even to his own ears.

'Stockings.'

'I approve of that. Now, let your hand caress that pretty pink pussy. Is it still smooth?'

'Yes.'

'Is it wet?'

'Yes.' Abbie's voice was a moan.

'Then off you go. Slide your fingers into that creamy juice. Put the phone down lower so I can hear you.' He wanted to be there, feeling her heat and wetness for himself. He fisted his cock, keeping the movement slow, imagining it was Abbie's hand on him.

Soon it would be. And Abbie's mouth. And Abbie's sweet, wet pussy. He couldn't wait.

'Move your wet fingers around your clit. Does that feel good?'

Another shaky moan was his only answer. A door banged and Abbie gulped. Someone else must have come in. She had been panting and sighing and occasionally muttering disjointed words. Now she was silent.

Jack could hear faint footsteps, a cubicle door closing. There was someone else there with Abbie. 'You stopped,' he told her. 'That was naughty. I didn't give you permission to stop.' She said nothing, remaining stubbornly silent. 'I'll have to do it. I'll feel how your juices are wetting your thighs, and I'll dip my finger in them. Maybe two fingers. I think you're wet enough for two fingers, don't you? I might kneel down in front of you and blow on your clit. I remember you liked that.'

She gasped, unable to keep silent.

Jack grinned. He was turning her on as much as himself. He kept talking, all the time gliding his hand up and down his cock. Abbie was going to pay for this, for arousing him like this.

A flush, a door opening, running water, a dryer. Finally the other door banged again.

'Now, you've got a job to finish, haven't you?'

Her breathing was shaky. 'You're evil.'

'You have no idea.'

She went back to her task with enthusiasm. Jack listened to the sounds she was making, the moans, the way her breathing speeded up. Finally, when she was at the point of no return, he said, 'Stop now.'

'No!' she wailed. 'You can't do this to me again.'

'I wasn't going to. But you disobeyed me and stopped halfway. So I'm stopping you now.'

'Please . . .'

His voice was as hard as his cock. 'No, Abbie. Maybe next time.'

'Next time?'

'Ring me back in an hour's time, and we'll do this again. If you're good, I'll allow you to come.'

Her wail was music to his ears. She slammed the phone shut and he allowed himself to come.

Abbie fastened her seat belt and stared out the window at the Los Angeles skyline. A small flutter of excitement danced low in her abdomen. She would soon be in the same city as Jack. Tonight they would be together again.

Jack was going to be mad at her. She hadn't had time to call him after the bathroom and Betsy had given her an odd look when she saw her flushed face. After that, she had raced to Kit's loft to collect her stuff and then hurried back to her apartment to pack. She had barely made the flight.

Stowed in the overhead compartment were her laptop and her precious notes about the Honduran story. Despite her best efforts, she hadn't been able to contact Tom Breslin. The only information she could get was that he was somewhere in Europe.

The flight landed on time, and soon Abbie had collected her bag and was in a cab to the hotel.

She watched the city avidly as the cab brought her through the streets, enjoying the warmer air and the glimpses of ocean.

Her hotel room was basic. The *New York Independent* didn't believe in spoiling its staff. Abbie unpacked quickly and rang the local office to let her editor know that she had arrived. She hesitated before calling Jack. 'Oh, don't be such a coward, Marshall. What is the worst thing he can do to you?' She pressed the call button.

Jack answered almost straight away. 'Where are you?'

Excitement hummed when she heard him. No 'hello,

Abbie', or 'I missed you'. Just that hint of menace that made her heart flip.

'I've arrived and I'm at the Canterbury. It's on –'

'I know where it is. You're not staying there.'

'But I –'

'No buts, and don't bother to unpack. I'll send a car. You'll be staying at my house.'

Staying with him, sleeping with him in his bed? What would they say at the office? She was supposed to be working on a story. 'Jack, I –'

'Do you have a problem with that, Abbie?'

'No, Sir.' God, she couldn't believe that she had just said that – called him Sir again.

'Good girl. Now, I want you to change into a skirt and heels and wear a pretty top. No bra or panties. Be in the lobby in twenty minutes. And one more thing. You disobeyed me and there will be consequences.' With that he hung up.

Abbie sat down heavily on the bed. She was really going to do this. Everything they had done up to now felt like a game. The phone calls, the cybersex. While they were living on opposite sides of the country, there was safety in geography. Now that she was in his territory, there would be no safety net.

For the first time since she met him, Abbie felt sick with nerves. Jack had a dark side. She had always known that, but what if she didn't enjoy it? What if she disappointed him?

She threw her bag on the bed and removed her clothes from the closet. She had only one skirt, a light silk knee-length one that she had brought to wear on a date with Jack. The top to go with it was strappy and probably too fancy for daytime. It would be obvious to anyone who looked at her that she was wearing nothing underneath it.

She picked up her favourite linen pants and then dropped them into the bag. She wasn't going to disobey another order. Jack would only find a suitably creative way to punish her.

Seventeen minutes later she was waiting in the lobby. The receptionist had given her an odd look when she checked out within an hour of checking in. She would probably bill the company for the room anyway. The air conditioning in the lobby had turned her nipples to peaks and Abbie adjusted her wrap, trying to cover them.

A dark-haired man in a chauffeur's uniform entered the lobby and scanned the guests before his eyes fell on her. 'Ms Marshall?'

'Yes, that's me.'

He bent down and picked up her bag. 'My name is Ben, Ms Marshall. Mr Winter sent me to fetch you. The car is just outside.'

Abbie didn't know why she felt disappointed. It wasn't as if Jack had said that he was coming, but she would have loved for him to be here. She followed Ben across the lobby and out into the sunshine.

Jack had said that he would send a car. She hadn't expected a limo. The car was pure Jack, long and sleek with dark tinted windows that concealed the occupants from prying eyes. Ben put her bag into the trunk and opened the rear door.

'Hello, Abbie.'

So much for playing it cool. She almost stumbled in her haste to climb into the back and touch him. Jack's beauty never failed to astonish her, but the dark intent in his eyes made her shiver. The door closed behind her and the chauffeur climbed into the front seat. Without being told, he closed off the partition, leaving them cocooned and alone.

Jack dragged her across his lap. She sucked in her breath as she found herself dazzled by his strength and the familiar scent of him. She had missed him so much.

There were pictures of Jack everywhere. His face stared at her from every movie theatre, but none of them conveyed the magnetism of his physical presence. Just being near him again made her slightly breathless. Having him train that astonishing intensity on her made her quiver.

Jack pushed her back just enough to create a small gap between them, and stared at her face intently. 'You've given me more sleepless nights in the past week than I had the whole time we were in Honduras, and you're going to pay for it.'

He lowered his mouth and took hers in a slow kiss. The potency of his embrace hit her like a glass of champagne. She squirmed in his arms, trying to touch him, to get closer so she could feel the warmth of his skin beneath the crisp cotton of his shirt.

Jack broke the kiss and buried his face in her neck. 'I missed the smell of you.'

The echo of her own thoughts made her smile. 'Anything else?' Abbie asked, giddy with the delight of being back in his arms.

'Oh, I can think of a couple of things.' Slowly, with anticipation, Jack pushed the thin straps of her top off her shoulders and tugged it down to expose her breasts.

Abbie was torn between her desire to have his hands

on her naked breasts and the feeling of being watched. She glanced at the partition that separated them from the driver. 'But won't he hear us?'

'Probably. So if you're shy, you'd better be quiet.' Jack bent his head to take one plump nipple between his lips.

The heat of his mouth and the flick of his tongue against her tender peak made her cry out.

Jack lifted his head. Amusement danced in his eyes. 'Not so shy then, Ms Marshall?'

He traced a path along her calf with the tips of his fingers, causing her toes to curl. When Abbie clamped her knees shut, he gave her a sharp tap on her thigh. 'Who does this body belong to?'

Abbie couldn't answer him. His hands stroked her lightly from calf to knee and his mouth latched on to her nipple again, giving her delicious slow swirls with his tongue, followed by sharp nips that bordered on painful. Her panting breath was louder than the quiet hum of the finely tuned engine.

Jack slid his hand under her skirt, stroking her inner thigh. 'Are you wet for me?'

She was helpless now. A low moan was all she could manage. Abbie parted her thighs, whimpering when one long finger entered her in a slow pumping stroke.

'Please, Jack.' She barely knew what she was begging for. Everything focused on one tiny, bright point of pleasure. He captured her mouth again in a rough, possessive kiss. Each stroke of his tongue pushed her need higher. She wanted him on top of her, inside her, fucking her hard until she was senseless.

The honk of a car horn startled her. She was sprawled

across Jack's lap in the back seat of a limo, legs spread, breasts bared and he was still fully clothed. Jack took her hand and pressed it against his erection. His eyes were teasing. 'I promised myself that I'd wait until I got you home first. Look what you've done to me. I'm not sure if I'll make it.'

He smoothed her skirt down and fixed the straps of her top in place. 'There, almost presentable, apart from the expression on your face that says what you've been up to.'

'It does not.' Abbie sat up and reached for her purse. The compact mirror told her that Jack was telling the truth. Her mouth was red, and she had bed hair. 'Oh my god, it does.'

She ran her fingers through her hair and reapplied her lipstick while Jack grinned at her. 'Abbie, I'm joking. There's going to be no one at the house except you and me.'

Her fingers shook as she replaced the compact in her purse. Her and Jack Winter, alone for the weekend. Her brain was in meltdown.

Electronic gates swung open and they swept up the drive to Jack's home. Abbie sat up. She was curious to see where he lived. It was small by Hollywood mansion standards. A modern house with clean lines; it probably had a pool around the back. The one thing that struck her was that the grounds were very extensive for the size of the house – large enough to protect him from the long lenses of the paparazzi. Jack valued his privacy. 'Have you lived here long?'

Jack shrugged. 'I bought it five years ago, but I've probably spent less than a year in the place. I've been working a lot.'

'So I noticed.'

She suddenly felt shy with him. They were lovers, cyber friends, but she barely knew the first thing about him. Where he grew up. What he liked to do or to eat. Jack Winter was still a mystery to her. When they talked, it was always about her and about what they were doing.

Jack drew her closer. 'You're thinking again. I can tell. What is it this time?'

She had promised him honesty.

'I know so little about you.'

A shadow crossed his face, then he smiled. 'I plan on changing that this weekend.'

The car stopped outside the front door and Jack helped her out, all old-fashioned courtesy, just as if he hadn't had his hands under her skirt moments before. Jack picked up her bag, leaving Ben to put the car away. 'Looks like it's you and me, Abbie. Let's go inside and I'll show you around. Starting upstairs.'

When Abbie hesitated, Jack winked at her. 'It's just a house tour. I promise to be good.'

She didn't know whether to be disappointed or relieved.

The house was perfect. Each room was beautifully decorated, as if she had stepped into the pages of an interiors magazine. But it was soulless. There were no personal touches, until she came to the master suite. A collection of photographs decorated one wall. 'Your family?' she asked.

'Yes.' But he didn't elaborate, and ushered her through a corridor with walk-in closets on either side and into a giant bathroom.

'Wow,' she said. 'The tub looks as if it could fit six.'

'Eight, at a push.'

When he saw her disapproving expression he burst out laughing. 'That's what the estate agent said, but I haven't tried it.'

Downstairs, she followed him through a state-of-the-art kitchen, study room, gym and media room.

'And what's this one?' she asked. She would never be able to find her way around the place. Jack had a room for everything.

'It's the playroom. Want a tour?' His voice was playful, but she could see a hint of tension in his shoulders.

Abbie swallowed. Did she want a tour? A mixture of excitement and dread pulsated through her. She wanted to know him, to know the real Jack. She stood on tiptoe and brushed her mouth against his. 'Lead the way.'

The room was high and wide, with lots of recessed lighting. There was an electric winch in the ceiling, a couple of oddly shaped chairs, an A-frame with tie points, a St Andrew's cross, two padded benches and a few other things she didn't recognize. Just like at the gym, she thought, where they had terrifying-looking machines that tone your biceps or hamstrings. But she couldn't quite convince herself that she was comfortable with what she saw.

One thing she did recognize was the display of whips on the wall. There was a selection of paddles and straps and crops, which ranged in size from one to four feet long. Her heart flipped. Oh dear god, surely he wouldn't use one of those on her? At the end of the room a gigantic four-poster bed took up almost one entire wall. The wooden posts were marked and scratched. She wondered how many women had been restrained there.

'God, I can read you like a book. The answer is none, so far – the bed is a recent acquisition. It came from the house of a notorious Madam somewhere down south. Her family took to religion and shut up the house. Everything was sold.'

He stroked the wooden posts. 'I've just had it restored, but I wanted the marks left on it as a reminder that where there is pleasure, there is also pain. Speaking of which, I believe you're due a punishment.'

Her tongue felt strange, as if it had forgotten how to form words. 'A punishment?'

Jack crossed the room and considered the selection of whips. He picked up a long crop with a small loop on the end and caressed the leather in his hand. 'A punishment for endangering your personal safety with the Honduran story and a further punishment for disobeying me earlier when you didn't call me back. And it's going to hurt, Abbie. Just like your disobedience hurt me.'

Abbie took two steps back. He couldn't be serious. 'You're going to whip me with that?'

'No. Not this time, Abbie. We'll start with something else.'

Despite the small swell of fear, she felt the first stirrings of excitement. Nothing that they had done so far had made her come as hard as she had done when Jack had spanked her.

'I can see by the size of your pupils that I have your interest. Don't worry, we'll start with something easy. Now, why don't you strip?'

26

Keeping her eyes focused on his face, Abbie pulled off the strappy top. Her breasts sprang free and her nipples pebbled into tight peaks.

'Good girl. Now, step out of the skirt. I want to see you naked.'

Abbie unzipped the skirt and let the silk drop to the floor. She forced herself to stand still while Jack stared at her. His hot, relentless gaze made her tremble.

'Nervous?' he asked.

Abbie licked her lips. They had gone dry. 'You know that I am. I don't know what you're going to do to me.' Her voice shook, and she had to clear her throat to get the words out. What had she let herself in for?

'Oh, I think you do know and you want this, almost as much as I do.'

He was right. Part of her did want it, wanted the extremes – of sensation, of emotion – that only he could drive her to. But another part, a big cowardly part, was terrified of what it would feel like. Maybe they could do it later?

He took her in his arms and her thoughts scattered. Jack cupped her hips, drawing her against the hard ridge straining against his pants. 'See what you do to me. I can barely think straight since I met you. I need to take the edge off before I –'

'Let me.' Her fingers tugged at the button of his trousers and she pulled the zipper down. 'I want to do it.'

He groaned when she slid to her knees. It had been a while. William hadn't been into oral sex so she thought she wasn't either. But at this moment her world was reduced to Jack's cock. She wanted to smell him and lick him and suck him and have him come in her mouth. She caressed him through the dark cotton of his boxers, running her fingers along his thick erection before pulling it free. She took a second to admire its strong thrust before she leaned in and tasted him. Jack groaned again.

His hands tangled in her hair. She wrapped her lips around him and was surprised at how big he was. She opened her mouth a little wider and sucked him deep into her mouth. God, he tasted delicious. A hint of soap and an aroused male.

She rested her hands on his hips and he thrust forwards in a small involuntary movement. 'God, that feels so good.'

She ran her tongue over the tip and was rewarded by another groan. She released him from her mouth and began a slow exploration with her tongue, lapping at him from base to tip. He made a tormented noise.

'I need your mouth, Abbie. Take me in your mouth.'

Abbie obeyed. This time she sucked harder, running her lips and tongue over the sensitive tip, driving him crazy. She could feel his tension as he tried to hold back. 'No, not yet.'

She flicked her tongue again to tease him and he shuddered. For once, Jack wasn't in charge. She gripped the base of his cock and sucked him deeper, savouring his musky taste. He growled with pleasure. His hands fisted in her hair as he drove into her mouth in short strokes. Abbie swirled her tongue lightly around the head again and took him deeper. She could feel his climax gather as she sucked harder.

'Please . . .' Jack was losing control. His thrusts became longer, tipping against the back of her throat. Her gag reflex kicked in and she closed her fingers around the base of his cock to slow his pace.

Jack stroked her hair, caressing it gently. 'Sorry, Abbie, sorry.'

She relaxed and, taking a deep breath, she sucked him deep again. Jack tried to pull back, but she wanted this, wanted him helpless.

He gasped, 'Don't. I . . .'

She loved having him vulnerable like this. In spite of her position kneeling in front of him, she was the one in charge. She opened her eyes and glanced upwards. Jack's eyes were tightly closed. His jaw was tense as he fought for control. She pulled him a fraction of an inch deeper and with a strangled cry, he came in a hot, salty torrent at the back of her throat.

She held on to his hips until he stopped trembling. All she could hear in the room was the sound of his harsh breathing. Jack lifted her in his arms and carried her to the bed, lying back so that she was sprawled on top of him.

Abbie smiled, pleased with herself. That had been astonishing, reducing Jack to pleas and moans. Then she spotted the rack of crops and remembered. This was only a truce. She was in Jack's playroom and she was still due a punishment.

She dropped her head against his chest and listened as the thudding of his heart returned to normal.

'I do believe you have hidden talents, Ms Marshall,' Jack said.

She lifted her head and saw the satisfied expression on his face.

'You think so?'

Jack dropped a light kiss on the tip of her nose. 'Mmmm, but they won't distract me from punishing you.'

Ah, they were back to punishment again. Jack had a collection of whips that would impress a saddlery store. He couldn't possibly think of using them on her. She had to work and her job involved sitting down. On an actual chair, not a pile of cushions. The other reporters would give her hell if they even suspected what she had been up to.

Jack sat up, taking her with him. He led her across the room to what looked like an antique prie-dieu with a red velvet kneeler.

'Another purchase from the Madam's house?'

Jack grinned. 'Why don't you try it out?'

With a little shiver of excitement, Abbie knelt down and leaned over the top. The red velvet cushioned her breasts and she rested her chin on the edge. From a small drawer built into the base, Jack produced two lengths of silken rope and looped them around her wrists, then looped the end around the rope, holding her securely so that she could only move a few inches. He was really going to do this.

'Nervous, Abbie?'

'No,' she said defiantly, trying to sound braver than she felt.

'I can fix that.'

She turned her head, the one thing that could still move, to see Jack picking up a white cloth. He folded it and put it over her eyes. The smell of hemp, strong and exotic, overwhelmed her, masking Jack's distinctive scent.

Abbie wriggled. Without her vision, the world changed. She was deeply aware of Jack's closeness, the sound of his breathing, the touch of his hands. He was still dressed and she felt his shirt all along her back when he leaned over to check her bonds. The velvet of the little bench cushioned her skin.

'Did you have to do that?' She hoped that holding a conversation would make this feel normal, but even her voice had changed. Or had it always been that husky before?

Jack laughed in response. 'Some people like it. They say it increases the anticipation. What's the nasty Dom going to do now? Will he use the crop, the whip or the flail? Or perhaps you'd like to make the acquaintance of a paddle?'

Abbie stayed silent. She had seen the size of the paddle and it looked as if it would really hurt.

'Or maybe you'd just prefer my hand.'

A sharp swat landed on her butt and she squealed. 'Fuck!' She had forgotten how much it stung.

Jack laughed. 'Fuck is not a safe word, you know.'

Three more followed, interspersed with caresses. Abbie squealed each time. The next smacks were harder and she tried not to cry out. Holding her breath, trying to anticipate where each stroke would land.

His hand rested on her inflamed skin. His touch was soothing. 'OK so far?'

'Yes,' she said. She wasn't sure how comfortable she

was being restrained but there was something about surrendering control that was turning her on.

'Good, I'm just getting warmed up.'

Jack's voice sounded further away. Abbie twisted her head round, trying to gauge where he had gone. The dull sound of wood on flesh gave her goosebumps. He had the paddle.

The next blow wasn't as sharp as his hand but the sting was deeper, hotter. She groaned with each blow and gave herself up to them. Her breath came in short gasps as the paddle hit her flesh, striking sparks into her skin. She wriggled, trying to control where the blows landed. Through the pain, the stirrings of arousal bloomed low in her abdomen.

'Like that, do you?' Jack spoke against her ear. She hadn't heard him move. He knelt down behind her, his knees bracketing hers. His heat overwhelmed her and she felt his erection pressing into her hot buttocks. He stroked her hair. 'Good girl, I've got something nice for you next. You'll like this.'

He moved away again and resumed spanking her. Abbie was dizzy. She had lost count of the smacks and was consumed by the ache between her thighs. She wriggled her hips again and was rewarded with a cool hand against her skin.

'Hush, Abbie. Soon, I promise you.'

A row of butterflies landed on her back and Abbie jerked. Well, maybe not quite butterflies. They stung a little, but not as much as the paddle. The soft tips caressed her calves and back, avoiding her inflamed butt. It almost felt relaxing. She must be crazy: she couldn't actually be enjoying this. She was panting and she felt heady, as if her body belonged to someone else.

'Good girl.' She smiled at his praise.

He moved away from her and she heard the rasp of a zipper. The tip of his cock nudged against her aching centre and he drove into her in one slick stroke. Pleasure and pain mingled together and she cried out. She couldn't take much more of this.

On his next thrust she almost lost her mind. 'Please, more, harder.'

She couldn't believe the hoarse voice was hers. Short, hard thrusts pushed him further into her, inflaming her. Each stroke touched something deep inside her. It was like being prodded with an electric goad, so intense she had no control of her body. With one hand in her hair and the other clamped on her hip, he drove her on. She had never felt so restrained, or so free.

Her inner muscles clamped around his pumping shaft. Her world was reduced to the smell of sex and Jack's body overwhelming hers. Abbie cried out again, desperate to come.

'Not yet, Abbie. Not yet. Almost there.' Jack's thrusts became more frantic. She welcomed the pain as it pushed her over the bright edge into ecstasy and shuddering into blessed darkness.

She was aware of his weight pressing on her back. His ragged breath against the damp skin of her neck. Soft, soothing words against her hair. She was his: his best girl, his love.

Jack untied the bindings on her wrists and kissed her hands, before lifting her in his arms and carrying her to the bed. She rested her face against his damp chest and listened to the thudding of his heart.

'You are amazing, Abbie. Fucking amazing.'

She didn't feel very amazing. Every inch of her body sang with ecstasy or pain and she couldn't seem to string two coherent words together. After a while, Jack rolled off the bed and returned with a glass of cool water. He helped her sit up and pressed it against her lips. 'Drink now.' She did, then yawned and closed her eyes.

When she woke, Jack was watching her. He ran his index finger along her jaw. 'You're so beautiful.'

Abbie snorted. 'I know what the mirror tells me, Jack, and beautiful doesn't come into it.'

'Hey, you're natural. There's not a thing false about you. No Botox, no hair extensions.' His hand strayed to cup her breast. 'And these are natural too.'

'There's a little too much of them.'

Jack's face changed, became stern. 'What did I tell you about being self-critical?' He flipped her over on to her stomach and landed half a dozen sharp swats on her abused rear end.

'Ow!' She pushed herself up and glared at him. 'What the hell was that?'

'It's what you can expect any time I hear you running yourself down.'

Abbie's stomach rumbled loudly.

'When was the last time you ate?'

She had almost forgotten that the whole food thing was high up on his list of rules. Abbie tried to be evasive. 'Sometime yesterday. I can't remember.'

Jack frowned. 'What's your favourite food? And please don't tell me salad.'

'Ice cream,' she announced.

'OK, ice cream it is. Wear something warm. We're taking the bike.'

The bike turned out to be a Harley. Abbie eyed it dubiously. She preferred something with four wheels. It looked dangerous. She had to admit, though, that the bike didn't look quite as dangerous as Jack Winter in jeans, a dark T-shirt and a scuffed leather jacket. He was positively edible.

He put on a pair of sunglasses, handed her a helmet and smiled. 'Your chariot awaits.'

Her ass still stung from earlier and she wasn't sure how she would fare on a long bike ride. It had been difficult enough to put her jeans on. She climbed on to the bike behind him. The leather seat cushioned her butt. Maybe this wouldn't be so bad after all. He revved the engine and they took off down the drive and out through the gates on to the street.

Abbie held on to Jack's solid body as he sped along the highway, weaving between the traffic. She hated to admit it, but he was a good driver and it wasn't long before they reached Pasadena.

Abbie followed Jack into a small ice cream parlour. The interior was cool, with pale yellow walls. Jack took off his sunglasses and perused the menu. 'So, what will it be?'

Abbie stared at the list, bewildered by the array of exotic flavours. Blueberry and thyme, spiced strawberry with balsamic vinegar, cucumber sorbet. There were too many choices. 'How about a Guinness ice cream?' she suggested.

'Nah, I've tasted that one already. I always like to try something different.'

'Honey and lavender?'

Jack gave her a dark look. 'I'm not a lavender kind of guy, or hadn't you noticed? Maybe I should take you back to the playroom and refresh your memory.'

Abbie shifted in her seat. 'No, thank you. My ass remembers just fine.'

'I'm glad to hear that. Now, for you, I'd recommend the vanilla bean and brown sugar.'

'Vanilla?' She pulled a face. Despite their earlier encounter, was she still too vanilla for Jack?

He leaned across the table and took her hand. 'Hey, I happen to like vanilla. Maybe we can get some to take out and I can lick it off your breasts.'

Abbie looked around her, hoping that no one had heard him.

He gave her an unabashed smile. 'If you don't want vanilla, how about some Phish Food? You know, sex on the beach? I'd really like to see you naked, rolling around in the surf.' Jack was shameless and he didn't care who was listening.

She flushed, trying to ignore the stares coming from the couple at the next table. 'I think there might be a law against that. Besides, you might have underestimated me. Maybe I'm really into Rocky Road.'

'Rocky Road, huh?' Jack didn't look convinced. 'A lot

of people don't understand Rocky Road. They think it's all about the hard bits, but it's not. The marshmallow plays a very important part.'

'I do? I mean, it does?'

'Sure.' Jack stroked her hand, tracing a path along each finger in turn, kneading gently at the tender skin between each joint. 'When the nuts and the marshmallow get mixed up with the chocolate, they don't know where they're going to end up. They have to trust each other. Rocky Road needs huge dollops of respect, trust and emotion from both sides. But if it works out, well, it can be pretty spectacular.'

In a roundabout way, this was the most personal conversation they had had about their relationship. Abbie had to ask the question that had been plaguing her. 'So, how do you feel about sharing some Rocky Road? With me, I mean.'

Abbie held her breath, waiting for his reply.

'I think I'd like that.' Jack lifted her hand to his mouth and kissed it in a gesture that was somehow more intimate than anything else they had done that day. His gaze was hot, almost predatory, and she shivered, wondering just how rocky the road would become in a relationship with him.

He flashed her a smile, the one that never failed to take her breath away. The waitress came to take their order and Jack ignored her 'don't I know you from somewhere' stare. He ordered two Rocky Roads and they ate them in silence. Even though they were eating the same ice cream, Jack insisted on feeding her some of his. She didn't understand why, but it tasted better off his spoon.

Afterwards, he draped his arm around her shoulders as they walked back to the bike. He gave her a tender kiss before putting her helmet on. When Jack was like this, she felt cherished, as if she were valuable and worthy of protection. His attentiveness was comforting and a little unnerving. She was still uncertain what she had done to earn it or how long it would last.

'Hey, no more sad faces. I have a surprise for you.'

She couldn't wait.

27

Abbie was reading the papers when Jack came into the lounge. He had a grin on his face and was up to something.

'What are you up to? I don't trust you when you look so happy. That angelic smile is misleading.'

His smile widened. 'Angelic? Me?' He swooped down and gave her a quick kiss. 'You must be confused. I'm pure devil. But in this case, I have nothing evil planned. I thought you would like this.' He handed over two tickets.

Abbie read them twice before she believed it. *Romeo and Juliet.* Jack was taking her to a play. She squealed and threw herself at him. 'You're taking me to the theatre? That's fabulous.'

He tightened his arms around her. 'I promised you a date, didn't I? An evening at the theatre should count as a proper date.'

She gave him a severe look. 'You have a lot to make up for, after that performance in the ice cream place. I didn't know where to look.'

'As if I could forget. You blush like an angel when you are embarrassed. Or aroused. Which reminds me . . . have you any marks from yesterday?'

Abbie's face heated up. She had planned to check in the mirror, but when she woke up cuddled against him that morning, Jack had made such sweet love to her that it had brought tears to her eyes. She didn't understand how he could go from being the aggressive Dom who pushed her limits to such a tender lover, but she was addicted to him. Jack Winter had become her obsession. Not that she would ever tell him that.

'No, I'm fine.'

'Show me.'

Her eyes widened. 'What?'

Now he was pure Dom. 'Show me. I want to see for myself.'

Abbie gazed at him, disconcerted, but he wouldn't yield. This wasn't the playroom. This was late afternoon in a lounge that opened out on to his swimming pool; there were other people in the house – the housekeeper, a gardener, Jack's assistant – anyone might pass by. But Jack's gaze was a challenge as well as a command. 'Oh, very well,' she muttered ungraciously. She turned her back to him, flipped up her skirt and revealed a pair of skimpy blue panties.

He moved in close and, ignoring her squawk of protest, pulled them down and ran his hands over her ass. Against her will, her breathing speeded up and she trembled. She couldn't control or hide her reaction to him.

'You're a bit pink, and here.' He pressed a spot at the join between thigh and buttock; the sensation made her hiss. 'You're going to be tender. But I don't think you'll bruise.'

His finger slipped down between her lips and teased her, gliding along the delicate folds and flicking against her clit. She twitched and jumped. God, that man had fingers that should be registered as lethal weapons. She was so exposed but she couldn't move away from those hypnotic fingers. 'Mmm, you're wet for me,' he murmured. She shifted, opening herself more fully to him, begging without words for him to increase the pressure. Until he finished by trailing his damp fingers between her cheeks. That made her jump and squeal in protest. He gave her a light smack on her bottom. 'Go and get dressed. You can't go to the theatre like that.'

She stared at him, incredulous. 'You're going to let me get dressed? Panties and all?'

He pretended to consider. 'Yes, panties and all. Don't want you to be embarrassed if a breeze blows your skirt up.'

'I could wear trousers.' Even now, she couldn't resist teasing him. Bratting, he called it.

'To Shakespeare? I'm shocked at the idea.'

An hour later, she was ready to go, dressed in her favourite silk wrap dress. It was two years old, but comfortable and flattering. She carried a light trench coat – even in LA it got cool in the evening.

'You look gorgeous. I want to do all sorts of decadent things to you,' Jack told her. 'Now, pull your panties down and bend over. I have a gift for you.'

'You're kidding. You're not really going to do more kinky stuff to me, are you?' But she couldn't hide the flicker of interest and anticipation.

'Of course I am. You'd be disappointed if I didn't.' He held something up.

Abbie looked at it with curiosity. It looked like a small blue dildo, less than three inches long and quite thin. 'This isn't too bad.' It didn't look threatening.

'It's not.' He eased her over the back of his overstuffed couch. It was the perfect height for this. She wondered if he had chosen it deliberately. With her head down, she couldn't see what he was doing, but wasn't surprised to feel her panties being tugged down to mid-thigh. She grinned. Jack had a fixation with her ass.

She was sure she would be going to the theatre with a warm backside. But no smacks landed. She twisted round to see what he was doing and saw Jack coating the little dildo with lube.

'What are you –?' Her eyes widened as comprehension hit. 'Oh no, no, you are not doing that.'

His large hand held her in place.

'Too late,' he told her, and pushed it in. The cold of the lube hit her first, then the sensation of something alien sliding into her butt, where she hadn't been expecting anything. She wriggled and squealed but was helpless to prevent him.

'You bastard. You –' She cursed until he put his finger over her lips and clicked his tongue.

'Language.' She glared at him, but let him pull up her panties and help her stand. That small movement made the little dildo shift and move. 'How does that feel?'

'Just the way you think it feels, you sadist.'

Jack raised one eyebrow at her. 'You think this is sadistic? That sounds like a challenge.'

Abbie put up her hands. 'No, no, I'm sure you are only a semi-sadist.'

He laughed. 'Don't worry, it's not very big, you'll get used to it.'

'I doubt it.' But she followed him out to his limo. As

she lowered herself, the little toy shifted inside her and she hissed. He laughed again.

She tried to ignore it as they travelled into LA. They chatted about her work, especially the story she was building on Tom Breslin, but the dildo jerked inside her when the limo braked or turned a sharp corner.

Abbie loved the Ahmanson with its water fountain, huge columns and modern architecture. It was a theatre that could swamp a small play, but this was *Romeo and Juliet*, played with a full cast. They took their place and the lights dimmed. Jack put his hand into his pocket. The little plug in her butt vibrated.

She jumped and squealed. It was the strangest sensation she had ever felt. 'What the hell?' she demanded in a whisper.

He held up a small remote control. 'Didn't I tell you that it was a vibrator?'

She gave him her filthiest look. 'No, you neglected to mention that little fact.'

'Oh well. I've just set it to go off at random intervals, but it's quiet enough that no one else in the theatre will hear.'

Her mouth opened in shock. 'Random intervals? During the play? Oh no, you can't do this to me.'

He put his finger over her lips. 'As long as you're discreet, no one will know what you're doing.'

She gave his finger a sneaky lick, and laughed when he groaned.

The orchestra warmed up, forcing her to stay silent, but she wasn't going to forgive him for this. She was tense, waiting for it to go off again.

The play was a revelation. It was years since she had been at traditional theatre and she had forgotten the power of a live play. Romeo was a little older than ideal for the role, but the actor was so good it didn't matter. By the time the tragedy unfolded, she was sniffing into a tissue, despite the intermittent buzzing of the vibrator. 'That was amazing. I've never seen anything like that.' She stood up. 'Let's go backstage and meet the actors.'

Jack rose more slowly. 'I'm not sure that's a good idea.' There was something strange in his expression, a shadow that scared her. She tried to ignore it.

'I'm a reporter. Right now, I'm working on the Lifestyle section, which means I have to cover this sort of thing. This show deserves a five-star review. And I have to interview Romeo. Come on.'

She headed for the backstage area. Jack followed silently. Her press pass got them through the stage door and as far as Romeo's dressing room. The name 'Kieran O'Dwyer' was on the door.

She knocked and a voice said 'Yes'. She opened the door and stuck her head in. The actor was wiping off his make-up. He grimaced, then looked up, smiled and waved her in. Jack followed her.

Kieran O'Dwyer was tall, blond and aristocratic, a picture of elegant male beauty. He managed to look stylish while leaning against a mirror with half his face covered in make-up remover.

He stood up and bowed over her hand, kissing it with old-fashioned grace. 'My lady, to what do I owe this honour?' She hadn't noticed it on the stage, but he had an accent that sounded just like Jack's.

The butt plug jerked, shocking her. She glared at Jack. What was he playing at? She turned back to the actor. 'Mr O'Dwyer, I'm so pleased to meet you. I'm Abbie Marshall of the *New York Independent.* And this is –'

O'Dwyer took his attention away from her cleavage and looked up. 'Mick. I might have known.'

Abbie looked from one to the other in confusion. Jack pressed the remote control again and she jerked and gasped. She was going to kill him.

Jack leaned back against the door. 'Long time, no see, Kieran.'

The men knew each other. And didn't much like each other: behind the fake smiles the animosity was palpable.

O'Dwyer smiled at Jack. 'It's great to see Hollywood agreeing with you, Mick. You've become quite the urbane man of the world. George Clooney will have to watch his back.'

That was the second time he had called Jack 'Mick'. What was going on? 'Mick?' Abbie looked from one to the other. 'Who –?'

Jack buzzed her again. She frowned but kept command of herself and turned to Kieran. 'Why do you call him Mick? How do you know each other?' She was in full reporter mode, and no annoying little vibrator was going to stop her.

O'Dwyer beamed at her. 'Oh, Mick and I go way back. I knew him when he was plain old Michael Delaney. Long before – but, no, no point dragging up old times, eh Mick?'

Abbie had whipped out her notebook. 'Tell me about meeting Mick, Mr O'Dwyer.' She emphasized the name and ignored him buzzing her again.

Kieran made a dismissive motion with his hands. 'Oh,

no big secret. Mick and I were in college at the same time. We were all so impressed with him, the boy from Fairview who got a Trinity scholarship. Everyone thought he was destined for great things, until fate took a hand. But, sure, didn't he end up here, so all's well that ends well, as the bard himself would say.'

He turned to Jack while Abbie scribbled notes. 'I caught a bit of *Steel Jacket 3* on the plane here. Fair play to you – it's certainly the kind of stuff that gets the punters in and keeps them entertained. Bread and circuses and so forth. Good work.

'But tell me, do you never miss playing decent roles? You know, where it's not all about how you look and you can really get into character.'

Jack spoke through gritted teeth. 'I do get into character, all the time.'

'Of course, you do. Of course. What am I saying?' O'Dwyer sounded condescending, as if he was talking to a child. He turned to Abbie, handed her his card and told her, 'Anything you want, anything at all, just call me. I'm entirely at your service.'

She was examining the cursive script on the gilt-edged card when Jack reached for her arm. 'Come on, Abbie, time to go. You can interview him tomorrow.' He added another quick buzz to reinforce his order.

She scowled at him, but closed her notebook and asked O'Dwyer if he would be available for an interview the next day. She was leaving when O'Dwyer spoke again. 'By the way, Mick, I ran into Sarah recently. You'll be glad to know she eventually recovered from the incident. Your father never got over it, though, did he?'

Jack shoved Abbie out the door, but turned back. 'You fucking bastard, you had to do it, didn't you?'

They were in front of the theatre waiting for Ben to return with the limo when Abbie finally managed to wrench her arm free from his grip. 'Do you mind telling me what that was all about? Why was he calling you Mick? Who is this Sarah? And what was the incident he talked about?'

He set his jaw. 'It's none of your business.'

'It is my business, I'm your –' She stopped abruptly and looked away. She didn't know what she was. She didn't know what to call it, or what she could expect from him. 'I need to know what he was talking about. I need to know about you.'

'You don't need to know about this.' His voice was hard. 'Abbie, leave it.'

'No.' She wouldn't back down. 'As soon as we get back to your house, we will discuss this.' For the first time, she saw a crack in his façade; she could get an insight into the real Jack.

'No, we won't. I think it's best if you stay in a hotel tonight.'

She stared at him, shocked. Finally she found her voice. 'They may have given my room to someone else.'

'Not the Canterbury. I'll get Ben to take you to a decent hotel'

'I don't have anything with me.' She was dazed. What had just happened? One minute he was keen to drive her wild and now he wanted to send her to a hotel.

'Order anything you need from room service. Send me the bill.'

She stared at him, shaken. 'Why? I thought . . . I thought we had something good together.'

'We do. But you can't be with me tonight. You need to go to a hotel and be safe.'

'Safe? What do you mean?'

She thought he wasn't going to answer but when the limo arrived, he did. 'I can't be near you tonight. Otherwise I'll do things to you that you can't handle and that you won't forgive. I'll see you tomorrow when I have more control.'

He bundled her into the car, lifting her legs in and fastening her seat belt for her as if she were a child. She hardly registered him telling Ben to drive her to the Four Seasons.

28

Jack ran until his legs trembled and his lungs burned, but he couldn't outrun the memory of Abbie's wounded look when he closed the limo door on her. That expression would haunt him. It was the hardest thing he had ever done, but it was for her own good. He couldn't be around her tonight.

When he staggered back to the house, he was still full of impotent rage which needed an outlet. He considered looking for a party or event somewhere in LA where he could find a willing and experienced sub, but he knew it would be a waste of time. If she wasn't Abbie, he would just be going through the motions. He headed to his gym and beat the hell out of a punch bag.

The security alert took him by surprise. Someone was at the gate. He had given the staff the night off because he had expected to be with Abbie, so there was no one to answer it. It rang again.

Abbie's nervous face looked back at him through the security camera. 'What are you doing here? Something wrong with the Four Seasons?' He kept his voice non-committal, but his heart pounded. Abbie had come back to him.

'I . . . I want to be with you.' She sounded nervous, but wasn't backing down.

He took a breath. 'Abbie. If you come in, you know

what will happen? Tonight won't be feathers and velvet. It's going to be leather and bruises and hard fucking. If that's not what you want, go away now. Come back tomorrow.'

'Jack.' Her voice shook. 'I want that too.'

He didn't believe her, but he buzzed her in and met her at the door. She was barely in the house before he grabbed her and devoured her mouth in a deep, endless kiss. He wanted to take time to savour the sweetness of her mouth, the softness of her lips, but he couldn't restrain himself. Instead, he held her head while he plunged into her mouth. He pressed her up against the front door, imprinting himself on her soft curves, absorbing her taste and smell into his being.

Abbie responded sweetly, sucking at his tongue in welcome and running her hands up his back. The tips of her nipples were distinct points against his sweat-dampened T-shirt. He looked down.

'Holy fuck! What are you wearing?'

Abbie's trench coat had opened, revealing that underneath it she was naked. Deliciously, sweetly, mind-bogglingly naked.

She blushed deep red but managed a smile. 'This old thing? I've had it for ever.'

Jack laughed. In the middle of a battle where he was losing out to his demons, she had managed to make him laugh. He gave her a quick, tight hug, then stepped back and told her sternly, 'So, you are appropriately dressed for the occasion. That's good, I might go slightly easier on you.' He smiled, a smile he knew was full of menace. 'Or maybe not.'

She shivered, but stood her ground. 'Bring it on.'

He brought her into the playroom, anticipation tightening his muscles and making his cock swell. His hands trembled slightly with eagerness. She turned to him, shaking slightly. Her mouth, swollen and already bruised from his kiss, smiled in nervous welcome. She still wore her trench coat, which was open to reveal a swathe of baby-soft pristine skin. He wanted to mark that skin, brand her as his, to ensure that no other man ever put a hand on her.

The strength of the impulse shocked him. He had thought he didn't do contracts any more, never mind the sort of forever arrangement that she inspired. He took a step back. 'Are you sure?' He forced himself to give her one last chance. 'Go to bed now, we'll talk in the morning.'

He didn't know how he made the offer: his demon was howling at him to seize her, tie her up, fuck her until she couldn't walk. He kept his hands at his side, fists clenched against the urge to grab her. 'Last chance, Abbie.'

She moved in closer, crowding him against the door, and reached up to plant a soft kiss on his mouth. 'I don't know what is going on with you now. I do know that I want to be with you tonight. And I know that you won't hurt me.'

Her unreasoning faith in him triggered a surge of rage and lust he couldn't control. He hauled her up against him, forcing her mouth to yield to him, dominating her with his kiss. She tilted her head back to allow him better access and he took everything she offered and more. He used his tongue mercilessly, as if to show her what he intended to do to her later. She clutched him desperately.

She already knew too much about him. He couldn't

pretend to be civilized any longer. Tonight Abbie was going to see the real Jack Winter.

When he lifted his head, she was panting and her eyes were dazed.

Jack pulled her into the centre of the large room. 'Strip,' he commanded.

She kept her gaze pinned on him while she slowly slid the coat off her shoulders and let it drop to her feet, leaving her standing in only a pair of black heels. There was a hint of rebelliousness in her eyes, but the submissive act was a pure aphrodisiac.

'Give me your hands.' She did, holding them out palm to palm, like a child saying her prayers. Perfect. He grabbed a length of rope and looped it around her wrists, twice, three times, then finished the knot by looping it between her wrists and tying it off. He checked. Perfect tightness. No danger to her circulation, but she would never wriggle free.

'What are you –?' He didn't give her a chance to ask any more. He pulled her hands above her head, hooked them to the winch and raised it until she was forced to stand on tiptoes, with her heels not quite able to reach the floor.

Nervous now, her eyes followed him when he went to the rack where he kept his whips and floggers. He took down a neat flail with twelve strips of leather, and a riding crop. There was apprehension in her eyes but she didn't protest.

'Tonight is different. There are no limits. We're going to do what I want. You chose to come here. You'll take the consequences.' He wasn't acting to scare her. He knew he was going to lose her, and something was driving him to scare her away first.

Abbie's breathing was too fast, her pulse thundered in her neck, but she looked him in the eye. 'I trust you. I know you won't hurt me more than I can bear.'

'Then you're a fool.' Without warning, Jack whisked the flail against her hip, so that the tails curved around her and caught her buttocks. It was a hard, direct strike. He wanted to make her react.

She gasped and jerked, but smiled at him. 'I trust you.'

Damn her. How was she doing this to him? He stood behind her, still dressed in his sweaty gym clothes, and pressed against her naked body. 'How does it feel to be so vulnerable?' He ran his hand down her body slowly. 'So open to whatever I do to you?' He dipped his hand into the warmth between her thighs.

She moaned, helpless to stop him, and her thighs quivered. Her moisture dampened his hand and he couldn't resist milking it. She whimpered and moved her hips back against him.

He stepped away, picked up the flail and flicked it across her ass. She gasped again. The backhand stroke caught her the other way and she jerked in her bonds. He did it again, giving her no quarter, intent on bringing the blood to the surface and turning her skin a rosy red. She panted, trying to catch her breath.

He wouldn't let her. He wanted – no, he needed – to drive her past her comfort zone and out of control. He flicked the flogger up and down her body, listening to the sounds she made when it hit different parts of her flesh.

Abbie's thighs were sensitive, and a stroke there made her wheeze. He did it again, just to hear the sound a second time. Her back could take more punishment than her calves, but alternating hard strokes and soft flicks kept her off balance and drove her crazy.

Then he moved round to the front. When the first blow landed against her stomach, she flinched and protested. 'You can't –'

'Of course I can.' He struck again, this time higher up, closer to her defenceless breasts. He teased her a little by flicking the flogger up and down her body before he flashed it against her breasts.

She gasped, then struggled to catch her breath. Her nipples tightened even more, their points now a bright red lure. He couldn't resist bending down to catch one between his teeth and biting down gently. She made a strangled sound that shot heat to his cock.

God, he wanted to do this to her all night.

'Are you all right?' He had no idea how he managed to ask that. Or what he would do if she said no.

Abbie took a couple of breaths before she answered. 'I think so.'

'Good. Then it's time to make it interesting.'

He went back to flicking the flogger up and down her body, back and front, trying to see what drove her highest, made her give the loudest response.

Without warning, he dropped it and picked up the crop. He flicked it against her once in warning, then struck harder. She wailed and kicked, but didn't ask him to stop. He did it again and watched two dark marks forming on her perfect ass. He needed to mark her. He struck again, lower down, and she screeched. One more time, another yell, and he couldn't resist her any longer.

He tossed down the crop, shoved his pants down his

legs and picked her up. 'Grab the rope,' he told her. Without untying her, he shifted her so that she was in position, then pulled her down on to his cock.

Abbie shrieked as loudly at that as at anything he had done to her earlier, but the cream coating her thighs was proof that she needed this as much as he did. He had no patience and no control and rammed into her hard, again and again. Gripping the rope above her desperately, Abbie rode his cock, frantic for release.

He wanted to draw this out, torment and tease her, but her heat dragged him into her. He felt his juices racing to the head of his cock and couldn't prevent it. He angled her so that her clit was under pressure and lowered one hand to grip her punished ass.

That was all it took. With a wail, she tumbled into orgasm, her internal muscles milking him mercilessly. His back arched as he followed her over and shot jet after jet into her welcoming warmth.

She slumped against him, boneless, and he managed to release her and carry her to the bed before collapsing beside her.

Finally, she stirred. 'That was . . . astonishing. Why have we never done that before?'

Jack propped himself up on one elbow and looked down at her. 'Are you serious? You'll be black and blue tomorrow. You won't be able to sit down to type.'

She gave a half-laugh. 'No one is likely to be looking at my ass, so the colour doesn't bother me.'

'Not everyone takes that attitude.'

'No?' Her smile had a cat-got-the-cream quality that made him smile too.

Jack had planned to torment her all night long, but his demons slept. Abbie was exhausted and so was he. He pulled a cover over both of them and turned out the light.

Abbie tried half-heartedly to tear herself from Jack's embrace. He was still wearing a dressing gown and she was fully clothed. Well, almost. Her ass still stung from the previous night and she couldn't wear any of her panties. Jack had lent her a pair of silk boxer shorts.

He nuzzled her neck again. 'Are you sure that you can't stay and play some more?'

She brushed a kiss against his lips. 'Don't tempt me. I know that it's a temporary assignment, but I can't not turn up on the first day because I've had a booty call.'

'But what a booty call.' Jack nibbled her lower lip while his hand stroked her still-tender flesh. 'Would you like a cushion for the car, Ms Marshall?'

Abbie frowned at him with mock severity. 'No, thank you, Mr Winter.'

'Make sure you're home by five. I'll expect my boxers to be returned by then.'

'Yes, Sir.' She gave him a mock salute and climbed into the car.

Ben dropped her outside the office and she took the elevator to the sixth floor. The receptionist called through to Lifestyle and a short, dark-haired man arrived to greet her a couple of minutes later. 'Hi, I'm Matt Lincoln, glad you could join the team for a while. My office is this way. Good work on the Jack Winter piece. I gotta say, you really hit the ground running.'

'What piece?' Abbie followed Matt into his office. She had arrived less than ten minutes ago. How could she have had time to file a piece about Jack?

He flopped into his chair and picked up the morning edition. 'Well, let's just say that you were instrumental. You interviewed Kieran O'Dwyer and he rang up afterwards to fill in the full story. We gave you a credit on the byline.'

'The full story?' She felt like a parrot but she wasn't sure what had happened.

'O'Dwyer knew all about Winter's past. Or should I say, Michael Delaney's?'

Michael Delaney. Jack's online name; the name Kieran O'Dwyer insisted on using last night. The name that Jack said meant nothing. Matt Lincoln pulled up the story on screen. 'Jack Winter's Secret Shame – Irish Actor in Sex Scandal Cover-Up.'

> Sources close to Mr Winter have confirmed that the Hollywood A-lister left his native country under a cloud more than a dozen years ago, when a scandal involving a sex assault on a college student threatened to put him in prison.
>
> The unnamed woman alleged that Jack Winter had tied her up and whipped her with a riding crop. The charges were withdrawn before the case reached court and Mr Winter left Ireland shortly afterwards.

Abbie felt as if she had been punched. Twelve years ago Jack would still have been in college. There was no way that he would strike anyone unless they were involved in a BDSM relationship. She closed her eyes as a wave of nausea washed over her. Was that why Jack was so paranoid about his privacy? Why he had insisted on a clause in their agreement about not revealing details of their relationship? Safe, sane and consensual was Jack's mantra. He would never become involved with someone who was unwilling. Had the girl in Ireland betrayed him?

Abbie looked at the byline: Matt Lawson and Abbie Marshall. 'I didn't write this.'

'No, but you found it. Good work getting the tip-off. Josh Martin was right, you've got great instincts for a story. We just filled in the gaps. It's just gone to print. We've just been on to his agent, Zeke Bryan, but he's playing dumb.'

Oh dear god. Jack would think that she had written this. She had to speak to him. She grabbed her purse and punched in Jack's cell phone. 'Come on, please answer. Please answer.' It went straight to voicemail.

OK, she would go there, explain to him what had happened. Jack could call the newspaper to confirm how they got the story. It would be OK.

The cab dropped her outside the metal gates and Abbie buzzed the intercom. There was no reply. She pressed the buzzer again and Ben answered. Oh thank god. 'Ben, it's Abbie, please let me in. I need to talk to him.'

'Mr Winter is indisposed, ma'am. He's not available to visitors.'

Abbie tapped impatiently on the metal plate. 'Please, Ben. I'm not visitors. I need to talk to him.'

She heard a reluctant sigh and the low sound of a motor running as the gates opened. Abbie raced up the driveway to the house and found Ben waiting beside the limo, her bag at his feet.

'He says to take you back to the hotel. He doesn't want to see you.'

She could feel the tears pricking behind her eyes. Jack had to see her. She had to explain what happened. 'I can't do that, Ben. Not until I speak to him.'

Ben shrugged. 'I wouldn't recommend it. He's inside, punching the hell out of whatever he can get his hands on.'

'In the gym?'

'No, ma'am. He's already trashed that. The cleaning staff are going to be busy this week.'

Abbie stepped into the hall. The shattered remains of a glass sculpture lay on the black and white tiled floor. The piece was one of a matching pair she had admired when Jack had shown her around the house. She heard a crash and followed the noise. In two hours he had turned from being her playful, tender lover into this fierce creature that the paparazzi liked to see: wild, angry and drunk, pacing around like a hungry lion. The whiskey bottle in his hand was half empty. He picked up a photograph and threw it at the wall as she entered.

Abbie flinched back and stumbled, dropping her jacket and purse with a clatter.

His head shot up when he heard it and his face filled with rage. 'You bitch, Abbie. You lying, deceitful bitch.'

Jack crumpled the printouts he was holding into a ball and threw them with as much force as he could muster. 'It's going to be all over the press, and the TV stations have already picked up the story too. Zeke has been fielding calls non-stop.'

'Jack, I didn't –'

He snarled, 'Don't. Don't lie to me, Abbie. I thought a cheap gossip piece was too sleazy for a news journalist like you to put her name to?'

Abbie winced at the insult. Jack was furious. His eyes were red-rimmed, as if he had been crying. 'Jack, listen to me. I didn't—'

'Jack, listen to me,' he mimicked her cruelly. 'I *did* listen to you, Abbie. I listened to you when you told me you cared about me. Listened to you when you said I could trust you, that you would never betray me. I loved you, for Christ's sake.' He took a deep swig from the open bottle. 'Loved you.'

He dropped the whiskey and lowered his face into his hands. Transfixed, Abbie watched the liquid spill on the pale silk cushions.

His words were like a punch in the gut.

Jack loved her. Had loved her.

He didn't believe her.

He would never trust her again.

Jack raised his head. The blue eyes that had blazed with lust for her were cold and empty.

'Get out of here, Abbie. Just go. I don't think I've ever hated anyone as much as I hate you right now. I never want to see you again.'

Abbie backed away from him. She scooped up the things which had fallen from her purse, shoved them back in, and fled.

29

Ben drove her back to the Four Seasons. She tried calling Zeke Bryan to explain, but his secretary said that he was too busy to take her call. Abbie sat on the edge of the bed and stared at her suitcase. It had arrived at her hotel room only minutes after she had. Jack obviously wanted every trace of her out of his life. There was little point in unpacking it. She couldn't do it. She couldn't stay in LA while Jack was here. To see him, to know that he despised her, was more than she could bear.

With shaking fingers she rang the airport. They could get her on a flight later that evening. After that she rang Josh and left a message that she was taking an indefinite leave of absence, effective immediately. She would take some time out, maybe do a bit of freelancing.

The trust fund that she had ignored for years became as seductive as a chalet in an ice storm. It would soon be Christmas. She couldn't bear the thought of sitting around the table for a big family dinner, pretending that she was happy. She could just imagine Miffy's pitying looks at the Christmas Eve cocktail party and the last thing she needed was to run into William and his mother. No, Christmas in New York was not an option. She would talk to Kit. Maybe they could go someplace together for a few days.

*

The first snowfall of the season started just as the cab pulled up outside her apartment early the next morning. Winter had most definitely arrived. The thought of it made her tearful. Without Jack, her apartment felt empty. Even there she felt his loss. There would be no more chats, no late-night phone calls, no teasing about what colour lingerie she was wearing. There would be no one to nag her about having food in the freezer or knocking her terrible taste in romantic comedies.

There was just her, alone without Jack. She had never felt so lonely. Abbie tossed the suitcase on the couch, sending a cushion tumbling to the floor. A single white feather floated free and drifted in the air before landing on the coffee table. Abbie picked it up and brushed it against her skin. There was no escaping him.

She had far too many memories of a man who had only spent a single night here. The touch of his mouth on hers. His rough hands as he took her, driving her wild with passion. She lay on the bed and dozed for a few hours, exhausted by the trauma of the previous twenty-four hours, but she couldn't sleep properly. She couldn't bear to be alone with her thoughts. Jack had brought her such joy, but all that was left now was torment.

Abbie got up and changed into her jeans and boots. She found a heavy jacket in the cloakroom and shrugged into it. The winter season was just beginning and it would torture her until next spring, just as she wished its namesake would. She pulled the door behind her and set out for Kit's place.

The lights of her friend's loft apartment shone brightly to brighten the gloomy winter day. Abbie tramped up the stairs and rang the buzzer. Inside she could hear music and it wasn't the indie stuff that Kit usually played. Kit must have company – she should have called first.

The muffled sound of laughter came from behind the door as it jerked open. Kevin's jaw dropped when he saw who it was. He was bare-chested, his skin was damp and a towel hung low on his hips. Behind him, Kit asked who was there.

Kit was with Kevin now. How could she have forgotten that? There was no point in talking to her. Jack and Kevin were best friends. She would hear about him all the time: his latest escapades, who he was dating and how much he despised her. Abbie turned and fled.

Pelting sleet struck her face as she walked aimlessly through the shoppers. She could no longer hold back the tears, and so she stopped trying. Abbie walked for miles, ignoring the occasional stare from a passer-by, suppressing the instinct to stomp through the groups of carollers. How was she going to get through months of this?

Back at her apartment, she opened the freezer door. One tub of Rocky Road ice cream and four pre-packed meals for one stared back at her. She slammed the door closed, poured herself a glass of wine and turned on the TV.

Jack's face stared back at her and she turned up the volume. 'In an update on today's big story from Hollywood, it has been revealed that Jack Winter is out of the running for the coveted lead role in the multimillion-dollar remake of *The African Queen*. In a statement issued today by his agent Zeke Bryan, the actor was said to be devastated by the recent reports about a sex scandal . . .'

Abbie switched off the TV; she couldn't listen to it any

more. The role that Jack had craved would go to someone else. Another reason for him to hate her guts. She couldn't forget his face: the hurt, the anger, the vulnerability. Jack had trusted her and thought that she had betrayed him.

He hadn't wanted to listen to her explanation. The bottom line was that Jack Winter trusted no one and without trust there could be no relationship. He told her he never wanted to see her again – that he hated her. There was no coming back from that. Abbie's cell phone vibrated on the table. Four missed calls. Kit's number appeared in the display after each of them. She couldn't face talking to her now. She would call her tomorrow.

Abbie paced the floor of her apartment and stared at the snow falling outside, blanketing the pavements. Across the street, she could see a Christmas tree in an upper-floor window. She hugged her sweater around her. How was she going to get through this?

She rinsed the wine glass and put it on the drainer. She would have to let the cleaning service know that she was back in New York. As she switched off the sitting-room lamp on her way to bed, a winking red light caught her eye. She was sure that she had forwarded her calls. She pressed the button.

'This is a message for Ms Abbie Marshall. Ms Marshall, I'm afraid Mr Tom Breslin will not be available to meet you any time soon. He has been posted to Ireland. If you call again, one of the other staff may be able to assist you with your questions.'

Ireland? Abbie sat down on the arm of the couch. Why had Tom Breslin been posted there? She drummed her fingers against the desk while she thought. Ireland was small – she could track Breslin down there, and it wasn't as if she had a lot to do in New York except be miserable about a man who didn't love her.

Her uncle Martin and aunt Barbara lived in Ireland. She hadn't visited them in years but during their annual visits to New York, Barbara was always urging her to come and stay with them. Barbara was her mom's sister. She had fallen in love with an Irishman too – Abbie wondered if there was something in their genes.

Ireland was the best solution. There was nothing left to keep her here. Mind made up, she punched in the number for the airport. There was a flight to Dublin leaving at 11pm. She booked it and got packing. There was no answer from Martin and Barbara when she called their home so she left a message. If they couldn't have her, she'd stay in a hotel. She could follow the Breslin story; it might help to take her mind off Jack Winter.

The concierge summoned a cab and the ride to the airport was uneventful. At the check-in desk a smiling girl in a blue-green uniform handed her a ticket and wished her a pleasant flight. Abbie blinked back the tears. The accent sounded so much like Jack's that it made her heart ache.

She hadn't thought of that: what would it be like being surrounded by people who all sounded like Jack? But it was too late to change her mind and she allowed herself to be shuffled through security and on to the plane.

The stewardess handed out blankets and pillows to the passengers. Abbie's eyes closed almost as soon as they climbed into the air. There was only one saving grace. She was heading to the only place in the world where she would never run into Jack Winter.

30

Jack had ceased measuring time; it had become meaningless. Now the only thing he counted was bottles. But he stopped counting when the number got high. He didn't care any longer.

Abbie had betrayed him. Every time he remembered that, his gut twisted again and the only way to numb the pain was to drink more. He was vaguely aware that eventually he would run out of whiskey and would have to face her deception. But not yet.

He lifted the bottle to his mouth and took another swig, then flopped back on the couch. He could picture her bending over it as he had inspected her marks after their first session in the playroom, and her astonished response when he pressed the dildo into her ass. He remembered the things he had planned to do to her. He punched the back of the couch. It absorbed his blow, mocking his efforts. He contemplated going to the kitchen and finding a knife to slash it with. Later. When he had finished this bottle and needed another.

He took another mouthful and let it slosh around his mouth before he swallowed it. He scarcely noticed the bite of the spirit any more.

Bitch! How could she have fooled him like that? He was good at spotting bitches. Ask anyone. She must be a new breed of super-bitch, bred in a laboratory to fool him. She could look so innocent and still be a bitch. How did she make her eyes dilate like that when he touched her? Even the memory caused his dick to give an interested twitch. Down boy. We don't do bitches.

He had to stop thinking about her.

OK, think about the bad stuff. Think about how she disobeyed his orders in the jungle and put everyone in danger. How she insisted on dragging around that bloody laptop. How it rubbed her shoulders raw.

No, don't think about her breasts bouncing gently as she walked. Don't think about them swaying when he burned the leeches off her. Don't think about them cuddling into his hands when she finally slept. And definitely don't think about how her ass felt under his hands in that cave.

She's a bitch.

She has an empty fridge because she eats men for breakfast.

She can lie with a pretty tremble of her lips and a flicker of her eyes.

She'll do anything to get a story, even allow a guy to tie her up and crop her and fuck her until she almost passes out.

There's a name for someone like that.

The bottle was empty. Jack tossed it out the patio door, straight into the swimming pool.

Where was his staff? Why was no one cleaning up this shit? Oh yeah, he'd told them all to fuck off. Maybe he should tell them to come back and clean up. And get more booze.

He needed more booze.

When the door opened, he didn't bother checking to see who it was. 'Do you have any more whiskey?' he called.

Kev stomped in and stood in front of him. 'No, you've had enough.'

Jack considered that. He could still remember what a bitch Abbie was. 'No, not yet.'

Kev looked grimmer than Jack had ever seen him. 'What the fuck are you doing? Are you determined to kill yourself?' Kev asked.

'Might as well.' Even as he said it, Jack was appalled at the words.

'You're a fucking eejit. You've spent two weeks hitting the bottle, getting into fights, practically fucking Kym Kardell in front of the paparazzi.' Kev sounded more pissed off than Jack could remember. 'I know how you feel about Kym Kardell. God knows you told me enough.'

'She had cut her hair a bit like Abbie's,' Jack said. 'Needed to see if she was wearing the same sort of bra.'

'Some people don't deserve to live,' Kev announced to the room. 'Kym fucking Kardell?'

'Better than Abbie fucking Marshall.' His voice slurred. Jack blinked. Christ! When had he gotten so drunk?

He peered up at Kev, who seemed to be thinking about something. Then he grabbed Jack by his arm, hauled him off the couch, dragged him through the patio door, outside, and threw him into the swimming pool.

Jack sank down, down, down into the clear water. He considered allowing himself to stay down there. Would Abbie be sorry? Would she come to his funeral? For a few moments, he allowed himself to imagine a huge Hollywood funeral with Abbie crying and blaming herself.

Then his sense of self-preservation kicked in and he pushed off the bottom of the pool and fought his way to the surface. He grabbed the edge of the pool and pushed his sopping hair out of his eyes to glare at Kev.

He had enough time to take a breath before Kev pushed the top of his head and submerged him again. Fuck him. What was he playing at?

Jack struggled against the hand holding him down. Was Kev really trying to drown him? He fought harder, and grabbed Kev's arm. One good yank and Kev was in the pool beside him.

'Are you out of your fucking mind?' he roared.

Kev grinned at him. The bastard had enjoyed doing that. 'Are you sober yet?'

Jack cursed, then stopped. 'Yes, I think I am.'

'Great, then let's get out of this pool. I came a long way to talk to you. The least you can do is offer me a coffee.'

Ten minutes later, sitting in Jack's state-of-the-art kitchen and drinking extra strong coffee, Kev asked, 'So, what's going on?'

Jack had no defences left. 'She betrayed me. I trusted her and she just wanted a story.' He didn't bother to say which 'she' he meant. There was only one woman who mattered.

'Are you sure?' Kev took a sip of his coffee, cursed, and dumped in three spoons of sugar.

'She'd do anything for a story. You saw that.' The memory of how ferociously Abbie had clung on to her laptop because she needed it for her story haunted him. Abbie was a born reporter.

'Did you ask her?'

How could Kev ask that? 'Why? Her name was on the fucking story. Who else could have done it? She's the only one who was there when that poncy little fecker O'Dwyer spilled the beans. And she fucking spent the night with me. Bitch!'

Kev looked at him in disgust. 'O'Dwyer is the sort of little bastard who would have gone to the papers himself. I bet he was jealous that you're a big star and he's not.'

'O'Dwyer is right. He's a real actor.'

The words were harder to say than Jack had expected.

'You're a real actor,' Kev said. 'And people have heard of you. I bet that little fucker is still making minimum wage.'

Jack gave a dry laugh. The wages in theatre were a joke.

'Look, we all got to know Abbie well in the jungle. And you've got to know her a lot better since. Besides, if she spent the night with you, when did she get time to write? I don't believe she would have done this without at least asking for your side of the story.'

Jack stilled, his alcohol-fuzzed brain struggling to pull together what he knew. Abbie had been going mad waiting for a comment from . . . he gave up trying to remember who, but he did remember she wanted a comment from someone before she ran a story. She said it was good journalism.

'She knew I wouldn't give her a comment.'

Kev stirred his coffee again. 'Well, what did she say?'

Jack blinked, trying to remember. She must have admitted it. Hadn't she? But his memory came up blank. 'I don't remember,' he mumbled.

'You're a fucking danger to yourself, do you know that?' Kev wasn't mincing his words. 'You go on a bender without actually finding out what the hell is going on? Jesus, I'm going to dine out on this for years to come.'

'Her name was on it. Abbie Marshall, in black and white.'

Kev shrugged. 'So what? I've seen enough of the media to know that bylines are often about politics, not who wrote the story.'

Jack swallowed. 'Why would they use her name if it wasn't Abbie?'

'How the fuck would I know? I wasn't sleeping with her. All I know is that I'd have asked her before I went on a bender that is making headline news all over the world.'

Mind made up, Jack stood up. 'You're right. I'll ask her now. Is she still in LA?' He reached into his pocket for his phone and was vaguely surprised to find it wasn't there.

'No, and she's not in New York either. She's vanished.'

Jack hadn't expected this. 'What?'

Kev looked grimly satisfied at breaking the news to Jack. 'No one has seen her in over a week. No one knows where she is. Kit's very upset at not hearing from her, and her office says she has taken leave of absence. If her family knows anything, they aren't saying. So, good luck tracking her down.'

31

Sobering up was more painful than Jack had expected, but he didn't spare himself. He had to get sober so he could find out where Abbie was. He put the gym back together, spent agonizing hours working out, and got himself back to normal.

As if he'd ever be normal again, he reflected bitterly. His life was completely fucked-up. He was being reviled in every newspaper and gossip show as a sexual predator. Zeke took a certain pleasure in telling him that he was unemployable: no one would hire him to wait tables. He had also, he discovered, trashed his house pretty thoroughly and it would require tens of thousands of dollars to repair. But none of it mattered when he thought about Abbie.

He was completely fucked-up. He still didn't know if she had betrayed him and sold him out for a newspaper headline.

He did know that he was obsessed with her. He couldn't rest until he had her back under his roof and in his bed. He wanted her naked and trembling and begging him to do whatever he wanted to her. And he would.

Every time he closed his eyes, his dreams filled with her and all the things he would make her do. All the things she would want him to do to her. All the things she would do to him. The way her eyes darkened when she was aroused.

The way her skin flushed when he shocked her. The delicious colour her ass turned when he spanked it. The noises she made when he pushed her out of control. The sassy responses she would zing at him as soon as she got her breath back.

First, he had to find her.

He rang her cell phone, but wasn't surprised when she didn't answer. He guessed he wasn't on her list of favourite people right now. He kept trying but she never picked up.

Next he tried the paper. Like Kev had said, no one there knew where she was, only that she had taken a leave of absence.

Kit was bound to know where she was by now. Abbie told Kit everything. Of course, Kit was bound to hate his guts, but that was too bad. What the hell was Kit's surname?

He called the one person who would know. 'Hey, Kev, do you have a number for Abbie's friend Kit? She might have heard from Abbie.'

Kev sounded breathless, as though he had been interrupted in the middle of a workout. 'Bad timing, bro. And she still doesn't know.'

Jack pushed his hair back off his face – when had it got so long? 'I want to ask her myself.'

'She doesn't know.'

'Just give me her fucking number. I'll ask her myself.'

He heard a scuffle, a muttered curse and then a feminine voice came on the line. 'I don't know where Abbie is, and if I did I wouldn't tell you. You've caused her enough heartache.'

Another brief scuffle and Kev was back. 'She really doesn't know. She's worried. If Abbie contacts us, I'll let you know.'

Us? When had Kev and Kit become 'us'? Jack thanked them and hung up, feeling more desolate than ever.

He wandered around the house, remembering Abbie there. The more he thought about it, the harder it was to believe that she had sold him out. He needed to talk to her.

He didn't know what to do with himself. He picked things up and put them down again. He put his hands on the mantelpiece and leaned on them, trying to figure out what to do with himself. Then he spotted a cell phone. It wasn't his. He picked it up and turned it on. A screensaver of a white feather showed up. It was Abbie's phone. Had she left it behind? He couldn't imagine that. She never went anywhere without it. She had joked that she'd rather lose an arm than her phone.

He scrolled up and down through the contacts list. It was impressive. Private numbers for the White House and international movers and shakers, just about every senator and congressman in the country, most of the big-city mayors, all the political names that counted, and quite a few of the criminal ones too.

This was her business phone. It must have fallen out of her bag when she dropped it. Now he had the means to find her. He started dialling.

After the seventh call Jack wanted to hit something. Or someone. Possibly that ultra-annoying sister of Abbie's. How could two women who were so unalike be related? The bitch knew where Abbie was and wouldn't tell him.

He remembered the break-in at her apartment, the

push into traffic. Someone didn't like Abbie. His bones ached with the need to protect her.

There was one person in her personal contacts list he kept avoiding. He'd rather lose his left nut, but it was time to man up.

'Hey, William. It's Jack Winter here. I need to ask you something.'

The voice on the other end of the line was as annoying as he remembered. 'How did you get this number?' he asked, as if Jack were something he'd picked up on his shoe.

With a supreme effort of will, Jack restrained himself. If the dweeb knew where Abbie was, he would be polite. He asked him if he knew Abbie's whereabouts.

William sniffed. 'Why would I tell you anything? You have done nothing but drag Abbie's name through the mud.'

'Hey, she was the one who hitched a ride on my plane. I didn't ask her.'

William's voice got even more pinched. 'She wouldn't behave like that. Abbie wouldn't disgrace her family in any way.'

'Oh yeah?' Jack found it next to impossible to let this twerp talk about Abbie. 'You don't know her as well as you think.'

'You are a bad influence on her. She never behaved like this until you came along.'

'There's a lot of things she never did until she met me.'

Memories of Abbie begging him to punish her harder rushed through his mind. And then he thought of her with her legs splayed, her pussy open and glossy and pleading with him to make her come. He couldn't believe he'd never smell her or taste her or fuck her again. Or that any other man would. And the thought of this guy sleeping with Abbie, putting his hands on her, putting his – No, he couldn't go any further with that thought or he'd commit violence.

William spluttered. 'No wonder she ran away from you.'

Jack winced. It was true.

'At least she's too far away for you to find her now.' There was a wealth of satisfaction in William's voice.

Wait. The twerp knew where she was?

'Where is she?'

'I have no intention of telling you.'

He did know. Jack straightened up. 'Where is she?' he repeated, his voice edged with a subtle threat.

William laughed. 'She's better off without you.' He was gloating.

Oh fuck. He was going to have to do this. Jack shoved his hand through his hair and braced himself. 'Please, I'm begging you. Tell me where she is.'

The bastard laughed again. 'Not so much fun now, is it? How does it feel to know there are some things your Hollywood charm can't buy?'

'It's not fun,' Jack said. 'Where is Abbie?'

'What do you care? You've made her a byword for scandal, ruined her marriage prospects and upset her family. She's better off without you.'

It was true, and hearing it cut like a scalpel. Jack winced. 'At least tell me that she is well, and safe. There are some bad people after her.'

'She's fine. I always knew that job of hers was dangerous. But unless those bad men of yours are leprechauns, they won't bother Abbie.' William hung up on him.

Jack stared at the blank phone. Leprechauns? There was only one place in the world with leprechauns. Abbie was in Ireland.

Abbie pulled back the curtains and stared at the snowy landscape. As far as her eyes could see, the rolling countryside was white with snow and frost. Martin said that this was the first white Christmas the country had seen for years, and she had to land right in the middle of it.

Two weeks of snow. Two weeks in which she had barely stepped outside the house. Two weeks in which she hadn't stopped thinking about Jack. Her aunt had known what was wrong with her straight away. Barbara was so much like Abbie's dead mother that it was scary. That same intuitive instinct for how another person was feeling. She had taken one look at her woebegone expression in the lobby of the Shelbourne Hotel and said, 'Broken heart, is it? Poor pet.'

Abbie had burst into tears then and had barely stopped crying since. Delayed reaction, Martin had called it. Barbara had called him a big eejit. The expression reminded her so much of Jack and Kevin that she had cried even harder. She barely remembered the drive to Meath. She had no idea where Meath was except that it had taken two boxes of Kleenex to get there.

Now it was Christmas morning and she couldn't hide out in her room any longer. She had promised Barbara that she would come downstairs and help cook the huge Christmas dinner. The housekeeper had left everything prepared and Barbara had been up for hours cooking a giant turkey. Abbie felt bad that she had no present to give anyone except a bottle of champagne she had bought in duty free. She dressed quickly and headed downstairs to brew some strong coffee.

Two staghounds waited in the hallway, hoping that someone would take them for a run. They were so tall that Miffy's twins could have easily ridden on their backs. The dogs were called Doheny and Nesbitt and, despite their size, they had the run of the ground floor of the house, except for the kitchen. Barbara gave Martin an arch look every time they misbehaved. Apparently there was a long, involved story about Martin bringing home two small puppies to help a friend. Barbara hinted that there had been drink involved in the transaction. Martin never bothered to deny it.

Her aunt and uncle's easy companionship caused Abbie the occasional pang of jealousy. Barbara had evolved with ease from spoilt New York society princess to owner/manager of a working stud farm. She obviously adored the quiet Irishman she had been married to for more than thirty years.

Martin emerged from the small parlour at the front of the house. 'D'ya fancy a walk, before all the hoo-ha starts? Only I have to give the wee boys a run before the dinner.'

Abbie grinned at the understatement. There was nothing wee about the dogs. Barbara had spent hours decorating the table for her guests and Martin hated fuss of any kind. She would welcome a walk, so she borrowed a waxed jacket from the cloakroom and followed him outside.

The dogs raced around, barking with delight. Abbie

tramped after them through the crisp white snow. It was beautiful here. There was something still and peaceful about the Irish countryside. She wondered how Jack had ever left this place.

Martin surprised her. 'You're thinking about him.'

Abbie gave a wry laugh. 'What gave the game away?'

Martin laughed. 'I had the same miserable expression on my face for weeks after I left Barbara in New York.'

'So, what did you do?'

'Well now, I decided that I had to get her, or forget her. The problem was that I couldn't forget her.'

'So, you got her?' Abbie laughed.

'Aye, but it helped that she was miserable as well.' They tramped across the paddock towards a small copse of trees. 'Is he miserable too, Abbie?'

She shrugged. 'Jack? I've no idea. He hasn't been in contact.' She had attempted to call him a couple of times. He hadn't answered his phone and she hadn't left a message.

Martin whistled for the dogs. 'Well, maybe you should find out. Can you ring him?'

What would it cost her? Maybe she would phone Kevin and find out if Jack was still mad at her. Jack was five thousand miles away. She could just hang up if he sounded angry. At least she would know, one way or another.

'So, are you going to ring the lad or what?'

Abbie sniggered. She could hardly imagine Jack as a lad, but Martin was right. If she was trying to put Jack Winter behind her, she had to know for certain that they had no future. Her stomach flipped at the thought of it. *Oh, come off it, Abbie. He's already told you that he loved you and that he hated you. What more can the guy say?*

Decision made, Abbie quickened her pace to catch up with Martin and the dogs. It was Christmas day. The season of goodwill to all men, including Hollywood superstars. She could do this. She'd call Kit and then Jack.

Christmas lunch was much like Thanksgiving at home. The same gigantic turkey and a big crowd around the table with lots of teasing and toasting. Suddenly Abbie missed her family. She glanced at her watch. It was noon in New York. A decent time to call Miffy and her dad. Her cell didn't work in Ireland but Barbara said she could use the phone in the study.

Abbie punched in the number and listened to the phone buzzing at the other end of the line. Miffy answered. 'Abbie Marshall, why on earth has it taken you two weeks to call?'

Abbie held the phone away from her ear as her sister ranted without pausing for breath. How worried they were. How haggard their dad looked. How the girls wondered why their Auntie Abbie wasn't around to take them ice-skating. How she missed their annual outing to Bergdorfs. *That was one thing I didn't miss*, Abbie thought as Miffy went on and on.

She had asked Barbara and Martin not to say that she was staying with them, but she hadn't known that they would take her so literally and tell Miffy they didn't know where she was in Ireland. 'It's OK, Sis. I'm with Barbara and Martin.'

'She's with Barbara and Martin.' She could hear Miffy repeating the news to whoever had come into the room. For crying out loud, this was supposed to be a casual 'happy Christmas' phone call, not the Spanish Inquisition.

'Sis, I'm OK.'

'OK?' Miffy's voice got louder. 'It's not OK to disappear like that. We were worried. It was embarrassing having the police inform us that you had flown to Ireland and there was nothing more they could do.'

Abbie sucked in a breath. She couldn't believe that they had involved the police. All she had intended to do was lie low for a while.

Miffy was still talking: '. . . And I invited William for Christmas dinner just so you could make up with him, and you don't bother showing up, leaving the poor man without a partner. Really, Abbie, what sort of manners do you have?'

Ah, this was familiar territory. When Miffy moved on to manners Abbie knew her sister was winding up her statement against the accused. Defending her so-called bad manners she could deal with.

'Hold on.' Abbie finally managed to break into Miffy's rant. 'I never said I was coming for Christmas. If you invited William, that was your doing, not mine.' It felt good to stand up for herself.

Miffy continued. 'You do realize that everyone's been calling here looking for you? That friend of yours with the strange hair has been very annoying. Josh Martin from the newspaper called asking where to send your cheque. And that dreadful Jack Winter was horribly rude yesterday –'

'Jack called?'

Abbie wanted to dance around the study. Jack had called. He missed her. He wanted to see her. Her euphoria quickly turned to bitterness. Yes, he called two weeks after he dumped her.

Miffy sniffed. 'Really, Abbie, whatever is going on with him, you have to stop it. He's in the middle of the most hideous scandal.'

She tried to sound casual. 'Did he say what he wanted?'

'He said he had your phone and wanted to know where you were. He was extremely rude.'

With a sinking heart, Abbie realized where she had lost her work phone. It was in Jack's place. He was probably trying to return it to her, nothing more than that. 'Thanks, Miffy, put Dad on.'

Abbie listened as the girls squabbled over the phone to tell her about this year's Christmas extravaganza. Miffy tackled Christmas like a military campaign. She had a 'list' at several stores so that there could be no Christmas faux pas. The holiday season would proceed in an orderly fashion in the Marshall-Baker household. Abbie was glad to have missed it.

Eventually, her father came on the line. 'Hi, Abbie, how is Ireland?'

'Snowy, would you believe? They have a white Christmas here for the first time in twenty years. I'm fine, Dad, just fine. I'm following a story. Well, I will be when Christmas is over. I'll be in touch soon.'

There was no more mention of Jack.

32

Abbie replaced the receiver in the cradle and slumped into the battered leather chair. Doheny – or was it Nesbitt? – pushed into the room. His nails clicked loudly on the wooden floor. He cocked his head to one side and stared at her.

'Another walk, huh?'

He wagged his tail in response.

At the back of the house, she could hear the sound of music starting up. Martin had promised dancing but she couldn't face it. Maybe she could slip out while they were busy. She grabbed a coat and scarf from under the stairs and pulled on one of Barbara's hats. The second dog appeared when she reached the front door. 'OK, guys, let's go.'

Abbie followed the barking dogs across the paddock. The sky was clear and filled with stars. In New York she rarely got to see the night sky because of the light pollution but here it was a wonder and she stared until the stars began to blur. What was Jack doing tonight? Was he partying with some starlet who had eyelashes longer than her skirt? Maybe he was at an exclusive A-list party.

The thought of him being with someone else made her heart ache. She blinked at the stars. 'OK, Abbie, it's time to stop crying about Jack Winter. It's over.'

There, she had said it. She was over Jack Winter. Well, maybe not over, but moving on. She would go back to the house and call Kit, and in the New Year she would resume work on the Breslin story. Abbie whistled for the dogs. 'Come on, guys, we're going home.'

Back in the house, the dancing was in full swing and had moved from the kitchen to the hallway. A few more cars had arrived since her departure. Barbara and Martin's place was obviously party central on Christmas night.

In the time it took her to get to the study, Abbie had fended off two invitations to dance and an offer of a glass of whiskey. The Irish were a friendly lot who didn't take no for an answer. Despite herself, she laughed and promised to come back after she had called Kit.

The phone rang steadily but no one picked up. Maybe Kit was out. Abbie was just about to hang up when she heard her voice. 'This better be good.'

'Kit, it's –'

'Oh my god, Abbie. Is that you? Where the hell are you?'

Abbie could hear a male voice in the background and Kit telling him to be quiet. 'I'm in Ireland.'

'Ireland? What are you doing there? I've been worried sick about you. Why didn't you call me?'

Abbie twisted the cable on the phone. She had meant to call Kit dozens of times, but she couldn't face talking about Jack. 'Sorry, my cell phone doesn't work here and, well, I guess I wasn't ready to talk to anyone.'

'How are you feeling now?' Kit lowered her voice. 'You know that he's been looking for you?'

Abbie sighed. 'I heard. Miffy told me.'

'Are you going to call him?'

There was no going back to him. Jack didn't trust her. After the initial flood of joy at hearing that Jack had been looking for her, she realized nothing had changed. He didn't trust anyone. He had set the rules of their relationship from the beginning, and expected her to blindly follow them. It wasn't enough for her any longer.

'No, I'm not going to call him. It's over.'

'I see.' Kit was using her therapist's voice.

Abbie wasn't in the mood for being the client. 'So, any news? How is New York? Did Santa Claus bring you anything nice?'

She heard Kit laugh. 'Nice distraction, but I will get the full story from you. As a matter of fact, Santa did bring me something nice. A cute Irish guy with a diamond ring.'

Abbie almost fell off her chair. Kit and Kevin. Engaged. 'You're getting married?'

'No, I happened to admire the ring and the idiot bought it for me. How can I possibly marry a man I've known for less than two months?'

Abbie giggled. If anyone was going to marry a man she had known less than two months, it would be Kit. 'So, you're not going to accept him?'

'I didn't say that either. I'm considering my options.'

Abbie could hear the sound of kissing and then Kit's low laugh. Kevin was there with her and they sounded happy. 'I'll leave you to your options, then. Call you soon. Night, Kit. Happy Christmas.'

Barbara tapped on the door and appeared carrying two glasses of champagne. 'If you won't come to the party, the party will have to come to you.'

She took one gratefully and took a sip. 'Sorry, Barbara, I was just calling home.'

'That's OK, but you've spent far too much time on your own these past two weeks. Besides, I've a nice man that I want you to meet.'

Abbie pulled a face. 'I'm not in the market for a man. They're too much trouble.'

'This one won't be, I promise. He's talking to Martin about horses. You probably know him already. It's Chris Warrington.'

Abbie's head shot up. 'American ambassador, Chris Warrington?'

'The very one.' Barbara left the room with a smug smile on her face.

Abbie raced upstairs and riffled through her wardrobe. Lots of jeans and business skirts, but at the back was the dress she had worn to the theatre with Jack. She ran her hands over the silky fabric. It held painful memories, but it was the only dress she had with her.

Abbie put on some make-up and hurried downstairs. If she wanted to find an American citizen who had recently moved to Ireland, Chris Warrington was the man who could open the way for her.

She was aware of a few admiring glances from some of the partygoers. It was amazing what a flirty dress and a pair of heels could do. Abbie made a beeline for Martin and the ambassador.

'Chris, I'd like you to meet my niece, Abbie. Abbie, this is Chris Warrington.'

'Ambassador.' Abbie smiled and offered her hand.

A pair of blue eyes twinkled at her from beneath a

shock of white hair. Chris Warrington was on his second posting to Ireland and had a reputation as an astute politician and a decent man. 'It's first names only while I'm here. Martin and I go way back.'

'Aye, I sold him a nice little filly about eight years ago.'

'And made a nice profit too.' Both men laughed.

Abbie decided to strike while the iron was hot. 'I was wondering if you might be able to help me. I'm doing a follow-up on a story about Honduras, but the official in the State Department who was helping me has just been transferred here. I was in a plane crash and lost a lot of my notes.'

'I heard about that.' He suddenly sounded interested. 'Weren't you with that actor, what's his name, Winter?'

Beside her, Abbie watched as Martin stopped pouring a glass of whiskey. *OK, you can do this, Marshall. It's not going to be the only time that someone mentions his name.* She put on her brightest smile. 'That's right. Jack Winter.'

The ambassador winked at her. 'That's the one. My teenage daughter is crazy about him. Any chance you could get me an autograph?'

Abbie's smile froze. She would rather chew her own toenails than ask Jack for anything. 'I'll see what I can do.'

'Now, who was the man you wanted to contact?'

'His name is Breslin. Tom Breslin,' she offered.

'Ah, Tom. Good guy, he's only been with us for a couple of weeks. Big into the horses too, I understand.'

Martin rubbed his hands together. 'Bring him along to the hunt ball, then. I could do with another bit of business.'

'Only if we split the commission.' The ambassador laughed. 'Do you want me to give Tom a message?'

And warn him in advance? Not a chance. The ball would be a perfect opportunity to find out just what Breslin's involvement in Honduras was.

'No, let it be a surprise.'

Someone tapped her on the shoulder and she turned. It was Barbara. 'There's a phone call for you in the study. It's from America.'

Abbie left the party behind and hurried to the study. It had to be Miffy or Kit. Maybe the girls had opened their gifts and wanted to say thanks. 'Hello?'

'Hello, Abbie.'

She closed her eyes. Jack. Almost a full minute of silence passed while she tried to stop the words from spewing from her mouth. How hurt she was that he had believed she had betrayed her. How angry she was that he had tracked her down. How much she had missed him. Instead, she steeled her voice to be as curt and professional as possible. 'How do you do, Mr Winter?'

'We're back to that again, huh? You weren't so formal in LA.'

Her head flooded with the memories. Jack's mouth kissing her, Jack's arms holding her, Jack's hands as he . . . No, she wasn't going to think about that. 'I remember a lot of things about LA. Not all of them were pleasant.'

Jack laughed, a low earthy tone that sent a shiver down her spine. 'That's my girl. Still sassy.'

'I am not your girl.'

'Oh baby, you'll always be my girl.' His tone was silky with menace and she shivered. He had used that same tone when he told her in explicit detail what he was going to do to her.

It excited her now as much as it did then. There was no way that she was giving in to this again. 'Save the theatrics for the silver screen, Mr Winter. Don't you have a party to attend? Some sweet little starlet who's begging for your attentions?' God knew how many women Jack had invited to his playroom since she left. 'Don't let me keep you.'

She half expected him to hang up, to respond with a sarcastic one-liner as only Jack could. Instead he laughed.

'Did I say something funny?' She found it hard to keep the edge out of her voice.

'No, you said exactly what I wanted to hear. The best Christmas present ever. You still want me.'

'I do not –'

'Yes, you do, and you're jealous as hell that I might have played with someone else. The truth is I haven't been near a woman since you left.'

Abbie gave a disbelieving snort. 'Thanks for the update, but I'm no longer interested. Now, if you'll excuse me, I do have a party to go to.'

'Abbie.' His voice had an edge to it now.

If she was in LA that tone would signal a punishment. Against her will, her nipples hardened. It was infuriating: five thousand miles away and he could still arouse her. She had to finish this. 'Thanks for scratching my itch, Mr Winter, but I'm not interested in playing and –'

'Abbie, get out of that sulky mood you're in or there will be consequences.'

With that he hung up. Abbie sat down on the arm of the chair. Nesbitt crossed the room and put his head on her lap. She scratched behind his ears. What did he mean, consequences? How could there be consequences? He was thousands of miles away.

Dublin looked different. Even the airport wasn't the way he remembered. When he left Ireland twelve years earlier, there had been one terminal. Now there were two, and the maze of roads leading to car parks, bus stops and drop-off points was like doing a jigsaw in the dark.

He had only brought hand luggage. It wasn't as if he planned to stay in Ireland for one minute longer than it took to find Abbie and drag her back to America with him. This time, she wasn't getting away. He had plans for sweet Abbie. On the journey from LA to Dublin, he had time to imagine what he was going to do to her when he got her back in his bed.

Anything to avoid thinking about what else he faced in Ireland. His family. What would Ciara look like now? She had emailed photos over the years, her engagement, wedding, pregnancy, the birth of her baby, but it wasn't the same as seeing her in the flesh. She had chatted on Skype but refused to turn the webcam on, claiming she'd crack the screen. There had been fewer pictures of his mother, and fewer still of his father. The old man's face was always the same: stern and unforgiving.

Jack didn't want forgiveness. He had done nothing wrong. It was his father who had turned his back, not him.

'Michael! Michael! Over here!' He didn't register the name – it was so long since anyone had called him that – but the screaming woman in the bright-red snow jacket was impossible to ignore.

‘Ciara? What are you doing here?’ Even as he spoke, he couldn’t resist sweeping her up into a rib-cracking embrace. She hugged him back with equal fervour. Even her smell was familiar, and something inside him eased at her welcome.

‘You thick eejit, I came to welcome you home.’ Finally she stepped back and looked him up and down. ‘You’ve lost weight. You’re thinner.’

Perhaps it was true, but he shrugged it off. ‘The camera makes you look fatter than you are, that’s all.’

Ciara gave him a salacious grin. ‘Still, if you weren’t my brother I’d say you were a fine-looking thing – not bad, not bad at all.’

He checked out the arrivals hall to see if he had been recognized. A few people were looking at him and nudging each other, but no one approached or asked for his autograph. His newfound fame as a sexual predator had obviously proceeded him.

‘Why didn’t you tell me you were coming?’ Ciara demanded as she led the way out of the airport. ‘I only found out when I rang up and that trainer fella told me.’ She put money into a machine to get her ticket stamped and led him out into the slush-covered car park.

At least Ciara was dressed for the weather, in a snow coat and heavy boots. Jack’s Converse trainers were already soggy and his leather jacket was not doing a thing to keep him warm. He had forgotten the weather in Ireland. Ciara stopped beside a scruffy Civic and motioned Jack into the front passenger seat.

‘So, is it Michael or Jack now that you’re here?’ she asked as she put the car into gear and pulled out carefully.

'It's Jack. Michael ceased to exist the minute I left Ireland.' Everything felt strange. He was on the wrong side, the car was far too small for a man of his height and Ciara had grown up.

She snorted. 'Try telling Dad that.'

He couldn't help it. 'Does he ever talk about me?'

'Not much. But he watches every film you're in, and reads all the letters you send to Mam.'

Jack didn't know what to say to that. He had never forgotten the night his father had thrown him out.

They fell into silence as Ciara gave all her attention to negotiating the slushy roads. They crawled along. He was glad of the chance to get his head around the fact that he was actually back in Dublin. Finally, they got to a stretch where the traffic was flowing. Ciara gave him a sideways glance before saying, 'So, what did happen back then, Jack? I remember all the fuss, but no one would tell me any details.'

'You were too young.'

She stopped at a set of traffic lights on to the main road and looked right at him. 'Well, I'm not young and innocent any more, so spill. Or I'll assume the worst. And you have no idea how vivid my imagination is.'

'It was nothing. Or it should have been nothing. Do you remember Sarah who was one of my gang in college?'

'I used to slag her about her D4 accent, but I thought she was all right.'

Jack gave a reluctant laugh. 'Me too. But we had a lot in common.' He couldn't tell Ciara just how much they had in common. Ciara might be an adult now, but she was still his little sister.

'Anyway, we had been at the Horse Show. She bought a riding crop in the Exhibition Hall and that night we played with it.'

Ciara surprised him with a dirty laugh. 'I'll bet you did.' So, his little sister wasn't so innocent any more.

'We were a bit surprised at how strong the marks were, but she liked it. Then her mother took her to Brown Thomas to buy a dress for the Horse Show ball. She saw them and raised hell. And Sarah was too scared of her mother, and of what everyone would think, to tell her that it was consensual. She made out that I had lost it and attacked her.' Jack shrugged, trying to sound casual. 'I was arrested and charged with assault, and locked up in the Bridewell.'

Ciara winced. 'I didn't know about that. Are you still claustrophobic?'

He grimaced. 'A bit. I hate small planes or confined spaces.' That was an understatement.

'Dad pulled a few strings and got me out and he went and spoke to her parents and the charges were dropped.'

'If he did that, why did you fall out? Why haven't you talked in twelve years?'

'He never asked me what happened. Just assumed I had beaten her, and told me to get out of his sight.' All these years later, the hurt of that was still fresh.

'Give him a break. A cop – a sergeant, at that – whose son was arrested for kinky stuff? Of course he wouldn't react well. Talk to him. He'll forgive you.'

The idea made Jack's fists clench. 'I didn't do anything that needs forgiving. He assumed the worst.' He took a breath. 'Anyway, I won't have time to talk to him. I'm only here for a day or two, until I can pick up,' he hesitated, 'a friend. A special friend.'

'Abbie Marshall. I know.' Ciara wasn't even looking at him, she was watching a tractor towing a sports car.

He nearly pulled a tendon in his neck, he whipped round so fast. 'What? How did you know?'

'Of course I know. As soon as I saw her on the news when you were found I could see that she was just your type. And Kev said that she had gone missing.'

'Kev?'

'Well, sure. Even though you scared him out of asking me out, we're Facebook friends and e-mail occasionally. He follows me on Twitter,' she added proudly, 'which is more than you do.'

Jack felt as if he had fallen down a rabbit hole. Why had he assumed that what happened in America wouldn't reach Ireland?

She pulled out and overtook a lorry salting the road, a bus and a Ford Focus in one manoeuvre. He might have survived a crashing plane and a Honduran rainforest full of poisonous snakes and man-eating cats, but if he got through Dublin in one piece it would be a miracle.

'So, are you staying with me or going home?'

'Neither. I've booked a room in the Clarence.'

Ciara took her attention off the road and gave him an incredulous look. 'No bloody way. My house or Mam's. I am not taking you to a hotel. Not unless you want to have photographers chasing you all over Temple Bar.'

He winced. He hadn't thought of that. 'OK, your house it is, if you're sure Johnny won't mind.'

She kept her attention on the road. 'He'll be fine. And Aoife is mad to meet the uncle who sends her all the presents.' Ciara pulled into a side street. 'Here we are. Grab your bag and prepare to enter Bedlam.'

For the moment, the subject was dropped.

33

Abbie unwrapped the dark-blue tissue paper and gasped. She lifted the green silk dress and shook it, trying to shake out the creases. 'It's fabulous.'

'I wore it the night I met Martin.' Barbara gazed at the dress wistfully. 'It doesn't fit me now but it will look lovely on you.'

Abbie held it up against her and looked at her reflection in the mirror. The dress brought out the colour of her eyes. Jack would . . . *No.* No more thinking about Jack. It was almost a week since their conversation and she hadn't heard a word from him since.

His threat of making her pay had been empty. She wasn't sure if she was glad or disappointed. She had thrown herself into helping Barbara with the preparations for the hunt ball. Tonight she would meet Tom Breslin and get back to work. It would be good to have a story to focus on.

'There's a headdress to match.' Barbara opened a second, smaller tissue parcel. A jewelled headband glittered in the paper. Wrapped separately were two feathers, dyed to match the colour of the dress.

Abbie sat obediently as Barbara fitted the headband and attached the feathers. Even without make-up the elaborate band made her look sophisticated. It wasn't a look she did often.

'You won't be able to sit down all night.'

'What?' Barbara's words startled her. The last person to use those words meant something else entirely. Abbie blushed and Barbara gave her a knowing smile.

'I meant dancing. You won't be short of partners. You go and get ready. I'll iron this for you.'

For once, the shower didn't turn cold halfway through. Abbie took a while to moisturize her skin. There were no bruises on her ass, no burning rasp from five o'clock shadow, no marks on her wrists from restraints. All traces of her adventures in D/s were gone. She felt naked.

But it wasn't just any marks she wanted; it was Jack's marks. Kit had been right. She was a natural submissive, but it didn't matter. There was only one man that she would ever submit to and that was never going to happen again. For all Jack's talk about trust and openness in a D/s relationship, in the end he hadn't trusted her.

She applied her make-up carefully and pulled a face at her reflection. 'Stop thinking about Jack. You're worse than a teenager.'

Barbara had laid the dress out on the bed. Creases gone, the silk shimmered under the lamplight. Abbie adjusted her headdress and attached the feathers. An exotic creature stared back at her from the mirror. She painted a Cupid's bow on her lips. 'Very Louise Brooks,' she approved. 'Now, let's see if the paint job will tempt Mr Breslin.'

She had never made an entrance before, but the green dress certainly drew attention. She spotted Martin in the crowd, wearing a formal dinner jacket. He was chatting to the ambassador and another man in his forties. Barbara was at the centre of the crowd as usual.

An octogenarian friend of Martin's who had been at the Christmas party offered her his arm. His suit was shiny in places and he smelled faintly of mothballs. 'You haven't forgotten you promised me a dance tonight, have you?'

Abbie smiled. He was a sweet old guy. 'Of course not, lead the way.'

Three dances passed before she could politely disentangle herself from his grasp. For an old guy, he had a lot of moves and some of them weren't polite. She made her way through the heaving crowd to where Martin and the others were still chatting. Drink in hand, Martin was holding forth about his favourite subject.

'Do you ever stop talking about horses?' she asked.

He glanced around the room at the swathe of female flesh on view. 'Sure, what else would we talk about? Mind you, there's a few fine fillies about the place tonight, including yourself. Have you met Tom? He's with the ambassador.'

So this was Tom Breslin. Forties, handsome, dark hair and beautiful tailoring. Thanks to Miffy, Abbie knew enough about clothes to recognize that Breslin's tuxedo was handmade and that the black pearl stickpin was real. His sharp eyes drank her in from head to foot before returning to her boobs. Abbie ignored his impolite stare and offered her hand. 'I'm Abbie, Martin's niece.'

There was no recognition on his face. Good. Maybe he hadn't associated her with the reporter who had been trying to get an interview with him for weeks.

'Delighted to meet you, Abbie.' He took her hand in his.

Abbie tried not to grimace when she felt his clammy hand. She hated men with sweaty palms. She forced a bright smile. 'So, you work with the ambassador. My, that must be interesting. I bet you get to travel a lot.'

Breslin returned her smile and moved closer. 'Yes, I do. Europe, South America –'

'South America? Wow! I'd love to hear about that. That part of the world has always fascinated me.'

Breslin took the bait. 'Why don't we dance?'

Jack eyed the house where the East Meath Harriers' Hunt Ball was in full swing. He didn't have an invitation and he had no interest in horses, hunting or the horsy set, but if this was where Abbie was, he was definitely interested.

No one was going to keep him from Abbie.

He marched up to the wide front door, where a group of men were smoking and discussing the prospects for hunting the following week, if the snow melted enough. He had no doubt he could mingle with them and get in but their slow pace would drive him mad. He needed to see Abbie.

When a pompous little man with a list tried to stop him, Jack waved him away. 'I'm here to see Abbie Marshall. Can you direct me?'

'Um.' The man with the list was thrown. He looked from Jack's face to the list. 'I'm sorry, I'm sure I know you, but . . .'

'That's OK,' Jack said, walking past him. 'Happens all the time.'

He strode down the hallway towards the sound of music, voices and laughter at the back of the house. All the partitions between the living room, dining room and conservatory had been pulled back, creating a long, high room which was thronged with brightly clad, boisterous partygoers, all intent on having a good time.

There was a small band playing Tom Jones at one end of the room, and a dozen couples were dancing with more energy than grace. Ten tables seated large groups of diners who chatted loudly and occasionally cheered for no reason that Jack could see.

The men were dressed like him, in dinner jackets and suits, apart from a few in hunting pinks, and the women wore long dresses which revealed a lot of cleavage. The makeshift ballroom was decorated with a ceiling-scraping Christmas tree, tinsel, balloons and rosettes. The revellers varied in age from a babe in arms to an elderly lady with a walking stick, thinning white hair and bright red lipstick.

Where was Abbie? If this was another dead end, he wouldn't be responsible for his actions. She had been away from him for too long.

The crowd parted, and he caught a glimpse of green and a couple of waving feathers. Abbie looked as if she had stepped from a 1920s movie. She eclipsed every other woman in the place in a vintage dress that made her eyes seem like pure jade. The silk gown shimmered with every step she took. She wore a beaded headband trimmed with feathers that should have looked ridiculous, but instead made him want to strip her and use those feathers to torture her.

He strode forward, anxious to claim her and put her back where she belonged, in his arms and in his bed.

She threw back her head and laughed. She was dancing

with another man, a man who had his arms around her. And she wasn't fighting him off.

'Hi, Abbie,' he said, stopping right beside her and keeping his voice level, which took some effort. 'My dance, I believe.'

He got a certain amount of satisfaction from the shocked expression on her face. Her jaw slackened and her eyes rounded. There was a mix of elation and anger in her eyes but she recovered herself quickly.

'Sorry. What do they say at these things? My card is already full.' She turned her attention to the man she was dancing with. 'What were you saying, Tom?'

No way. No fucking way. He had come halfway across the world for her, faced down his father for her, gatecrashed a stupid hunt ball, and she was blowing him off. He fed his anger so the desolation inside couldn't take over.

Jack turned to the other man, using his extra height to intimidate him. 'You won't mind if I cut in, will you?' He was pretty sure he'd once used those lines in some crappy historical play.

Something in his face must have been a warning. The other man backed away, hands up. 'No, that's fine, you have your dance.'

Jack took Abbie into his arms. She fitted there as if she had been made exclusively for him. Her perfume, subtle and enticing, teased his senses. The sense of rightness was overwhelming. Abbie leaned against him for a moment, letting him take her weight, before she pushed back and stared at him coldly.

'What are doing here, Jack? You sent me away, remember?'

She held herself stiffly in his arms. Her expression was a mask of cool indifference, but the small pulse hammering at her throat told a different story. Abbie was hurt and she was still angry with him. She wasn't going to give in easily.

'Just tell me one thing. Did you write that story?'

'You have to ask?' The hurt in her eyes was his answer.

She wrenched herself away from him and marched back to the man she had been dancing with before. Jack didn't hear what she said to him, but he smiled at her and swung her back on to the dance floor.

Jack was about to go after her when a hand on his arm stopped him. Fists clenched, he swung round, but the elderly man with shrewd blue eyes carefully kept a non-threatening stance. 'No need to get riled, son. So you came to get her?'

'Yes, and you're not going to stop me.'

The old man grinned. 'You don't think she's going to just let you take up where you left off? That girl has her mother's temper and something tells me you'll be getting a taste of it shortly.'

Jack wasn't paying much attention. Abbie was dancing too close to the stranger, smiling at him flirtatiously.

'Who the hell is she dancing with?' he said to the old guy.

'You don't learn, do you?' The older man held out his hand to Jack. 'I'm Martin Locke, Abbie's uncle.'

Jack shook hands briefly, without taking his eyes off Abbie. When her partner swung her out and pulled her back against his body, he had had enough. He pushed through the other dancers, pulled Abbie away from the other man and into his arms. This was where she belonged.

'You're mine,' he told her. 'We signed a contract and I haven't released you from it.'

Abbie stiffened. She muttered furiously. 'Are you out of your mind? I've had enough of D/s to last me a lifetime.' She laughed at him. 'I'm not a sub. You are not my Dom and you can take your overbearing attitude and shove it where the sun don't shine.'

Abbie stamped on his foot, her spike heel doing enough damage to make him wince. She tore herself from his slackened grasp. 'Martin, this gentleman is leaving. Can you show him out please?'

To Jack's fury, four men surrounded him and indicated that they wanted him to leave. He had no option but to go.

Abbie watched as her uncle and cousins manhandled Jack and escorted him from the hunt ball. It felt so good to see him at a disadvantage for once. When she had heard his voice and looked up to see him standing beside her, the flood of joy had been so strong it was terrifying. He was a son of a bitch, he had treated her like dirt, but as soon as she saw him she'd wanted to throw herself into his arms and beg him to make love to her.

So not going to happen.

Even if he was the most ravishing man she had ever seen. The way Jack looked at her, the intensity in those glittering blue eyes made her feel as if she was the only woman in the world. All his attention, all his passion was focused on her. But now she knew she wasn't content to have that for the duration of a contract. She wanted it for ever.

What was it Jack had said – a strong Dom needed a strong sub? *Well, Sir, you're getting your wish. I'm about to become the most difficult sub in the world. Let's see if you're ready for me.*

The little scene had attracted the attention of all the guests. She could see some of the women whispering to each other 'Was that Jack Winter? Oh my god!'

Barbara came over and patted her on the back. 'Well done, dear. It's time you stood up for yourself. Do you want me to call the police and have him arrested for trespassing?'

For one moment, Abbie was tempted. The idea of Jack locked up in a cell, perhaps an old-fashioned one where he would be manacled to the wall and she could visit him and . . . OK, not somewhere she wanted to go. Abbie shook her head. 'No, that's fine. He won't bother me again.'

She knew – or at least, she hoped – she was lying. She wanted Jack to bother her again. She wanted him to pursue her with the same ruthless intensity he had used to get them out of the jungle. Not that he was going to catch her, but she would enjoy his efforts.

Her stomach lurched at the thought of Jack's pursuit and heat coiled low in her belly. Unconsciously, she shifted her thighs together, trying to ease the ache that Jack always inspired. OK, perhaps she might let him catch her eventually, when he had suffered enough.

There was still a trace of Jack's distinctive man-and-musk scent on her skin. She took a deep breath to inhale it then caught herself. She was over Jack. She had thrown him out – and it felt good. No more running after him. It was time to get back to work.

She turned back to Tom Breslin, whose gentle features were belied by the intelligence in his steady gaze.

'I'm sorry about that,' she said. 'Now where were we?'

'You're *that* Abbie Marshall, aren't you? I didn't realize that reporters lead such interesting lives. Crashing in a jungle, and now being pursued by Jack Winter.' His smile took the sting out of his words. He had a Connecticut accent that reminded her of home.

It was time to take the gloves off. 'I've had enough excitement, thank you. But you had your adventures in Honduras as well, didn't you? Why don't we talk about your involvement with the DEA there? What was your impression of the country?'

The music changed to something slower. Breslin took her into his arms and circled the small dance floor. He was a good dancer and although he held her close, there was still an air of impersonal politeness about him. 'Such a poor country. I hope that American influence might help. We have to help stop the trans-shipment of drugs through there.'

It was a stock answer, one he had clearly rehearsed and used many times before. She asked him more questions and he gradually loosened up.

'How well do you know Antonio Tabora?' she asked, just as the band started to play Horslips' 'Trouble'. It was a loud, rousing song and the dance floor was inundated with boisterous dancers.

Breslin shook his head, frustrated. 'It's too noisy here.

Why don't we go for a walk outside? It's quieter there and I'll tell you all about Tabora.'

She agreed, eager to get him to answer her questions. She was close, she knew it.

Breslin led her down to the stable yard, where the snow had been cleared and night lights lit their way. The half doors on the stables were still open and a dozen horses poked their heads out, eager to see what was happening. Breslin led her through the yard to where a sports car was parked in front of the hayshed. 'It's cold out here. Get in and I'll tell you about Tabora.'

'I don't think . . .' Abbie stopped, uneasy. They were still close enough to the house that the music was audible, but it was dark and they were alone. The thin silk of her dress offered little protection against the biting wind. 'Maybe we should go back to the house?'

She tried to pull away, but Breslin had a firm hold on her elbow. He didn't let go. 'Don't be silly,' he said. 'You wanted to know about Tabora. I'm going to tell you. Now get into the car.'

He unlocked it with a click, still holding her arm. Abbie's journalistic instincts warred with her feminine ones. She didn't want to be near anyone who wasn't Jack but she needed this interview.

The strength of her revulsion took her aback. Bloody Jack Winter – he had ruined her for other men. She couldn't even sit in a car with someone to ask him questions. She was tougher than that. If she had to interview someone, she would do it.

'Let me get my notebook,' she said.

'I have paper in the car, you can use that.' His grip tightened, urging her further into the car.

There was something wrong here. 'No, I'd rather get my own notebook.' She tried to move backwards, but Breslin prevented her. He pushed her on to the seat and closed the door.

34

'Take your hands off her,' a furious, familiar voice snarled.

Jack lunged out of the darkness and grabbed Breslin by his lapels. 'When a woman says no, you should listen. Do you hear?' He hauled him up so that he could look the smaller man in the eye. 'She said she wants her own notebook.'

Abbie scrambled out of the low-slung car and stared at Jack in astonishment.

Breslin tried to pull away from Jack's furious grip. 'Let go of me. What are you still doing here? You were asked to leave.'

'I'm looking after Abbie. Protecting her from scum like you. Just be grateful you didn't touch anything but her arm. Next time you won't be so lucky.'

Jack dropped him and the American ran up the yard. He turned to Abbie. 'What the hell were you doing out here with that loser? You're mine.'

The lights from the yard were faint, but enough for her to see the feral expression in his eyes. Jack was at the edge of his control, and something deep inside her exulted. She wanted more of that. 'I'm yours? In your dreams.'

He grabbed her and pulled her tightly against his chest. 'In my dreams,' he agreed, his voice dropping to a growl. 'And in every waking minute too. You're going to stay with me.'

'Oh yeah?' Abbie despised the breathy quality of her voice. She took a breath and firmed it. 'Make me.'

She felt the change in him when she threw down the challenge. His body hardened in a rush. 'Why, you little brat!'

She didn't care. This time, they were playing by her rules.

Jack lifted her off her feet and invaded her mouth. His lips were cold but his kiss was so hot it scalded her. There was no slow build-up, no gradual seduction. This was pure, raw passion, urgent and demanding. She wrapped her arms around his neck and opened to him. She slanted her mouth against his and opened wider, inviting him in.

The taste was intoxicating and addictive. His mouth was furnace hot and it branded hers. Vaguely, she acknowledged that no other man would ever do for her after Jack, but now she didn't care. She was too busy inciting him to further depredations. He thrust his tongue into her mouth, seizing control and dominating her. She nipped it sharply. Not enough to draw blood, just enough to make him aware that she had teeth and would use them.

He growled and held her head still while he took possession of her lips and mouth and gave her no quarter. She didn't want any; she gloried in his strength and determination. She met his hunger with a matching passion, squirming to get closer to him, to feel more of his glorious heat.

All the anger and misery she had felt earlier had turned into flaming, passionate, unstoppable desire. Jack was hers, and no one would take him away from her. Not even Jack himself. She clung on to his shoulders and demanded that he keep kissing her.

By the time he raised his head, he was panting and she felt boneless. If it weren't for the steely arms around her, she would have tumbled to the icy ground. Somehow Jack knew. He picked her up as if she weighed nothing, checked around the yard and headed for the dark hayshed.

The warm, heady smell of sweet hay was almost as enticing as the musky aroma of the man who held her so tightly to his chest. All her senses were on overdrive. Abbie took a deep breath as Jack lowered her along the length of his muscular body. She was no longer Abbie Marshall, reporter; she was a woman who hadn't had her man in far too long.

The hayshed was warm and dark, and there was no reason not to yank Jack's clothes off. So she did. At her first grab, Jack stilled, but he allowed her to pull the jacket off over his shoulders and drag the shirt tails out of his trousers. She slid her hands underneath his shirt and hissed with pleasure at the heat of his skin. She skimmed up along his ribs, enjoying the way he twitched when her fingertips tickled him and tangled in the hair on his chest. When she reached his nipples and pinched, he lost control.

Jack grabbed her head, holding her still for his voracious kiss then his hands ravaged her body. He moulded it as if he owned it, caressing her ass and her stomach and breasts through the silk of Barbara's antique dress.

'More,' he growled, barely lifting his head from her mouth. He pulled up the silky cloth until his hand was on her bare thigh. She shuddered from the contrast of his hot hand and the chill of the winter air on her skin.

'Cold,' she managed.

'Not for long.' He dragged the material up to her waist and pulled her tightly against his erection.

Her mouth dried. Had he always been that big? To hell with it, she didn't care if it had grown while she was away. She put her hand down to his crotch, grabbed his straining shaft and watched Jack's eyes roll back in his head. 'Oh yes, the big bad Dom has a weak spot, and I'm holding it in my hand.'

'Keep that up, and you'll see what my hand can do.'

She laughed, taunting him. 'Bring it on.'

'What an excellent idea.' With deliberate fingers that shook only slightly, Jack undid his trouser buttons, pulled down the zip and pushed them off his narrow hips.

Her breath shortened as she looked at the impressive cock which was pointing straight at her. God, she wanted to feel that inside her again. But Jack deserved a little more torture. 'You know the old Chinese expression?'

'Which one?'

'Woman with skirt up can run faster than man with trousers down.' With that, she whirled and raced for the door of the barn. But she had only taken a few steps before a weight crashed into her from behind and Jack tackled her to the hay-covered floor.

'You didn't run fast enough. Now you pay.'

'Oh shut up, you're not a Bond villain,' she said, and grabbed his head to kiss him. This was a meeting of equals, both as strong, both as hungry as each other. She held on to him with arms and legs, preventing him getting away from her. He took over the kiss, blasting away any lingering reservations she might have had.

She gloried in the coarse silk of his hair, pushing her

hands through it while he strung biting kisses down her neck and along her collarbone.

Jack's hands were busy, stripping away her panties in one ruthless movement and taking ownership of the heat between her restless thighs.

'Still smooth. Good girl,' he said, and something inside her melted.

Oh god, the things he could do to her with those words. But she had no intention of letting him know. 'I'm not a good girl, I'm very bad,' she said, and pushed herself on top of him. He lay on his back in the hay while she straddled him. She didn't want to wait. She was hot and wet and hungry, so she rose up on her knees, positioned him carefully and slid down on his cock. 'Ahh!' The sensation of him filling her, completing her, was so exquisite that she felt as if part of her brain had short-circuited. Just remembering how to breathe took all her concentration.

Then he pulled her down to kiss her and she forgot that too. Who needed to breathe when she had Jack? She wanted this to last, but the feel of him was too much to bear. Her hips were moving without any instruction from her.

'Slower,' Jack said, but she couldn't stop. He rolled her over so that the hay was prickly under her buttocks, then he held her ass in his hands while he drove into her again and again. With each overwhelming lunge, her nerve endings wound tighter and tighter until she could not think, only feel and react.

She was aware that she was making noises – loud, primitive noises that echoed through the barn. Jack loved it. 'Shush, you'll scare the horses.' He put his hand over her mouth to silence her.

Abbie bit it. She hadn't planned to, but she had no control left. She needed him to move faster and urged him on with heels and nails and teeth. Finally, finally, Jack moved faster, speeding up until she became one continuous mass of breathless ecstasy, unable to form any word except 'Jack'.

It was too much, too overwhelming, and with a last scream and a fizz of delight, she fell into a shuddering climax. Jack gave three more thrusts and followed her over.

They lay there, panting, while they tried to collect themselves. Finally Jack raised his head. 'Do you know that you're still wearing that feathery headdress? And I have plans for it.'

She ran her hand down his back. 'Nothing like the plans I have for this body. I'm going to have you on your knees, begging.'

He frowned, the euphoria gone. 'Are you mad? I'm the Dom.'

'You're the Dom who screwed up. You want me, you're going to have to beg.' Abbie pushed him away, climbed to her unsteady feet and began straightening her clothes.

She was on her way up the yard when Jack called. 'Do you know you've got hay on your back and in your hair?'

She turned to tell him where to go, but he was already gone.

Abbie stomped back to the house, trailing hay behind her. Nothing had changed. Jack was still an arrogant Dom and she was still crazy about him. As she reached the house, she saw Tom Breslin drive away in a Porsche Carrera. If she couldn't get the truth from him, perhaps the ambassador could.

In the small downstairs cloakroom, she repaired her hair and clothes as much as she could. At some point during her interlude with Jack, she had lost one of the feathers from the headdress. She removed the other one with shaking fingers. It was time to talk to Chris Warrington.

The ambassador's sceptical expression turned serious when she showed him some of the files on her laptop. Murders, gang warfare, drug running, all organized by Tabora. She outlined Tabora's connection with Breslin and finished with the question: how could a middle-ranking diplomat afford a $250,000 car?

When they finished talking, she was shattered. Breslin was going to get a very early wake-up call and she would get her exclusive: *Warrington Exposes Corruption in State Department.* Not a bad night's work, but she still had to deal with Jack and she hadn't seen him since the stables. She refused Barbara's offer of a nightcap and headed to her room.

The lamp was on and Jack was lying in the middle of her bed. His jacket and tie hung over the back of a chair and his dress shirt was open at the neck, exposing several inches of tanned flesh. How could he be that handsome and unattainable? 'I suggest you put your jacket back on, it's cold outside.'

'I'm not going anywhere.' Jack patted the bed beside him. 'Why don't we talk?'

Abbie began to remove her make-up. 'Talk about what? About how I'm a good little subbie? About how much fun we'll have together back in the States? Sorry. The answer is no.'

For the first time that evening, he looked uncertain. 'Abbie, I'm not good at this.'

'At what? Relationships? Well, doesn't that suck? You said sane, safe and consensual. So far, so good. You also promised honesty, but so far I haven't seen a lot of it. OK, why don't I start?'

She took a deep breath. 'I'm in love with you, Jack. But it's not enough.'

His mouth firmed into a thin line. He was closing up. Jack was slipping away from her.

'What's the matter? Too much honesty?' She wiped away the remains of her mascara with a tissue. Then she met his eyes in the mirror.

'Jack Winter isn't enough. I want Michael Delaney too. Not half a man who's running from his past.'

She held her breath, waiting. The seconds ticked by in the stillness of her bedroom. There was no tender kiss, no reconciliation, no words of love. Just Jack, battling his inner demons.

He reached for her hand. 'You don't know what you're asking. It's too much.'

Abbie closed her eyes. She had done it. Laid her cards on the table, told him what she wanted, but Jack couldn't or wouldn't connect with her. He was still the same closed-off Jack he had been from the very start.

'Then I want you to leave.'

She didn't move until she heard the soft click as the door closed behind him. When she opened her eyes again, she was alone. This time it was really over.

35

There were only two seasons in Ireland, Abbie decided as she packed her bags. Rainy and cold or rainy and not-so-cold. The first stirrings of spring were making her homesick. She missed New York and her family. It had been wonderful to have some time to start writing the novel she had always planned, but Josh was screaming for her to come home and work for the paper. It was time to pick up the pieces and move on.

Tucked between her clothes was her 'Jack' box with the small fragments she'd collected during their time together: a paper napkin from the ice cream parlour in Pasadena, a feather from the night he'd spent in her apartment, a tiny pressed orchid from Honduras. The flotsam of their relationship that she'd held on to when she fled to Ireland. It pretty much summed them up, but there wasn't a lot to show for five months of her life.

The bedroom door opened and Nesbitt pushed his way in. She ruffled his thick coat. She would miss her canine confidants. They had borne the brunt of the second Jack Winter meltdown. Barbara had fielded the phone call the day after the hunt ball and told him that Abbie had returned home. Since then, there had been no word. Not a single shred of gossip to feed her aching need of him. He hadn't returned to New York or LA, and according to his website, there were no scheduled appearances.

The *African Queen* saga continued. Jack's replacement as Charlie – for it leaked out that he had originally been cast in the part – broke his arm on the first day of shooting. Maria Richards had pulled out due to an unexpected pregnancy.

'What did I tell you about being upstairs? Get out of there,' Barbara shouted as Nesbitt ran past her. Barbara handed Abbie a newspaper. 'There's something in there you might want to read.'

Automatically, Abbie turned to the news section but Barbara snatched back the paper and flicked on to the entertainment section. 'Look at this,' she said, pointing to the 'On the Town' column.

TRIUMPHANT RETURN TO THE STAGE FOR JACK WINTER

In what must surely be Dublin's best-kept secret for many years, last night the newly opened Barry Theatre scored an impressive coup in featuring a surprise appearance by Hollywood leading man Jack Winter in its first production, Brian Friel's *Faith Healer*. Producer Jonathan Wilde later revealed that he had persuaded his old friend to tread the boards again on condition of absolute secrecy. 'It was a hell of a challenge keeping it under wraps,' Wilde said at the after party, 'but Jack has been through a difficult time and the rest of the cast and the whole team were determined that someone of his genius would get the chance to remind people what he does best. He was a pleasure to work with and won everybody over with his craft and his dedication.'

> Better known for his roles in Hollywood action movies, Winter played the part of hard-drinking, egocentric Frank Hardy with a depth of anger and anguish that was almost painful to watch. His final soliloquy had the audience on the edge of their seats. It is an astonishing return to the stage by an actor who was last seen in Dublin while still a student. Back then he was tipped to be one of the leading actors of his generation and many considered his global success as a film actor to be the greatest loss to theatre since Richard Burton.
>
> This is Jack Winter as his fans have never seen him before. Anyone who has been lucky enough to get tickets for the remainder of the five-night run can look forward to a once-in-a-lifetime theatrical experience.

The paper slipped from Abbie's hand as she sat down heavily on the edge of the bed. Her heart thumped like a drum at a Fourth of July parade. Hollywood might be finished with him, but Jack hadn't given up.

'Pity it's sold out,' Barbara said.

'Sold out?'

'Yes, that piece is from last Saturday. Tonight is the last performance.'

'But it can't be sold out.'

Barbara's expression was sympathetic. 'Maybe you should have let him know that you were still in Ireland. He was looking for you.'

Abbie followed her down the stairs and into the study. 'I'll ring the box office.'

The girl on the other end of the line laughed at her. There was no hope of a ticket, even for a reporter for the

New York Independent. Abbie replaced the receiver in the cradle. There had to be someone she could call. She couldn't leave Ireland without saying goodbye. She picked up the receiver again and punched in a number. 'It's Abbie Marshall. I need to speak to the ambassador.'

The return journey to Dublin was uneventful. There were no boxes of tissues this time, just a sadder, wiser woman. Martin deposited her at the hotel for her last day in Ireland. She would get a gift for Kevin and Kit's wedding. After that she would watch Jack one last time and slip away.

Abbie tugged the suitcase open and tossed its contents on to the comforter as she searched for the parcel of tissue paper. The green silk dress had been cleaned, Barbara's parting gift. She opened the Jack box, took out the feather and put it in her purse. He had used a feather to inscribe her breast with an 'M' the first time they made love. His true self. Michael. It was silly, she knew, but it was like an amulet that would protect her. Abbie dialled reception. 'I want someone to do my hair and make-up and I need a taxi for 7.30pm.'

'Ten minutes, Mr Winter.'

Jack pulled on the jacket of his grey suit and looked at his unshaven face in the mirror. 'Hi, Frank.'

It was like this every evening, pulling on the clothes and getting inside the head of Frank Hardy. When Jonathan had suggested that he take on the role he had been stunned and flattered. This had been one of the best weeks he'd had in a very long time. Five nights on stage, in his own city, playing the role of an Irishman in exile. Five nights of rave reviews. His father in tears after the show one night; he had embraced him and without either of them saying anything, the poison drained out of their relationship. The only thing that was missing was Abbie.

Her aunt had told him she had gone home, but no matter how much he begged Kit, all she would say was that Abbie was tucked away somewhere remote, writing a novel. She hadn't tried to contact him. He had messed up again. Every time he got close to expressing his feelings, to telling her that he loved her, how much she meant to him, how much he needed her in his life, he lost the words.

He always did something to hurt her, but in the end, the person he hurt most of all was himself. He had wanted her since the first time he saw her in Honduras. Now he loved her, craved her like a drug.

Abbie had seen through the Hollywood façade he had tried to maintain so carefully. She had cut through his arrogance and bullshit with her quick wit and intelligence. She aroused the Dom in him more than any woman he had ever known. He wanted her back. Would get her back, he told himself, and then would do whatever it took to keep her.

'Five minutes.' The knock came again. Jack dropped his head in his hands. It was time to become Frank.

He didn't remember the performance. He never did; he was always too deeply buried in his character. But the final line of the play, about renouncing chance, always brought him back to himself. He had to renounce the old Jack if he wanted to move on. The one who was afraid to admit what he truly was. The Jack who lived a double life, half

Hollywood superstar, half sexual Dominant, and who was no longer sure who he was. The Jack who had sabotaged every single one of his relationships because they all had involved hiding some aspect of himself. He was done with hiding. He was one man – good and bad, actor and Dom, son and, maybe one day, father.

The applause came again. Taking the hands of his two colleagues, Jack stepped into the spotlight. The warmth, the adulation and the glory were real and tangible when you were face to face with the audience. The crowd rose to their feet and roared his name. The others dropped his hands and he stepped to the front of the stage. 'I'd like to dedicate this performance –'

The crowd fell silent. His voice faltered. Jack cleared his throat and started again. 'I'd like to dedicate this performance to Abbie Marshall. The woman I love, the woman who saved me. Wherever she is tonight.'

The curtain closed for the final time and Jack made his way to the dressing room. Sweat had glued the shirt to his back. He was wiped out.

'That was amazing.' Jonathan clapped him on the shoulder on the way back to the dressing room. 'You know, we could do a tour with this. A month in London and then maybe a short run on Broadway. Of course, the salary wouldn't be anything like what you'd earn from starring in a Hollywood blockbuster. Equity rates only, I'm afraid.'

Jack grinned. Zeke Bryan would have a fit. He spent more than that on manicures in a month. He held out his hand. 'Sounds great. Where do I sign?'

Back in his dressing room he dropped his jacket on the back of a chair and opened the buttons of his sweat-stained shirt. He sat down at his dressing table and poured himself a cup of tea from the waiting pot. If Kevin could see him now, he would laugh himself sick. No booze, no starlets, no wild sex in the dressing room. Just a nice pot of tea.

A knock came on the dressing-room door and he frowned. One rule he had imposed was no visitors for at least thirty minutes. It took him that long to get Frank out of his head. 'Who is it?' His voice was sharper than he had intended.

The grey-haired wardrobe mistress popped her head around the door. 'Someone to see you. I wouldn't normally let anyone back here, but she says her name is Abbie Marshall.'

His hair was slicked back, his white shirt open to the waist and his laser-blue eyes were accentuated by the dark stage make-up that he hadn't yet wiped off. Jack looked as sensual and decadent as a libertine. She had forgotten how handsome he was in the flesh. So beautiful. So intoxicating. Abbie fingered her beaded purse to give her hands something to do. This was a mistake. She shouldn't have come.

'Hello, Jack.'

She felt a small thrill that the hand holding the teacup shook slightly as he replaced it on the saucer. Jack stood up and inclined his head. 'Abbie.'

'You were wonderful.' The words gushed out before she could stop them. *Great, now you sound like a teenage fan. Why can't you talk to him, tell him how you feel?*

He flashed a smile that was pure Jack. 'Thanks. It was Jonathan's idea for me to play Frank. He's talking about a tour, starting with London.'

'That sounds great.' A tour. He couldn't go on tour, she'd only just found him again. Abbie's smile froze on her face as she thought of all that adulation he'd get, to say nothing of all the willing females.

'So, how is the writing going?'

'It's OK, but I'm going back to New York tomorrow. Josh wants me to cover another South American story.'

'South America, huh?' Jack shrugged the shirt off his shoulders and he stood bare-chested before her.

'South America.' She was distracted, trying not to stare at his abs. She had come full circle – back to staring at his abs like that first morning in the jungle. *Oh, control yourself, Abbie. You've seen him without clothes before.* Her eyes darted away from his torso and she glanced in the mirror, but was still conscious of his heated stare.

'Maybe we should talk about this.' Jack advanced steadily while she retreated, until her back touched the cool surface of the wooden door.

'T-t-talk about what?' she stammered.

Jack lowered his head. His breath fanned her cheek. He pressed his mouth against her neck and held it there, not kissing, not biting, just waiting.

The beaded purse thudded to the floor, its contents scattering. Abbie turned her head and was rewarded with a sharp nip of his teeth. She let out a gasp. 'Don't.'

His tongue swirled around the bite mark. 'Don't what?'

Jack traced a path along her shoulder until he reached the thin strap of her dress. Mesmerized, Abbie could do nothing but watch as he pushed it away then did the same with the other strap. The fine silk fluttered to the floor, leaving her standing in a strapless bra, heels, stockings and panties.

Jack unclipped the bra, then pressing his mouth against one nipple, he sucked hard on the tender peak. Abbie yelped at the sensual assault.

'Now, where were we?' he murmured against her neck. The vibration of his voice sent a jolt of pleasure through her. 'Oh yes.' Another nip, this one more painful than the last. 'South America. There's just one little problem with that.'

Another caress. This time his hands slid along her waist, cupped her hips and drew her against the hard length of him. 'I don't believe that you asked for my permission to go.'

Abbie couldn't think straight. She could never think straight when Jack touched her. Jack wanted her. He didn't want her to go away.

Her mind was in tumult.

No, it had been a mistake to come here tonight. She had to go back to New York. She had a job waiting for her. She should be back in her hotel room, tucked up in bed. Not standing half-naked in a theatre dressing room.

'That's the kind of dangerous behaviour that could get you into a lot of trouble.'

'It could?' The high, breathy tone didn't sound like her voice.

'Oh yes, and there will be consequences.'

Jack wanted to punish her. A hot thrill shot through her, like fire in her blood. It was wrong and decadent, but no one else could make her feel like this.

'Step out of the dress and place your hands on the clothes rail.'

Ignoring the pile of silk on the floor, Abbie crossed the room and placed both hands on the chrome bar. She heard a rustle as Jack tugged the leather belt free of his trousers and doubled it over.

He slapped it against his palm with a loud crack. Abbie closed her thighs. The ache between her legs was getting worse. She wanted him so badly. She wanted the punishment to be over so that Jack would touch her. She heard a soft click as the key turned in the lock, then his warm hand cupped her breast.

His bare chest caressed her back, the dampness of his skin reminding her of other times he had taken her. Dominated her. She tensed, waiting for the first blow. Instead, all she felt was the light touch of a feather against her bare skin, trailing down her back like a whispered breath. 'Oh,' she gasped.

'Don't turn round. Keep your eyes closed, until I say.'

'Yes, Sir.'

The first sharp crack of the belt landed on her ass, followed by three more strokes in quick succession. It didn't hurt, she told herself. Not as much as the months spent without him.

The next one hurt and the one after that. Abbie tensed, waiting for another blow to land. Instead she felt the brush of a feather. Her skin flamed as he continued. Light flicks of the belt, followed by touches of the feather, until she was dizzy. Her soft cries filled the dressing room.

Jack threaded his hand through her hair, holding her in

place while he took her mouth in a searing kiss that left her dazed and breathless.

'Had enough yet?'

'No, you bastard. I can take whatever you give me, and more.'

His amused expression turned serious. 'You really shouldn't have said that.'

The leather belt landed on the dressing table. Abbie heard the scrape of a chair against the floor. She turned slowly, heat pooling between her thighs. Jack sat on a wooden chair in the middle of the dressing room. He patted his thigh. 'Get over my knee.'

She took her sweet time closing the distance between them, watching as his eyes ate up her body, enjoying the thrill of knowing that Jack wanted her, only her. One step away from him, she stopped, knowing that her disobedience would arouse him further.

'Ms Marshall, you are in so much trouble already, don't make this any harder on yourself.'

She lowered herself across his lap, savouring the rough feel of his woollen trousers across her breasts. The chair was too high to let her put her hands on the floor, so she gripped his ankle for support. Jack traced a circle on her tender skin before he raised his hand and smacked her.

Her body jerked. She had forgotten what it felt like. He struck her again, four times in quick succession.

'Ow!' His hand was hard.

Jack laughed. 'Missed me?'

'Not a bit,' she said.

His hand flashed down against her thighs and she squirmed. The hot stinging strokes woke dormant nerve endings, sending sharp darts of pleasure through her core. 'Oh god,' she cried out. She covered her mouth with her hand, afraid that someone would hear her.

The next strokes landed in a random pattern, moving from cheek to thigh and back again. She writhed. She had forgotten the sharp sting of pain, followed by the slow soothing circles of his palm against her heated flesh.

'That's for not returning my calls.'

Smack.

'That's for making me crazy with worry about you.'

Another smack.

'And that's for not filing your lingerie reports for months. You've earned this, Abbie.'

She felt his fingers at the seam of her panties and he pulled them roughly down. The sharp blows lessened in ferocity, becoming slower and more sensual. She gave herself up to it as he continued, each blow now focused on the area where her ass met her legs, sending jolts of pleasure up her stinging thighs. Her breath came in uncontrolled gasps, smothered by her hand.

She writhed again, straining on her tiptoes, trying to ensure that he struck the same sweet spot. 'Ah!'

Jack took it for the invitation that it was. His hand flashed light and fast, sending a flood of sensation through her. Abbie bit down on her hand, crying out as it became too much to bear. Pleasure shot through her, arcing out through her fingers and toes, and she crashed into nothingness.

When she came through, Jack was holding her, stroking her trembling body back to awareness. Her ass was on fire, the rest of her felt punch-drunk. She smiled lazily at him as he stroked her hair away from her face.

'I missed you so much, Abbie. Losing you tore the heart out of me.'

His thumb traced a path along her mouth. 'What if I were just Jack Winter, actor? No private jets. No limos at the airport. Just you and me together. Could you cope with that?'

Abbie held her breath. He wasn't joking. This was a Jack that she hadn't met before: he was nervous. 'Let me up and I'll think about it.'

Jack released her reluctantly. She crossed the room and picked her dress off the floor. The green silk shimmered in the light of the dressing room. She eased it over her head and looked at her reflection in the mirror. Her face was flushed from the spanking. Her eyes sparkled. She looked like a woman in love.

'For how long?' he asked. 'How long do you need to think about it?'

It wasn't fair to torture him, but Jack had tormented her plenty over the past few months. She walked to the door and he got up and followed. Abbie reached towards the lock and he covered her hand with his, preventing her from turning the key.

She looked over her shoulder into his blue eyes.

'For as long as it takes you to kiss me.'